MW01126101

Secrets

carla dietz fortier

carla dietz fortier

AuthorHouse™
1663 Liberty Drive, Suite 200
Bloomington, IN 47403
www.authorhouse.com
Phone: 1-800-839-8640

First published by AuthorHouse 6/7/2007

ISBN: 978-1-4343-0094-2 (sc)

Printed in the United States of America
Bloomington, Indiana

This book is printed on acid-free paper.

Dedication

For Fianna River Brooks

Acknowledgements

I am deeply indebted to the members of the Troubadours Writers Group for their endless encouragement and helpful critique; to my husband, Jerry, for graciously playing second fiddle to the many hours a project of this magnitude requires; and to my daughter, Nicole, for being my constant source of inspiration.

Chapter One

The elevator door slid aside as quietly as a velvet stage curtain on opening night. No actors appeared, though, only nurses and aides hurrying by on rubber-soled shoes.

Clea Reilly stepped out, noting her feet landed as usual on the G and H of the Green Haven Nursing Home logo stamped onto the tile floor. The letters seemed as worn as she felt. She wondered if every visitor contributed to the slow disappearance of the G and H or if she alone was responsible for their steady demise. Perhaps next time she would make a conscious effort to avoid the letters altogether...take a bigger first step, or a smaller one.

Next time.

She sighed and headed down the corridor. The walls had been painted a pleasant enough shade of yellow, but Clea was unaffected by the pointless attempt to add cheer to a place devoid of hope. Georgia O'Keeffe posters lined the way, evenly spaced and finishing-school straight. She knew them all by heart—the yellow orchid, the petunias and calla lilies, the huge red poppies by the nurse's pod—and hated every one. She hated being in this place and especially doing what had become by now routine.

In front of her a frizzy mound of hair rose like a black sun over the countertop.

"Mornin', Miz Reilly."

"Lydia? This is a surprise. I thought you were moving to a later shift."

"Next week that surely be the case."

"Good luck to you then. I hope your replacement is as thoughtful as you've been."

"Miz Josie an' me goes back a good many years. I just be keeping a special eye on her from four to midnight." The woman laughed, her whole body put in motion by the effort. "And don't you worry none, dearie. I'll make sure the new day gal is up to snuff." Lydia winked. "If you know what I mean."

Clea smiled her thanks. "So, what's in store for me today?"

The nurse's eyelids drooped, as did her enormous body. Slowly she shook her head.

Another bad day then. The slender volume of rose poems felt heavy in Clea's hand. She had hoped not to use it today, rather to pass the hour talking, even though her mother regarded her as a stranger. But on bad days she merely read aloud. In theory familiar words, softly-spoken even if uncomprehended, gave a measure of comfort. In practice they seemed only to further burden an already weighty melancholy.

Nodding to the nurse, Clea moved on around the corner where she paused at the second room on the right. The name Josephine Worth had been crudely punched onto a narrow plastic strip and stuck on the door just above the 303 room number. Clea's fingers lightly traced the raised letters. Lydia had been wrong before. The nature of the disease allowed for small windows of lucidity, spikes as well as valleys in temperament.

She hesitated a moment then pushed open the door and stepped into the homey if overheated room. Her compliment of Lydia's ministrations had not been exaggerated. The occupant was clean, dressed neatly in a sweat suit of aquamarine velour and seated in a rocker facing the window. Beyond the glass, the crown of a venerable maple, showy with yellow, russet and orange, rocked in the breeze as gently as the woman did in the chair.

"Hi, Mom."

Josephine looked up, displayed no sign of recognition, no change of expression. "Are you the nurse?"

"No, Ma. It's me, Clea."

"It's nice to meet you, young lady, but you must have the wrong room."

"Mind if I stay anyway?"

The pale bird of Josephine's hand fluttered, an involuntary tremor betraying inner fear. For a moment Clea thought her mother would order her from the room. It didn't happen often, but she had been dismissed like that before.

Instead the older woman shrugged and said, "No one ever visits me, you know."

"Now, now," said Clea, dropping to her knees in front of the rocker. "Try to remember. I come every morning after dropping Addison at school and before I head out to work."

A vacant stare was the only reply.

Rising, Clea went to the bed and sat on the corner. She fanned open the book. Today it wouldn't much matter which verse she read or whether she began the poem at the end and ended at the beginning. Absently she flipped through the pages, paused now and then and recited a line.

The rose, like hues of insect wing,/May perish in an hour....

Red Rose, proud Rose, sad Rose of all my days!

'Tis the last rose of Summer,/Left blooming alone....

Her brow wrinkled at the maudlin selections, so she thumbed to other pages, seeking cheerier poems.

What is fairer than a rose?/What is sweeter....

That was better, she thought.

The rose is the grace of the earth....

Sometimes, though, she caught herself mentally visualizing the words instead of actually saying them. She forced herself to pay closer attention. The doctors had urged her to engage familiar sights and sounds and this *was* her mother's favorite book. However, after twenty minutes, she gave in and prepared to leave.

"How's my little granddaughter Addy?"

Startled, Clea peered into her mother's face, encouraged by what she saw there. Haunting memories of better times flooded over her, so much so she almost missed the opportunity the moment afforded. When she found her voice, the words tumbled out.

"Addy's not so little anymore, Mom. A bumpy adjustment to high school but she'll be fine. Homecoming's a few days away. That'll help. She wants—but certainly isn't going to get—a navel ring. I'm putting my foot down on that one."

Clea's chuckle was cut short when she saw the spark of understanding die and a cloud obscure the sky blue of her mother's eyes. She picked up the book again and read in earnest.

Deep-hearted, pure, with scented dew still wet—
One perfect rose.

However, the flame that had once been Josephine Worth refused to reignite. Soon the scrape of walkers and slap of slippers on the hallway tiles broke her concentration. The residents were being marshaled toward the dining room for breakfast. It was time to go.

She bent to kiss her mother's cheek, bracing for, but stung as usual by the subtle recoil from the unwanted contact.

"I'll see you tomorrow."

"It's not mine, you know."

"What's that, Mom?"

"That." Josephine pointed to the window ledge. "Take it. Take it away."

Only two things occupied the shelf—a framed photo and a straw basket from which trailed a needlepoint ivy. Clea touched the delicate green leaves.

"You don't want the plant here anymore?" But she could tell by Josephine's continued agitation it was the picture that had caused the alarm.

She closed in on the photo. A six-month-old, hands raised in secret glee, sat baby fashion within the bounds of the wooden frame. It was a picture of Clea, the only one she ever remembered seeing of herself as a child. Josephine had forbidden photographs, dismissing any criticism with religious zeal. Besides, her mother always said, the best photo album was her mind, filled with memories, easier to organize and didn't collect dust.

It seemed now a cruel irony.

"You don't mean *this*?" The question doubled as a plea.

Josephine waved toward the door as if to spirit a hated object out of the room.

"Okay, Ma. Try to stay calm. I've got it." Clea stacked the frame on top of the book already cradled in her arm and with her head bowed over the last few things that defined her mother's essence, she slipped through the door and hurried away.

Shaken by the abruptness with which the one remaining mother-daughter link had been severed, Clea hid within the tinted cocoon of her vehicle and bit back tears that threatened her makeup. She plucked tissues from a box on the dash and blotted her eyes at the same time a shiny black Wrangler pulled into the space beside her.

Rikki Kinderset waved through the window, then exited the Jeep, balancing two steaming grande-sized cups from Starbucks.

"Got us big ones," she called, hoisting the drinks. "Think we're going to need it today."

"You have ESP or something?"

"No, but when you schedule three appointments in one day, I plan ahead. Let me in, huh."

Clea leaned over the seat, popped the lock and gave the door a shove. While Rikki wedged the coffee into side-by-side cupholders, Clea shed her silk jacket. She folded it neatly across the book and photo lying in her lap and was about to deposit the lot in the old Explorer's cargo hold when her assistant stayed her hand.

"Nice frame. Where'd you dig this up? Did I miss one of your marathon antique-hunting excursions?"

"No, and I'm warning you not to refer to this particular picture as an *antique*." She lifted the corner of her jacket, enough to reveal the toothless grin of the child.

"You?"

"Uh-huh."

Suddenly serious, Rikki stole a glance at the imposing façade of Green Haven. "Your mom…she didn't…?"

"No, no, nothing like that. Just another memory cell that's vanished into thin air is all."

Clea's eyes filled again. To cover a weakness that embarrassed her, she made a fuss about finding the perfect spot behind her in which to secure the pile without displacing the trove of camera equipment stashed there.

The younger woman filled the awkward moment by releasing her ponytail, smoothing a veil of brunette hair and twisting it into a more reserved, if slightly flyaway knob on the back of her head.

"Do you want me to drive today?" she said when Clea had finished her task.

"Thanks for offering but I'm okay."

"Sure you are." Rikki powered on the radio and with an undisguised effort to brighten the mood, spun the dial until Marc Anthony filled the car with a kicky mambo beat. On this lighter note she repeated herself. "Sure you are. You're the most okay person I know. What say we hit the road?"

Between the bouncy music and Rikki's eager smile, Clea knew her sullen mood didn't have a chance. She threw her hands into the air in surrender.

"You ought to be more careful what you ask for, Rik. By the end of the day you'll wish I'd left you standing in the parking lot."

The engine sputtered to life, and Clea steered the SUV into traffic. At the first stoplight, she patted Rikki's arm.

"It's good to have someone standing by to pitch me a life ring whenever I feel like I'm drowning. I don't say this often enough. What would I do without you?"

Rikki grinned. "For starters, you'd recognize a whole lot sooner that green means go. Which I suggest you do—and quickly—before we become the victims of road rage."

"I meant what I said."

"And I mean it when I say we're good for each other. Now go!"

Clea settled into the drive, the neighborhoods of Portland a good forty-five minutes away. Her own problems faded as she thought of the girl beside her. A half dozen years younger than Clea, Rikki Kinderset had not had an easy life. Bounced from foster home to foster home, she had managed to dodge the twin bullets of cynicism and bitterness and emerged into adulthood with a sparkling personality and a bushel-load of optimism.

Luck had brought her to Clea's door to beg for a job as photographer's apprentice. There was not one day in the last three years that Clea regretted signing her on for a six-week trial period.

Today she knew they would both earn their stripes.

For the next seven and a half hours they dug in. They hauled studio lights. They emptied camera cases and equipment boxes, only to pack them up again and repeat the exhausting work at the next sitting...and the next... all the while representing Clea Reilly's Family Photography efficiently and professionally. Clea usually enjoyed the family portraiture part of her business, but by four-thirty she was convinced the lunar phases were malaligned with the rest of the universe. Though dressed in Sunday school attire, the day's gaggle of little boys and girls had behaved like the devil's own. Throw in one bawling baby and two uncooperative Great Danes and Clea's head throbbed.

Construction detours delayed their return, landing them on I-5 in the middle of the evening rush.

By the time she dropped Rikki at her car, all she could think of was home. Visions of a hot bubble bath simmering away tensions brought a smile to her face, though she knew such luxury was impossible. Tedious work lay ahead. The day's canisters of film had to be logged in and prepared for the lab. At minimum, she assured herself, peace and quiet awaited.

That also was not to be.

The low murmur of a distant TV greeted her at the back door.

"Addy?" she called. "Is that you?"

A voice, faintly recognizable as her daughter's, limped down the dim hallway and staggered into the kitchen. If there was any intelligible language in the answer, it had been lost along the way.

Clea tried again. "What are you doing home so early?"

Another muffled response.

"I thought you were staying at school to help decorate the class float."

This time nothing.

"For Pete's sake, Addison," Clea yelled. "Come here where I can figure out at least part of what you're saying."

Clea kneed shut the door and had unloaded her arms onto the kitchen counter when Addy appeared, displaying much the same enthusiasm a prisoner reserves for his executioner.

Though baggy jeans and faded flannel shirts had been the attire *du jour* since day two of Addy's recent high school experience, the sight of her daughter was still disconcerting. Addy's chosen hair style brought another involuntary grimace. The short locks had been dyed black with flame-red tips and gelled into rigid spikes which resembled the business end of a Medieval weapon.

Clea forced her lips into a thin, tight line, barring escape of the criticism that sprang readily to her tongue. Instead she feigned preoccupation with the pile of stuff she had brought in from the car and offered herself this solace: "If this is the worst of living with a teenager, I should consider myself fortunate indeed."

Aloud she said, "I thought work on the float started tonight."

"Yeah."

"And?"

"I didn't go."

"That's obvious. I guess I'm asking why?"

"I didn't know anybody there."

"Oh, Addy, I realize making the move from St. Gerard's to the public schools has been tough from the standpoint of friends, but they're not going to come banging on the front door. You have to put yourself out there."

"By stuffing colored napkins into chicken wire?"

"It's a way."

"Pretty stupid if you ask me."

A silent moment intervened in which Clea sighed and Addy backstepped into the hall. Just before the girl slipped out of sight, Clea stopped her with, "Grandma asked about you today."

"Yeah, sure."

"She did. This weekend you come with me. It'll be good for both of you."

"C'mon, Ma. Grandma's a zombie."

"Addison Reilly, you watch your mouth. I won't have you—"

"You know what I mean. Grandma's not *grandma* anymore. That's why she's in the nursing home."

"They say Alzheimer's is genetic. I hope your attitude changes when it's *your* turn to visit *me* at Green Haven."

Addison moaned and took a second wary step backwards.

"Let's start over, honey. How was your day?"

"Okay. Nothing spectacular."

"Want to hear about mine?"

A shrug.

Clea blew out her breath. "What do you want for dinner then?"

"Pizza?"

"I wasn't planning on your being here for supper, so pizza it is. Why don't you make the call."

Addy fled but a moment later popped back into view. "Mrs. Gibson called. She'll be here at six-thirty to pick up her order."

"Tonight? She's not scheduled until tomorrow."

"Said she wants both eight by tens in a frame."

Clea stopped short. "Good Lord, people can be so thoughtless. How am I supposed to do this with…" She looked at the clock on the microwave. "…with 45 minutes' notice? Mrs. Gibson should know better than—"

"Actually, Mom, she called on Saturday."

"What?" But having delivered the bad news, Addy disappeared.

Since her divorce from Michael over ten years ago, Clea had taken an avocation and built a business. His sporadic support checks left no choice. In order to stand out from the several dozen other photographers listed in the *Yellow Pages*, Clea offered to mount portraits in unique frames, most scavenged from resale shops and area flea markets. She refinished them herself in a small workshop off the kitchen.

She raced there now and from one of the many shelves pulled out the box containing the Gibson order. Carefully wrapped in tissue, the first eight by ten was already framed in a rough wood which Clea had lightly stained with green. The second photo, however, was matted only and to frame it properly would require a style she knew she didn't have. Her supply of that popular size was dangerously low. Nothing appropriate came to hand, even after rummaging through the inventory twice.

"Great," she groaned, aware of the jackhammer at her temples. Every day had been a struggle to build her professional reputation. And now this. One giant step backward. A dissatisfied customer meant loss of potential future business—not only Mrs. Gibson but most probably everyone willing to listen to the woman's complaints.

Clea stood in front of the shelves as if wood and glass would materialize under a relentless stare. Soon her vision blurred and didn't refocus until her eyes wandered to the kitchen counter and lighted on the book of verse and the neat and perfectly suitable frame beside it. Reluctantly Clea moved toward the table. She needed to use that frame, yet at the same time was loath to separate it from its photo.

What if in a rare moment her mother asked about it? Would she notice a substituted frame? More important, would the shock of so familiar a thing being altered cause irrevocable harm?

This picture was a fragile bridge. It supported Josephine's memory of the past, of the years which included Clea and Addison. Dare she risk a crack in the structure, or worse, that the bridge crash down altogether, leaving her mother stranded across the river and she alone on the near shore?

In the quiet room the clock picked away at her resolve.

With no other choice, she removed the brads from the back, lifted out a piece of card stock, the picture, the glass. That the photo was doubly thick struck her as unusual. She fingered it and discovered the picture was actually one half of a larger one which had been folded in two.

Clea spread it flat. What she had for all her life thought was a picture of herself posed alone revealed a woman, sitting in profile, smiling softly at the baby balanced on her knee.

"Pizza'll be here in twenty."

The announcement startled her, for Clea had not heard her daughter reenter the room. She barely recovered from Addy's unexpected presence when a beringed finger with its ghoulish, black nail polish slid into her field of vision and tapped the photo in front of her.

"That's you as a baby, isn't it, Mom?"

"Uh-huh."

"So..." The finger trailed sideways. "...that's grandma?"

An answer, if there was one to be had, never broke the surface of silence, for just as Clea knew she most certainly was the pictured child, just as certainly she realized the woman was not Josephine Worth.

Chapter Two

3:11.

The red blips on Clea's alarm glowed like neon. Even when she closed her eyes, they retreated only momentarily, and reappeared as ghostly gray echoes on the wall of her retina. She rolled away, then back again.

Still 3:11.

An eerie wash of color spilled from the clock face onto the as-yet-unexplained photograph lying next to it on the nightstand. Turning the clock around offered scant relief, for the image of the woman and child had imprinted itself in her brain as firmly as two times two equals four or blue plus yellow yields green.

It was no use. Sleep was impossible.

After pizza and Mrs. Gibson, after work on the day's film and the usual argument with Addy over the eleven-o'clock-lights-out rule, Clea had taken a magnifying glass and studied every inch of the picture. The woman—girl really, for she appeared to be in her twenties—wore a sleeveless, flowered shift. Matching alligator clips on a dainty beaded chain tethered a white angora cardigan so it draped neatly over her shoulders. Her hair had been teased into the signature style of the late sixties—bouffant, chin length, half-circle flips on the ends. Its color matched the wheat-blond fringe which wreathed the baby's face. Their eyes were four buttons off the same card.

They were so alike they could have been related, giving rise to the question that kept Clea awake most of the night.

Who *was* the woman?

Her mother had never intimated the existence of aunts, cousins, or younger sisters. Over the years there had been no reunions or wedding invitations from nieces and nephews. Christmas cards arrived from friends or the parents of her mother's sixth grade students. None came from family.

Clea had grown up in the sure knowledge she and her mother were alone. Facing the rough times as a team of two had always struck her as romantic, especially when her mother would come to her side and say, "Remember, Clea, we're like two sticks from an oak tree. Nothing can break us as long as we stand together."

And nothing had, neither scraped knees nor a wounded heart, nor the years when a teacher's salary didn't stretch quite far enough.

But at this moment Clea felt like a puny twig, tinder dry and ready to snap.

She punched the pillow with her fist and buried her face in the hole.

"Sleep," she told herself. "Something'll come to mind in the morning."

What miracle might be in the offing she had no idea, for the sole guardian of the elusive information could only occasionally remember her own name.

"Sleep, Clea. Sleeeep!"

And somewhere between the earnest appeal and the pale light of dawn, she did.

As it did every day, a small knot tightened in Clea's stomach as she crossed the third floor lobby at Green Haven. The unpredictable hills and dales of her mother's moods slowed her steps and dampened her palms with a thin sheen of perspiration.

Today more than usual.

Today she had a purpose other than filial duty.

Today she would try to coax a memory from the locked vault of her mother's mind.

The ever-present book of rose poems had gained a page—the photo Clea had tucked inside its covers. She would prod with an innocent "Who's this, Mom?" and listen closely for a clue.

She looked to the nurse's station for a sign the plan had the remotest chance of success. Her hopes plummeted when Lydia's fingers bobbed up and down in front of the white ocean of her uniform bodice like a line of storm-fed sea swells. A warning. Even before Clea navigated the turn onto the residents' hallway, she prepared for the tempest, so was little surprised at what greeted her behind the door to her mother's room.

An aide—or was this Lydia's replacement?—fended off with one hand an armada of swats and slaps. The other hand, gripped around a hairbrush, made aborted sorties on a matted nest of gray.

"Please," the girl pleaded. "Let me fix your hair a little—just a little—before Big Mama out there has my ass."

"Perhaps I can help," said Clea.

The girl whirled, her cheeks blazing crimson. One of Josephine's blows caught the brush and sent it spinning to the floor.

"Oh, shoot," said the aide, her eyes now riveted on Clea. "Are you from the office? This isn't.... I wasn't.... It's only that Mrs. Worth...."

"I know what Mrs. Worth can be like. I'm her daughter. Sometimes it's best to give up and let her have her own way. Let me see what I can do."

When the girl didn't move, Clea said, "Why don't you take a break."

"I'm supposed to make the bed."

Clea nodded and fished the hairbrush from under the nightstand while the aide threw the spread over rumpled sheets and plumped the pillow.

Bed made and girl gone, Josephine calmed. She had circled to the rocking chair and was sitting quietly. This boded well. Though she stiffened when Clea laid a hand on her shoulder and clenched the chair's armpads until her knuckles lost all color, Josephine remained seated and if not pleased at least resigned to have her hair groomed.

For awhile Clea worked without speaking, smoothing and separating until bit by bit the gray tangles gave way and fell into a soft pageboy. Even after all had been put to right, Clea continued brushing. With each stroke a slide show of other days clicked, frame by frame, onto a screen only she could see. There she sat—as a four-year-old, an eight-year-old, a ten-year-old—safe and loved, on a pink chintz coverlet while her mother combed and braided, laughed and chattered.

Before too long the air in the stifling room congealed in Clea's throat, and the head in front of her fell out of focus.

She dug deep for courage and finally spoke, no louder than a whisper. Like intruders, the words rushed forth, and once she started there was no calling them back.

"I found a picture last night. Actually I didn't *find* it. It's my baby picture, the one you used to have right there by the window. I guess I never really saw the whole thing before. I'm sitting on someone's lap, Mom. Addy thought the woman was you. We know better, don't we?"

She waited for a reaction.

Not a muscle quivered. Josephine seemed transfixed, though on what Clea hadn't a clue.

"Addy was excited to see you so young," she continued. "Said you were pretty 'way back when.' I'm afraid I lied to her. Oh, not directly. I simply didn't contradict. Who is that woman?"

This time Josephine stirred, a barely perceptible movement, yet enough so the seat cushion wheezed at the shift of her weight. Hopeful a long-dormant synapse had fired, Clea pressed on, retrieving the photograph and holding it up for her mother to see.

"Bah-brah."

Two strangled syllables escaped her mother's lips, like stubborn buckthorn yanked roots and all from the soil.

"What did you say, Mom? Was that a name? Barbara? Was it Barbara?"

But there would be no clarification. Josephine whipped the rocker into a full-out gallop and drowned out Clea's budding optimism with a disjointed, tuneless hum.

Ten frustrating minutes later Clea tiptoed from the room. The odd duet of squeak and hum played on.

In sharp contrast, a noisy, efficient buzz enveloped the nurse's desk.

"I hear Miz Josie still be in quite a state," said Lydia from behind a stack of medical charts.

"You're so right, and I'm afraid I made it worse."

"You're not to worry yourself, Miz Reilly."

"I hate to upset her."

"You know as well as I this afternoon she'll take a fancy to something else. Things'll be better. I can almost guarantee it."

"Almost, huh?"

A good-natured laugh burst from Lydia and infected Clea who smiled in spite of her wretched mood.

The smile didn't last long.

If Clea hoped all would be cleared up with a single question, she was mistaken. Instead of resolving anything, her mother's curious reaction only heaped flour into the broth.

She tried to wrestle a Barbara from the murky depths of her memory to no avail. Had she misheard? Perhaps the name her mother actually uttered was a surname. Barber? Barbeau? Or was Josephine merely calling for the nurse's aide? Clea chastised herself for not having the presence of mind to read the girl's ID tag.

And, of course, it could mean absolutely nothing at all.

Habit guided her through the halls and down the elevator. She spoke to no one. Preoccupied with her mother's strange behavior, she had forgotten all about the morning's weather. When she shoved through the exit door, the air wrapped itself around her like cotton batting.

Rikki approached. "Rotten weather," she called.

"What? Oh, yeah." Clea looked around as if seeing the fog for the first time. The earlier wisps had thickened, settled and lay curled like sleeping cats on a carpet of grass. "I'm sorry. I should have called and canceled. I'd hoped it would clear. Instead it's gotten worse."

"No kidding. If the fog's like this in town, the coast's sure to be socked in."

"I agree. No sense driving all the way to Florence to photograph a wall of gray."

"Right, the dunes. This was going to be your entry to the National Parks contest, wasn't it?"

"Fame and fortune...foiled again."

"It came with some nice prize money too."

"Which I could really use, but for that to happen, I'd have to actually win."

"If I were the judge, you'd be a shoo-in. Michael late again?"

A brittle laugh escaped Clea's lips. "Still is more like it. If I had a dime for every one of his excuses, I wouldn't need his checks at all. But for now you're the winner, and the grand prize is a day off. How about that?"

"Do you hear me complaining? By the way, how's your mom doing?"

"No better...worse actually. All my fault too."

While Rikki raised a curious eyebrow, Clea flip-flopped between confiding or keeping the matter of the photo to herself. There wasn't much that slid by Rikki, and maybe this too she would divulge. But not yet.

They returned to their respective cars and headed out, Rikki in the direction of her apartment and Clea into town.

Caught up in her private thoughts, Clea hardly remembered the drive. The old Ford came by rote to a diagonal slot on Sixth Street directly in front of Mitz's One Hour Photo. The day's chores beckoned, and dropping off film was number one on the list.

Clea slid from behind the wheel. Before she cleared the curb, she saw Mitz through the plate glass. From the outside looking in, it appeared the woman's hand, raised in welcome, had grasped the brightly-painted "O" in "photo" as if it were a life ring and Mitz about to cast it to a victim at sea. The gesture stoked an inkling into an idea. Clea returned momentarily to the car and slipped the photograph into her purse.

Even though Mitz was well into the years when most people opted for the slower pace of retirement, she steadfastly refused all offers to buy her out. Nearby businesses changed hands two and three times. The bookstore became a hair salon, the craft store a wallpaper shop. The flighty nature of the street, though, was balanced by the constancy of Mitz's One Hour Photo.

A cheerful bell announced her entrance, and as always Clea marveled at the tastefully cluttered displays, showcasing paraphernalia to please both shutterbug and professional. The woman had a talent for anticipating what fads would come and go and what would remain forever classic.

Habit brought Clea's eyes to the row of framed decorative art strung out on the wall above the cash register. Her mother had always admired the one titled "Love Is Like...A Red, Red Rose." Clea was fond of it too. A tall crystal tube held a single, bold red rose, its head high and proud over a cluster of leaves. Two leatherleaf fronds extended outward like familiar arms welcoming a loved one home.

In the past Clea had offered to buy it, a gift for her mother. Mitz had kindly shook her head. "Ah, Clea, my dear, that one's not for sale."

Other photos came and went from the gallery. The rose remained. Forever fresh, never fading.

Unlike her mother.

Clea sighed just as Mitz sang out her name.

"Clea, you're just in time. I'm expecting FedEx any minute. You've got something for the lab?"

Clea upended a bag onto the counter, and the film from yesterday's shoots spilled out.

"Oh my," said Mitz.

"Only those numbered one through six are high priority, so if Fred shows up early...."

"If that boy makes so much as a fuss, his mother will get an earful." Clea smiled inwardly for *that boy* was a good fifty years old. "Now, dear," Mitz went on, "you sort. I'll write up the envelopes. I see you have a page of special instructions."

"Two."

"Hand them over."

The drone of fluorescent bulbs filled the small shop, for no other customers broke the silence of their work.

Mitz's hands skittered like mice as she scratched names and numbers onto delivery envelopes then duplicated the information in a logbook. She bent low over the counter, compensating in distance what her eyes lacked in focus. Clea noted the stark white of the older woman's hair, so tightly bunned it looked as if a snowball had hit the back of her head and stuck there.

Mitz had been around for a long while. If anyone knew of her mother's past, the past beyond Clea's memory, it was Mitz Maguire. Clea's fingers danced around the clasp to her purse, but as with Rikki, she hesitated, not sure how to broach the question without embarrassment. After all, her mother had obviously known of the folded-away portion of the picture, yet had chosen never to mention it, not even once.

The imprint of Mitz's hand on her arm surprised her, not only the coolness of the touch but knowing her mind had wandered to another place and she had missed what had been said.

"You okay, dear? Are you thinking about your poor mother?"

Was she so transparent? What other of her thoughts was this woman privy to?

"I'm sorry," Clea stammered, flustered.

Mitz persisted. "How *is* Josie these days? I confess I haven't been up to see her at Green Haven in weeks. She thinks I'm there to sweep the floor. It's so much more pleasant to remember what used to be."

Here it was, thought Clea, the opening she sought—the lull in conversation, Mitz's nostalgic sigh. An offhand remark now about the photo would be as easy as dropping a coin in a slot.

"You're going to think this funny," she began, forcing a smile. "Mom's had this picture of me around forever, yet only last night I realized there's someone else in it. Someone I don't know."

She resurrected the photo and carefully laid it out for inspection. She hoped for recognition. In the least, she expected curiosity, but Mitz stiffened as if Clea had just offered her a poisoned cookie.

Clea caught her breath. "Do you know her? Her name may be Barbara."

Mitz averted her eyes and retamped the edges of a stack of catalogs that had already been piled razor straight next to the cash register. "I don't know any Barbaras," she said dismissively.

"That name's a guess." Clea pushed on. "It could be a last name that sounds similar to Barbara like—"

"I can't help you."

"But you and Mom have been friends since high school, surely—"

"I said I don't know." The testiness in her voice stung.

Clea tried again. "The young woman would be much older now, sixtyish. If you looked at the picture a little closer, you might—"

A rush of air and the frantic jangle of the bell interrupted. Both women spun to face the door.

"Fred! Oh my, it's Fred." Mitz gasped as if she had been holding her breath and only now remembered to exhale. She waved him inside. "I'm not quite finished. So much. Piles and piles of envelopes. I'll hurry. You mustn't get behind in your route." She busied herself with papers and forms, ignoring Clea entirely.

Clea picked up the photo, slowly refolded it and tucked it back into her purse. At the door she paused for one last inquiring glance. The older woman raised her head, her gaze a mix of sympathy, understanding…and something else that Clea could not quite decipher, not even after Mitz quietly but firmly said, “Let it go, Clea. Let it go.”

Chapter Three

In the time it took Clea to shrug off the business district and the trailing ill ease of Mitz's parting words, she had reached the outlying grid of quiet residential lanes. A wintry front had moved in, and the morning's nasty overcast had spawned an icy drizzle.

She turned into the driveway and sat clutching the steering wheel while gazing through the rain at her mother's house.

The dirty gray light accentuated the homestead's flaws. Clumps of moss oozed from under broken shingles. Crusty scabs of paint curled upward to expose raw wounds in the wooden clapboard beneath. Two corner trees pegged the house to the gloomy sky, and there it hung, a sodden blanket too heavy for the line. It was as if the house had passed beyond mourning and come to weary terms with the final stage of grief while Clea had yet to relinquish her anger that her mother would never return there.

The rain showed no sign of abating, so Clea sprinted to the porch and let herself in.

The house was cold and damp. She hadn't been there for a week, nor had she foreseen the recent downturn in the weather. The day's rain made matters worse.

She looked around and shivered, only partly because of the chill. It seemed a sorcerer had aimed his wand and poof! What had once been a home was now nothing more than a house, filled with furniture, but stripped of life.

The sterile rooms struck her the same with each visit, though none of it should have come as a surprise. After all, she herself had boxed her mother's belongings and locked them out of the way in the small bedroom upstairs.

The ambitious plan to entice renters, however, had idled at a standstill. Soft market, everyone told her. Bad timing, end of season. All Clea knew for sure was the much-anticipated rent money to ease the strain of Green Haven's endless stream of expenses had failed to materialize.

No dwelling on that now. She had come for a different reason. She intended to snoop.

But first, some heat.

Quickly Clea crossed to the thermostat. As soon as the furnace clicked on, she circled around the massive stone fireplace which dominated the center of the wide open living area, and headed toward the kitchen.

It too was bare. Clea had long ago emptied the cabinets of perishables and tossed appliances dating to her childhood. The microwave she bought her mother a few Christmases ago, and which she suspected had never been used, was the only keeper. Considering the needs of future occupants, she spared a set of old dishes and for her own use, a few basics. These last had been segregated from the tenant-ready goods and huddled like sad refugees on a far corner of the countertop.

Clea heated water in a mug and dunked a teabag, warming her hands for a moment over the steaming brew. A package of saltines had gone stale but she grabbed them anyway. Thus armed, she reentered the great room and mounted the steps to the second floor.

Her once-upon-a-time bedroom, more recently the sewing room, resembled a fortress. Boxes stacked head high lined the perimeter, an unbroken defense which blocked both window and closet door.

Where to start?

At the time, when the emotion of packing away her mother's things had been overwhelming, she had merely upended drawers and cleared out cupboards in a broad sweep, flinging all into unmarked cartons. Now she lamented the lapse in her usually more organized self. A glance gave no clue as to contents. Randomly she selected a box and broke the seal.

Vast stores of memories spilled from the boxes, along with godawful art projects from kindergarten, souvenirs and trinkets. A slim manila file held newspaper clippings. Clea sorted through the yellowed snippets but found only her own life in review—academic triumphs, graduations, a wedding notice in which she appeared far too young and naïve to have made such a life-altering decision. The occasion of Addison's birth followed and a series of advertisements she had placed to draw customers to Clea Reilly's Family Photography.

Time and again her thoughts drifted from the task, so she literally had to shake them from her head in order to continue, but in hours of searching, nothing helpful emerged. Her mother kept no journal, seemed to have saved everything but letters.

When a ragtag address book surfaced, Clea felt a rush of excitement. She sat in the middle of the carpeted floor and scoured the alphabet for a Barbara.

There was none.

If that's what she was looking for at all. And why was she bothering anyway? She'd already lived thirty-three years totally unaware of the existence of this Barbara. Would another thirty-three really matter?

Clea sighed, awareness seeping in that she was stiff and sore. Knotted muscles at the base of her neck refused to loosen despite rolling her shoulders this way and that. When she rose on rubbery legs to stand on feet tortured by a thousand pinpricks, she conceded.

"Okay, Mom. You win. Keep your little secret." Then she laughed, for it brought to mind a few secrets of her own she had hidden from her mother. "Tit for tat, huh? Guess that's the way it'll stay."

She slipped out of the room, careful to resecure the lock. Before descending the stairs she detoured into her mother's bedroom, drawn there out of habit more than curiosity. Only the bed, a side table and chair, and the heavy mahogany dresser remained. Small geometric shapes in a thick layer of dust were faint reminders of knickknacks, though the voids too were filling in. Clea made a mental note to give the place a thorough cleaning.

She turned to leave, had no reason to stay, but found herself pulled toward the closet. She dragged the chair into the narrow walk-in and using it as a stepping stool examined the shelves for anything that might have been left behind. A thumbtack skittered drunkenly and fell to the floor.

Clea hunted it down but left it lying and inexplicably began tapping the wallboard, listening closely for a sound that might suggest a hollow space beneath. Crouched in the back of the closet, she was well into the game when a noise from the street startled her. She rocked back on her heels, suddenly aware of the spectacle she presented.

For Pete's sake, Clea, she thought. You're acting like a fictional detective, and not a very good one at that. If someone saw you now, they'd think you were nuts.

The judgment, though overly harsh, was the impetus she needed to bolt from the house. She forced aside nagging questions and dismissed Mitz's *warning* as the bane of an avid mystery reader where anything one tick off center spelled high drama.

Outside, the rain had stopped A thinning veil of clouds allowed a peek at the sun. To Clea's dismay, it appeared much lower in the sky than she expected. It was almost three. She hurried home, glad to find the back door still latched, meaning Addy hadn't yet arrived from school. She dropped her coat across the back of a kitchen chair and immediately went to work on dinner. Soon the aroma of garlic and basil filled the room, and a pot of sauce gurgled gaily on the stove.

A gust of fresh air swirled ahead of Addy as the girl burst into the house.

"Hi, sweetie," said Clea.

Addy rushed by on her way to the pantry. Crackling plastic wrap betrayed the girl's mission. "Yeah, hi," she mumbled.

"Hey! We'll be eating soon. Don't ruin your appetite."

"Okay," Addy said through a mouthful of chips, the opened bag under her arm.

"Please, don't...." Clea stopped mid-sentence when she realized her admonition had no audience. Her daughter was nowhere in sight. "Addy," she called loudly, "I forgot to collect the mail. Would you...?"

"Got it," came from the depths of the living room.

The chip bag protested noisily, and Clea heard what sounded like two failed attempts to balance an unruly assortment of, she guessed, junk mail. Finally Addy reappeared and dumped an armload on the center island.

"Anything interesting?"

"Nah. Oh, wait. There's a package."

"A package made it through the mail slot?"

"Yeah. It's little."

Clea turned from her preparations. A number of envelopes and sales catalogs lay scattered on the counter. Her daughter stood quietly examining a small bundle the size of a pack of cigarettes.

"It's addressed to grandma," Addy said barely above a whisper.

As the girl flipped the box over and over in her hands, Clea saw the familiar yellow forwarding sticker slapped on the backside by the Post Office. She stepped closer to her daughter's side, trying to more clearly see the handwriting.

"Who's it from?" she asked.

"No one. I mean, there's no return address. Can I open it?"

Clea hesitated. "I *do* check everything else that comes in the mail for her. Bills and such. I guess there's no harm."

But Addy hadn't waited for permission. Her black-painted nails sliced into the wrap to reveal a small, ivory-colored box.

"I wonder what...?" Clea began, but again Addy was a beat ahead of her mother. The lid joined the brown paper scraps on the floor.

At last, Clea and Addison fell into sync, both open-mouthed yet speechless.

An exquisite pin rested on a velvet cushion—a finely-crafted pink rosebud atop a gracefully curved golden stem.

Addy found her voice first. "Wow!"

"I second that." Clea ran a finger over the rose's smooth enamel surface. Accents of gold sparkled under the kitchen light. "This is beautiful."

Lifting it from the box to the palm of her hand, she nodded in appreciation. The pin was weighty, obviously of high quality and equally lofty price.

"Do you think grandma has a secret lover?" said Addy over her mother's shoulder.

The idea struck Clea as ludicrous and she said so.

"What if he lives in a foreign country and doesn't know she's in that *place*? It's possible."

"No, it's not. First of all, the stamps are U.S., and grandma would never—"

"How can you be so sure?"

"Simple. We're very close, your grandmother and I. Always have been. I know all her friends and—"

"Then who's this from? See, you don't know anything about grandma... and it's too late to ask, isn't it?"

At that, Addy tossed the box onto the pile of mail and ran down the hall. Clea followed a few steps behind, though not fast enough to avoid the door to Addy's room, slammed with such ferocity it knocked akilter a pair of sconces on the wall.

By the time Clea twisted the knob and yanked open the door, Addy was already slumped in a chair, her arms folded tightly over her chest. In front of her, as if mocking the scene, bright yellow smiley faces floated aimlessly across the computer screen.

When Addy swiped a sleeve at the corners of her eyes, Clea's anger at her daughter's behavior dissolved.

"Sweetheart, what's wrong?"

"Nothing."

"You're crying."

"No, I'm not."

"What's this about? Grandma's illness? I wish I could reassure you."

"It's not like she has the flu, Mom."

"Of course not. Alzheimer's is serious, but we're dealing with it."

"Yeah, yeah. One day at a time. You're always saying crap like that."

Clea tried to put an arm around her daughter's shoulders. They twitched. Unspoken, yet certain rejection. Clea backed off. "That's the only way to live," she said. "Otherwise you drive yourself crazy."

"But you're the one who said it. You're gonna to get it. I'm gonna to get it. My life's already ruined. What's the use about anything?"

"Nothing's hammered in stone. The future isn't so easily mapped out—good or bad."

Addy didn't answer.

"If I could give you guarantees, I'd do it in a minute."

"A lot that means. You never keep your word anyway."

Stunned, Clea swiveled her daughter's chair until they were face to face. "Are we still talking about grandma?"

"Daddy says I should've stayed with my friends and gone to Catholic Central."

The giant leap in the conversation hit Clea like a one-two punch. At first dazed, she could only stare at Addy's face set in defiance, damnation blazing from the girl's eyes. It took a moment to regain her voice.

"Your father said that?"

Clea grit her teeth. If Michael had lived up to his obligations, she could have afforded any high school Addy wanted. How dare he, in one broad stroke, paint her as the bad guy.

"I'm the new kid that nobody wants to talk to. Daddy's on my side. He understands."

"Your father hasn't managed to call or drag himself up here since you were in second grade, yet he knows all about school and your friends?"

"We email."

"He uses email? How did you find that out?"

Addy hung her head. "I memorized the postmark on his last letter to you, and I searched on the computer until I found his address. I know I didn't tell you, Mom, but I wrote and sent him my email name and he answered."

"Just how long has this been going on?"

Avoiding the question, Addy said instead, "He has lots of time to write since he's not working for that old lumber company anymore."

How typical, Clea thought. The absent parent always lands the breaks. Michael remembers he owes child support once every six months or so, won't spend a quarter on a phone call, but a few clicks on the computer and he's nominated Father of the Year. And it sounded like he'd lost another job. Fat chance of seeing a check from him anytime soon.

A flash of anger brightened her cheeks, but when Clea looked closely at her daughter's misery, she willed herself into a calmer, cooler state. The failed marriage was not Addy's fault. And if Michael came across as a white knight to a sad and lonely teenaged damsel, she admittedly owned a portion of the blame. Vowing never to bad mouth him within Addison's hearing, she had erred in the opposite extreme and rarely mentioned him at all, including his well-earned shortcomings.

A remedy was in order, though now didn't seem the best time. Addy would claim sour grapes, and on that particular point she might be right.

Softly, hoping her voice would soothe, she said, "Dry your eyes, honey, and come to dinner."

"I'm not hungry."

It was pointless to insist. "I'll keep a plate warm in case you change your mind."

Clea slipped from the room.

Damn that Michael! He acted no wiser than a fourteen-year-old himself. Clea fully intended to skewer him with a few nicely-honed comments about his parenting skills, but when she reentered the kitchen, the torn wrappings still scattered on the floor reminded her of what had actually started the row with Addy.

Clearly the girl missed her grandmother—the funny grandmother, the indulgent, approachable grandmother—and suffered by not knowing quite how to handle the loss. Addy wasn't alone in her feelings, but Clea worked through her grief by making herself useful. She showed up at the nursing home and shouldered the thousand little details involved in arranging her mother's affairs with the least number of snags.

Addy's suggestion of secrets had been painful, but the last forty-eight hours proved them all too true. Part of her mother's life had been private, closed to Clea, hidden and unexplained.

It hurt.

She'd feel better if it weren't such a mystery, and with that in mind, Clea gathered the scraps and laid them on the dining room table where she worked them like a jigsaw puzzle, taping each piece until the brown paper square was once again whole.

Block letters told nothing other than they had been boldly written. Together with the stamps, little room remained for the postmark. Clea imagined a distraught postal clerk attempting to affix the mark without obliterating the address and smudging the ink in the process. It yielded no information about the sender.

She swept it aside and meant to repackage the pin but noticed the box's lid was missing. Hunting around, she found it under a chair. When she tried to reunite it with the box, she discovered a small white card stuck inside. No bigger than a gift enclosure card one might get at a florist, it was nonetheless tightly wedged. Clea prized it out with a utility knife. Formally embossed across the face were the words "Thank You."

Clea turned it over, crowing to herself that at least one question was about to be answered. Her half-formed smile abruptly disappeared.

The card was signed "#21."

Chapter Four

"*What* in God's name is this?"

Sinking heavily into the nearest chair, Clea stared at the card.

How many more surprises did her mother have tucked away?

She popped to her feet with the need to walk around. Let activity generate a clue. But immediately the room closed in, leaving her lightheaded and none the wiser. She tried to visualize each unknown as a new piece of clothing and how the drape and color fit her mother. Nothing clicked. In fact, she could barely conjure an image outside a narrow definition of "mom" or "grandma."

Worse yet, she found it impossible to deny how little she actually knew about her mother. What had the woman been like as a girl? What aspirations and dreams kept her awake at night with the sheer intensity of wanting them so badly? Had her hopes been fulfilled or had she spent her life in silent disillusionment? Clea knew none of this, and it didn't take much soul-searching to realize—and admit as God's truth—she had been too wrapped up in herself to make an effort to find out.

To be sure, her own life had been chaotic. It wasn't easy the many roles she'd had to play, first as wife, then single parent, sole provider, caretaker.

Excuses all.

The years had been rife with opportunities to step beyond the threshold and open the door to the inner world of Josephine Worth. For one reason or another Clea had failed to even jiggle the handle, and now that she wanted in, was thwarted by a door securely locked. The cost of indifference verged on physical pain, and a leaden ball of regret hung beneath her heart.

Like Addy, Clea lost her appetite.

The sauce still bubbled on the stove. The pasta was way beyond *al dente.* She crossed the room to shut off burners and scoop the meal into a Tupperware bowl which she set on the counter to cool. Without enthusiasm she attacked the day's mail, segregating junk from bills. Midway through, the phone rang.

Half a ring, actually, for Addy had an extension an easy grab away from her computer. At first Clea gave the call no more than a passing interest. A moment later she thought of Michael and prayed he had decided to splurge on long distance. There was a message she wanted to send sizzling through the wires. She dropped a handful of advertisements into the trash and was about to head toward the bedroom when Addy appeared at the end of the hallway holding a cordless.

"It's for you."

Stealing a glance at the kitchen clock, Clea said, "Who would call me at this time?" She puckered her mouth, irritated at the after-hours intrusion, yet when she took the receiver her hand shook visibly.

Her side of the conversation consisted of lone syllables, so when she clicked off and looked at her daughter, the girl's eyes were huge with alarm.

"What is it?" said Addy. "Who was it?"

"The evening supervisor at Green Haven. The doctor wants to see me."

"Tonight?"

"He's making rounds. If I can get there before six, he'll still be at the home."

"Is grandma okay? I mean...you know what I mean."

Not wanting Addison to gauge the level of her concern, Clea sucked in her breath. Like pumping air into a balloon gives it shape, her shoulders squared and her chin lifted. She slapped on a smile and lied.

"Of course she is. Don't worry, honey. It's probably time for one of doctor's periodic updates."

"You're sure that's all?"

"Nothing more, but I don't know how long it'll take. Will you be all right here alone?"

"Mom, I'm not two years old." Hands on hips, elbows spread wide, she looked every bit a dragon defending its lair. "Just go. Besides, I'm babysitting the Westin kids. They pick me up in an hour."

For the second time in less than an hour, the air crackled with tension. Clea felt a numbing ripple of guilt which she could neither control nor fully understand. Addy's stance was rigid, an obstinate wall that Clea didn't have the energy to scale.

"Okay," she sighed and circled the kitchen, collecting car keys, purse and jacket.

On the porch she almost tripped over a mound of dark gray fur the size of a football. She couldn't tell if the response to her shriek was a purr or a growl, but the cat disappeared behind a bush.

"That stray is here again. Just can't seem to discourage it. You're not feeding it, are you, Addy?"

Clea didn't wait for the answer, but once in the car she glanced back toward the house. Addy was on the stoop, balancing a paper plate of spaghetti in one hand, a plastic bowl in the other.

"Here, kitty. Here, Kitty-Face."

"Kitty-Face? Oh, no," she groaned to herself. "Why did you have to go and name it, Addy?"

Little wonder the cat kept returning. One look at her daughter gently coaxing the kitten into the open and she guessed the smorgasbord had been a nightly affair from the beginning. No use protesting. Adoption had obviously already taken place.

The drive to Green Haven took barely fifteen minutes. Clea parked and hurried across the lot. The colorful posters along the third-floor corridor blurred into one huge Expressionist collage as she passed.

Fresh in her mind was what she hadn't told Addy: the nurse supervisor's hushed mention of a decline in her mother's condition. Dr. Foley would explain when she arrived. The nurse would divulge nothing else.

The doctor stood at the central pod, scribbling in a case file, his back to Clea. Good. She needed a moment to compose herself. Once he noticed her there, she wanted the presence of mind to measure the seriousness of the situation. The distance she was led away from the sensibilities of other patients and their relatives would tell her a great deal. She was glad then when Dr. Foley motioned her toward a pair of chairs along the wall, removed from the hubbub but not behind closed doors. A good sign, she thought. The news might be bad but not dire.

"How is she?"

The doctor referred to the chart in his hands as he spoke. "I'm afraid Mrs. Worth suffered a rather significant setback today. She had been nicely stabilized for quite awhile. It was only a matter of time before a new decline set in, yet I'm puzzled as to what brought this on."

"What do you mean?"

"In our Alzheimer's patients, it frequently takes a stressor—an accident or illness—to initiate a change in status like the one I see now. Health-wise, your mother is in fine shape. I know you've kept up regular visitation. That generally has a calming effect, so I have no explanation other than to say it's the unpredictable nature of the disease."

For the first time the doctor looked at Clea and continued, "You realize, each patient is an individual and as such reacts differently to different stimuli. Your mother's speech has slurred and the staff reports a marked increase in anxiety level. We've sedated her for now."

The palms of Clea's hands began to sweat. She buried them in her jacket pocket and lowered her gaze, so no one could read there the shame she felt for the part she no doubt played in this recent turn of events. The doctor rose to his feet. She made no attempt to enlighten him. She sensed rather than witnessed his departure, but when she glanced up he was but a few feet away, peering at her with doubtful eyes. Her cheeks burned. Still she said nothing.

Foley tipped his head. "Have a good evening, Mrs. Reilly."

He had made no accusations, quite the contrary, nevertheless Clea felt thoroughly reprimanded, a penitent admonished to "go and sin no more." She vowed to take the warning to heart. No matter how curious she might be, never again would she confront her mother, neither with questions nor pictures, and now especially not with the rosebud pin.

For awhile Clea wandered the halls, alternately avoiding and approaching Room 303. Eventually, to see for herself what damage she had wrought, she entered the room.

Tightly drawn blinds threw shadows along the walls with the only light a pale blue wash from a fluorescent tube at the head of the bed. The faint smell of antiseptic wafted from the bedclothes, which rose and fell with her mother's every breath. Josephine's hair was mussed, a stray lock limp across her cheek. Clea brushed it aside, then leaned in to kiss the gently snoring woman.

She lingered at the bedside, buffeted by sorrow yet at the same time intrigued by an aspect of her mother she never knew existed. A woman with secrets.

The frail figure slept on. Clea leaned over her and whispered, "If only there were a way to step back in time and do it right. I'd pay more attention, Mom, get you to talk. And I swear I'd listen a lot better too."

If Clea hoped confessing her shortcomings would prove therapeutic, she was mistaken. It only sharpened a hunger that could never be sated.

Josephine stirred. Fearing the sound of her voice had caused her mother unrest despite the drug-induced slumber, Clea backed away, turned, and tiptoed out.

In the car she fished the cell phone from her purse and punched in her home number. No answer. If she called the Westins, Addy would only think she was checking up on her.

With no reason to hurry, Clea set out for home, allowing her thoughts to wander on the way. Passing landmarks only vaguely registered. A good hundred yards beyond an asphalt parking lot, realization of where she was belatedly connected with an idea scratching at the corners of her mind. She swung the wheel and executed a misshapen U-turn.

As it was still within the dinner hour, only a few patrons wandered the library's aisles. Several elderly gentlemen claimed the few overstuffed chairs and napped over the pages of newspapers or magazines. The reading room was empty. In the reference area, the lone librarian sat at the desk, a piece of needlepoint spread on her lap. With a small Stork scissors she snipped extraneous threads. When Clea approached, the woman dropped her handiwork into a bag on the floor and looked up.

"Oh, Clea. How nice to see you."

Clea recognized Merriam from the church choir. Over the years the woman's wrinkles had deepened and her waistline thickened, but her soft-spoken voice and eager smile had remained welcomed constants. They greeted each other warmly.

"What can I do for you tonight?"

"Do you keep old copies of *The Sun*?"

"Last two years in paper. I'll show you where."

"Actually I'm more interested in earlier editions. Say, around 1970?"

"That would be on microfiche. The slides are kept in a back room. I'll need a date."

"Therein lies the problem. Other than the year, I have no idea."

"What are you looking for? Maybe I can hunt up a cross reference."

"Again, I'm not being very helpful. I thought I could just browse and see what pops up."

Merriam raised an eyebrow, compelling Clea to explain further. "*The Sun* has always been big on photos of community events, and I'm trying to identify a woman who might have lived or visited here in that year. Her name may—or may not—have been Barbara."

When Merriam's puzzled look didn't fade, Clea showed her the photo.

"Oh my," said Merriam, clutching a small gold cross that hung by a chain at her throat. "Wherever did this picture come from?"

"It belongs to my mom." Clea cocked her head. "Have you seen it before?"

"Me? Oh no…oh my no."

"Well, if this woman happened to attend a parish carnival, fund-raiser, or some type of public function, her picture may have been taken and she'd be identified in the caption. Hopeless, huh?"

"No, of course not. I mean, it's worth the try. Why don't I get you situated and familiar with the viewer first."

Clea followed the librarian to an ancient card reader that wheezed and grumbled when Merriam flicked on the switch. She settled into a plastic chair, giddy with anticipation.

As a small-town newspaper, *The Sun* prided itself in spotlighting local comings and goings, even more so in previous years when filling space with advertising was less of a priority. Clea pored through the paper, greedy for sight of the pretty blond woman. Over the course of the next hour, though, excitement waned as page after page, issue after issue, month after month flashed across the screen. Soon her eyes watered. Her back ached. The batch of cards representing December dwindled until the last one had been scanned and set aside.

Merriam returned for the twelfth time to collect the month's worth of microfiche. "January of '71?" she asked.

"Nope."

"You shouldn't give up so easily, young lady," said Merriam, glancing nervously over her shoulder. "It's no trouble for me. In fact, it's a terribly slow evening."

"Thanks, but I've had it. Don't know what made me think finding this woman would be as easy as a quick trip to the library."

"You young people. Always in such a hurry. Uh, surely you can stay and—"

Just then a bearded man came up behind Merriam and placed his hands on the woman's arms. Only after he'd gently eased the woman to one side did his face come into Clea's full view. "Mr. Sheznesky!" she exclaimed. "I haven't seen you in years."

Mr. Sheznesky grabbed the lapel of his sports jacket and, striking a rather flamboyant pose, recited, "'There is no good in arguing with the inevitable.' James Russell Lowell," he added with a look that left no doubt he considered neglecting due credit a cardinal sin. "Research beckoned me here. I was occupied in the reading room when you came in, but couldn't resist the opportunity to say hello to one of my more promising students."

Amazing how the passage of time skewed one's vision of reality, thought Clea, remembering the man as the somber task master of the English Department who had threatened her with a D and relented with a C minus. His junior level class was universally dreaded for its essay tests, weekend-devouring papers and points off for misspelling his name. When he opted to exchange his teaching seat for the school counselor's role, upcoming freshmen and sophomores sighed in collective relief.

Clea sighed now. "Research?" she asked to cover a too-long break in the conversation. "I'd heard you'd retired."

"Ah, yes, but idle hands, you know. And what brings you to this quiet little corner of the world this evening?"

Clea counted on Merriam to offer an account of the fruitless hunt for information, but when she turned to the librarian for assistance, the woman was hurrying into the stacks.

She was trapped. Trapped and nervous, as if facing him armed only with a limp excuse for a missed assignment. Sixteen intervening years made her no less flustered at the prospect of not only composing an explanation but delivering it with grammatical precision.

Annoyed he still affected her this way, Clea chose to cash in on the old adage: One picture is worth a thousand words. She showed him the photo.

"I've been sifting through the newspaper's archives, trying to identify this woman. Came up empty-handed."

She could shut up now, bid him good night and be gone, but she knew she'd hate herself later, first for her embarrassing display of timidity, and for not making good use of one more opportunity to attach a name to the woman.

"You wouldn't happen to recognize her, would you?" she asked.

Mr. Sheznesky—Delbert, please, he insisted—pumped Clea for details, a true scholar hot on the trail of minutia. Clea repeated what little she knew.

In the best tradition of theater, Delbert examined the photo—at varying angles, under different lights. Finally he said, "I'm quite positive this was one of my former students. A name escapes me at the moment. Someone of no consequence, I'm sure. Long departed—from town, that is, not from this life." An uncharacteristic titter ended his pronouncement.

"But why would I be photographed with her?"

"Clea, dear, your mother was a very popular teacher during her stint with the school district. She developed many long-lasting attachments to her students."

Case closed—at least if Clea read finality into the conspicuous check of his wristwatch. Delbert pecked her on the cheek, another disconcerting departure from the expected, and departed.

More perplexed than ever, Clea did too.

Once in her car she sat with the engine idling and reviewed the strange encounter with Delbert Sheznesky. She empathized with Barbara who had suffered like so many others through a semester of World Lit at the mercy of this man, a man who even now with a few words and gestures continued to intimidate full-grown adults.

There ought to be a law.

Clea laughed at her own assessment of the incident, yet the thought of the law gave her pause. She shifted into drive and made her way downtown.

Now, though, sitting in her car outside the sheriff's office, second thoughts stopped her from entering the building. What did she expect? That they would print Barbara's picture on a milk carton? Or call in John Walsh or Eliot Ness? She had to smile at the idiocy of it all, yet driving away was giving up, and she refused to do that.

The station house was lit against a backdrop of darkening sky. Activity within played out like a TV drama with the sound turned off. The busyness of the place impressed her. She studied the faces. Found none familiar.

Thank God, she thought. If she was going to be labeled a nut case, it was best done by a stranger. But the more she considered it, the more she hoped to spot someone she knew. Spilling her story to a friend felt more comfortable. A little shot of nepotism never hurt either, for her request no doubt fell outside the realm of standard procedure.

The car grew cold.

Still she was undecided.

A sharp rap on the driver's side window lifted her two inches off the seat. Pain shot through her knee where it banged the steering wheel, and the sound that broke from her throat was somewhere between a sob and a scream.

"Out of the car, miss."

The no-nonsense order and the broad expanse of uniform outside and a little to the rear of her door were authority enough. Clea scrambled to comply.

"I've been watching you for at least five minutes. You got business here or you just like to sit in the dark and stare through windows?"

The man's voice boomed. Clea feared policemen would rush from the station *en masse* and circle her car.

"I can explain, officer. I was about to go inside. Had to work up the courage."

"Courage, is it?"

"Not a good choice of words. Nerve, then. Really, all I wanted was to talk to someone, the sheriff maybe."

"Why don't you show me ID first. For the sake of formality, you understand."

"Of course, no problem." She held out her license.

He didn't take it immediately but unhooked a flashlight from his belt and swept a beam of light over the photo equipment in the back of her van.

"What's this stuff?"

"Cameras. Tripods. I'm a photographer."

"Let's see that ID now."

She waited while he read.

"Clea Reilly? Hmm. I've heard that name before. You ain't related to a Josephine Worth?"

"My mother."

"Well, I'll be a devil from down under. Josie Worth's little girl?"

Clea was startled at the rapid transformation in his attitude, more so when he draped an arm over her shoulder and steered her toward the building.

"C'mon in. C'mon in."

In tandem they walked beneath the sign that identified the Regional Sheriff's Department within the Law Enforcement Center. Once inside, glaring overhead lights half blinded her, and after the coolness outside, the temperature seemed stifling. Plate glass no longer muted the phones, the chatter, or the whir and hum of computers and copy machines. The noise of men at work, however, was nothing compared to the boisterous officer beside her.

"Bet you don't remember me, do you, Clea?"

She wished he would lower his voice. To nudge him toward a more private conversational tone, she answered softly. "I'm afraid I don't...."

"Frank Peterson," he interrupted. "Known your ma forever." He pointed to his prominent gut. "No wonder you don't recognize me. I've put on a few." He raised the same finger to his head. "And a little snow on the roof too."

Peterson's laughter drew a spattering of head shakes and groans from nearby desks.

"I'm sorry, I still don't quite place you."

"Not to worry. Sit." He pointed at an empty chair next to an empty desk. "Heard about your ma," he continued. "A shame. A damned shame. What brings you here? My shift hasn't started, so for the time being I'm all yours and invisible to everyone else." He laughed at his own joke.

"Well...."

"Out with it, young lady. Out with it. Get yourself a speeding ticket?"

"Oh, no. Nothing like that. I wanted to speak with the sheriff about a matter that—"

"The Queen Bee, huh?" he said at much lower volume. His head jerked toward a glass-partitioned fishbowl of an office. Inside, behind an impressively large desk, sat a pleasant-looking, middle-aged blonde.

"Queen Bee?"

"Sheriff Beatrice High and Mighty Summers." A chuckle exploded from Frank's lips, yet he whispered like a conspirator. "We'll keep that Queen Bee thing between us, huh?"

"Uh, sure. Okay."

"No sense bothering her royal majesty," said Peterson, then dialed up the sound and added, "Have a seat. How can I help? Anything for Josie's daughter."

Moments before when Clea sought an ally, she was disappointed at finding none, but now confronted by the loud and demonstrative Frank Peterson, she had a change of heart, though not the courage to get up out of the chair and walk away.

Reluctantly she opened her purse and produced the photo. She laid it on his desk and tapped the slick surface. "See this woman? I'd like to find out who she is."

Frank reached into a chipped coffee mug and fiddled among an assortment of pens, gnawed-on pencils and what looked like a cheap, red plastic flower for a pair of drugstore reading glasses. "Need my cheaters. Now, let's take a good lookie-see at what you've got." He centered the picture on the well-worn desk blotter and studied it, chin resting on his thumb.

Clea continued. "We may be related or she might be a friend of my mother's. Either way, with Mom's health as it is, I feel I should at least attempt to locate her. Give her the news, you understand. By the way, the infant is me, so this woman is much older now."

She explained how she came upon the picture and ended by detailing her unsuccessful search at the library. She waited for a comment, but Peterson had fallen mute. His beaming smile disintegrated into an expressionless mask, and he sat immobile as if poured into an enormous sack of overly-starched skin.

Clea's mouth gaped at his sudden alteration in demeanor, for she had so recently seen the identical change in the face of Mitz Maquire.

"You know who it is?"

"No." His answer was brusque.

"You're positive?"

"Absolutely."

"I thought for a moment I detected—"

"You thought wrong. Listen, I've been around a good many years and have never laid eyes on this here lady."

"And there's no way you can help, no records to pull, no computer databases?"

He frowned, shook his head. "Too little information. Thirty odd years in between. A pure waste of time to even try. Sorry."

Clea tried to hide her disappointment. "I guess deep down I knew before I asked that if this wasn't outright impossible it would be a Herculean task."

Frank sized up a chunk of air about three feet across and grabbed it with beefy hands. "Yeah, colossal. Gargantuan. Like you said, impossible." Jovial, and once again the benevolent family friend, he slid open a file drawer under his desk. "Tell you what. I'll hang on to this. You know, in case something comes up."

He swept the photo close to the blotter's edge, about to launch it into a pit of ragged folders and papers when Clea seized it.

"No! I understand if you can't help, but I won't part with the photo." It was in her purse before he had time to react.

Eager now to be away from this man, Clea made her excuses and almost sprinted for the door. A duty board hung from a peg near the exit. Magnetic dots behind each officer's name recorded those present. According to a printed header, the shift changed within the quarter hour.

As Clea stared at the roster, a plan took shape.

Though the temperature had plummeted and she shivered in a jacket far too light for the night air, she bypassed her car and entered a side lot where employees parked. A large sign identified space number one: Reserved For Sheriff.

Recent events had ratcheted Clea's intuition to high alert. Peterson's behavior struck her as bizarre though she was at a total loss to explain why. If she hoped to make any inroads into the whereabouts of Barbara, she needed to go straight to the top. Queen Bee or not, Sheriff Summers was the logical choice, and if that meant lurking in a parking lot away from the prying eyes of Frank Peterson, so be it.

By ten after eight a dozen officers had arrived, replacing another dozen who signed out for the night. The sheriff was not among them. Clea chafed at her neglect of the obvious. She had failed to take into account the extent of Summers' dedication to public service or how much a woman elevated to an important position might need to prove her ability in a man's job by putting in long overtime hours.

Nervously she glanced up at a security camera affixed to a lamppole. If she waited much longer, she might find herself in a cell. Ten more minutes, she promised herself. Then she'd bolt.

In the meantime, she was cold. Her fingers prickled with numbness. She rocked from one foot to the other. No feeling in her toes either.

Thank goodness her other senses still worked. A light current of air carried forward the flowery scent of a woman's perfume, followed closely by the tap of heels. Clea stepped to the driver's side door of the Buick occupying space number one. Summers slowed upon approach and remained three or four conservative paces away.

Clea rushed to explain her presence. "I wondered if we might speak in private. I only waited out her so I'd be sure not to miss you."

"My office would be more comfortable."

"Here is fine, if it's okay with you. It'll only take a moment." Quickly Clea related her story. When she'd finished, the sheriff moved nearer but while appearing sympathetic, in the end said, "Unless you have grounds to suspect foul play, it would be irresponsible of me to commit public resources to something like this. I can recommend several excellent investigators closer in to Portland, but beyond that...." She shrugged. "I'm truly sorry."

"I had to at least try."

"Stop by tomorrow. I'll pull together a list of firms that specialize in that sort of thing."

"Thank you, sheriff. I'll keep your offer in mind, though right now I'm afraid any additional expenses are out of the question."

The conversation was over. As Clea prepared to leave, the station's side door opened and framed a man wearing a dark suit. He proceeded to descend the steps two at a time. Long, deliberate strides propelled him toward the lot as if trying to outpace the penetrating chill. The sheriff also paused. Together the two women watched his progress as he crossed the sidewalk, negotiated a maze of parked cars and disappeared into the shadows of a far row. A birdlike chirp pierced the darkness. A car door slammed.

Clea started to turn away, but Summers laid a restraining hand on her arm. "Stop by tomorrow anyway," she said. "I have a different idea."

Chapter Five

She's not bitchy at all, thought Clea. Thus far their meeting had been beyond civil, friendly even. Beatrice Summers had shared tongue-in-cheek comments about the weather and related an amusing anecdote from her recent election campaign. She had expressed compassion upon hearing Clea talk of her mother and only interrupted their conversation to acknowledge a clerk idling outside the office door. The sheriff waved the worker in. While she autographed a sheaf of forms, Clea reflected on Frank Peterson's unflattering sobriquet and chalked it up to an advanced case of nose-out-of-joint disease. Frank was a long-timer and no doubt unused to being under the command of a much-younger superior. A woman to boot.

"Sorry about that, Ms. Reilly. The paper mill cranks this stuff out twenty-four hours a day."

"My sympathies."

"None wanted. I'm not complaining. Now, where was I?"

"My rather unorthodox request."

"Yes. Like I explained last night, ordinarily what you asked is out of the question. However, not a week ago I had an unexpected assignment to my jurisdiction which might prove the answer to my…to your dilemma. I would be willing to direct this project to him."

Clea sat a little straighter in the chair. "That's wonderful, but I was under the impression department policy as well as budget were overriding factors."

"Let's say, under normal circumstances that would be the case."

"Then why…?"

The sheriff smiled warmly. "Try not to overthink the offer. Of course, if you'd rather go the way of a private investigator, I totally understand."

Summers reached for a plain white envelope lying on the desk between them and slid it closer to Clea. "Here's the list of PI's I promised."

The sheriff leaned back into the overlarge leather armchair, so obviously part of the décor intended for her many male predecessors. As she did the springs squeaked. Clea worried that if the chair protested a second time, it would be from Summers rising, a sure signal the interview had drawn to a close.

"You're more than generous," she said. "I assure you I won't monopolize his time. If he could only make some inquiries or whatever it is you do, I'd be most grateful."

Sheriff Summers raised a hand and Clea fell silent. "He's yours."

Odd way of putting it, thought Clea. She wondered too at the scowl that had replaced Summers' pleasant smile. A frigid blast of panic raised gooseflesh on her arms. Could the sheriff be referring to Frank Peterson? As much as Clea desired professional help, Frank's loud and overbearing manner put her off. How could she possibly work with him? Besides, he'd already rendered his verdict on the chances of locating the woman in the photograph.

Clea was about to say something when Summers picked up the phone and punched in two numbers. "Davis. My office. Now."

So it wasn't Peterson. Who then? And why had Summers so harshly addressed him?

Clea shifted in her chair until she could see the squad room over her shoulder. Nobody jumped in answer to the summons. Business as usual. Against the far wall a dispatcher worked his equipment like Solti conducting the London Philharmonic. The only other uniformed officer in evidence hunkered over a desk stacked high with manila folders.

The rest of the work force, men and women alike, was divided between detectives and go-fers. If attire was the benchmark, Clea could barely tell which was which. The dress code was relaxed. Dockers and golf shirts or sporty blouses reigned supreme. No one glanced their way.

During Clea's second scan of the room, one man rose to his feet. Clad in a dark suit, crisp white shirt and charcoal gray tie, he stood out like a zebra in a horse corral. In no particular hurry, he buttoned his suit coat and shot his cuffs. As he approached, Clea's curiosity was piqued, for here was the same man who had darted across the parking lot the evening before.

This morning slow motion best described his gait. Granted, he came from a distant corner, the path narrow and riddled with misplaced chairs and evidence boxes. However, Clea sensed the pace was more a deliberate act than the result of any obstructions, a feeling echoed by the impatient thrumming of Summers' fingernails on the polished mahogany desktop.

He halted at the door and stayed there, arms crossed, expression immutable. Cool blue eyes swept the room, pausing only briefly on Clea before locking with those of the sheriff.

Beatrice Summers rose, apparently unfazed at still having to look up an extra six inches into his face. Her voice was spiked with scorn. "At ease, soldier."

The order made no difference. Neither backed down, and the atmosphere remained charged.

Clea leaped purposefully to her feet, a Switzerland between warring nations. "I'm Clea Reilly," she said as casually as if introducing herself to a new customer.

Summers' stance relaxed. She gestured toward the man.

"Agent Ren Davis."

"Special Agent."

"Of course. *Special* Agent Davis is from the New York office of the FBI. He's been placed here for reasons I've yet to discern, though I'm at liberty to assign him cases as I see fit." Meaningfully she tapped a file lying by itself on her desk. It had been stamped in red with the word Personnel. "And I'm assigning him yours."

The pronouncement made, Davis shifted his weight and cocked his head at Clea. She submitted to his inspection—up, down and up again—though not without growing resentment.

"Mr. Davis, if you're unhappy with this arrangement—"

The sheriff cut in. "He has no choice."

"In that case, I'd best fill him in on what I know and what I'm hoping to learn."

"That would be an excellent idea." Summers' features brightened noticeably. "And why not do it at Clark's across the street. The coffee's better than here, and you'll have more privacy for going over details."

Clea didn't think there was anything sensitive about the nature of her request, and she certainly didn't have enough information to warrant more than two minutes of Davis's time, but she wasn't about to object and risk a retraction of the sheriff's offer. Having help—reluctant though it appeared—from the FBI was more than she had dreamed. If following the sheriff's instructions to the letter sealed the contract, coffee at Clark's it was going to be.

"I'm right behind you," she said to Davis.

He walked from the room. With his back toward her, Clea heard a low, unintelligible grumble. At the first unoccupied desk he picked up a pad of yellow paper, then aimed for the exit.

"I'm afraid he's all I can do." When Clea turned at the sheriff's remark, she found the woman once again amiable. Summers handed her the white envelope. "Hang on to this," she said. "You may want these names yet."

Quickly thanking her, Clea dashed out. She fully intended to make the best of this opportunity but not as a third class charity case and that meant not trailing Special Agent Ren Davis out the door like a simpering puppy.

"**And** you did *what*?"

Rikki leaned across the Formica-topped island, ears perked at the story of Clea's mystery photo and all that had ensued. The two had been arranging proofs in a presentation album and now with white-gloved fingers Rikki carefully picked one by its corner and dangled it in front of Clea.

"In or out?"

"In. But let me start from the beginning. He ordered two black coffees without even asking what I wanted."

"You always order plain coffee anyway."

"That's not the point. You know, be polite, ask."

"East Coast public servants light in the manners department, huh?"

"And then some. I told him about finding the picture. I think he expected a piddly, housewifely concern. An errant husband maybe, or something equally beneath his exalted FBI title."

"Of *Special* Agent." They both giggled. "What a dreadful morning you must have had."

"Actually it didn't turn out quite so bad. The young woman's picture obviously aroused interest. It didn't matter we were talking about information cold enough to have developed frostbite. In fact, the part I thought would be the biggest stumbling block perked him up. He paid for the coffee—a buck fifty on a credit card, if you can believe. Then we left to go to the copy place."

The telephone interrupted. Clea excused herself. "I'll catch it on Addy's phone."

Rikki had continued to select photos and slip them into plastic sleeves and had already filled and closed the final album when Clea returned.

"Afternoon appointment's confirmed. We've got to finish up here by two."

"Already done. Now on with the story, please."

"First, what's this?" Clea picked up a five dollar bill lying on the table.

"I wanted to give that to you before I forgot. It's for Addy's stash. When I drove her to school for you this morning, she told me how she was saving her babysitting money for a stereo system. It's to help her along."

"Rikki, you're a sweetie. I've secretly been doing the same."

Clea fished into her own purse until she hooked a crumpled five. Then she opened a cabinet door above the refrigerator, took down a pig-shaped cookie jar and tucked the bills inside.

"Addy means business. There's quite a bit of cash in here."

"Okay. Quit stalling," said Rikki. "So you've got Mr. Hotshot FBI Man eating crumbs from the palm of your hand. I want to know how you two ended up at your mother's house."

"He's hardly doing that. And we didn't…yet. We made a photostat at Graphic Express. Did I tell you he ran the twenty-five cents through his credit card too?"

"Hmm. You must be glad you're not paying for time and expenses. Sounds like not a single nickel gets by him."

"I suppose I have to admit that may be a good thing. If he's meticulous with the small stuff, I'm counting on his being conscientious on the job. It's plain to see, though, he's not thrilled with his transfer to the Pacific Northwest. I'd venture to say he has a sequoia-sized chip on his shoulder about it. Anyway, he's been here less than a week. Is living at the Travelodge out by the highway. When he claimed he couldn't devote too much time to this project until he found permanent quarters, I solved his problem."

"And yours at the same time?"

Clea grinned. "His housing allowance was a thousand a month. I offered Mom's place. He's coming by at seven to look it over."

"And it slipped your mind to mention you were only asking eight hundred?"

Raising a finger to her lips, Clea whispered, "Mum's the word."

At quarter to seven Clea turned the old Explorer onto her mother's street. She had brought dustrags and a can of spray freshener. She wanted to clean the place a bit and get the furnace to sop up any damp air from the recent rains. No harm in making the house live up to its thousand dollar a month price tag.

Her plan disintegrated when she spied the dark blue Ford sedan sitting in the driveway. It screamed government issue. Davis acknowledged her with a curt upward motion of his head and followed her onto the porch. She unlocked, then stepped aside so his first impression was of the open expanse of the great room and its imposing fireplace. He entered and wandered the ground level floor, mutely surveying the space and the furniture, arranged as Clea knew it had been since she was a child.

Painful, wonderful memories caught at her throat. She saw her mother grading papers on the old maple wood table. The smell of banana muffins seemed to waft from the kitchen, and from upstairs the barely-suppressed laughter of five pajamaed twelve-year-olds unable to sleep because one or another had whispered a boyism in the dark.

She didn't notice Davis had finished his circuit until he stood at her elbow and said, "It'll do."

Instant anger bubbled up inside her. All her fond childhood memories, all the love and security she had felt within these four walls had been cruelly reduced to two dispassionate, indifferent words.

That was it. The deal was off. A stranger in her home, in her mother's home? Whatever made her think this a good idea? She squared her shoulders, prepared to tell Mr. Ice-in-his-Veins Davis it had all been a terrible mistake and he would have to look elsewhere, but when she faced him, he handed her a check.

Reality made her take it. Too many bills were finding their way to her mail slot. She needed the money.

"Most of my stuff's in the car," he said. "Some more in storage. I'll get that later."

He held out a hand, his curled fingers wagging a gimme. It took a moment for Clea to realize he expected the key. She dropped it into his open palm.

Everything had transpired so fast, Clea was momentarily flustered. Should she leave? Should she stay and explain the little trick to keeping the shower head from dripping or point out where extra fuses were stored?

While she remained undecided, Davis abandoned her in the entryway and began a second, slow and critical revolution around the room. When he disappeared behind the cavernous fireplace and into the kitchen, Clea sucked in her breath. With him out of sight she scolded herself for wilting in his presence like a schoolgirl summoned to the principal's office. As landlady, she had every right to lay down rules. To do so would show him she could be just as aloof in this business relationship as he was making every effort to be. She stood her ground. When he emerged on the other side of the room near the staircase, she ignored his surprised expression which intimated, "You still here?"

"I forgot to mention," she said coolly. "Second bedroom on the left upstairs is locked."

"And you're waiting to give me the key?"

She shook her head. "Off limits. I've used it to store my mother's personal items and papers."

"Then I insist on a key."

"No way. If you want me to move the stuff, say so, but I won't have you prowling through—"

"Thought you were all set on delving into the past? A past your mother is now incapable of explaining. I don't mind telling you I'm damned good at what I do, but that doesn't make me a magician. I'll need to see those papers."

"I've been through her things. There's nothing there to help you."

"And you read minds as a sideline? Know what I'd be looking for?"

How handily she'd been lured into that trap. "Tell me then, and I'll do the search."

"It's not a matter of rummaging through boxes for clues numbered one, two and three. One relies on impressions, hunches, the cumulative massing of seemingly unimportant and at the moment insignificant things. I have no idea what I'm looking for and won't until I find it, but your locked room strikes me as the perfect place to start."

How could she argue with that?

Chapter Six

With two people crouching on the floor on opposite sides of a packing crate, Clea's former bedroom—small to begin with—was doubly cramped. Davis still wore his suitcoat and tie even though the room was heating up and dust covered everything and drifted upward when they began shifting boxes.

The guy needed to loosen up, Clea decided, yet she kept her mouth shut.

Early on she discovered one of the lightbulbs in the room's overhead fixture had burned out. Davis brushed off the inconvenience as well as her offer to borrow a replacement from a downstairs lamp. Not wanting to leave him alone with her mother's things, she acquiesced. But in the half light, shadows cloaked the stacks of boxes, molding out of cardboard a corps of ominous henchmen that pressed uncomfortably close.

Although she had handled every object at least twice before, pawing through them now, with a total stranger, seemed clandestine and wrong. Her fingers trembled. She almost dropped a dainty figurine. Tension and stale furnace heat mounted in the airless, crowded room. Clea longed for relief, to call a halt while she adjusted the thermostat and eased her nerves, but like a machine, Davis never stopped.

Grab a box. Plunk it on the floor between them. Unpack. Inspect. Repack.

Occasionally he set an item aside, but not very often.

He insisted on seeing everything, some of which Clea found embarrassing. Being a teacher, her mother had a penchant for saving report cards, both hers and Addy's. Clea thought he lingered a little too long over the C's and D's she had scored in ninth grade—her rebellious period—but he made no comment. Only when he had finished leafing through the rest of the sheets, did he ask, "Who's Addison Reilly?"

"My daughter. Fourteen. Just beginning high school."

"And Mr. Reilly...?"

"Is of no account."

Davis's eyebrows shot up at the remark, but when she didn't elaborate, he moved on.

The chore developed a rhythm. Clea judged his pace then altered hers to match. Still she found it difficult to shake a host of uneasy feelings over what amounted to an invasion of her mother's privacy. When Davis suddenly rocked back on his heels, she stopped wrapping a bud vase to look up.

His arms were tightly crossed and he stared at the top of her head. "Relax, will you," he said. "You're ready to jump out of your skin. We're not a couple of grave robbers digging up corpses here."

"Then why do I feel guilty as charged?"

She ran a finger nervously over the rim of the vase. A chip caught her skin. The cut drew blood. "Damn!" she said.

He reached into his pocket and passed her a handkerchief.

"You're the one who went begging to the sheriff," he said.

"I'm perfectly aware of that."

"One phone call. Undo the whole thing."

"You'd like that, wouldn't you? Judging by our initial meeting, I'd say it was an understatement that you lacked enthusiasm for this particular assignment."

"Trying to read my mind again?"

"No. Just the facts, as you boys in law enforcement are fond of saying."

Davis eyed her curiously but said nothing, went back to work. By the time the last box had been ravaged, Clea sighed over the pitifully few keepers he had managed to uncover after two long hours and out of dozens of cartons.

"I told you, you wouldn't find much."

"Correction. You said I wouldn't find anything and look what I came up with."

"You call this something?" She poked at the pile. "A couple of credit cards, expired two years ago I might add. One old file of papers when Mom still had a mortgage on the house. I've gone over this address book already. There's no Barbara. And half the listings are people who've either died or are close to it." She didn't think the rest was worth mentioning.

"How much have you thrown out?"

"Lots, but all junk."

"Such as?"

"Old magazines and church bulletins. Outdated calendars. Twenty years of gas and electric bills and the like. But nothing important or sentimental. That's all here. And after picking through it, you've ignored at least 99.9 percent."

"Do you always consider the glass half empty?"

"Only when it is."

"Your problem is you see what's here and are blind to what's *not* here."

Clea rolled her eyes. See this, don't see that. What kind of logic was that?

As if the question wormed across her forehead like a marquee, Davis said, "Think. What's *missing*?"

"I don't understand."

"Your mother saved every old bill and canceled check but not a single personal letter. Why?" When Clea didn't answer, he held out his hands, palms up, scale-fashion. As one hand dipped low, he said, "Pack rat." The other hand floated shoulder high. "Dumps letters. See? Out of whack. My job is to figure out why there's a blip in an otherwise consistent pattern."

"I only want to find out who the woman in the photo is."

"Without knowing your mother's motives, that picture is nothing but a dead end. Remember, it was concealed when it could just as easily have been displayed…or destroyed. Again, why?"

Clea had wondered about that herself. She felt foolish not having a ready answer and resented Davis for pointing out in a roundabout manner that she hadn't known her mother very well at all.

He broke into her thoughts. "Rustle up some paper so we can make a list."

"How about doing it downstairs? If I kneel much longer, I'll be crippled permanently." As if to prove the point, her joints cracked and popped as she rose and hobbled toward the door.

She needed time alone to weigh satisfying her curiosity—for that's how it all started—against what was shaping up as a probe into her mother's life—and by proximity hers. She recalled her recent argument with Addy after the rose pin came in the mail. Her daughter had accused her of the very same ignorance that Davis now suggested by innuendo.

She disappeared into the kitchen, filled a pot with water and rummaged a cabinet until she found a jar of powdered coffee. All the while Addy's words resonated in the back of her head: *You don't know anything about grandma… and it's too late to ask.*

Well, it might be too late to ask, but perhaps not too late to find out. For Addy's sake. For her own as well.

The front door banged open. When Clea peeked around the corner, she saw Davis lugging a suitcase up the stairs.

"I'm making coffee," she called. "Instant'll have to do."

By his second trip, she had loaded a tray with mugs and packets of sugar and cream liberated from a Portland restaurant. By his third, she had it all laid out on the dining table along with a thick notepad and several ballpoint pens.

Davis removed his coat and hung it on the toprail of a chair. He folded back his cuffs, loosened the gray tie, preparing, it seemed, for a lengthy stint of physical labor which Clea thought had been put to rest upstairs. She sneaked a look at her watch. It was already after nine.

"Are you sure you don't want to settle in first?" she asked. "I hardly think Sheriff Summers meant for you to be on duty around the clock."

"You late for a date or something?"

"No, Mr. Davis, I am not. I was merely trying to be considerate of your time."

"Then let's not waste it." He squared the notepad in front of an empty chair and motioned for her to sit. While she took up the pen and poised it at the ready, he paced from one end of the table to the other, massaging his chin and squinting down his nose, lost in thought.

"What else is missing?" he said in an undertone.

"Not much that I—"

He interrupted. "I'll think. You write. Hmm, photos. Family photos."

"Permission to speak."

Davis stopped short. Suddenly afraid her sarcasm had angered him, Clea froze, but after a pause he merely swept an arm under a courtly bow. "Permission granted."

"Thank you. The reason there are no photographs is that for as long as I can remember my mother didn't want her picture taken…nor mine."

"Why?"

"I guess I never asked. It was a quirk of hers. We treated it like an inside joke and after a while it was so habitual it seemed the norm instead of the exception."

"I understood you were a photographer."

"Ironic, huh?"

"But why not other people's pictures?"

"I never gave it much thought, but you're right. Not even of Mitz."

"Who?"

"Mitz Maguire. She owns the photo shop downtown. She's Mom's oldest and dearest friend."

"So, your mother kept only one photo—you as a baby."

"Uh-huh."

"Write it down."

She did.

"Now, ancestral information not in picture form? Like a family tree."

Clea shook her head.

"What about...a passport?"

"Never traveled."

"Marriage license?"

"That's easy. Never married."

"Ah!"

"There's nothing to 'ah' about, Mr. Davis. You must have heard of single parenthood even in New York."

"Write it down. I also didn't find your birth certificate."

"Why on earth would that be important?"

"Why wouldn't it be?"

"You seem to have a tendency to talk in riddles, don't you? But honestly I don't recall ever seeing the thing."

"Didn't you need it to get married? I'm assuming by your name change and your earlier, fond comment about a Mr. Reilly that you went the more traditional route." He faced Clea, but his eyes lost their focus, perhaps mentally witnessing the ceremony which he detailed in a low voice. "Church wedding, white dress and veil, reception, champagne toast, five-layer cake, the whole nine yards."

"No—drunk, pregnant and Las Vegas. Satisfied?"

"Sorry," he mumbled. "But write it down anyway."

For the next hour and a half he dictated and she wrote, filling several pages with her compact handwriting. He bundled similar items and had her divide them into categories including documents and helpful databases, but the bulk fell under the heading of *Why?* Questions to mull and inconsistencies to puzzle over.

Clea balked when he asked her to compile a list of Josephine's friends, relatives, and acquaintances whom he would eventually interview. She wanted no field day among the gossipmongers nor a rash of heart attacks in little old ladies confronted on their porch stoops by an FBI agent...*special* agent.

When Davis insisted, she complied but only after extracting the promise he would be selective and prudent, considerate of her mother's reputation in the community and her own need to shield Addy from speculation. Even then she had her doubts. Davis didn't strike her as one who let discretion get in the way of bringing an investigation to a close. But he promised, and she fully intended to remind him of that on a regular basis.

He also wrote up a page of his own as she offered scraps of information about her personal history. Talking about herself was another thing she didn't like, especially when it all had nothing to do with the mystery woman, but Davis kept asking. Sometimes she glanced at his notes to see what he had written, but they were indecipherable, a shorthand of some sort or just the world's worst penmanship. His scribbling slowed when she spoke briefly of college and marriage but picked up speed as she reiterated recent conversations with Mitz and Frank Peterson and the sense of unease their twin reactions had fostered.

As the hour neared eleven and Clea stifled two yawns in as many minutes, he called a halt.

"We'll meet again tomorrow," he said.

"I do have a day job."

"At your convenience then."

She noticed the faintest hint of a smile twitch at the corners of his mouth. "You're enjoying this, aren't you?"

"It's what I trained to do. Besides, it beats all to hell sitting under the eagle eye of Sheriff Summers."

"You don't like her much."

"I believe the feeling is mutual."

He had *that* right. The sparks flying between the two this morning could have started a forest fire. Well, it was none of her business. She was grateful for the help and not inclined to snub her nose at a gift horse of any temperament.

She moved around the room, gathering her things, laid a business card on the table and accepted his in return. The nondescript card showed only his name and cell phone number.

"Ren," she said thoughtfully. "Is that short for something?"

"Yes."

"And that something would be?"

"A point of contention between my mother and me."

Despite his serious face, Clea laughed. "Let's see. A horrible moniker. How about Rensselaer? As in Indiana?"

A quiet growl was his only response.

"That's okay...for now. In the meantime Ren it is, unless you'd prefer Mr. Special Agent?"

"Ren'll be fine."

"And you can call me Clea."

Finally his face softened into an actual smile. "Which is short for?"

"Absolutely nothing."

He walked her to the door. "Remember, I need to see the photograph in its original form. All I have is the black and white copy we made." He handed her the address book. "Plus, go through the names in here and cross off the dead ones, so I'm not chasing ghosts."

"Had I known homework was involved...."

He ignored the remark. "I'll call you in the morning."

On the drive home, Clea's hands played over the steering wheel, the exhilaration of the evening expressing itself at the tips of her fingers. Despite some misgivings, she was glad. The search had begun. Even though she had nothing tangible to show for it yet, a first step had been taken.

First step? she thought and laughed out loud. Giant leap was more like it. Going to the police was so official, so...irreversible. The sheer recklessness of it made her shiver.

But deeper inside, something chafed at her mood. Not all the time. It came and went. One minute the nameless feeling irritated, the next it disappeared, leaving only the surety that like a pebble in one's sock it would soon pop up under a different toe and be just as annoying.

As she approached the house, the light still burned behind Addy's window blinds. It was well after eleven. They were going to have words over this. Rules were rules and meant to be kept whether she was home or not.

When she entered the kitchen, her daughter confronted her, fists firmly planted on her hips, the fiery orange-tipped spikes of her hair mimicking the flame in her eyes.

"Mom! Where've you been?"

"I told you I was going to unlock grandma's place for the new renter."

"That was five hours ago."

Clea tensed. It had not been her intention to reveal the details of who Ren Davis was and how he came to be the long-awaited tenant.

"I had to show him a few things. If you were worried, why didn't you call?"

Addy turned her back. "I wasn't worried. Besides your phone's off."

Clea dug into her purse. "Oh-oh! Dead battery. Honey, I apologize."

"You make me call if I'm gonna be like a minute late."

"I know." Gently she took the girl's shoulders and brought her around until they were face to face. "We're on the same team, Addy. Same set of rules applies. I'm sorry and promise it won't happen again. Truce?"

"Sure."

"Then it's bedtime. And so I don't forget, here's my plan for tomorrow. After I visit Mom, Rikki and I are driving out to Cannon Beach to meet a client. The weather's supposed to be clear on the coast. I'll be home well before you."

"Uh. School's letting out at two for the pep rally. All those cheerleaders and rah-rah spirit stuff make me want to puke. I'm coming home early."

"And doing what?"

"Nothing. Maybe use the computer."

Was that code for emailing her father? Would this latest incident be duly reported, and would the invisible Michael Reilly pass judgment and in doing so create havoc from afar? Very soon she would be obliged to set him straight, but for now she grit her teeth and attempted a smile.

"Do me a favor then. Sort the dirty clothes and throw in a load."

"Aw, Mom."

"And this time remember: red sweatshirt goes with the darks, not the lights."

Clearly she was teasing. A beguiling grin spread across Addy's innocent face. It brought to Clea's mind a cherished image of the little girl her daughter had been and at the same moment opened a window onto the woman she would become. If, in the meantime, she had to endure the crazy up-down, up-down teenage years, it was worth the effort.

"Now to bed—for the both of us."

Chapter Seven

"**Hey,** Ma. Come here."

"What is it, Addy? Can't you tell me while we're in the car?"

The clock on the microwave had raced ahead another five minutes since last she checked. Addy still hadn't finished breakfast, and the zipper on the canvas tote refused to budge beyond the halfway point, forcing Clea to wrestle pop cans, snacks, sunglasses and even a rolled-up sweatshirt through a narrow, five inch slit.

"No, Mom, you have to look. Some old guy's been standing across the street like forever. All he does is stare at the house. It's creepy."

Clea snapped to attention. "Get away from the window," she warned and hurried forward to pull her daughter from open view. With Addy safely in the shadows, she tiptoed along the wall, out of sight, and hooked a finger on the lacy sheers, parting them a crack.

"Oh, for Pete's sake."

"Who is it?"

"Our tenant."

"Yuck! What's he doing here?"

"Not a clue, but I intend to find out. You get ready, or you'll be late for school."

Retreating to the table, Clea grabbed the bag, plopped a baseball cap on her head, and shoved open the back door.

"Five minutes," she cautioned Addy.

On the way past her Explorer, she dropped the bag on the car's hood and headed for the curb.

Again Davis wore a suit, this day's selection a deep navy blue. His shirt was so white it almost glowed, and a steel-blue dagger of a tie hung from a precision knot at his neck. Dressed in jeans and turtleneck, Clea felt she filled the role of country bumpkin. But just because he boasted a big city wardrobe did not excuse his stalking her home at 7:30 in the morning. Drawing nearer, however, she noticed yesterday's scowl had also been replaced. A look that bordered on amusement played across his features. He had mellowed a degree or two. For that Clea mentally etched a mark in the victory column.

"You lost?" she asked.

"No."

"You're freaking out my daughter. How'd you know where I live anyway?"

"Have you forgotten I'm with the FBI?" In one gesture he intimated the vast network of government resources to which he had ready access. "We've got our ways."

He paused while her eyebrows arched and her lips rounded in an expressive "Oh."

"Or," he continued, plucking a little white card from his breast pocket, "I could have looked at your business card."

Clea rolled her eyes.

"Naturally I didn't mean to spook Addison. Please extend my apology."

"You may retract that once I tell you she described you not only as a pervert but an *old* pervert."

He leveled unblinking eyes at her. "And how would you describe me?"

A sly smile lit Clea's face, but she only consulted her watch and said, "Do you always start work so early?"

"When I'm on a case, I punch in once and don't clock out until the file is closed."

"If that's meant to impress me, it succeeded, but honestly, Ren, you've caught me in the middle of a rush. If Addy isn't to school soon, she'll be in hot water. I have to stop at Green Haven then out to Cannon Beach with my assistant."

"That would be Rikki Kinderset."

"I'm not even going to ask how you know that."

"What's at Cannon Beach?"

"Usually solitude. Especially during the week and especially after the tourist season. Today, work's involved. A family of six driving down from Astoria for an outdoor sitting. After that, landscape shots."

Vocalizing the day's demanding schedule reminded her of the fleeting time. She glanced over her shoulder, diverting her attention from Davis's comments to signs that her daughter might be on the move. She almost missed it when he said, "I thought you'd be interested in a progress report."

"What progress can you possibly have made overnight?"

"Your missing birth certificate."

"You found it?"

"No."

He paused. For dramatic effect, she figured, but when Davis remained silent, she slapped the sides of her jeans in exasperation. While she waited for him to continue, other sounds issued from the direction of the house. Sandwiched between the slam of the back door and the slam of the car door, she heard the faint mewling of a kitten.

"I've got to go." She took one backward step.

"According to the great State of Oregon, you've never been born."

"Ha, ha. Very funny."

"No, really. I searched county records from Tillamook to Wallowa. You are officially a non-person."

"Obviously there's been a mistake because here I am. And in a hurry. And finding it difficult to understand your single-minded curiosity about my birth certificate."

"That's why I'm the professional."

"And I'm just what, the dumb blonde?"

Davis wagged his finger. "Uh-uh. I didn't say that, wasn't even thinking it. Only that a birth record comes complete with other useful information—doctor's name, hospital, addresses, name of the father."

"Oh, I guess I need to explain that last a little further. But later, okay?" She backed up another step.

"I'll call." He waved her business card. "I have the number. In the meantime I'll dig deeper."

Clea was almost to her car when she called out, "By the way, Ren. I'd recommend you invest in a different set of clothes. Dressed like you are is liable to scare off half the population."

He looked down at his attire, giving Clea time to collect her bag, rev the engine and disappear down the street.

"*You* seem out of sorts today," said Rikki as she unpacked an apple from Clea's bag.

"Does it show?"

"Girl, if you were a lighthouse, I'd say visible about twenty miles out."

Clea puffed out a breath. "That bad, huh?"

"A darn sight worse."

Clea's answering laugh was muffled by the sweatshirt she tugged over her head. Despite the clear sky and brilliant sunshine, a steady wind blew along the shore, decapitating breakers and driving inland a veil of salty mist.

After the Carson family had piled into their Lexus and headed home, Clea and Rikki had spread an old towel on the sand near the tidewater mark. For protection they tucked themselves behind the naked carcass of a tree washed ashore long ago during a winter storm.

"You letting me in on an explanation?"

"We ran late this morning. Addy barely made the final bell. She didn't bother saying good-bye and left her lunch on the front seat. I had to hike it all the way to Student Services."

"Sounds like a normal day to me."

"Then I had to watch Lydia spoon feed Cream of Wheat to my mother because she's no longer capable to getting down to the dining hall."

"You knew that time would come."

"It came too soon, Rikki, and I blame myself."

"Hell, you're not responsible for every up and down in Josephine's condition. And don't bring up the Carsons either. You've dealt with enough personalities like them to fill at least one looney bin. Really, how could she think two hours in the wind and surf wouldn't wreck her hair? No, that's not it at all."

"Do you always have to be right?"

"Are you saying I am?"

"Maybe. I guess it's this thing with Ren Davis."

"Oh, you have a *thing* with him?"

"Down, girl. Nothing like that, but this morning he showed up unannounced in my front yard."

"Now we're getting somewhere."

"Let's walk and talk. I want to set up a few shots before it gets too late."

Five minutes later they had scooped up remnants of their lunch, hauled it to the car, and retraced their steps to the beach, carrying equipment bags and tripod. They doubled back to a tangle of driftwood where the Carson clan had posed and from there Clea framed in her viewfinder the offshore monolith of Haystack Rock. Near its base dozens of gulls hovered, their bodies gleaming white against the black, volcanic rock. Swollen waves rolled and broke. Wind beat water into foam and sent it flying. Clea mounted the camera on the tripod and set her stops, using her skill to capture more than visuals alone but the raw gladiatorial combat of one element pitted against another.

"I never tire of this place," she said wistfully.

"You're stalling."

Clea removed her baseball cap and hung it protectively over the lens.

"Okay," she said, pausing while she gathered her thoughts. It wasn't really stalling, she told herself. Just doubt. What exactly was she feeling? Anger, hurt, frustration, sorrow? All of the above? None of the above? While her creative eye remained crystal clear when she scanned the beach for perspective and composition, her inner eye had developed a cataract.

"What can I say?" she said to Rikki. "You know the roller coaster I'm riding with Mom and Addy. Then there's Michael putting in his two cents, and I don't mean in child support. Throw in the picture and rosebud pin. The last thing I need right now is another complication, and one drops in my lap."

She shared Davis's findings about her birth record.

"Wow! So you don't actually exist?" Rikki lightly pinched Clea's arm as if testing for flesh and blood.

"Not a joke."

"Listen. Don't go building an ant hill into a sand dune. Thirty-something years ago a piece of paper fell between two bureaucratic chairs. The government slipped up. Gee, imagine the chances of that happening?"

Tension drained from Clea's shoulders. "Of course, you're right again. I can't seem to think straight these days."

"That's why you keep me around. To do your thinking for you."

"And because you're so good at casting a spell over unruly pets and sugared-up kids."

"That too."

"Next time I see Davis I'll have him check the hospital's files. End of problem."

"And I'm disappointed. Here I expected confessions of a hot, steamy romance brewing behind my back."

Clea punched Rikki's arm. "Get real. The man may be good looking, but talk about an iceberg. He'd have no trouble sinking an ocean liner."

"He'll thaw."

Before Clea could respond, a powerful gust rocked the tripod and sailed her cap toward the water. She steadied the camera. Rikki lit out after the hat, her laughter a wind chime.

Clea wrinkled her nose at Rikki's observation, claimed it ridiculous and would have completely dismissed it from her mind if the cell phone hadn't rung. The incoming number was displayed. Ren Davis.

He had said he would be in touch, but Clea didn't think it would be so soon. Her first reaction was annoyance. She had envisioned her role in this case as that of catalyst. Provide the information and let him—an army of one—take care of the rest. A hands-off operation with resolution weeks down the road when he passed her a plain brown envelope containing name and particulars of the woman in question. It worked that way on TV. Why was the real life version becoming so complicated?

For a second she considered not answering the phone at all, explaining later how she'd been in the middle of an important shoot, but it rang a second time, and an insistent third.

"What the hell," she mumbled and punched the talk button. "Mr. Davis?"

"I thought we'd graduated to first names?"

"Of course. Ren. I was planning to call you in a bit to give you the name of the hospital where I was born. Good Samaritan. A quick check is bound to clear up your concerns on that score. Or I could do it if you want."

"Fine."

His lack of enthusiasm baffled her. A few hours ago the topic of her lost birth record had been hot enough to necessitate an early-morning stake-out at her house. The question had festered in the back of her mind all day. In one word he summarily dismissed it.

"Just fine?" A day's worth of fretting for nothing more than fine. His explanation had better rise to the status of masterpiece.

"Something else cropped up."

Too vague. She pressed him further. "Go on."

"The fireplace doesn't work."

Clea almost dropped the phone.

"You should—"

What Clea should or shouldn't do was cut short when she jabbed a finger on "power off."

She still stared, open-mouthed, at the phone when Rikki returned, waving the sand-covered cap. "What's up?"

"I don't know which is worse," she said, poking air with the cell phone. "Being a landlord or trying to work with a man."

"Unless it's *being* the landlord of the man you're trying to work with?"

"Yeah, the big double whammy."

She repeated her conversation with Davis. Rikki burst out laughing until Clea had no choice but to follow suit.

"If he expects me to drop everything and come fix a damned broken fireplace, he's in for a reality check. Tomorrow I'll call Tony the handyman.

Tonight he'll have to make do with toasting his marshmallows over the stove."

"And in the meantime?"

"We've got things to do, and they don't include worrying about Ren Davis. First, let's finish on the beach, then swing up toward Seaside. There's a resale shop along the way where I got some great bargains on old frames a few months ago."

"Sounds like a plan."

Forty-five minutes later they were heading north on Highway 101. The coast was golden. Not a hint of fog clear to the horizon. The shop's owner not only remembered Clea's previous visit but in the intervening months had stockpiled every frame he could lay hands on. She bought them all. They began their final inland leg, braced for delay, but found instead the ubiquitous orange cones of summer had been collected by construction crews, leaving the newly-resurfaced pavement smooth and obstacle-free.

They rode with the windows rolled down and the radio blasting. Rikki belted out numbers along with Springsteen and Billy Joel, while Clea used the change of pace and scene for a much-needed break from the problems waiting at home. Once or twice she thought of Davis's complaint, but the rest she put on hold. When *Dancing In The Dark* thundered through the speakers, she threw back her head and joined Rikki in carefree, off-key song.

Although traffic moved briskly, the side trip had added an hour, so it was after four when Clea's house finally came into view. She breathed a sigh. "Home. Safe and sound. Just the way I like it."

But as soon as she entered the kitchen, the absolute quiet struck her like a slap. No hum of the TV. No clicking keyboard. Not a scrape of a chair or a rustle of paper. Addy should have been home long ago. She dropped her load of frames and started toward her daughter's room.

"Easy on the panic button," called Rikki, who'd followed her inside. "Here's a note."

The piece of paper was anchored to the refrigerator with a ladybug magnet. Addy's back-slanted hand assured her the laundry was done and she'd accepted a last-minute babysitting job with the Westins. Left at three. Home late when Mr. and Mrs. returned from open house at St. Gerard's. At the bottom of the page, almost as an afterthought, was scrawled: Davis guy called 3X!!

Accusation flared in those last few words. Maybe it was the double exclamation points, or how reference to Davis had been segregated from the rest of the note by six inches of glaring white space.

She rounded on Rikki. "Settles that."

She would have said more except for the sight of Rikki making silly faces at a furry gray bundle cradled in her arms.

"Look what I found on your steps. I didn't know you had a cat."

"I don't. It's a stray, but I'm afraid Addy's been feeding it. Secretly—or so she thinks. Put it back outside before it—"

"She."

"Before *she* takes too much of a liking to the great indoors."

"Aw. Addy'd love a cat."

"Hey, you're supposed to be on my side. Besides both she and I are gone all day. There's no one around to take care of it."

Rikki shook her head. "That's the excuse you use not to get a dog. Cats take care of themselves."

"In that case, this particular feline can take care of itself outside. Now shoo."

"As soon as I bring in the other two boxes."

Instead of departing with the cat in hand, Rikki thrust it at Clea who more in self-defense than anything reached out and grabbed the squirming, squeaking kitten. She held it at arm's length while studying its white muzzle and matching paws.

"So," she said, wrinkling her nose, "you must be Kitty-Face. And I suppose you've brought along about a hundred of your very tiny best friends, huh?"

Just then a holler from outside demanded attention, and Clea transferred the cat to the crook of her elbow and held open the screen.

"Doesn't that little cutie have the bluest eyes?" said Rikki as she passed through to the workroom.

Clea groaned and shot her friend a withering look, but minutes later Kitty-Face was licking peanut butter from her fingertip. "Don't say a word," said Clea at Rikki's grin. "She's not settling in, but without something in her belly she'll only fuss at the door and never go away."

Rikki patted Clea's shoulder. "You have so much to learn."

Once the boxes were in and the cat out, the two women shared a pot of tea and sandwiches in the small workshop next to the kitchen. Rikki prepared the day's film for processing while Clea sorted the frames by size and the amount of work necessary to restore them. They nailed down the details of Friday's hectic schedule which centered around group shots of the high school football team and cheerleading squad followed by couples' poses during the Homecoming dance. It saddened Clea she would be the one attending the grand affair while her daughter missed out.

When it was time for Rikki to depart, they exchanged a hug and knowing glances, for tomorrow would be a challenging day.

With Rikki gone, Clea puttered around the kitchen, rinsed a few glasses and set a plate of leftovers on the counter to take the chill off. Since Addy's whereabouts were accounted for, the stillness of the empty house no longer spelled alarm but wrapped itself around her like a soft woolen shawl. She reheated tea in the microwave and wandered into her bedroom.

As promised, freshly-laundered, neatly folded clothes lay on the daisy print of her bedspread. "Ah, Addison Marie," she whispered. "Underneath the gangster clothes and hip-hop hair, you're a jewel."

She sank to the bed and paired the socks, the only thing Addy had neglected. When the job was done and everything ready to be drawered, she noticed one item remained. It was on her dresser. Wrinkled and wadded into a ball, it had been placed in a manner to isolate it from her bottles of perfume and jewelry boxes. Care had been taken so it not touch her brushes or hand mirror, her reading glasses or her small electric clock.

She crossed the room and picked it up.

The deliberate quarantine of Ren's handkerchief carried a message, and Clea knew exactly what it said.

Chapter Eight

"*Davis.* Leave a message."

Ah, that was abrupt. But then, why should she think the voice mail would be any different from the man?

Clea hung up. A note was better anyway, more business-like. And that's the way their dealings would be transacted from now on—clear-cut and sterile.

She bobbed her head in agreement with herself. No innocent visits or calls for her daughter to misinterpret, for clearly Addy had taken a work relationship and manufactured it into something far more personal.

Clea would deliver the message now, tonight while Addy was absent from the house. Go no farther than her mother's front porch and slip the note through the mail slot, a face-to-face totally unnecessary.

She slid open the kitchen junk drawer to find something to write with and remembered Ren had also asked her to cull her mother's address list.

Good, she thought, two birds...no three. He had wanted to see the photo as well. She pulled both from a shelf then paged through the book, annotating with a red pen those people still alive and whether or not they resided at the address given. She tucked the two objects neatly into a large Kraft envelope. After smoothing and folding Ren's handkerchief, she added it as well. On the outside of the envelope, again using the red pen, Clea thanked Davis for his diligence but requested all future meetings be restricted to daytime appointments only. In parentheses she added phone calls too.

Satisfied the language was properly beige, Clea signed her name and sealed the flap. In the event Addy came home early, she jotted a one-liner to her too, explaining she had run out to pick up a few things. Not an actual lie if she returned carting a loaf of bread. Checking the refrigerator, she added a gallon of milk.

Twenty minutes later her alibi from the Mini-Mart on Fourth Street rested on the car seat beside her. One stop remained.

Nearing her mother's house, an eerie, empty sensation settled into her stomach, though she knew better than to pass it off as hunger pangs. For the first time in her life, she would come to this house as an outsider, someone who rang the bell and asked to be admitted. At least tonight there'd be no idling on the stoop, landlady's hat in hand. She'd simply pull to the curb and execute her mission.

The plan fell apart the moment she mounted the porch, for the front door stood ajar. Her eyes narrowed. Someone in law enforcement, a New Yorker besides, ought to know better. No matter what regard Ren Davis had for his own possessions, her mother's furniture, books and art work still filled the rooms. Clea felt a lecture coming on, one she would adamantly deliver in person.

She took a deep breath and shoved open the door.

"Mr. Davis. Ren Davis. Where are you? I've something to say to you."

She cocked her head to listen, but no one responded.

"Mr. Davis!" she called again then stepped inside.

In front of her stood a half dozen U-Store-It boxes lined up like soldiers marching off to war. Even though hours of daylight remained, every bulb in the living room squandered its wattage.

"I certainly hope I didn't include utilities," she grumbled, annoyed with herself that, in her haste to rent the house, she had overlooked such an important part of the lease. One more thing to be clarified, along with the business about the proper use of locks.

And as long as she was here, it might be a good idea to see what else rated discussion. She ventured across the squares of tile that defined the foyer and looked around.

Funny how a few personal articles, unfamiliar and masculine, so completely transformed a house. The small rosewood table in the entryway had been stripped of its lace doily and now sported a Yankees cap and trophy baseball. Clea dragged a finger over the scrawl of ink in the sweet spot. The signature defied translation, but the items served to humanize Ren, and some of Clea's irritation washed away.

With anger on the wane, realization of where she was rolled in like surf to fill its place. She was planted a good six feet into his paid-for turf, very much the intruder she had come in to warn him about.

Her brain relayed a frantic signal. Get out, it said. She spun to do its bidding and collided with a wall of muscle.

"Holy shit!" she cried and reeled backward.

With a draw quick enough to make Wyatt Earp jealous, Davis grabbed her arms, preventing a fall that would have mowed down his packing cases like outlaws at the O.K. Corral.

Breathless, Clea fought for balance and at the same time tried to extract herself from the viselike grip of his hands.

"What are you doing sneaking up on a person like that?" she blustered.

"Not sneaking, simply walking through the door."

"Which, by the way, you shouldn't leave open to any shady character roaming the streets."

He raised an eyebrow. "Obviously."

"Not me—burglars. And let go of my arms."

When he complied, Clea brushed and batted her sleeves. The pretense they had somehow acquired a layer of dust that demanded immediate attention gave her a few moments to compose herself. Her heartbeat slowed from Indy 500 to a relatively sedate thrill ride. She huffed in her best imitation of a victim and thrust the envelope at him.

"Here, take this."

Davis saw the note and began to read while Clea looked for a graceful exit, but he steadfastly blocked the doorway and thwarted escape.

Tap, tap, tap. Her toe beat a nervous rhythm on the tile. Davis seemed to be one mighty slow reader.

Trapped and trying to appear occupied, Clea noticed the change in his attire and wondered if he had taken her comment about his clothes to heart. If so, a generous portion of the message had been lost, for while the black slacks and open-collared, white knit shirt were an improvement....

Clea slowly shook her head. The boy desperately needed help.

She was still shaking her head when her eyes lighted upon an object that stood just over the threshold, its long wooden handle upright and within easy reach of his hand.

"What's that?"

Without shifting his gaze, he replied. "A sledgehammer."

"I can see it's a sledgehammer. I meant, what's it doing here?"

"Remember? I called you about it earlier this afternoon."

"Uh-uh. There was no mention of heavy duty tools."

"Oh, right." He pinched his chin between two fingers. "I do seem to recall a sudden break in our connection. But since you're here now...." He pitched the envelope onto one of the boxes, shouldered the sledge, and hooked Clea's arm through his. "I've something to show you."

"If this is about the fireplace?"

"It is."

Before she could say more, he hauled her to the gaping facade and waited as if expecting she would slap her forehead and yell "Eureka!" when in truth she had no idea what mystery lay hidden in the brick and mortar.

"So?" she said.

"It doesn't work."

She was about to do the head smacking anyway, though for an entirely different reason when he lowered the sledgehammer to the granite hearth.

"Wait a minute. I won't have you trying to bludgeon it into submission. Tomorrow I'll call a repairman. Until then, you'll just have to be patient."

"Clea, did you never, in all your years of living here, notice there was no damper, no flue? The fireplace is a fake."

"In that case, what's the big deal?"

"Like I told you yesterday, solutions lie in the details. Among your mother's ownership papers, I found an architect's floor plan. This whole area was wide open." His eyes swept the great room. "The fireplace was added later. So I asked myself why go through the expense and bother of constructing an indisputably mammoth fireplace that's not a fireplace at all?"

"Decoration?" Exasperation sighed from his lips, and Clea had to admit her explanation was feeble at best. "Okay," she conceded. "Not decoration. I suppose now you're going to enlighten me."

"I'll pose another question instead. Why so massive?"

"Scale. You said yourself, this is a big room."

"And ruin it with something of no use?"

"Does the Bureau actually send you people to school for that?"

"What?"

"To learn how to never give a straight answer."

"What makes you think I don't give a straight answer?"

"There. You did it again."

His features softened just short of a smile, and he raised his hands in mock surrender. "You found us out."

"National security's been breached." Clea chuckled, surprised at his emergence from the special agent persona. But the altered mood lasted no longer than her thought, for once again his eyes hardened in focus, and the line of his mouth pulled straight and serious. The amusement had clearly staled, so Clea redirected her attention to the fireplace.

"I've got it," she said and snapped her fingers. "You missed the built-in pantry at the back."

She plucked at his shirt and led him along the outer wall of the edifice toward the kitchen where her enthusiasm died. Ren had obviously been there already. The place was a mess. The louvered pantry doors had been flung open, the shelves emptied of their contents, the shelves themselves removed and leaning against the sink.

In the larder an optimistic guess allowed for sixteen to eighteen inches of depth. Even with the additional two feet of "decoration" at the opposite end, a universe of unaccounted-for space stretched in between.

While she stared, Ren squeezed around her and rapped the back wall with his knuckles. The resonant sound attested to its hollowness.

"Do the words 'construction mistake' carry any weight?" she offered.

He shook his head.

"I didn't think so."

"Look closer," he said and traced a finger along a faint bulge in the plaster which began at the floor near the inside corner, ran upward approximately seven feet, across to the other corner, and from there back down to the floor. "At one time an opening led into whatever's behind this wall. It's been sealed over."

"And I imagine that's where the sledgehammer enters the picture."

"With your permission, of course."

Clea fell silent, transfixed by the blank wall and the thought of what, if anything, might lie on the other side. Ren's voice carried to her ear with a subtle eagerness as he urged her toward an answer.

"If you're worrying about damage, don't. As part of an official investigation, federal government pays."

"My tax dollars at work, huh?"

Davis's face glowed with little-boy excitement. His enthusiasm was viral and Clea caught it. She backed away and with a wave of her hand, said, "Sledge away."

Blows echoed through the house. White, chalky dust as fine as talc choked the small pantry. Plaster chips and bits of lath sailed in all directions.

Sweat beaded on Davis's forehead, formed a slurry with the dust and trailed milky streaks down both sides of his face. What a sight! Clea wondered if he realized how far he'd strayed from the uptight agent she'd met not thirty-six hours ago.

After ten minutes' work, he dashed away, yelling over his shoulder about needing more tools. When he was out of sight, Clea examined the Swiss cheese he'd made of the wall. The layer of plaster was thick, the holes deep. After inspecting one, she wrinkled her brow. She had expected to see clear through, but saw only black. In went her finger, up to her wrist. She encountered another surface, solid and smooth.

"The plot thickens," said Ren, coming up behind her, now armed with a claw hammer and pry bar.

"I see you've called in reinforcements."

In lieu of an answer he wedged the bar into a crevice and pounded it with the hammer until a section of wall broke free and fell at his feet. He moved the tools to another hole and repeated the task. The work wholly absorbed him, so Clea found a push broom and swept debris into black plastic bags.

When the entire back wall of the pantry had been excised, Davis called Clea over. "What do you make of it?" he asked, thumping his fist on a fully-exposed panel of wood.

"A wall over a wall?" She shrugged.

"Not a wall…a door. See the lock? It's a kind of latch without a knob and set at exactly the height of this shelf bracket. With the shelf in place and loaded with canned goods or whatever, it would be virtually invisible."

"I don't understand. For what possible reason is there a door behind the pantry wall?"

"One way to find out. Did your mother keep sets of old keys around?"

"Screw the keys. The place is a wreck already. And besides, you'll be paying to have it all repaired."

"Uh, not me personally."

"Ren, don't keep me in suspense. Smash the damned thing."

"With pleasure."

One whack was enough. The locking mechanism split apart. The door swung open.

Over their shoulders light from the kitchen spilled into the tiny room, illuminating gauzy curtains of cobwebs. Ren swiped an arm at the thickest veil, making a lopsided tear in the webs. Together they peered inside. But while he uttered sounds of interest, Clea shrank back, stunned by what she saw.

Clea didn't give much thought to the stares of nurses as she pounded down the corridor, but when one of Green Haven's teenaged aides giggled behind an upraised hand, she slipped into a visitor's bathroom and took stock of her appearance. One glance in the mirror explained the looks aimed in her direction.

She wadded a paper towel, soaked it under the tap to dab at red-rimmed eyes, hoping to pat away some of the puffiness. Cobwebs laced through her curls like a macabre hairnet, and white dust speckled her clothes.

"God! I look a fright. No wonder I'm drawing everyone's attention."

She brushed at the mess, not sure whether she was making things better or worse, for the webs seemed to dig deeper and the plaster smeared the instant it came in contact with the moisture on her hands. Her reflected image was of a skid-row drunk. She'd have to make a mad dash for her mother's room and pray security didn't come racing after her.

She'd been driven to the nursing home by a need she found difficult to explain. At first she'd tried to reach Rikki, her confidante and sounding board, but second thoughts compelled her to turn off the phone and make her way to Green Haven instead. Though she considered Rikki a close friend, and had shared details of the photograph and pin, this business at her mother's house still baffled her. Until she had a firmer grip on its meaning, she considered it a family secret, and like a family skeleton better locked away in a closet. The irony struck her and she almost laughed, for a closet was exactly where this secret had been moldering for decades.

It was bad enough Ren was party to it, but he was. She couldn't change that. The minute he had convinced her to enter the fireplace room bound them together with the knowledge of its discovery.

Clea wrinkled her brow, yet couldn't arrive at any conclusion other than it now seemed imperative to see her mother. Not talk to her, of course. That was beyond pointless. But to look at her and register if the meter of her feelings had slipped a notch or two.

The fluorescent bar above the bed was set to dim, the feeble light barely illuminating the occupant under the covers below it. Propped by pillows, Josephine gazed blankly at the ceiling. Clea wondered if she saw anything at all. Instead of going immediately to her mother's side, Clea bypassed the bed and stood at the window.

The glass had a two-way quality. Through it came the darkened world of the facility's grounds. Sidewalk lighting faintly shed a yellowish glow on the building's northeast wing, casting angular shadows in the corners and doorwells. The stately maple outside the window swayed in a primal dance, eerily human.

Despite the limited light, all what she saw was real and what she knew with a certainty existed.

Imposed across this reality was something else. A reflection. A scene, not quite true to life, but a mirror image, thus skewing what it portrayed. Dual outlines of her mother were visible in the thermopanes. In each the only moving part was a finger, idly tucking behind an ear a limp strand of hair.

Over and over. Mindlessly repetitious. A lifelong habit ingrained into the fingers when all else was an empty shell. Nothing about her mother seemed real anymore, a notion that had built slowly with the inexorable advance of disease and multiplied tenfold within the last hour.

Clea sighed and stepped closer to the window until so near her breath fogged the glass. A steamy circle flared and cleared, blurring her vision in waves, much the same sensation she'd experienced earlier in her mother's kitchen. One minute she had given vent to curiosity about the hidden room, then was bowled by surprise, with bewilderment close behind.

Though reluctant at first, she had allowed Ren to take her hand and coax her inside.

A stale, musty odor had assailed her nostrils as she passed through the pantry. The kitchen clock, the hum of the refrigerator, a neighbor's barking dog—familiar, common sounds woven into the fabric of the house—died away, unable to penetrate the solid walls. A spider web wisped across her face. Black spots on the floor burst to life and scattered on eight legs into dark corners. Clea barely noticed. Her eyes were riveted on the far wall where a faded paper border peeled away at the ceiling and spiraled downward, its row of yellow duckies on a death march into the nether worlds.

Beneath it stood an infant's crib.

A blanket had been turned back in readiness, a tiny pillow lay in waiting. What color they might have been was long buried under a ghostly gray layer of dust. Perched on the mattress, a glassy-eyed, moth-eaten teddy bear chose this moment to give in to gravity and slump on its side.

Clea's hand flew to her throat. "What in God's name is this place?"

"It appears to be—"

"Damn it, Ren, that was rhetorical. I see exactly what it is. This stuff hasn't just been stored here, it's been used here. The horrible question is: Why would anyone put a baby in this airless room?"

"Before you do a swan dive into the wrong conclusion, there *are* vents up near the ceiling. Suspicious—yes. Airless—no."

Clea gave him her back. He had missed the point altogether. No sane person kept an infant in a cramped cell. Cruelty. That's what it amounted to. Sick. Clea's mouth screwed up in distaste at the thought of a baby being treated like an unwanted wedding gift.

She shivered. "Let's get out of here."

"You go. Take a few deep breaths. I have to take a closer look."

"No. I want you out of here."

"You know I can't just leave this alone now that I know about it."

"But, Ren, it's obviously been here and like this forever. We simply seal the wall back up and forget about it."

He lowered his voice, murmured words Clea couldn't quite make out. In the softer tones she read a genuine concern. Her breath quickened. Had she convinced him? But his eyes had darkened over and flitted from one object to another.

"I'm afraid it doesn't work that way, Clea," he finally said. "This set-up suggests abuse, or at least child endangerment. Doesn't matter how long it's been collecting dust. I'm obligated to probe deeper and, if need be, make a report."

"Report? If you go and tell anyone about this, someone might get the ridiculous idea my mother could have...." She spun on him, horror segregating each word into a lone island of misery. "You think my mother has something to do with this?"

"I'm not drawing a conclusion one way or another before all the evidence is gathered and properly investigated."

"Is that FBI-speak for yes?"

Ren's chin dropped to his chest, effectively choking off any answer he might have intended and, at the same time, avoiding the slow flow of poison from Clea's eyes.

Anger flared again, heating her blood, so her snug-fitting turtleneck grew damp under the arms. Or was the heat pouring from a window register in her mother's room to blame?

Clea had been so lost in the memory, a good few seconds ticked by before she placed herself in Green Haven. She was still staring into the courtyard. The breeze had picked up, scooping fallen leaves and hurling them in a frenzy against the glass panes. She let out a pent-up sigh and turned toward her mother who now slept soundly, hands resting quietly on the coverlet. Slumping against the windowsill, Clea willed this night to be over or, better yet, to never have happened at all. When she spoke, her voice cracked.

"Why the roses, Mom?"

Horrified at seeing the crib, Clea had at first overlooked the dozens of long-stemmed roses crowded into a single vase which rested precariously on a small table at the foot of the crib. There were pinks and reds and whites, some fully unfurled, others tightly-wound buds. All were crisp and dry, perfectly preserved.

"Don't touch anything," Ren cautioned, but she ignored his warning and cupped a trembling hand around a flower head. A petal broke free and fell as crumbs onto a once-white table scarf.

Raking fingers through her hair, Clea said, "My God, what am I supposed to think about this? What happened here? I can't believe...I *won't* believe...." She clamped her mouth shut, for to articulate a theory, even so much as one lowly thought, might imbue it with substance that could be mistaken for truth.

Leashing in her tongue was one thing. Easily accomplished. How could she turn off her mind? The bouquet commanded her full attention with the same irresistible force of a hypnotist's watch dangling from a chain.

Roses. Roses.

The universal symbol of love and friendship and innocence had permeated her mother's life. Rose poems. Roses embroidered onto pillow casings. Two paintings of roses which graced the wall next to the bookcase not ten feet away. The heritage rose planted by the porch and lovingly cared for throughout the years. And a rose pin, newcomer to the list.

Dead roses in a vase.

"Damn you," she screamed at Davis, knowing full well as the words flew from her mouth she had pegged him as the sacrificial goat because to think otherwise was unthinkable.

Davis reached out to her. "Don't panic yet."

She slapped his hand away. "You're the second person to say that to me today, but in this case I've every right to my hysteria."

"Let's you and I sit down and calmly consider the next step," he suggested, this time keeping his arms cautiously at his side.

"No next step. I want you to stop. Go back to working for Sheriff Summers. You're fired."

"Be reasonable, Clea. You can't simply strike the tent poles and haul the circus out of town. You don't mess with the FBI for Christ's sake."

"Then damn the FBI."

With that Clea spun on her heels, stormed through the living room and out the door, the battle against a flood of tears all but lost. On the way she paused only long enough to backhand his baseball off its pedestal and send it rolling across the floor.

"That's what I did, Mom. I fired him. The problem seems to be how to keep him fired."

Without meaning to, Clea had rehashed the tale out loud. Now that she'd finished talking, an ominous silence pressed like fingers at her throat. A quick glance confirmed her mother's slumber appeared undisturbed.

"What should I do?" she said, more for the sake of adding sound than any expectation of an answer. "For sure, that bastard'll never let it go."

She exhaled, long and hard, then dragged to the bed and leaned over Josephine's upturned face. A flat affect and facial sag spoke volumes about the ravages of Alzheimer's. Gone were intelligence, wit, and personality—jewels stolen by a heartless thief. Clea missed most the gentle smile. An inventory of her childhood and adulthood generated only images of her mother's generous and loving nature. Nowhere was a hint of a flawed soul. Not one tiny fragment of memory rushed forward to even suggest it. So what explained the roses, the crib, the room?

Tired beyond belief, she moved to the rocking chair and sat. A worn sweater hung over the back rail, handy in case of a chill. Clea took hold of the sleeves, wrapped them around her in a hug, and began to rock, slowly as if cradled in a mother's arms.

"We used to decorate that mantle with Christmas lights," she whispered. "Remember? And you let me arrange the pieces of the manger scene. All the while, inches away.... Oh, Mom." Clea shuddered. "This is all a big mistake. Isn't it?"

A low keening intruded. Clea startled. Josephine had roused from sleep, her restless fists gathering the sheet into two knotted balls. One eye was open, a wink frozen in time. The look scared Clea. The pale blue eye was firmly focused, conveying a message. But a message of what? Accusation for unearthing a piece of history so long and carefully buried? Understanding of Clea's dilemma? Permission to delve further? Or was it warning her away?

If this was the fleeting moment where real communication was possible, Clea dared not let it pass. She half rose from the chair. "Mom?"

Just then the door to the room swung wide. Though backlit, the solid, square shape framed in the opening was unmistakable.

"Lydia," said Clea. "You surprised me."

"Well, I'll be, Miz Reilly. Fancy you visiting in the evening."

Flustered, Clea groped for something to say. "Gone onto second shift, I see."

"Yes, indeed. A few days ahead of schedule. But what are you doing here?"

How could she explain? "I was just in the neighborhood."

"I see your Mama's gettin' fidgety. She must know I'm coming with her sleeping pill." Lydia's laugh burst the bubble of gloom that shrouded the room. "Don't mean to chase you out or nothin', but in five minutes Miz Josie'll be snoozin' away like a baby on Prozac."

The side trip to Green Haven yielded neither solace nor answers. Clea's only recourse was to drive straight home. With any luck a sandwich washed down with some good, strong coffee would produce the fertile soil in which solutions could grow, especially what to do about Ren Davis. First, though, she braced for Addy's censure, for the quick run to the market had stretched into hours.

The moment she walked into the kitchen she knew something was wrong, or rather right, definitely different.

Addy fiddled at the counter, humming with the radio, her back turned toward her mother, but it wasn't the cheerful atmosphere that struck Clea. It was the clothes. The baggy blue jeans and double-X large shirt had been replaced by a neat pair of khakis and a pale blue T-top, sized to show developing curves and a narrow band of skin around the waist. The red spray and gel had been washed from her hair. Though the underlying color was still a dozen shades darker than natural, Addy sported girlish curls instead of spikes.

"Pinch me," said Clea. "I'm dreaming."

Addy whirled around, struck a pose. "Hi, Mom. Like my new look?"

"Very much." The words were out before she noticed the shiny silver hoop clinging to her daughter's belly button. "At least most of it."

"Daddy thinks I look like a gazillion times better this way."

Clea's jaw went slack. "Daddy?"

Before more could be said, a whiskered gray face poked between Addy's elbow and ribcage and announced its presence with a high-pitched meow. Addy plucked the kitten from the counter and cuddled it against her cheek.

"Daddy says it's okay if Kitty-Face comes inside. She's so little she won't take up any space at all."

"Daddy?" Clea shook her head, wondering when she had departed Planet Earth and landed in an alternate universe where her daughter, in both dress and demeanor, appeared as a normal human teenager and the word *Daddy* was bandied about with disturbing regularity.

"Whoa, sweetie. I'm a bit lost here."

"Daddy says you won't mind since it was me who asked."

"Mind what? Asked what?"

"For him to come visit. He says he'll be just fine sleeping on the couch."

Something exploded at the back of Clea's eyes, filling her head with heat and light. "Oh no, Addy. No."

One look at her daughter and a lump the size of Ohio hardened in the pit of her stomach. A second look over Addy's shoulder confirmed a diagnosis worse than cancer.

From the living room, where he'd no doubt been eavesdropping, he sauntered toward the kitchen and slouched against the adjoining door jamb, arms crossed, a Cheshire cat smile splitting his face.

"Good to see you again, Clea."

Clea uttered a single, frostbitten word. "Michael."

Chapter Nine

Sunlight flooded the kitchen as if apologizing in advance for the coming gray season. It did little to lighten Clea's mood. She leaned against the sink, her back to the room, and stared at tiny fragments of blue showering into the basin. She barely connected their steady accumulation with the blue sponge she maliciously twisted and crumbled in her hands.

Behind her she could hear Michael digging through the refrigerator, then attacking a utensil drawer, no doubt leaving disorder in his wake. That irksome click of his tongue dredged up past memories and pulled tight the skin at the back of her neck. Worst of all, he acted as if his presence was normal, as if he belonged, when all *she* wanted to do was haul his ass curbside to be collected with the rest of the trash.

In sharp contrast, Addy burst in, a whirlwind of high spirits and cheer. Her kiss on the cheek and "Good morning, Mom" heaped guilt into the black cauldron of Clea's thoughts. Why couldn't she accept that Michael's being here was good for Addy? Even if he was a world class lout. Even if she strongly suspected his appearance on the door stoop had more to do with what was advantageous for old number one than any desire to make his daughter happy.

Clea returned the kiss, smiling inwardly at Addy's attire, peasant shirt teamed with a knee-length skirt. "Hi, sweetie. Want breakfast?"

"Nah. No time. Daddy's driving me today, and I want to show him my locker. See you after school." A giggle. "Oh, I forgot. You've got that thing in the gym tonight."

"That thing, Addy, is my job."

"Well, don't worry. We'll think of something to do. Won't we, Daddy?"

"Sure thing," he said. "Why don't you go hop in the truck—red one across the street. Be out in a sec."

As soon as they were alone, Clea spun on him. "Don't get too comfortable, Michael."

With two steps he closed the gap between them, captured a blond curl near her ear and twirled it around his finger. "Is that any way to talk to your husband?"

"You're not my husband." She jerked her head out of reach. "I haven't quite figured out why you're here, but I suggest you make your usual pathetic excuses and hit the road."

Michael's gaze left Clea's face and wandered over her head, panning the cozy kitchen and well-stocked workroom. "The girl wants me to stay."

"That girl's name is Addy, in case you've forgotten. But she's a child and doesn't see the big picture."

"Which is?"

"We're better off without you. She's better off."

"You going to tell her that? Break her little heart? I don't think so." He ran the back of his hand up her arm. "Maybe you and me ought to give togetherness another shot? You know, for Addy's sake."

"Ptth. You haven't done anything 'for Addy's sake' since the day you provided sperm."

He laughed. "Always did enjoy your spunk, Clea, especially in—" The toot of a horn interrupted. "Gotta run. We'll continue this conversation another time, huh?"

"Not if I can help it."

Whether he heard her reply or not was unclear, for he turned away to snatch car keys and change from a pile of pocket detritus he'd strewn on the countertop. He tossed the keys into the air and caught them on the fly.

"Later, Clea."

The roar of a badly-tuned engine confirmed Michael's departure. A minute later the banging screen door announced Rikki's arrival.

The younger woman blew out a whistle. "No wonder you haven't introduced me to your FBI man. He's quite the hunk."

"Davis?" The comment caught Clea off guard, and against her will she found herself considering Rikki's assessment, leaning toward agreement. "What brought this on? Has he been pumping you for information?"

"Information about what? I never spoke with him."

"Then how...?"

Rikki quirked her head toward the road. "Outside. Just now. But shame on you for hiding him from me. You know I like swarthy Italian types."

"You must need glasses. That was Michael and he's definitely a redhead. Took off in his rust bucket of a pickup."

"No, green Chevy. And Michael who? Not *the* Michael?"

"Who else? Say, what are we talking about here?"

"I'm beginning to wonder that myself. Maybe I should go out and come in again. You know, pick a different door. One that doesn't lead into the Twilight Zone." Rikki stepped to the window and looked out. "Oh well, he's gone anyway."

Clea joined her, and the two of them quietly studied the empty street. Rikki spoke first.

"Let me get this straight. Davis is not the Mediterranean type."

"Sandy hair, blue eyes."

"And the long-departed, good-for-nothing ex was here, just drove off, and his hair is red."

"The curse of the Irish. Also blue eyes."

"Then who was the guy I saw?"

"Don't know. Maybe someone reading the gas meter."

"No, just sitting in his car—watching."

"That's it. I'm confiscating your stash of Grisham novels." Clea elbowed Rikki away from the window. "Enough with your thriller plotlines and shady utility men. There's work to be done."

"Right. Homecoming." A playful spark lit her eyes. "The word kind of takes on a different meaning now, doesn't it? What with Michael's being here...and at a suspiciously early hour."

Clea grimaced. "Addy asked him to come, and a miracle happened. He actually showed up."

"Hmmm."

"Don't worry, it's all temporary. He'll tire fast of playing father and pull his famous disappearing act. Addy'll be devastated. I'll be left in charge of damage control. And, in case you're wondering, he slept on the couch."

A succession of eyebrow wagglings and suggestive smirks followed and put an end to Clea's rotten mood. How lucky she was to have such a friend. Almost regrettably she picked up a handwritten checklist outlining the day's "to-dos" and waved Rikki to a seat at the table. They divided the chores and by 8:30 Rikki trundled out the door primed for the work ahead. Clea promised to meet her mid-morning at the high school. First, she had business to attend to, the nature of which she kept to herself. There were few things she didn't share with Rikki and maybe she was making a mistake with this one, but she couldn't help it. The secret room inside her mother's house was like an ugly bruise one hid under long sleeves or explained away as a clumsy accident.

Once refocused on this particular dilemma, her emotional roller coaster crested and began a gut-wrenching, downhill plunge. What choice did she have? Talking to people, exhuming the past, writing reports? No. Ren's way was far too public. She wanted to consign the whole crazy thing to a far corner of her soul and leave it buried there. That meant going to the sheriff with a reason she had yet to manufacture and having Davis yanked from his current assignment.

Clea thought about it all the way downtown but, pulling into the parking lot, she was no closer to an acceptable excuse than when she set out. That she simply changed her mind sounded lame, especially in light of her recent zealousness. A demand might arouse suspicion or alienate Summers and ultimately turn her last court of appeal against her. Still deep in concentration, Clea exited the Explorer and, head down, followed the sidewalk, aware only of the border row of purple salvia that led her toward the steps of the Law Enforcement Center.

A pair of black wing-tips appeared in her field of vision, planted directly in front of her. Automatically she veered left to avoid a collision, but the shoes moved too. A second correction to the right didn't help either, for the feet mirrored her steps like a well-trained dance partner.

Clea looked up.

Ren wore a charcoal suit and solemn face. "I had a hunch you'd come here." He took her arm and executed a brisk one-eighty. When she balked, he continued. "At least hear me out before you storm the castle. Over coffee?" He indicated Clark's Café but didn't wait for a yes or no. His grip tightened and he piloted her across the street.

The waitress came and went. Coffee cups were filled and drained before the first word was spoken. Caffeine had smoothed the edges of Clea's pique, enough so she could make eye contact and calmly say, "You can't change my mind, so don't even try."

Davis reached into his breast pocket, withdrew a leather bifold and laid it open on the table. His photo ID and badge stared up at her. "Listen, Clea. I'm obligated now...at least to question."

"What's that? A threat?"

"No, the truth. Involving Summers won't change the fact an inquiry will go forward, but working with me'll at least guarantee you'll know what's taking place. I promise to include you one hundred percent. It's your choice—in the loop or out of it."

She shook her head.

"The alternative is you become a number on a case file. Is that what you really want? Everyone in the department looking into your background, running down leads?" He bumped his chin in the direction of the government building. "Do it my way," he continued, a touch of mirth warming his eyes, "and I'll throw in a bonus. If I speculate myself too far into left field, you're welcome to come at me with guns blazing."

"As tempting as that sounds, I suspect there's more in this for Special Agent Davis than a shot at sainthood. What is it, Ren?"

"The little room behind the fireplace. If *you're* right about it, there's a perfectly logical, innocent reason it's there."

"And?"

"If you're not—and my gut's with me on this one—I intend to get to the bottom of it."

"All about you after all, huh?"

"Look, Clea, I don't deny some selfishness here. A chance to look good at the home office. But there's something in it for you too."

"Enlighten me. Please."

"Closure. You may not be ready to admit it, but not knowing is eating away at you."

She averted her eyes, hating that he was right. Although unable to fathom a set of circumstances in which her mother might be involved in anything illegal, let alone unsavory, the room's very existence was puzzling. A tiny grain of misgiving had wormed its way under the soft layer of her certainty. There it rubbed and irritated and largely refused her efforts to flush it away. And what if Addy came to her one day with a question for which she had no answer?

Ren broke into her thoughts. "Do we have a deal?"

"I won't agree to anything that will hurt my mother, my family."

Leaning back against the cushioned booth, Ren lowered his eyebrows a notch. "Does that include your present house guest?"

"You've been spying on me?"

Ignoring her remark, Davis produced a small spiral notebook and flipped it open. "Michael Patrick Reilly, born in Vancouver, Washington, date of birth July 27, 1969, PSU dropout, currently unmarried, currently unemployed, currently residing at—"

"There'd better not be anything in there on me."

He thumbed forward a few pages, winked and recited, "Clea Worth Reilly, five foot six, blond hair, green eyes, professional photographer, born in Portland—or so she claims."

At that, Clea rose, suddenly and awkwardly, jostling the table between them until the coffee cups rattled. She wanted nothing more than to go back to Monday and start the week out fresh, but Ren grabbed her hand.

"Wait," he said.

"No." She brushed him off. "I just want this all to go away. You. Michael. Green Haven. Everything."

"Believe me," he sighed. "Nothing goes away for good. You keep paying for it and paying for it."

What did he mean by that? she wondered. But to wrestle sense from his ambiguous remark required drawing energy from a wellspring that, at the moment, had none to spare.

"I can't think right now," she said. "There's so much confusion today."

"And a long day at the school ahead."

She nodded, giving up entirely being surprised he knew that bit of information. "I've got to go." She spun toward the door, then through it and onto the sidewalk outside.

A queue of first graders, strung together with teachers and aides like beads on a rosary, momentarily blocked passage. Their laughter tinkled, artless and pure. What would it be like to have no more to worry about than a field trip into town?

While she waited, Clea filled her lungs. The air smelled of fall and crisp enough to clear her thoughts. The notion of taking one step at a time made dealing with recent events easier to imagine and introduced a small measure of sanity among the problems that plagued her. Concentrate on the short term, she told herself. Get through photographing the teams, the floats, the class king and queen, the giddy girls and their pimply dates. Then worry about the rest.

The kids were gone now. Before she crossed the street, she glanced over her shoulder and through the café's plate glass window. Ren still sat in the booth. The waitress dropped a chit on the table. He reached for his wallet. Pulled out a credit card.

She was shaking her head when she noticed the booth to the left, the one that backed up to where she had been sitting. A man hunkered low in the seat, his head coming just short of the top of the backrest. His eyes were trained on an open menu. Nothing out of the ordinary, so why the sudden feeling of bugs crawling over her skin? She swung her gaze to Ren who had finished paying the bill and seemed to be studying her through the glass. Of course. His scrutiny had brought on the case of jitters.

The walk light flashed. She bobbed her head, acknowledging Ren's look, and hurried to the curb, forgetting the dark-haired stranger who no longer occupied the second booth.

A silver balloon lost its helium lift and floated to the floor where it lay amid strips of torn crepe paper and confetti sparkles, its graceful demise surreal when compared to the surrounding pandemonium.

Clea massaged her temples and shouted.

Rikki had been leafing through a stack of permission forms, marking those with missing information, numbering others. She cupped fingers behind an ear when Clea called her name and shook her head. "What? I can't hear you."

"My point exactly. Who in their right mind would call this music? You can't even dance to it."

A writhing mass of bodies crowded the gymnasium floor. "The kids seem to be doing okay."

Clea rolled her eyes. "Don't you know you're supposed to agree with the boss?"

"Oops!"

"Next time the DJ takes a break have him announce a 'last call' for photos. It'd be nice to hurry this along. We've been stuck in this corner since the game ended at four. I don't know about you, but I'm hungry."

As Rikki signaled her agreement with a thumb's up, a girl, slinky in a black slip dress, dragged a hesitant date to the cordoned off area where Clea had set up a backdrop, studio lamps, and camera. Despite the obvious, the girl asked, "This where we get our pictures taken?"

The couple's appearance triggered a surge of interest in their corner of the gym. Though some of the newcomers were there as hecklers, bent on embarrassing a posing classmate, others signed the proper releases and paired up behind a velvet rope.

Clea firmly believed in quality work no matter what, but the abbreviated attention span of teens at a party required she strike a careful balance timewise—enough to produce a good end result, not so much as to incite restlessness in those still waiting in line.

Bracing herself for the task, she thought, this is where teamwork pays off.

And it did.

Together she and Rikki swiftly processed the paperwork and coaxed picture-worthy smiles that would prompt a flurry of orders despite braces, acne and ridiculous hairdos. The line moved steadily forward until the last couple climbed off the stools provided for sittings. Clea led them through a narrow exit in the corral with the promise proofs would be in the mail within two weeks. She hoped her spiel didn't sound as lackluster as she felt.

Heaving a sigh, she dropped into a chair but had no sooner molded her body to the hard plastic contours than she heard a smattering of girlish voices behind her. Thinking a new line was forming, she reluctantly arranged her face in a smile and lumbered to her feet.

The last person she expected to see coming their way was Ren.

The creases in his jeans suggested a new acquisition while the sweater sagged at the elbows with a well-worn look. The incongruity of his appearance as well as his presence amid the satin and tux setting of a high school Homecoming struck her as amusing.

Rikki jumped up, a sly glint in her eye. True to form, she spoke her mind. "Hmm. Brown hair, blue eyes, no clue how to dress. If this is the mysterious Bureau man, Clea, by all means introduce me."

"First I want an explanation. What are you doing here, Ren? I'm busy."

"Looks to me like you're taking a break. Thought I'd offer dinner. By the way," he said, extending a hand toward Rikki, "Ren Davis."

What was it this time? Clea thought. Something as simple as food and drink was highly suspect. "Not possible," she said. "Much too much to do."

"Nonsense," Rikki broke in. "You just said we were close to done. I'll grab the film then enlist a couple of these fifteen-year-old stud-muffins to load the van."

Clea angled her head so only Rikki could see and mouthed a two-word message: Shut up! Her usually perceptive friend had apparently developed a blockage of brain matter, for Rikki completely ignored her, and before Clea could invent another excuse, had shooed them toward the door like a pair of pesky flies. She brushed the palms of her hands together and chimed, "Now go!"

Ren drove out along the highway where four big name motels competed for Portland-bound travelers. He wheeled in at the Westlake Inn and parked at the entrance to its Red Oaks restaurant. The softly-lit and polished mahogany interior invited—a perfect place to unwind.

The waitress steered them toward an isolated table, away from distractions of the bar and the twosomes and foursomes occupying tables up front. Clea smiled, wondering if the girl had mistaken them for lovers wishing to be alone. She didn't care as long as the food was good. A plateful of leftovers waited at home, while fragrant rosemary wafting from the grill's kitchen reminded her she was famished.

She scoured the menu, ordered chicken to his steak, zinfandel to his Heineken's. They made small talk over dinner, comparing East and West Coast autumns, then graduated to deep-seated loyalties to Yankees versus Mariners. Clea regretted abuse of his autographed game ball and told him so. She had a long-held opinion of Yankee fans as pompous blowhards, and told him that too. Ren added laughter to the banter.

Despite their differences, the evening advanced civilly, almost too civilly for Clea's comfort. She waited for the other shoe to drop on the real reason for Ren's congeniality.

The thunk came when he pushed his empty plate to one side and said, "You never did answer my question."

"Which was?"

"Do we have a deal?"

"I appear to have no choice. I'm damned if I talk to the sheriff and equally damned if I don't."

"It's the right decision. You'll see."

"No, Ren, *you'll* see. To you it's about winning, getting a gold star pasted next to your name. To me it's much more personal. You may think my mother's been embroiled in some shady business, but you're wrong and I'm going to prove it. I don't yet know how, but I will."

"Fair enough."

Well, the deed was done. She had officially agreed. If she now resented Ren's intrusion into her life, she had only herself to blame, for who had pushed the start button in the first place?

Going back in time was not an option. Neither was ambivalence nor token participation. In fact, the idea of keeping one step ahead of Ren Davis promised the most satisfaction. Difficult, of course, but not beyond the realm of possibility. FBI credentials afforded him an inside track to resources unavailable to her, but she was not without advantages—like familiarity with the area and its people, people who knew her and would open up to her.

The table decoration—a flickering, cranberry-scented candle—caught and held her gaze while she mentally pictured a line-up of her mother's long-time buddies. She would talk to them all. Teachers, shop owners, the postmaster and garage mechanic. Her doctor and….

A sharp finger-snap jolted her back to the restaurant and the man sitting opposite.

"Where'd you drift off to?" he asked. "Share if you've got ideas."

Clea had no intention of losing the upper hand. She had to think, and fast. "No, no," was her comeback. "I've just been wondering about the sheriff. She'll insist on periodic updates, won't she? Then all my private business will be floating around the squad room. I don't like to think of that happening."

"You credit the sheriff with being at all interested in the matter of an 'unknown woman in a photograph' when in reality the benefit to her is in banishing me from the office."

"What kind of logic is that? The police are always over-extended. An extra hand is an extra hand no matter where it comes from."

"Unless she sees men as a threat, especially one of superior training and experience."

"My, my, we're awfully fond of ourselves."

The chair creaked as Ren leaned forward and propped his elbows on the table. "Sorry. All I meant was Summers is defensive about my being here, a thing which I'm not too happy about either."

"Nevertheless, even I know a little about chain of command, and Bea Summers outranks you—at least out here, three thousand miles west of New York."

He shrugged. "Somebody else tried to tell me that."

"And you what? Didn't believe it? Didn't accept it? Didn't care? Do I detect some excess baggage you've hauled cross country and neglected to unpack?"

This time Davis chuckled but only briefly. His face sobered quickly as if mulling what she had said.

"Hmm. I'm beginning to think that Ren is short for *renegade*."

"I wish," he said and left it at that, but Clea had accomplished what she intended—to change the subject.

And now she wanted to leave. Committed to covertly contacting her mother's friends, she was anxious to set the plan in motion.

"Ready to go?" She raised a beckoning finger, trying to catch the waitress's eye. After three attempts, she gave up and turned back to Ren. He shoved her plate out of the way and laid the photograph in question in front of her.

"Apparently nobody's ever laid eyes on this woman before."

Surprised he had already been showing the photo around, Clea stammered, "Just how many people know about this now?"

He waved a sheet of paper at her. Immediately she recognized it as the list she'd compiled for him the first night at the house. A red checkmark preceded most of the names.

"You queried all these people?" she asked, amazed. "What did they say?"

"Nothing."

"Nothing at all? So a dead end?"

"Not saying and not knowing are two very different things. People out here are a tight-lipped bunch. Must be the air. Causes amnesia on a massive scale."

Clea assumed he was trying to be funny, but her stomach soured nevertheless, for not only had Ren thwarted her head start, but he had dashed any hopes that valuable information might be garnered by merely interviewing a string of people. All too clearly she remembered Mitz Maguire's frosty reaction when confronted with the photo.

A tapping sound disrupted her train of thought. What had he said? Something about jewelry, heirlooms?

She read his body language, followed the leap-frogging spoon handle that bounced from one item in the photograph to another, and finally understood. "No," she replied. "I've never seen the ring before, nor the earrings or pendant. Why should I?"

"How about the background?" he went on. "Look past the draperies. There's a sliver of a view out the window. Does…?"

"There I can help you…or rather not help you. Studio photographers used to pose subjects in front of a standard scene painted onto what looks like a roll-up shade. These days sittings tend to be more informal. Folks want to sit on their own sofas or pick a favorite outdoor spot. I've got a backdrop almost identical to this one moldering in my garage."

The conversation died. Moments later, the waitress appeared and laid the bill on the table. For a man who bought coffee with plastic, seeing Ren produce cash surprised Clea. Was he actually assuming the expense of this dinner invitation? She was about to comment on his generosity when he ripped off the bottom portion of the ticket and carefully stowed it in his wallet. Expense account receipt. The leopard hadn't changed his spots after all.

Clea refolded the photo and slipped it into her purse. They left the restaurant, each deep in thought.

The dance was still in full swing when Ren pulled into the student parking lot. Rock songs rolled in earsplitting waves from every pore of the building. Pizza delivery cars lined the drop-off zone near the entrance. Yet for all the noise, the cheap paper decorations and superficiality, Clea grieved for Addy who was missing out on the making of what should have been a very important memory.

Ren dropped her at the Explorer. True to her word, Rikki had packed the van and left a note promising to ready the film for processing. The book of rose poems lay on the dash. After a day riddled with hard work and emotional lows, a visit to Green Haven evoked mixed feelings, but in the end guilt won the tug of war. The stop added forty-five minutes to her day. It was past nine by the time she finally arrived home.

A quick check of Addy's bedroom found the girl fast asleep. Clea kissed her cheek. Before tiptoeing out, she tickled a purr from Kitty-Face curled on the pillow at her daughter's head.

Michael's pickup was nowhere in evidence. Out doing what came natural, she suspected, the very thing that had broken up their marriage.

Would serve him right to lock the doors and go to bed, though it would probably require something more on the order of a brick to the forehead to get the message across. Thinking it worth a try anyway, Clea reentered the kitchen on a bead for the back door. Halfway there she stopped, for the magnetic hook on the side wall of the refrigerator was empty, the spare key removed.

Had Michael pocketed it on his own or had he played on Addy's desperate need to please him?

Either way, what a rat.

Had he been there, she'd have unloaded both barrels, but alone, her irritation gradually cooled. As it did something else nibbled at the edges of her mind. Something she'd noticed at the restaurant while Ren peppered her with questions. Now in the quiet house, the impression grew stronger. Was it real or had she imagined it? She took the photo from her purse and laid it on the counter. The lower left corner had been mutilated, a portion torn away as if to remove an element of the picture. Clea knew what should be there and even with the naked eye could make out parts of a few letters. More curious than ever, she opened the drawer where she kept a magnifying glass and turned on the brightest light in the room.

Not much of the studio mark remained. A couple of D's on two separate lines. The "PHY" most certainly the end of the word *Photography*, and above the letters a few sketchy sweeps of a pen suggesting a graphic.

So little to go on. The skinniest of leads. But to puzzle out the mark would identify the studio and, in turn, supply a client list with the name and address of the woman her mother had called Barbara. A lot of "ifs" stood in between. *If* the studio still existed. *If* records were kept this long. *If* the photographer could be convinced to release them. Even barring cement walls along the way, what if Barbara had, in the meantime, died or moved or changed her name?

As daunting an undertaking as it seemed, it was at least a place to start.

Clea squinted through the lens. No other markings were visible. The back too offered no new information except for a row of numbers which she recognized as color developing codes.

"Whatcha doing, Mom?"

The magnifying glass clattered to the floor.

"Addy! You scared the daylights out of me. You were in bed a minute ago."

"I woke up. Hey, isn't that the picture of you and grandma?"

"Uh, no...I mean, uh...." Caught off guard, Clea couldn't recall how much she'd told Addy when she'd originally discovered the hidden half of the picture. She sidestepped the issue and pointed instead at the torn corner, took a deep breath and started again. "I only wondered who took the portrait. You know, professional curiosity. But that part's ripped, so I guess I'll never know."

"Let me see," said Addy as she grabbed the photo and studied it nose to paper.

"Mission impossible, huh?" A nervous laugh escaped Clea's lips.

"Bet I could find out."

"How? There's so little—"

C'mon, Ma. Let me try. I could use the Internet."

Eagerness lit her daughter's eyes, a sparkle that had been absent for months and revived only with Michael's arrival. Clea admitted to jealousy. She wanted back the special, two-against-the-world relationship she'd once enjoyed with Addy. Though she doubted the girl's search would yield anything useful, the effort promised a reconnection between mother and daughter. If, in the process, Michael's smugness took a few blows, so much the better.

"I'll bet Daddy would help us."

Clea rested a hand on each of Addy's shoulders. Their foreheads touched. "Sweetie, if you want to do whatever it is you do with the computer, fine. But let it be our little secret."

Chapter Ten

The scratch of sandpaper on wood broke the Saturday morning peace. Clea had risen early—not that she wasn't tired, but because sleep was elusive. Hours of tossing and turning had tangled the bedcovers into an ever more uncomfortable knot, until she gave up the struggle and was now bent over the sturdy table in her workroom, absently scraping stubborn layers of paint from a birchwood frame. Flecks of green and white discolored her fingertips, for she had forgotten to don gloves, a thing to which she remained oblivious even after twenty minutes' work.

Her thoughts were elsewhere.

At least what passed for thoughts. Mostly they were fleeting impressions and dark, troubling emotions that died before taking any real shape, like Polaroids that failed to fully develop. The effort to wrest a solid image out of the haze reflected in the mounting pressure of her stroke as she bore down on the sandpaper.

High-pitched shrieks of jays at the backyard feeder went unnoticed, footsteps entering the room unheard. When a hand clamped on her wrist and stayed its motion, sight of the all-too-familiar fingers snapped her back with a start. She batted Michael's hand away.

"Just rolling in from an all-nighter?" she asked. "Hope you've come to say good-bye."

"Clea, where's your hospitality?"

"In cold storage where you're concerned."

He clucked his tongue. "Here I am, trying my damnedest to turn over a new leaf and this is how you treat me. You always did read the worst into things."

"The worst, huh? How exactly should I have interpreted the reek of perfume on your shirts? Or the nights you didn't bother to come home at all? No, Michael. I don't believe you've changed one bit...or even have the intention of doing so." When he wandered to the other side of the room, she addressed his back. "Let me see. You don't have a job. Probably kicked out of your apartment. Suddenly you remember you have a daughter who eats regularly and has a roof over her head. Am I getting warm?"

"Ever the bitch. Who could blame me for looking elsewhere for a little sympathy, some good times."

"I don't care what you think of me or your warped view of our three years together, but don't you dare hurt that girl," she said, stabbing a finger toward Addy's room.

He didn't answer but stood by a rack of shelves and shuffled through envelopes in a box that held pending and completed orders.

"And leave my stuff alone, Michael."

"Business looks good."

"It pays the bills—just barely."

He yawned and strolled from the room, leaving Clea to grind her fist into the sawdust-laced tabletop.

Once he was gone, she breathed sharply through clenched teeth, and regretted ever thinking sheltering Addy from his crater-sized flaws was a good idea. Then again, his weaknesses were exactly why she did it. What caring person would burden a child with such a legacy? But look where it landed her. Addy obviously wanted a father in her life and had only Michael to pick from. By smoothing the ragged edges and hoping for the best, Clea found herself in the clutches of a lie. No, she argued, not a lie, not really, but an omission of the truth—and that was turning out to be just as bad.

Too edgy to sit, she rose and swept the paint chips into her upturned palm. A muted groan escaped her lips when she wiped a tack cloth over the picture frame she'd been working on. The intricately-carved design that had spoken of style and fine craftsmanship had been sanded to a whisper. Ruined. It would be so easy to blame the confrontation with Michael, but Clea knew better. The damage had been wrought by her own careless and preoccupied handling. She tossed the frame into the trash.

Two rooms away the sofa cushions whooshed and wheezed as Michael settled in. All hope of a productive day vanished, for not only was his casual claim to her territory a total distraction, but the even rasp of his breathing added further insult. He'd easily commandeered the sleep she had been denied.

The house now smothered her. The only way out was out. She picked up the telephone and dialed Rikki's number, pacing the length and width of the kitchen through six, seven rings before a sleep-groggy voice challenged, "Who is this?"

"It's Clea. I'm going for a drive. Pick you up in ten minutes." Promptly she hung up.

Whether or not Rikki signed on for the excursion was answered a short while later when Clea braked at the curb in front of Rikki's apartment and found the girl sitting on the outside steps lacing up her shoes.

On the way Clea had lamented her brusqueness. Neither her mood nor her problems were Rikki's fault.

"Hop in," she called. "I bought. Two cups of caffeine and a bag of chocolate-covered calories from Dunkin' Donuts. Yours, if you forgive me for dragging you out of bed."

"I'll let you know," said Rikki, tearing into the paper sack. "What's up?"

"Sitting in the house was slowly driving me nuts. I've got to do something."

"And you had to do it this early?"

"It involves a trip to Reedsport."

"Whew! That's a haul. What's down there besides the dunes? And if it *is* the dunes, I don't mind telling you, they'd still be there if you'd waited another hour."

"Call it a mission."

Rikki perked up. "You're being secretive. Care to elaborate?"

Clea switched to cruise control and launched an explanation, followed by a plan still cradled in infancy. When she'd called Rikki, her only desire had been to put distance between herself and the snoring lump on her couch, but almost immediately she admitted a more deeply-rooted need. Find Barbara. Prove Ren's suspicions wrong. Return at least one portion of her life to semi-normal.

"What's in Reedsport?" asked Rikki.

"Not what...who. Chet Martin. He was never a close friend of Mom's, but I'd put him solidly in the category of acquaintances. Then about eight or nine years ago, they had a falling out. I don't know why, but shortly afterwards he moved to Reedsport and opened a small used book shop."

"And the reason for today's junket is to grill him about a thirty-year-old picture?"

"You could try to be a little more subtle, but yes. Ren has shown the photo to a good many of Mom's cronies and come up empty-handed. His approach is obviously not working."

"Time to sneak into the opposing camp and scrounge among the unfriendlies."

Clea laughed. "Not quite that dramatic, but Martin's name didn't show up on Mom's address list, so I'll get to him before Ren knows he exists. Since I won't be waving a badge in his face, maybe he'll talk to me."

For a weekend, traffic on the Interstate was light. The wind helped rather than hindered, so the old Explorer devoured the miles like a frisky coupe. About the time they exited the freeway, the sun made a showy entrance, the final fifty miles along the Umpqua River transformed into a picture fit for a Visitors' Bureau poster. Nearing Reedsport they happened upon two yard sales side by side. The stop rewarded Clea with a replacement frame for the one she'd mangled as well as a small blue bowl stenciled with paw prints, a find sure to score points with Addy. Clea couldn't help but feel optimistic about the rest of the day.

Once in town, the bookshop proved a cinch to find. One inquiry led them to Martin's Twice Sold Tales, a block off the main drive, around the corner from a pharmacy. Clea stopped at the drugstore.

"Buy a four-pack of batteries," she told Rikki, "then mosey down the street. I want to approach Chet Martin alone. Less intimidating."

"No posse ganging up on the ol' bugger, huh?"

Clea lifted her shoulders, let them fall. "It'll just be innocent little me, wanting to ask an innocent little question."

"Then zap." Rikki smacked her palms together.

"Sometimes, Rik, I wish I had your flair, but no. No torture will be used in the process."

"Wimp."

The easy banter and the morning's successes inspired confidence, so when Clea parked at the curb in front of Martin's, she didn't bother to rehearse what she intended to say, just crossed the walk and entered.

The moment she opened the door, a musty, dusty smell poured forth, the by-product of poor ventilation and the sheer volume of aged leather and paper packed tightly together. Insufficient lighting and the maze of towering book shelves conjured up ancient catacombs. Deep within the belly of the store came a muffled sound. Clea ventured quietly forward, mostly out of curiosity, for the uninviting atmosphere of the shop had dealt a disabling blow to her high spirits.

The sound drew her along narrow aisles, around a table stacked haphazardly with books, and into a small clearing. There, behind a counter, sat an elderly gentleman. The man hovered over an open book. He mumbled as he read, following his progress on the page with a bony finger.

Clea realized she had no clear memory of the man she had come to see, only that he was unusually tall. She debated how to approach. Assume this man was Mr. Martin and risk showing her ignorance, or question his identity and risk showing the very same thing. In the end she needn't have worried, for the man suddenly looked up and seeing her, rose to heights that left no doubt who he was.

"Uh, Mr. Martin." Clea groped for a suitable opening and decided on a straightforward introduction. "Mr. Martin, I'm—"

"I know who you are."

"You do? I mean, of course you do. You and my mother were friends."

His bushy eyebrows wagged higher.

Clea fumbled in her bag and withdrew the photo. "Since you've known Mom for so long, I hoped you could help me put a name to a face. The woman in this picture."

"I wondered how long it would take before someone came knocking on my door."

"Huh?"

"Josephine's in trouble, I suppose, and wants to drag me into it. I won't allow that, do you hear?"

"Trouble? What trouble are you talking about?"

"You go back and ask her your questions and leave me out of it."

"I don't understand and I can't...ask, that is. Mom's at Green Haven and is quite incapable of much of anything."

"End of story then."

Clea bristled at Martin's disdain and his curt write-off of her mother's current situation. She took a step closer. "What's so troublesome about this picture?"

"Nothing," he replied. "Nothing."

"Yes there is. Tell me."

Martin burrowed in his jacket pocket for a cigarette, lit it and, despite the surrounding mounds of kindling, discarded the match without benefit of an ashtray. Clea recognized a stall and opted for a different tack. If pleading wouldn't budge him, maybe a veiled threat would.

"There's this man I know," she said. "He's with the FBI and full of questions."

Before she could finish, Martin rounded the counter and stormed past. Startled, Clea froze. But not for long. She spun and followed his retreat—down the History aisle, past Politics, into Classics. He kept going. To the front door. Through the front door. He flung it open squarely into Rikki's face, shoved her aside, and on long legs dashed down the street.

"Wow! What was that?" Rikki steadied herself at a parking meter as Clea appeared at the door.

"Which way did he go?"

"Who? The old guy? Left, I think. Into that alley."

Clea bounded in pursuit but had covered only a few yards when a car sped out of the same alleyway and careened out of sight.

"I'll say it again," said Rikki, coming up beside Clea. "What was that?"

"Something weird's going on. That was Chet Martin and he darted off like a scared rabbit after suggesting my mother was in some kind of trouble."

"And I thought what happened to me was strange." Clea's wrinkled brow encouraged Rikki to continue. "Remember yesterday morning when I told you there was a man sitting in a green car outside your place?"

"Yeah."

"I just spotted the same guy when I left the drugstore. Same green car. He was leaning against the fender with a puzzled look on his face, like he didn't know quite what to do."

"Where was that?"

"At the corner." Rikki turned to point toward the pharmacy. "Whoa. There he is. On the other side of the street. How's that for coincidence?"

The dark features and furtive slouch of the man struck a chilling chord. Clea too had seen him before. Not at her house but in the café, seated in the booth behind her and Ren. The moment their eyes met, the man halted, did an about-face and hustled back from where he'd come.

Clea grabbed Rikki's arm. "Quick. Get in the car."

"Why?"

"I'll explain later. Right now, move."

The tires screeched as Clea wheeled away from the curb. She avoided downtown traffic, seeking instead concealment in the labyrinth of side streets. A quick turn here, another there—a sure test of the stranger's intentions. Every few minutes she checked the rearview mirror. The sight of empty pavement eased her mind, though she opted not to return to the Interstate and chance an accidental crossing of paths.

At the 101 junction sign she swung north on the coastal highway. A mini van followed suit. A splash of red joined the parade. A black sedan. The road snaked back and forth. Clea ignored the posted speed and pressed to gain distance. Finally a straightaway offered the first unobstructed view behind them.

"All clear," said Rikki, who'd been twisted in the seat keeping a constant lookout. "No green car. Hey! Now what are you doing?"

"A little extra insurance is all." Clea detoured into the entrance to the Oregon Dunes. At the far edge of the parking lot a stand of fir promised cover, so she nosed the car as deep into the trees as possible. Killed the engine.

Quieted the swaying ring of keys as if even the faintest clink of metal on metal would give away their hiding place.

For a while the two women sat unmoving, unspeaking, staring through the windshield at the branches that fanned across the hood of the car. When a garrulous seagull broke the hush, Clea whispered, "I think we're safe."

"Yeah, but safe from what?"

Clea related her own sighting of the man. "You see, you weren't the only one to encounter him before. Don't you think his showing up here stretches happenstance to the breaking point and beyond?"

"Some kook is following us?"

"Appears so. Or better put, in the past tense. We seem to have outsmarted him." To prove her point, Clea indicated the half dozen other cars lined up at the trail head. "Same bunch as when we arrived. We lost him with all my fancy maneuvers back there."

"Now who's been reading high-crime novels?"

"Not me. That's your passion." Clea scanned the lot again. "So, how long does the heroine wait before she concludes it's all been a bad case of overactive imagination?"

"Oh, twenty minutes, or however long it takes you to fill me in on why we're having this conversation in the first place."

Rikki's estimate proved accurate. For twenty minutes Clea recounted all that had transpired since Monday—the complete version, as well as her doubts, her fears and her denials.

When she finished, Rikki patted her arm. "There's a logical explanation for every bit of what you said. From what I know of your mom, she's too sweet to...you know...secret rooms and all."

"Yeah."

"So, what's next?"

"For you, a vacation. This mess is mine to figure out. I won't put you at risk."

"What risk? You can't even say for certain we were followed. Even if we were, wouldn't you say the guy's pretty inept?"

Clea chuckled. "Regardless...."

"No way, sister. I'm your friend. Your problems are my problems. Besides, this is the most excitement I've ever had. Imagine, a real live mystery. I'm signed on for the duration, so don't try to talk me out of it."

Clea sighed. "Okay, and maybe you're right after all. My imagination in overdrive."

While they talked, two additional cars had arrived and spilled their families and gear onto the gravel. Children bounced with pent-up energy and adults conferred with hiking maps. A dog yapped at the end of a leash.

People already on the trails and more likely to come as the weekend morning progressed reassured Clea that the stranger was gone for good. She reached behind her for a camera bag and gestured.

"Up for a walk?" she asked. At Rikki's nod she unlocked the car door and stepped out. "I've been meaning to photograph the dunes in the fall for a long time. Too late for the contest now, but maybe I can interest a calendar company in buying them."

Rikki jumped out the other side of the car, tripod in hand. "Big bucks, here we come."

Rikki's optimism boosted her spirits as they walked the boardwalk that led to the dunes and down which the entourage of couples, kids and pet had already disappeared. Clea anticipated a later encounter with them when she would ask permission to pose the children by the shore.

Once the boarded walk ended, the trail sloped steeply and awkwardly downward. When they reached the interdunal stretch of fine sand, their shoes immediately filled with the stuff, making this part of the trek uncomfortable as well as difficult. Clea stopped often to snap pictures.

At the crest of the foredunes the marram grass had been cut away to accommodate the trail. Here they could see the ocean. The unpredictable, sometimes terrifying Pacific gently sloshed onto the beach. There was not another soul in sight.

Clea continued to take pictures, though disappointed she'd missed the children. She and Rikki traveled a good distance along the shoreline. They spotted no one the entire way. Clea's pace slackened, her gaze drawn ever more frequently inland. The isolation, at any other time a boon to a photographer, today brought a particular chill, as if dark eyes shadowed the women and measured their vulnerability.

Finally Clea stopped walking altogether.

"What's wrong?" asked Rikki.

"Nothing. Just a feeling. Silly of me."

"Silly ha-ha or silly like a whole circus of fleas using the back of your neck for showtime?"

"You felt it too?"

"I didn't want to spook you."

"I've gone through plenty of film. Let's call it quits."

"Amen to that."

The two hurried back to the break in the foredune that marked the return trail. As they crossed over, a sharp rustle in the beach grass startled them. It was impossible to tell exactly where the sound had come from. One thought it was near, the other far. They took one last, quick look at the lonely beach and the lonelier path ahead and took off at a run, as fast as the bulky equipment allowed.

Safe return to the parking area had them hugging each other, joking about their skittishness. Rikki clambered aboard while Clea circled to the driver's side. A sandy outline on the running board brought her up short. The spot had been whistle clean when they set out. Patterned grooves suggested the tread of a shoe. Gingerly Clea placed her own narrow foot over the track. It easily fit inside.

Someone had approached the car, looked inside, perhaps even tested the door lock. Despite a heavy sweater and the exertion of the run, Clea shivered, for the face of the dark-haired man flashed before her inner eye.

Chapter Eleven

The note she'd slipped under Addy's door that morning, detailing exactly where she'd be and when she expected to return, was now anchored to the kitchen countertop with a can of soup and bore one additional word—*Out*—in Addy's backhanded script.

So much for improved communications.

Clea remained at the counter and rehashed the morning's episode. On the long drive home her fears calmed. She convinced herself Ren was behind it all. He mistrusted her from the start and had arranged to have her followed. Eyes where he couldn't see, ears to hear, a hireling to report back.

Rikki had readily taken up the cry of foul.

It made sense. The stranger had appeared at her home only after Ren learned where she lived. And at the café? A gung-ho, special agent FBI man should have spotted a skulking low-life a mile off, unless, of course, he'd expected one to be there.

Now who couldn't be trusted?

Clea slid open the junk drawer and grabbed a pen. *Me too*, she wrote at the page bottom and left the note where she'd found it.

The car seat was still warm when she climbed back in. No sense letting good body heat go to waste, she reasoned by way of justification for her hasty turnaround.

Already Clea knew her destination.

Ren answered on the third knock. A split-second and recognition later his apparent bad mood changed. Deep lines across his forehead, which had clearly spelled annoyance at the interruption, melted away.

"Come in." He moved aside to let her enter. "What do you think of this?" he asked as if he'd been talking with her all the while and only now paused to elicit her opinion. He didn't wait for an answer, but turned on his heels and headed to the back of the house.

The reason she'd come was placed on hold, second to Ren's distracted reception which roused her curiosity. She trailed him past the dining area and into the kitchen. Small white cartons of take-out flanked the sink. Automatically she made a move toward them, intent on neatening up the area, thought better of it and continued her pursuit. She shied at the pantry door, but Ren walked on through. A moment later his head reappeared. "You coming?"

At her hesitation, he fully emerged and extended a hand accompanied by a look of resigned frustration at her reticence.

"We still need to preserve the site. Step carefully. Watch so you don't touch anything."

He made it sound so clinical, so non-personal; and since Clea knew what to expect beyond the doorway this time, she didn't fight the tug that pulled her inside.

Ren deposited her in front of the small table in the corner. The vase of dusty roses overpowered its diminutive surface. He plucked a chopstick from his breast pocket and directed the pointy end at a tightly-wound red bud.

"See this?"

"Yeah."

The wooden stick moved to another and lightly brushed a partially-unfurled petal. Ren looked at her, triumph animating his face.

Clea never considered herself dense, but she had no idea what he expected her to glean from the two flowers. She wrinkled her nose. "And?"

His shoulders sagged while his voice became that of a frustrated professor in a lecture hall filled with tiresome freshmen. "That one's a bud. This one has started to open. And this one over here..." The chopstick found another rose, a white one this time. "...is withered around the edges, distinctly different from the other two. If all the flowers were from a single bouquet, they would have bloomed at the same rate. These clearly did not."

"So?"

"And I counted them. Twenty-nine. An odd number, wouldn't you say? Not two dozen. Not two and a half dozen. Unless the number twenty-nine held a special significance to your mother...."

Clea shook her head. "You've overlooked the obvious. One rose spoiled and was thrown away."

That explanation gave Ren no more than a moment's pause. He dismissed it curtly and plowed forward. "I believe each rose constitutes a single occasion, added one by one to the vase over a period of time."

"Like an anniversary?"

"Yes, commemorative in some way."

"But you don't know what."

"This is where you come in. What sort of occasions necessitate giving a woman flowers…or, in this case, receiving them?"

"You mean to tell me you've never given a woman flowers?"

Immediately Clea frowned at the unnecessary dig, though she made no effort to call it back.

"That's beside the point," he continued. "Think specifically about your mother. What would be meaningful enough to *her* to preserve a flower she'd either bought or been given? Twenty-nine times."

The question stumped her. Not being married, her mother celebrated no wedding anniversaries. Since the roses had been sequestered behind plaster for longer than Clea had been alive, they also had nothing to do with a daughter's passing years. Nor her mother's, for that matter, as Josie had become a parent late in life, not even close to twenty-nine but past forty when Clea was born.

Clea considered her mother's career. As a teacher she might have received a bouquet as a class gift. Twenty-nine students. Twenty-nine roses.

When she mentioned this to Ren, he reminded her the flowers had not all been received at the same time.

"All right, a single student then, expressing appreciation over the years."

Ren rubbed his chin while he mulled the possibility, and in the patch of quiet the image of a gold enameled pin flashed briefly across Clea's mind.

Silly, she chided herself. How did the two fit into the same picture other than by subject matter alone? And surely a thankful student wouldn't have been so mysterious, would have openly signed his name instead of a cryptic number.

When Clea glanced at Ren, she was surprised to find him staring back at her.

"You've thought of something?"

"Unrelated. Totally."

"Let me be the judge."

The comment poked at her pride. Who did he think she was? The sorry little woman unable to put two and two together? Maybe this was payback for her earlier remark about the flowers? Under other circumstances she might have agreed she deserved it. Nevertheless, she decided to hold her tongue and just tell him about the pin.

"With all that's been going on, it slipped my mind until now. A few days ago a package arrived for my mother. It was a gorgeous pin in the shape of a rosebud. Probably has nothing to do with the dried flowers here because of the way it was sent." She filled him in on the plain wrapping, the neglected return address, and the card signed only with a number.

"Twenty-nine?" he asked.

"We should be so lucky. No. Twenty-one."

When she was through, Ren started to pace.

"Your mother was partial to roses?"

"Quite."

He worked his way from the secret room to the kitchen and on to the dining area where he stopped in front of the wall which showcased two framed oils, each depicting roses.

"In case you're wondering," said Clea. "I've no idea where they came from."

But she didn't stop there. She stepped around him, lifted the paintings from the wall, and carried them to the table where they could be examined more closely. The paintings were related in theme only—different artists, different styles, different palettes, different frames. Clea and Ren exchanged blank expressions before she carefully flipped the oils so they faced down on the table. Then she checked the backs for personalization—a note or gift card similar to the one that had arrived with the rosebud pin. There was nothing tucked behind the keys and the only thing adhered to the stretchers were worn paper labels on which was written the artist's name, a lot number, and what might have been an inventory code. Each painting had obviously made its way through one or two sales before ending up on Josie's walls, for brokers' names and home cities were also noted in script.

"I'm impressed," said Clea. "I never paid much attention to these paintings other than to think they were pretty, but you don't sell garage art through pricey East Coast auction houses."

"Would your mother have bought these for herself?"

"On a teacher's salary?" Clea stifled an outright laugh.

"Gifts then."

"That makes three we know of."

"And three makes a pattern. Weren't there also some floral knickknacks in those boxes upstairs? We should take a second look at them—and whatever else even hints of roses. While you do that, I'll google these auction places for current information, phone numbers and such."

He crossed to an end table and picked up the thin, black notebook computer, leaving the table depressingly bare, when in fact it had always held a basket with her mother's needlework at the ready. The adjoining armchair too had suffered an alteration—its ever-present patchwork pillow removed and placed somewhere out of sight.

Like a reluctant farewell kiss, a disturbing sense of loss fluttered across Clea's cheek, so real her hand flew to her face. Or had the furnace merely kicked on and delivered a gust of air through metal grates and the courtesy of Pacific Gas and Electric?

The fireplace—and what lay within its bowels like a storybook monster—dealt a far more telling blow. Wearily Clea swiped a hand over her eyes. Nothing was the same as it had been—nor would it be so again. In a matter of days, a force greater than time and memory had blurred all that Clea held dear. It was as if a counter magnet had been dropped onto the compass of her heart and the needle which had always unerringly pointed at her true north now spun wildly in circles.

Ren spoke her name and broke her inward focus.

"Unless you'd prefer to switch," he said, the laptop in his hand, a question on his face.

"Switch?"

"You search the Net. I tackle the boxes."

"Oh, no. I'm still a beginner on the computer. Addy's the whiz and I let her handle anything I need. My talent lies in grubbing through old cartons. I'll go upstairs."

When Clea later rejoined him, she deposited her haul of items next to the paintings. She had amassed quite an assortment: a small porcelain figurine of a child holding a rose, a head vase of an exotic, black-eyed woman with a rose behind her ear, various trinkets, a keychain, two mugs, a music box, and decorative plates. The book of rose poems was still in her car.

She sank into the armchair while Ren pored over the pieces one at a time. He examined each meticulously, then turned to the laptop and typed a description before moving to the next item. The silence stretched on and on. Clea wished he'd hurry, for it was difficult to keep her thoughts from straying into places she'd rather not go alone.

"By the way," he said as if he'd read her mind, "I *do* know when to give flowers. It's just the details I could never get quite right."

It took Clea a moment to link the comment to the conversation begun over an hour before. "What details? Flowers are a wonderful expression any time. The why and what and how don't really matter."

At this he faced her, leaned against the table, arms folded over his chest. "Believe me, details matter." Clea's puzzled expression urged him on. "If I gave daisies, the occasion called for roses. If I bought roses, orchids would have been better." He sighed. "I never had a chance."

"Girlfriend?"

"Wife."

"Oh," she said, startled by the information. "You're married?"

"Hardly. Apparently I got the bride wrong too."

Clea remembered the frigid reception she'd received at their first meeting and Ren's less than gracious opinion of the female sheriff. This explained a lot. She let him continue without interrupting.

"It wasn't just the little stuff either, but my job, my friends, even my dog. Probably sounds like I hate women." He shrugged.

"Well, if you've moved all the way out here to escape one, it does leave the impression you have strong feelings in that department."

"At that point I was more than willing to chuck the whole marriage scene, but Lauren couldn't stand not having the last say-so. She wasn't much good at this thing called Holy Matrimony, but she sure managed to get revenge straight. My being out of sight was infinitely better than simply being out of mind."

"What happened?"

"Money talks. A bigshot father talks even louder. Bellows, in fact. Daddy called in a favor or three for his little girl, pulled strings into a hangman's knot, and before the ink was dry on the divorce decree, I had walking papers to the back of beyond." Here he spread wide his hands, a gesture which embraced much more territory than the house on Chestnut Street.

"Oregon isn't such a dreadful place to be."

"It isn't New York either."

"If you opened your eyes, you might discover that in being exiled you got the better part of the deal."

"Mmm." With a sigh, Ren shook his head. "Let's forget this whole conversation, huh? I don't know what made me tell you all that nonsense in the first place. Correct Bureau procedure is to keep a healthy distance from a case."

"Well, it certainly wouldn't do to compromise a *case,* now would it?"

"That didn't come out exactly how I meant it."

"Apparently not."

For what seemed long minutes Ren regarded her through shaded eyes, his thoughts and conclusions closely guarded. Eventually he redirected his attention to the computer program and the list being compiled. The window that had slivered open, affording a mote of insight to his private life, closed, leaving Clea on the outside wondering what else lay behind the pane of frosty glass.

She balled her fingers and bit on a knuckle. "I reacted harshly too," she murmured. "Sorry. I'm not usually like this."

When he failed to respond, her body settled lower into the chair, pressed down by an iron glove of helplessness. It had been one hell of a week. A bed of quicksand sucking at her heels. She'd become ill-humored and short-tempered, a side of herself she barely recognized, didn't like, and yet one she seemed unable to keep in check. The view, as far as she could see into the future, was just as bleak, and on over the horizon more of the same. If her mother's apparent secrets were left unexplained, doubt would mushroom. Of that she was certain. Already feeler roots crept outward from the knot at the base of her spine. Soon they would take firm hold, plant themselves deep and damaging.

Silently Clea renewed yesterday's vow. She would not stop until recent events were properly and satisfactorily laid to rest. As much as she hated to admit it, for that to happen she needed Ren. And being a constant thorn embedded under his skin was no way to gain the required cooperation.

Friendly was better. She thought for a second, took a deep breath and finally asked, "So, where's your dog now?"

Without turning and with no inflection to betray his feelings one way or the other, Ren said, "Run over by a car."

Clea groaned. "I said the wrong thing again, didn't I?" She managed a sterile laugh. Back to square one, which brought to mind the reason she had made the visit to see him in the first place.

"Since the plan is to work together, Ren, everything out in the open, and we *will* be doing that, it's hardly necessary for you to have someone following me. Besides it's unnerving. I'd appreciate your calling him off."

Clea watched his back for a hint the message had been clearly sent and received. His reaction surprised her. Like an animal catching scent of another, bigger and more dangerous than itself, Ren went motionless, every pore of his body testing the air. Slowly he straightened, turning as he did. His face came into view, degree by degree, until the full force of those steel blue eyes sent shivers racing down her arms.

She had so thoroughly persuaded herself the dark-haired man was in Ren's employ, an alternate scenario never crossed her mind—that Ren would have no idea. Quickly she stood, feeling far too vulnerable slumped in a chair. As she did Ren closed the distance between them and gripped her upper arms, firmly, perhaps too much so.

"Say that again," he demanded.

"The man from the diner. Rikki saw him outside my house too, and he was in Reedsport this morning. I think he followed us into the park at the dunes. You don't know?"

Ren released her only long enough to slam a fist into his palm and swear under his breath. When he touched her a second time, his hand was gentle, his voice softer, more in control.

"You're trembling," he said.

"You're frightening me. If this guy doesn't belong to you, then who?"

"Are you positive he was following you?"

"Ren. My house? The café? Nearly two hundred miles down the coast? You said it yourself: three makes a pattern."

"What did he look like?"

She told him, though the man hadn't come close enough for more than a cursory description.

"What about the car? License plate?"

"I never saw the car. Rikki said it was green, an old boat of a Chevy, but that was about all."

The scowl on Ren's face spoke of his frustration and a mounting anger. "What were you doing so far from home?"

For a moment it occurred to Clea not to disclose her disastrous meeting with Chet Martin. The brief hesitation was met with a tightening of Ren's fingers on her arms. She gave in and related the entire story. At the end she searched his eyes, but it was his hands that told her more, trailing heat down her arms, capturing her own in their warmth. The pressure applied was of comfort not censure, though when he spoke again, his words were stern.

"Clea, I want you to go home, stay put, stay out of this. Let me handle it."

"As simplistic and perhaps desirable as that sounds, it wasn't our agreement, Ren, and this is very much my business."

"No, this is police business and you're a civilian."

"What, are we in the Army now?"

"Don't get fired up, Clea."

"I won't be shoved aside, Ren. We're talking about *my* life. I'm involved and fully intend to stay involved. With or without your consent."

He freed her hands.

Having won the point, Clea wasn't sure how the victory translated from rhetoric into action, but she would see it through to the end. The sooner the better. A faint smile tipped the corners of her mouth. There were more terrible things in the world than working with Ren Davis. And unless her eyes deceived her, there was a hint of a smile on his face as well.

"Agreed then," she said.

Ren dug his fingers in his hair. "God save me from women," he muttered.

Chapter Twelve

Ren climbed into his blue sedan and followed her home, so close she expected a cruiser to appear at any moment, lights ablaze, and pull them to the side of the road. When she wheeled into her driveway and braked, Clea braced for the crunch of metal. None came.

"Lucky break for him," she snorted under her breath.

Before the Explorer finished its knock and shudder routine, Ren was at the driver's side door, tapping on the glass.

"I think I can make it to the house all by myself," she said, the window cracked a notch. "Just like a big girl."

"I'm immune to sarcasm, Clea. I said I would see you safely home and I'm doing it."

"And a real boy scout you are."

He cocked his head. "Again, about the sarcasm."

"I'm only pointing out door-to-door service is unnecessary. I've been taking care of myself for a good decade and some and haven't muffed things up too badly."

Having said that, she shoved open the door, swung her legs sideways and attempted to step down. Her heel snagged a stringy carpet edge, and before she could catch herself had pitched forward into Ren's arms.

They grappled like wrestlers until her shoe popped off and the once-captive foot landed firmly on the ground. She extricated herself from his grasp, tugged her jacket back around her hips, retrieved the errant shoe. The muscles in Ren's face twitched at the effort to squelch ready laughter.

"As I was saying," Clea began, but got no farther before a giggle bubbled up in her own throat.

Ren took her by the arm and aimed her at the house. "Door to door it'll be," he said.

She let him lead, surrender being more practical at this point than trying to convince him the karate lessons she'd taken two years earlier had rendered her at all competent in the art of self-defense.

On the small wooden porch that led to the kitchen, Ren stooped down. "What do we have here?" From under the remnants of summer petunias, he hauled up a gray kitten by the scruff of its neck and delivered it into Clea's outstretched hands. "Yours?"

"No, Addy's." She snuggled the kitten close. "What the devil have you been up to?"

If looks were an accurate indication, Kitty-Face had seen brighter days. Scraps of leaves and grass clung to matted-down fur. A thin red line, evidence of a newly-acquired scratch, angled across its nose like a checkmark. The tiny heart pounded against Clea's fingertips.

"We'd better get you in the house."

"Good idea," said Ren, edging toward the door.

"I meant the cat."

"Of course, you did." Ren chuckled as he backed off the step onto a piece of flagstone that with three others linked the driveway to the house. Methodically he scanned the shrubbery up and down Clea's lot line. "Remember," he warned. "No more long trips unless I'm with you. If you see that green car, you call my cell. And, for God's sake Clea, keep a low profile until I have a chance to find this guy and drag his sorry ass to the sheriff."

"You've probably already scared him half way to Jackson County, so as long as you're here, why not come in and let me show you the pin I told you about."

Clea hooked a finger on the screen's latch and yanked it wide. She bumped a hip against the solid back door. It flew open.

"I want your doors bolted too," said Ren as he followed her inside.

As soon as they entered, the kitten squirmed out of Clea's grasp, hit the floor running, and skidded around a corner.

My God! she thought, that cat must have had one bummer of a day. She'd tell Addy in a bit. Together they'd find the kitten and administer a little animal first-aid. Then they'd have a talk about the responsibilities of owning a pet.

Right now she had an entirely different trio of affairs to contend with: a tantalizing smell permeating the room, a gnawing pang in her stomach that screamed "Feed me!" and Ren in her kitchen.

He was still at the back door, by outward signs rating her lock on a scale of "breaks in a breeze" to "withstands nuclear assault." Knowing what he'd find, Clea mentally calculated the cost of a new lockset.

In the meantime, the oven beckoned. She peeked inside. "Ooh. Addy's been busy. She's made my Irish casserole and apple crisp."

The doorknob rattled, drawing Clea's attention back to Ren. A frown dragged at the corners of his mouth. No doubt security on the homefront left a lot to be desired. Since her divorce and more recently since her mother's health began its downhill slide, the burden of such things had fallen to her. Ren's critique and judgment had not been sought, and she hated he found her efforts lacking, but the initial spark of resentment that ignited behind her eyes died quickly. She couldn't deny the appeal of his concern for her safety—even if mandated by his job description: serve and protect.

She wondered if his escort home constituted above and beyond the call of duty. Did it tip the scales for a reciprocal offer of dinner?

Just as Clea decided the answer was a definite probably, Addy appeared in the hallway, strumming an air guitar with obvious gusto and mouthing lyrics in sync to a tune audible to her alone through a portable headset. As the performance spiraled toward its climax, Addy spotted Ren. The instrument evaporated and Addy's lips froze around a vowel.

"Come in, sweetie," said Clea. "I want you to meet Mr. Davis. He's the gentleman renting grandma's house."

"What's he doing here?"

"I was about to invite him to join us for dinner."

"No!" The protest was a cocktail of challenge laced with whine.

"That's not very polite, young lady. I think you owe Mr. Davis an apology."

"I made supper for you, me and Dad. Just the three of us."

Addy's eyes glistened. She crossed her arms firmly over her chest, a smugly-defiant teen superimposed over a hurt, little girl. And, having painstakingly baited a parent trap, she stood her ground.

Great! thought Clea. She was in a pickle now. Having indirectly delivered the invitation, how did she gracefully uninvite Ren and avoid the double mortification of eating while her ex spewed God knows what and her daughter flung daggers over the biscuits?

In the end Ren saved her the trouble. With a cautious glance that rolled from mother to daughter, he said, "I'll take a raincheck, if that's okay. Fast food'll go better with my plans for the evening anyway. And it looks like you've got your hands full here."

"Appears so."

She followed Ren as far as the driveway. A car rumbled by on the street, and they both reacted to the sound, immediately on the alert and straining to see the driver. When the vehicle pulled up at a house three doors down and a teenaged boy emerged with an over-large laundry bag slung over his shoulder, Clea laughed at their jitters.

"Tommy Aberlane," she explained. "He moved into his own apartment last summer but shows up on a regular basis, usually right around supper time and with a week's worth of dirty clothes. At least mothers are good for some things."

"Don't be so hard on the institution. You seem to be doing okay at it."

"Ptth. That from a man who's survived the arctic chill of a disgruntled fourteen-year-old. I'm surprised your toes aren't dropping off from frostbite." Clea sighed and glanced toward the kitchen window in time to see a face duck behind the curtains. "She thinks she's being subtle. In reality she might as well plaster her intentions on a billboard. Poor Addy wants a *family*"—two fingers of each hand hooked around the word—"and is unable to see Michael for the disaster he is."

"You know, in my line of work, I often see the absolute dregs of humanity. I'm constantly amazed that kids choose to be with their parents despite home situations that've made experienced agents vomit on their shoes." He lifted his shoulders in a shrug and peered into space. "The devil you know is better than the devil you don't, I guess."

"That sounds horrible, Ren, but this town is a far cry from New York. It's quiet, almost boring, and I expect Addy to have considerably better manners."

"I like Addison. She's not a pushover."

"More like a concrete wall. Anyway, you deserve an apology even if it comes from me."

"Not necessary."

"Oh, but it is."

Neither Ren nor Clea made an effort to depart despite an awkward span of silence. The wind kicked up, skittering leaves across the shingles and showering them with ovals of amber and brown. Clea held out a hand and caught one on the fly. It disintegrated instantly into chips.

"So, you're going to be busy this evening," she said.

"Yeah, phone calls, web searches, grunt work."

"I'll see about a lock."

Ren nodded. "Have that car of yours looked at, too. Engine needs tending."

"Sure thing."

"I'm not kidding. You don't want a breakdown on the road."

Another stretch of silence. "Well, good night." The words rang with a pleasant harmony, for both Ren and Clea had spoken at exactly the same time.

Once Ren's car was out of sight, Clea returned to the kitchen fully prepared to engage battle. Her opening salvo: "I didn't raise you to insult my...my...." What the heck *did* she consider Ren? She started again. "Your behavior tonight was a disappointment, Addy."

"I don't want him here."

"On certain things you don't get a vote."

"It's my house, too."

"Of course, it's your house and you'll be seeing more of it this weekend because you're grounded."

"No fair!"

"No argument."

Addy stomped away but Clea called her back. The cat was problem number two; and if the yelling hadn't driven it into permanent hiding, they needed to find Kitty-Face and doctor her injured nose. Tensions eased only slightly while this was being done.

Repeatedly and dejectedly Addy watched the clock, tracking the minute hand while it slid past six, rounded six-thirty on its way to seven. The casserole dried around the edges, the apple crisp decomposed into a soggy mess. In the end the two ate alone, in stony silence, sad bookends to the one empty plate.

Mercifully the meal was over quickly. Addy slunk to her room, leaving Clea to clear the table and face the day's accumulation of mail. On top of the heap was a letter. Addressed to her. Plain white envelope. Curious, she picked it up.

Immediately underneath, however, was something of greater interest. An unstamped orange flyer boldly headed SPECIAL COUNCIL MEETING! The notice reminded residents of the planned open forum to hash over an upcoming referendum—construction of a new town hall facility. Controversial. Expensive.

Shoot! Clea thought when she saw the date and time—tonight, within the hour.

The letter she held disappeared into a pocket without a second glance as she rushed to the bedroom to change out of the clothes she had hiked the dunes in.

Now dressed in a long gray skirt and maroon sweater, hair brushed, lipstick fresh, Clea barked orders at Addy to keep the doors locked and the porch light on.

A meeting like this, with turnout high and emotions higher still, could drag on. A late night, she sighed, but the issue threatened her pocketbook and she wanted to know how much.

She was halfway through the door when she thought of Ren. A sprint to the Law Enforcement Center hardly constituted the long trip he'd forbidden her to make alone, but the uncertainty was enough that she backstepped into the room.

No, this is ridiculous she chided herself. I'm just running into town. She turned around, getting as far as the flagstones this time.

"Damn, I'll never hear the end of it." She ran back inside.

He answered her call while the first ring still echoed in her ear. "Clea," he said. "How are things—"

"Ren, I'm dashing to a town meeting. Wanted to let you know in case you called here for some reason." There, obligation—requisite or not—dispensed with.

"I'll pick you up."

"What?"

"I'm going with you."

"For heaven's sake, why?"

"Be there in five."

He hung up.

For the next ten minutes Clea groused about the delay, peering through the window up the darkened street every thirty seconds until finally headlights pulled a car to a halt in front of her house. She waited for the dome light to blink on and confirm it was Ren, but the car remained dark while the phone came alive.

"I'll wait at the curb," he informed her. "C'mon out."

Chicken, she thought, as she stepped into the night. He's afraid to tangle with Addy again.

Forgotten was her earlier anger at Addy's behavior, replaced by a growing bubble of pride. In a contest of wills with the mighty FBI, her daughter had proved a worthy opponent.

By the time Clea reached the car, she was humming her favorite Helen Reddy song.

They made their way down narrow steps, along a drab uncarpeted corridor to a door marked Council Chamber and entered to a crush of bodies, so dense the crowd swayed in unison from side to side like a perpetual wave machine. Voices rumbled, a restless undercurrent to the high-pitched squeal of someone testing a mike.

Ren leaned close, to within inches of Clea's ear. "Hot topic tonight?"

"Taxes, what else?" she said, shouting to make herself heard. "You should've stayed home."

"What? And miss all the fun. Nothing sparks fireworks more than people about to be separated from their hard-earned dollars."

"Namely me. Just watch."

He squeezed her arm. "While you're waiting your turn on the soap box, how about looking around. Point out anyone even remotely associated with your mother who didn't show up on her address list."

Clea nodded and up on tiptoe panned the room. Mitz Maguire had procured a front row seat. Her hands flew as if she were signing to a deaf person, though the one on the receiving end had no such affliction. He was Lance Gorman, long-time owner of the local Century 21 office. Had sold Clea her house. Had more recently offered to buy Josie's, though at a time when Clea still clung to the fantasy her mother would one day return home.

Off to one side sat Delbert Sheznesky, nattily dressed as always. He peered into the audience as if about to grade the upcoming performance.

She recognized Andy Hale though it had been ages since their paths had crossed. He and his wife had converted an ancestral home into a thriving bed and breakfast. The duties of host kept him busy. Maintenance ate up the rest of his time. Concern about the burden of additional taxes brought him to the surface tonight. Clea chanced a wave but couldn't catch his eye.

Some people she was sure Ren had already spoken with: Jonas Fenster, the pharmacist, for one; Will, the town's lone taxi driver; parents of former students; the florist, though only the name of his store came to mind—All Occasion Flowers. Stupid name, she thought, shaking her head as she did every time she passed the shop in town.

All this she relayed to Davis, at the same time amazed at the sea of faces she didn't recognize at all. The community was changing, growing despite her naïve insistence to the contrary. A "small town" label fit no better than a watermelon stuffed into a paper lunch sack.

As the number of acquaintances dwindled, so too did her hopes of learning about the past, those blanks that would never be filled in by her mother.

The sharp thwack of a gavel, followed by a good many "shusses" and "quiet downs," brought the meeting to a semblance of order. It wasn't the last time the gavel was heard. Debate was impassioned on both sides of the issue, occasionally vehement. A few hand-lettered signs cropped up among participants. The room heated to stifling, and the need for a new ventilation system quickly became apparent. Even though Clea hadn't yet the chance to speak her views, after an hour and a half her feet hurt and her back ached. She had heard more than enough.

In turning to signal Ren her intention to leave, Clea spotted a police uniform at the outer fringe of the crowd. Quickly she ducked behind the shield of Ren's shoulder, out of view and the accidental chance of eye contact. She was tired and in no mood to deal with the overly-exuberant Frank Peterson.

For the second time in five hours, Davis deposited Clea at her back door. She thought it best not to invite him in, and he showed no hint of wanting to offer up his hide for target practice to the troubled teen inside.

A narrow bar of light shone from beneath Addy's door. Clea passed it by, at this moment craving only privacy and a hot bath. She headed straight to the tub, ran water until steam billowed upward. Added oil. Sprinkled crystals. Feeling better already, she stripped and tossed her clothes into the hamper with the jeans and denim jacket she'd worn that morning.

The day's worries faded on a sigh as Clea eased into the fragrant water. With her body molded to the curve of the tub, she pushed aside thoughts of customers and deadlines, of taxes and nursing homes, of roses and strangers, until there was nothing left but Ren.

Chapter Thirteen

"**Please,** please, please!"

"Shh! We'll talk about this after church."

Clea shifted uneasily in the pew, already mad at herself because she knew she'd cave to Addy's pleas.

The night before, Michael had returned late, contrite over having missed Addy's dinner, and promising an excursion into Portland for an afternoon at Lloyd Center. This afternoon. A splurge at the Rave or Charlotte Russe. How could Clea refuse without being cast the ogre? Besides, the grounding had rolled from her tongue in the heat of the argument, before she fully weighed the consequences—that in order to monitor compliance she too would be grounded. It irked that Michael's offer actually saved her.

Addy whispered in her ear. "We'll buy something nice for you."

"Shh!" said Clea, a finger at her lips.

The organist struck a chord and the choir rose for the entrance hymn, *Gather Us In*. As she did every Sunday, Clea marveled at the soloist. For one who spent her days in the library speaking in undertones, Merriam's hearty soprano was both surprising and pleasant. The priest marched up the aisle and, with hands spread over the congregation, began the solemn prayers.

Immediately Clea's mind strayed. The jingle of altar bells became background noise to thoughts that had nothing to do with the Mass in progress. So much had changed since the previous Sunday that her participation in the liturgy consisted largely of private solicitations that this too would pass. She had hoped for an hour of solace but came up empty. When by 9 a.m. they filed out of St. Gerard's and Addy impaled her with doleful eyes, her resistance was gone.

"Okay, okay. You can go. Just quit acting like I've served up Bambi on a spit."

"Thanks, Mom."

On the ride home, Addy talked a streak, mostly excuses for her father's lapses, but her animation spilled over to fashions and the stereo she'd been saving to buy. It heartened Clea to see her daughter excited and smiling for a change. When they turned the final corner and Clea saw the red pickup at the curb, she breathed easier. At least Michael hadn't stood up his daughter again. More selfishly, she pictured a day to herself, to catch up on chores or tally reprint orders or pay bills or....

"Aren't you getting out of the car, Mom?"

"Huh? Oh, sure." What was wrong with her today? Her thoughts rolled in all directions like marbles scattered on linoleum. Better forget the paperwork and....

"Mom!"

"Uh, I'm right behind you, sweetie. Motor's been making a funny noise. Wanted to listen to it, is all."

Maybe what she really needed was a nap. But if a lazy Sunday was meant to be, it would have to wait. The minute Clea walked inside, Addy bombarded her with chatter and the raw enthusiasm reserved for teenaged girls about to embark on a shopping spree.

Michael put in an appearance and announced he and Addy would leave after breakfast. That sparked a flurry of activity in the smallish kitchen. Clea, determined to avoid any physical contact with him, hastily poured coffee and withdrew to the table while Addy and her father scurried around collecting cereal, juice, toast and rolls.

Michael's eyes were on her. Clea knew it, could feel it, though she never looked up from her cup even when it offered nothing more than a teaspoon of cold brew laced with grounds. Eventually Addy pecked her on the cheek, the outer door banged, and the kitchen fell silent.

Clea roused herself, gathered up the dirty dishes, wondering how her day would unfold. She was up to her elbows in dishwater when the hint of a cool draft brushed the back of her neck. She caught her breath, uneasiness knitting her brow. Slowly she glanced over her shoulder and saw the shape of a man. The plate in her hand bobbled, plopped into the sink, sending a spray of suds onto the wall, the counter and the front of her dress.

"I thought I told you to lock these doors," said Ren. He stood planted mid-kitchen, face scowl-darkened.

"You nearly scared the hell out of me."

"Good. Maybe now you'll actually listen to reason."

"For Pete's sake, it's broad daylight. No one's going to come sneaking around on a bright Sunday morning." The instant she said it, Clea realized the fallacy of her logic. Hadn't Ren just done exactly that? She backpedaled. "Tell me, does the FBI manual condone breaking and entering these days?"

"On occasion." He stepped beside her and picked up a towel. "Hurry up. We have to get to the airport."

"The airport? Why?"

"Paul's plane lands at eleven thirty."

Clea waited for some clue, either an identification of Paul or a reason why his arrival concerned her. When none was forthcoming, she said, "Who's Paul?"

"Friend of mine. I'll explain on the way."

"How did you know I'd even be here?" she said. "Addy and her father pulled away a few minutes ago."

Ren reached for a cup and wiped it. "I know."

"I might've gone with them."

A silly smirk conveyed how ridiculous an idea he thought that was. He laid aside the towel and glanced at his watch. "Almost done?"

"A minute to change. I'm all wet. Your fault, so don't complain."

In the privacy of her bedroom, Clea shimmied out of her damp clothes. Ren wore black slacks and something gray with long sleeves, so whatever he had planned called for casual. She dug into her closet for ironed jeans and a heather green pullover. When dressed, she crossed to the mirror and studied herself, uncertain why she should feel faint criticism at the image reflected there. Why did her appearance matter? And why had she chosen the sweater that complimented her eyes instead of the turtleneck, readily at hand and more appropriate to a brisk fall morning?

No explanation came, at least not one she was willing to own, so she averted her gaze. Opted against picking up the comb, instead absently tunneled fingers into her hair then fluffed it with a shake. She left her lips without color.

What else? she asked herself.

Her eyes flitted over the dresser top until they rested on the enameled pin and the packaging she had saved. Turning it over to Ren had completely slipped her mind the night before. She wanted him to see it, to add it to the collection of rose memorabilia. And a photographic record of all the items spread out on the table at her mother's house seemed a good idea. But Ren was in a hurry. Later. When they returned, she'd bring it up.

To be prepared for the eventuality, Clea snatched up the canvas bag she always carried when on an outdoors shoot. Already packed inside were the sunglasses and baseball cap she usually wore. Quickly she gathered her camera, a small leather case with close-up lenses, wallet, spare rolls of film and keys and stuffed them all inside. In a zippered side compartment she secured the pin and its brown wrapper which she'd already folded into a square.

The trip into Portland was by an old familiar route made curiously new by the fact she traveled it with Ren and viewed it from the passenger side of his car. The landscape rolled by, at first unadorned stands of evergreen, thick and dark. Now and again a flame-red sumac appeared, pinned like a prom corsage on an emerald dress of pine. Gradually the suburbs intruded, then city, and Clea lost interest in the passing scene. She shifted in the seat to study Ren's profile. He seemed fully occupied with driving, though Clea didn't think the moderate traffic called for such concentration. The radio was tuned to a football game, but the volume was so low she could hardly make out the broadcaster's calls. Was he listening? Was he pondering his next move on her behalf? Or was he daydreaming about nothing in particular?

"Are you going to tell me about this Paul?" she asked.

He stirred at the question. "What's to tell?"

"Like who is he?"

"Friend from New York."

"Work?"

"Uh-huh. I've begged a couple favors the last few days. He's not *persona non grata* in the department as apparently yours truly is, so he's better able to tap into the old network for information. You know, other field offices, guys working the street. Anyway, my calls must have piqued his interest because he volunteered his two weeks of vacation. He's landing in half an hour. I wanted you to meet him."

"He's helping us?"

"Yeah. He'll stay at the house. I've slept on couches before, so doubling up won't be a problem." He shot a glance at Clea. "Or will that raise the rent?"

She laughed. "I'll have to think about that one."

"Paul's specialty is missing persons which'll come in handy when we work with tracing the photograph. He's pretty smart overall. Enjoys a good mystery."

"Glad to oblige."

"With two of us working together, we'll—"

"You mean three of us."

"Right. The more heads the better. Is this our turn-off?"

They swung onto I-84 and soon passed an exit that would have taken them to Lloyd Center Mall. Addy would be there by now, prowling the stores. Briefly Clea wondered how much of a thrill the shopping was going to be considering the state of Michael's finances, but that wasn't her problem.

Eventually the northbound 205 branched off, and Ren asked her to watch for airport signs.

A phone chirped, and Ren slipped the cellular out of his pocket. His end of the exchange consisted of a string of "okays," no doubt putting into motion a prearranged plan to meet Paul outside the baggage claim area. When Clea pointed at the "Arrivals" sign, he changed lanes and slowed, crawling alongside the pedestrian walkway.

"Keep an eye out," he said, though Clea had no idea what Paul looked like. A second later there was no need. "Never mind, here he is."

A tall fellow in his late twenties stepped forward, his hand raised in greeting, face alive with recognition. Even if Ren had not braked right beside him, Clea would have pegged him as FBI. She shook her head at his stereotypical attire—dark suit, white shirt, black tie. Is this how he dresses even on vacation? If it weren't for his jet hair and eyes to match, he could have been mistaken for a clone of Ren on the day she first encountered him.

Paul was clean shaven except for his upper lip which sprouted a day or two's growth of heavy, black bristles. He leaped into the back seat and hauled a sizable duffel bag in behind him.

Once settled, he slapped Ren on the back of the head. "Hey, buddy."

"Clea Reilly. Paul Francesco," sufficed as their introduction, for curbside security waved them on, and Ren swerved the car into traffic.

On the home-bound drive conversation flew between the front and back seats. First Ren outlined what he knew of Clea's situation, followed by recent developments. It was apparent from the sketchy nature of some of what he said that he and Paul had already discussed details at length. At other times Clea got the impression he skipped over talk of his suspicions to spare her having to listen to theories coldly and matter-of-factly involving her mother.

Paul fired a barrage of his own questions. Sometimes he asked Clea to retell an incident in order to hear it from her point of view.

Interspersed were jokes about his annual mustache.

"I do it for my mother," he explained. "Two weeks out of fifty-two she recognizes me."

"And the rest of the time," broke in Ren, "we had to look at the whole damned mug."

"What do you want, Davis? Hazard pay?"

The easy camaraderie between the two exposed a side of Ren Clea hadn't seen before. She liked the interplay, and she liked Paul. He reminded her a lot of Rikki. She wondered if he was one of the friends Ren's ex-wife hadn't approved of. Then she wondered why she cared.

When her mother's house came into sight, Ren said, "Thought I'd drop Paul first. Let him get unpacked while I run you home."

"Wait a minute. I've got that pin with me, Ren. I thought we'd look it over together. Paul too. Besides I brought my camera along. If the need arises to show around any of those items we set aside, how better to do it than with a handful of photographs."

"Great idea," offered Paul, to which Ren added a concurring nod.

Clea beamed, knowing her photographic skills would make a solid contribution, and for the first time she felt part of the team.

They exited the car and trooped into the house.

While Paul banged around in the upstairs bedroom, Clea moved the rose-related articles closer to a window bathed in natural light. Ren had disappeared into the kitchen. She could hear water running and cabinet doors opening and closing. Just as well. She preferred to work alone. She allowed several exposures for each of the items, shooting from different angles, often with a close-up lens. Just as she finished the task, Paul descended the stairs, a leather case slung over one shoulder and a piece of equipment in his arms.

"Fax and scanner," he said by way of explanation, as he placed the apparatus on the dining room table. "Outlet?"

She pointed.

From the satchel he unpacked a laptop and placed it next to Ren's. When he opened the lid, a soft whirr told her he'd powered it on.

A moment later Clea stifled a laugh. The two computers were identical and stood side by side, ready for use. The screen saver on Ren's was a staid field of blue with the Bureau logo perfectly centered, whereas Paul's flicked from one scantily-clad swimsuit model to another. When he saw her stare, a blush spread over his olive skin and he hastily lowered the cover on his parade of beauties.

"Lunch," announced Ren as he entered with a plate of sandwiches, but stopped short at the sight of Paul's red face and Clea's amusement. He eyed them curiously but in the end only quizzed Clea about her progress.

"All done. One hour processing at Walgreens ought to do the trick."

"Don't you also have a book about roses?"

"Poems about roses. Yes, but I keep that with me for my visits to Green Haven." At Paul's puzzled expression, she identified the nursing home.

"Are there any inscriptions inside the book?"

"No," she said, her attention once again directed to Ren.

"Where'd it come from?" he asked.

"Mom's had it forever. I believe it was a Christmas present."

"From whom?"

Clea shook her head. "Though I do seem to remember it came through the mail. Like the pin. But it was years ago and I had no reason to question it then."

Ren crossed to his computer, pecked at a few keys until the inventory program filled the screen. He typed in the new information.

The three shared lunch, then examined the pin, its gift card, and the wrap with its barely legible postmark.

"Francesco. Here's your first assignment," said Ren. "Try to figure out where this was sent from. Clea and I are going to see a florist. Those roses didn't get here by themselves."

"I don't know," said Clea. "Don't you remember my pointing out the owner at the meeting last night? He's way too young to have managed the store when those flowers were delivered."

"Considering the universal reticence of your mother's contemporaries, that might prove to be a plus. You told me the shop's been in existence much longer. Maybe records have survived."

"That's a bit of a long shot."

"Yeah, I know, but sometimes long shots end up being three-pointers."

"Would you mind swinging by my house first, Ren? I want to check on Addy's whereabouts."

It took no more than five minutes to drive Clea home. Michael's truck was parked at the opposite curb. The shopping spree was history. Ren hesitated a moment before he got out and circled to her door to open it.

"Want me to wait out here?" he asked.

"Not at all." Clea grinned. "Unless a face-to-face with a card-carrying moron of a former spouse scares you."

"Hell no…but then I do have a gun."

"You do?"

"Of course," he said to her startled face. "It came with the badge." He took her arm and led her up the drive, saying nothing more.

As soon as they entered, Clea called her daughter's name, but it was Michael who sauntered in from the living room.

"Where's Addy?"

"Don't know," he said.

"What do you mean you don't know?"

"Hey, I'm not the traffic cop here. She got a phone call the minute we walked through the door. Something about babysitting. Pretty soon a woman drove up and…"—a flourish of his hand—"…she's gone."

"Damn it, Michael. Don't you ever think? You let her get into a car with someone you don't know?"

"What's the big fuss? She's not a two-year-old. If she's old enough to babysit someone else's brats, she's…."

Clea couldn't hear, much less care what else he said, for she'd grabbed the portable phone and stalked into the living room, stabbing at the keypad as she went.

In the worry of the moment, she forgot she had left Ren standing in the same room with Michael, a fact that didn't register until, satisfied at reaching Addy with the first number she'd called, she returned to the kitchen.

The two men were fully engaged in a stare-down contest. The rules seemed to require utter silence, for the kitchen was so quiet, a drip from the faucet hit the sink with a surprisingly resonant plunk.

Well, if Michael thought she was going to introduce them, he'd better think a second time. Long and hard. In fact, she actually derived some pleasure from letting him stew, so held her tongue. As for Ren, he had an upper hand in the name game and had been indoctrinated enough to understand she'd scarcely be civil let alone social during such an encounter.

The added strain of two mutes against one proved the breaking point for Michael. After a throaty grumble, he flung a jacket over his shoulder and vanished with a slam of the door.

Clea blew out a breath. "If we have time," she said to Ren, "I'm going to throw some dirty clothes in the washer. If you want a soft drink, look in the fridge."

She went straight to the bathroom and emptied the hamper, detouring into Addy's room on the way out. Piled on the bed were bags from various stores. Clea resisted the urge to peek at the purchases.

The call to babysit had apparently interrupted a project, for papers littered Addy's desk and the computer was still running. A troupe of smilies danced across the screen. When would that child learn not to waste electricity. Annoyed, Clea flipped the switch and banished the happy yellow faces to cyberspace.

A notebook lay on the desk, opened to a page filled with notations. What they meant remained a mystery even after Clea picked up the book and tried to make sense of the strange-looking names. Someday, she thought, when she had more time, she'd have Addy explain the rudiments of the Internet. For the moment her equipment of choice was the Kenmore washer parked in the garage, and her only search a hunt for dirty jeans, tops and underwear strewn about the room.

Arms laden, she returned to the kitchen. Ren sat at the far end of the table, a can of cola in his hand.

"Washer's in the garage," she told him. "As soon as I sort out a load, we'll go."

She dumped the clothes on the table and began to separate the whites from the colors. When she tossed the denim jacket she'd worn Saturday morning atop a pair of slacks, a soft, crinkly sound compelled her to snatch it back and search the pockets. Out came an envelope, the same one she had shoved inside with the urgency of the Council meeting. Again it sparked her interest, as much for the boxy, almost childish handwriting as for the lack of return address.

Her finger slid under the flap. Ripped it open. Extracted a single white sheet. As the creases unfolded, her mouth gaped and color bleached from her cheeks.

"What's the matter?" asked Ren, looking at her sharply.

Too stunned to speak, Clea reached over the mound of rumpled clothes and handed him the letter.

Chapter Fourteen

"**What** do you think it means?"

Clea whispered. To do otherwise would acknowledge the gravity of the message and encourage her astonishment to grow into fear.

She had rounded the kitchen table and laid her hands on Ren's shoulders, leaning in close for a view of the page he held by the corners between the tips of his index fingers and thumbs.

Sharply creased folds divided the plain white sheet into three equal rectangles. In the middle section a single sentence appeared, not written but constructed out of letters and groups of letters scissored from various sources and pasted in a line.

Secret things belong unto the Lord

"It sounds almost biblical," she said.

"But delivers a threat. Or at least a warning."

"Stop poking into things best left buried?"

"Something like that."

But why? she asked herself. Why would anyone want to keep her from identifying a woman in a thirty-year-old picture? For what else could have prompted the letter? Until she'd found that old photograph, her life had been as dull as unpolished nails. Since then…well, it *had* to be the photo. No one else knew about the room hidden in her mother's house. No one except Ren and Rikki…and now Paul.

The hairs on her forearms rose. Those on the back of her neck followed suit.

"Who do you suppose sent it?" she said.

"Not a clue."

"So what do we do? Call the police?"

Ren turned his head a notch, his lips inches away from Clea's cheek. "I *am* the police."

His breath warmed her skin, as unsettling a fact as the note in his hands. Clea straightened suddenly and blundered a step or two away from the chair. "I meant the real police…uh, that is, the local police."

"First things first. Can you dig up some kind of a plastic sheath? A baggie will do if you've got it. Two. One for this and one for the envelope it came in."

Thankful for a distraction, a reason to tear her eyes away from the letter as well as to widen the distance between herself and Ren, Clea rummaged under the sink until she found a package of sandwich bags. The envelope fit, but not the other. It took a search of Addy's room to come up with a see-through report cover for the letter.

The activity succeeded in calming her nerves—and raising her ire. Once the evidence was safely secured, the thin sheet of plastic seemed to provide a barrier between herself and the letter's implications, allowing her to study it more impersonally and analytically. Even to Clea's untrained eye, it was obvious care had gone into obscuring the identity of the sender—no telltale handwriting sample; no recognizable source of the snipped-out letters, for the bits of paper ran the gamut from heavy, high-gloss stock to ordinary newsprint.

"I'll get Paul to work on this," said Ren.

"What's to work on?"

"Paper source could tell us a lot."

"Right. We can narrow the list of suspects to anyone who reads magazines and newspapers."

"Paper composition might point us to a certain publication, and the choice of magazine or newspaper could be significant. Reading habits shed light on particular types of individuals; and if some of the clips came from trade magazines, the field is much smaller."

"You're making it way too complicated. It's more reasonable to think our guy cut the letters from a dozen different sources precisely to confuse the issue. There's a recycling station down the road a few miles. Let's say he made a pick-up instead of a drop-off. No way to trace magazines back to him."

"In that case, it would stand out," said Ren. "A worker at the facility might remember someone collecting stuff instead of leaving it."

"Unless done at night. I doubt there's any security, after all, it is just trash. Not even a fence that I recall."

"Then we have fingerprints." He held up his hand, a barricade against her next comment. "I know, gloves, but let's assume he's not so smart. Which means I need your prints for exclusion purposes since you touched the paper. We can do that later."

He scraped his chair away from the table, gathered the evidence and walked toward the door.

"Wait a minute. Where are *you* going?"

"I still want to question the florist before he closes."

"Not without me you're not."

"Clea, it's getting a little sticky now. Sending threats through the mail is a crime. In fact, notifying the sheriff's not a bad idea."

"And what's she going to do—circle my house with officers? You're already camped on my doorstep. And now there's Paul. I want to get to the bottom of this. The sooner the better. And I can pump information from the florist as well as the next guy. You may have your lists and computer programs and a whole Bureau full of contacts, but I can help too. You have to admit I knew about the recycling angle and you didn't."

Even though Ren didn't answer and appeared to mentally debate a rash of pros and cons, when a minute passed and his hand still rested on the doorknob, Clea knew she'd won the argument. At best the victory was tenuous and probably temporary unless she quickly got him out of the house with herself in tow. If she left the room, even for the minute it would take to grab a coat, she feared he might not be there when she returned.

A slash of white caught her eye, the sleeve of a heavy sweater buried in the tangle of laundry. She tore into the pile, dragged the sweater over her head and crossed the floor.

"What are we waiting for?" she said. "Open the door. Let's go."

The exceptional day—cloudless overhead, smell of burnt leaves in the air—had no doubt energized shoppers, for they were out in droves. Cars clogged the parking lot, forcing Ren to circle the block on the prowl for twenty-two feet of empty curb.

All Occasion Flowers occupied the end slot of the strip mall. Its choice location allowed a few extra yards along the outer wall for seasonal displays. At this time of year, the owner—his name continued to escape her—used the area for pumpkins and baskets loaded with green, orange and yellow gourds.

A single chime rang when Clea stepped on a mat inside the entrance door, and repeated its cheery welcome when Ren entered behind her. A teenaged girl, arms around a huge potted plant, glanced their way and smiled.

"Be right with you," she called, then set about wrapping a sheet of protective paper around the blooms.

"S'okay," answered Clea. "We'd like to speak with the owner. Is he in?"

"Out back. I'll get him as soon as I ring up these mums."

The customer paid and left. The clerk locked the register and disappeared behind a fogged door into the greenhouse.

"I'll do the talking," said Ren.

Then they waited. He feigned interest in an arrangement of straw flowers stuffed into a papier-mache jack-o-lantern while Clea nervously acknowledged other browsers. Her palms felt damp. She wiped them on her slacks.

The salesgirl reappeared, bringing with her a rush of warm, moist air and the shop's owner. He was short and stocky, forty at the most. His sleeves were rolled to the elbows, and there was dirt under his fingernails. His expression, one of annoyance, changed abruptly when the employee pointed at Ren and Clea.

"Ah. You folks need assistance with a special purchase?"

A name tag identified him as Dave M and was the tip-off Clea needed to jog her memory.

"Hello, Mr. Murray," she said, completely ignoring Ren's frown. "I'm Clea Reilly. This is Mr. Davis. We're not here to buy anything. We need a favor. It's really important."

The man balked. His smile fled. "The young lady over there can—"

Ren nudged Clea aside. "Perhaps there's somewhere we can talk?" he said to Murray at the same time he flipped open his Bureau identification. "Somewhere more private."

Murray absorbed the credentials. "Ho!" he chuckled. "The feebies. Just like on TV." At first his face lit up like a kid confronting Santa. Then his eyes narrowed furtively and locked onto an elderly couple examining a Boston fern. His voice dialed down to a whisper. "Feds looking for a cover? Need a place for a stake out?"

"A quiet place…to talk," said Ren. "Where *I'll* talk," he added for Clea's benefit.

The man fairly danced back into the heat of the greenhouse and beckoned them to follow. In a matter of a few steps, they transitioned from a Pacific Northwest chill to high noon in the tropics. Clea regretted her choice of the bulky sweater. The temperature change didn't seem to faze the florist, dazzled as he obviously was by the imagined melodrama unfolding in his presence. "Conducting a sting?" he went on enthusiastically. "Top secret, I'll bet."

Ren assumed the pose of fellow conspirator. "The Bureau *would* appreciate your discretion, though not for a special op. Our visit involves your store's records."

"My records?" Mr. Murray sobered fast.

"Orders and delivery confirmations. You feed stuff like that into a computer, right?"

"What the hell's this all about? Are you insinuating I didn't pay taxes or something?"

Clea interrupted. "Nothing like that at all. Old files, from years and years ago. Long before you owned the store."

"Oh." He relaxed somewhat and directed his answer to Clea. "That would be Mrs. Cooke."

"Are any of her records archived in your system?"

Murray laughed. "Mrs. Cooke couldn't tell the difference between a computer and a microwave—or a microwave and a breadbox for that matter. Her recordkeeping system was a truckload of boxes filled with a million pieces of paper. Try loading that into a database."

Crestfallen, Clea turned to Ren. "Which probably means it ended up at the dump."

"Don't I wish." Murray snorted. "The old lady was a pack rat. Made me sign a paper never to destroy her accounts if I wanted to buy the store. I'm shelling out four hundred seventy bucks a month on a storage unit behind Mike's Car Wash."

"Records still exist?"

"Yeah, but they have nothing to do with me, mind you. My business is on the up and up. Totally. One hundred percent."

"No one ever suggested otherwise," Ren assured him, before taking a deep breath and adding, "But you'd be doing a patriotic service for the United States government if you allowed us to have a look in your storage unit."

Murray puffed up his chest. "Always willing to do my part." At that the man strode to a wooden panel alongside a set of sprinkler controls and lifted a key off a hook. "Can't tell you how often I've wanted to torch the lot of it. Of course..." A nervous glance at Ren. "...I wouldn't. That's against the law. And lucky for you."

"Your cooperation is deeply appreciated. It'll be given prominence in my official report."

"In your report? My cooperation? Really?"

"Absolutely."

With a beaming David Murray standing tall among the flora, Ren and Clea withdrew to the sales area and closed the greenhouse door.

"Patriotic service for the government?" said Clea.

"Shh!" He hustled her toward the exit. "This is our first real break. I saw no harm in colorizing the truth a bit."

"So the patriotic service refers to the Ren Davis Get-Me-Out-Of-Jail case," said Clea lightly. "The one that's going to have New York begging you to return."

She expected a good-natured comeback and was surprised by the thoughtful look that came into his eyes.

They had nearly passed through the sales area, when Clea paused by the flower cooler. "I'll be out in a minute," she told him. "There's something I need to do."

He nodded and left.

Though fully aware it wouldn't matter to the recipient, Clea nonetheless shuffled through the assortment of mini-bouquets in small vases lined up on the shelves until she found one with a single bud of graceful proportion and delicate color. Like the dying refrain of a love song, an oft-recited line from her mother's book of poems tweaked her heart.

Deep-hearted, pure, with scented dew still wet—
One perfect rose.

Quietly she paid and even more somberly clutched the purchase to her breast as she walked through the door to the accompaniment of a melancholy chime.

In the car Clea closed her eyes and let her head slump heavily against the headrest, though it wasn't fatigue that drained her. And the sting behind her eyelids? Not tears. No, that was surely something else too.

The engine revved. The car rocked and swayed as Ren maneuvered onto the street.

What were they doing? she thought. What was *she* doing?

She had always encouraged natural inquisitiveness in her daughter. Good parenting, right? Yet it was her own impulsive curiosity that had popped the lid on this Pandora's Box. A cartoon image flashed across her mind—a rubber boat inflating uncontrollably in a closet while a frantic character struggled to undo the damage. Only this was no joke.

The car rolled to a stop. Clea blinked open her eyes, expecting the familiar sight of her porch and the ruins of her summer garden. Instead, rows of cars crowded a parking lot.

"Where…?" But she knew. Ren had driven to Green Haven. "You didn't need to go out of your way. I could have come later."

With his finger he bobbled the spray of baby's-breath enveloping the rose in the vase propped on Clea's lap. "It's about time you introduced me to Josephine Worth."

Though Clea would have preferred to pick the time and circumstance, she could come up with no logical reason to refuse. She recognized a stubborn set to his mouth and knew better than to challenge it. Besides, the car was already parked. A visit now would save her a trip, and her mother would undoubtedly not even realize Ren was in the room. She nodded her head. Agreed.

As if collaborating in Clea's hesitance, the elevator took forever, both to arrive and to make the two-floor ascent. Out of habit, as Clea exited she watched her feet scuff the Green Haven inscription on the tile, at the same time noting that Ren's stride, long and sure, easily cleared the letters.

At the third floor desk, Clea inquired if Lydia was on duty. An aide shrugged. Another nurse pointed to a station at the far end of the corridor. There Clea spotted the large black woman, clad entirely in white, glide down the hallway like an ocean liner on a tranquil sea, this despite the burden of a metal tray filled with numerous bottles and tiny paper cups. Time for evening meds.

Unable to gain Lydia's attention, Clea set off around the corner. "Mom's in 303," she said to Ren. Without waiting for a reply, she forged ahead and pushed open the heavy door. The suffocating heat struck her like a fist. Again she regretted the sweater.

Tinny theme music echoed off the walls. Its source an overhead TV monitor where Regis Philbin urged a contestant to choose a lifeline. Propped in bed between two over-stuffed pillows, Josephine stared at the screen with unresponsive eyes.

"Hi, Mom." Clea approached the bed. "See what I brought you?" The dainty vase with its solitary rose evoked neither acknowledgment nor appreciation. Clea held it out to her mother longer than necessary, hope against hope, but nothing registered. She abandoned the offering to the night stand in order to take up her mother's limp and clammy hand.

"Mom, I'd like you to meet a friend." The word *friend* came so naturally it shocked her, and she almost flubbed the rest of the introduction. "This is Mr. Davis...uh, Ren. His name is Ren."

"It's a pleasure, Mrs. Worth." Ren advanced and took the woman's hand from Clea, though it remained lifeless even after it disappeared into his genuinely earnest embrace.

"What did I tell you?" said Clea.

Ren continued to speak to Josephine. "Mrs. Worth, you've certainly given us quite a mystery to solve. If only you could clear up a few things."

"No!" Panic threaded through Clea's voice. "Don't mention her house. It'll only upset her."

"Well now, Miz Reilly. What's this about Josie's house?"

Both Ren and Clea startled, totally unaware Lydia had entered on crepe-soled shoes and witnessed at least part of the exchange. The nurse stood with one hand on her hip, the other holding a clipboard. Her face was a mask.

Regis read a question. Gave four choices. A woman hemmed and hawed over an answer. During it all, no one spoke in Room 303.

Clea waffled—not wanting to explain Ren's comment, yet unable to manufacture a lie. In the end it was Ren who said, "The house has been rented. To me."

The tension eased. Lydia's usual smile reappeared.

"Just as well for you, dear. With all you got to do, ain't no picnic takin' care of them two big houses."

"It *is* a load off my mind. Thanks for caring, Lydia. You've been a pillar, watching out for Mom, and here you are worrying about me too."

"Ain't worth the mention." The woman waved a hand in the air. "But now I got to have your gentleman sign in."

"Sign in?"

"The visitor's log, don't you know."

"No. I didn't know there was such a thing."

"Not for family, of course, but…." She leveled the clipboard at Ren.

Clea intercepted it, noting as she did the page of lines, all of them blank. She passed it to Ren who scribbled his name.

Once the formality was dispensed with, Clea expected Lydia to leave, but the woman lingered—to turn off the TV, to ease Josephine into a more restful pose, to dim the light, to reposition the flower vase on the bedside stand, to inspect the table's surface for dust. Finally she leaned over her patient and patted smooth a flyaway strand of hair. "You sleep well, Miz Josie. Hear?"

"Guess we'd better be off," said Clea. She gave the nurse an impulsive hug. "Lydia, you're a gem."

Chapter Fifteen

Monday morning. Usually a hectic time. A scramble of activity to round up misplaced homework, make and sack a lunch, bark reminders at Addy to check the kitchen calendar for last-minute appointment changes, and wheedle from her daughter school events that would have to be considered and accounted for in the five ensuing days.

But not today.

The energy inherent in a Monday morning seemed strangely missing, almost ominously so.

Still clad in pajamas, Addy emptied corn flakes into a bowl, announced a free-lunch day in the school cafeteria, and poked at a backpack, loaded with books and ready to go. And for once, the clock assumed the role of friend and savored each minute instead of spitting them out in rapid-fire succession.

The atypical mood even extended to Michael who engaged his daughter in lively battle over the merits of one model computer versus another. From the looks of it, both camps were equally armed, firing high-tech terminology like missiles, lobbing RAMs and ROMs like grenades. Clea's working knowledge of computers hadn't advanced much beyond the occasional game of solitaire, so she stood mutely by, a neutral nation, though secretly rooting for Addy.

She wasn't bothered by the exclusion. The contented glow on Addy's face more than made up for the fraction of self-esteem she sacrificed at not being able to join in. In fact, she had no recent memory of a more enjoyable breakfast, so with reluctance she consulted her watch.

Before she could open her mouth to hint at the passing time, Addy jumped up and deposited her dish in the sink.

"I'd better get dressed," she said, kissed both parents, and darted down the hall.

At Addy's departure, Clea stared across the table at Michael, unsure what warp in the universe had wrought this morning's change in attitude, for he too was upbeat, a bit breathless even from the spirited discussion. It wasn't like him and put Clea immediately on guard. A frown of concentration carved deep grooves across her forehead while she tried to figure him out.

"And a good morning to you," he said.

Did she detect a sour note in his voice? Or was she simply being paranoid? It wasn't every day a leopard donned a new coat of spots. Today of all days she wanted to believe change was possible, to dare to trust a man whose whole history could be summed up in a single word—untrustworthy.

Because she needed a favor, and she needed it now.

Asking couldn't wait. Addy had to get to school, and Clea had promised Ren an early start—although the part about Ren would never find its way into her explanation, nor would the whole truth for that matter.

Bracing—Lord, was she really about to do this?—she smoothed her face into a smile.

"Glad to see you're in good humor because there's something you have to do for me."

He winked. "Getting a little randy, are we? What with having a man around the house again."

Clea sighed. Same old Michael. What had she been thinking? "Never mind that," she said. "As long as you're parked on my couch, I want you to stick close to the house and keep an eye on Addy."

"What for?"

"Because she's your daughter and your responsibility too. I have a late afternoon job today, and I'd like you to be here when she gets home from school."

"Why?"

"I don't like her being alone."

"As if you never—"

"This is important, Michael. I'm worried."

"About what?"

Clea's fingers sprang to her forehead but could not rub away the gathering tension, nor the image of a letter-writing stalker in a green car. To explain risked going into detail, details as yet disjointed, and some like sores, still tender to the touch. From there it was but a tiny step to Ren, a subject to be avoided at all costs.

And what if Addy overheard? Clea's gaze shifted suddenly toward the hallway, fearful of seeing her daughter there, privy to what little had already been said. But the hall remained deserted.

"Worried about what?" said Michael again.

"I don't know. It's a mother thing, all right? You just have to promise me."

"Yeah, sure."

"A *promise.*"

"I said okay. Is that all?"

"I'm going to start the car. Send Addy out as soon as she's ready."

At the back door Clea paused, looked behind her, and in a tone as dead calm and dangerous as the eye of a hurricane said, "A promise, Michael."

The Explorer rattled to life. No sign of Addy yet. Clea backed down the drive until clear of the house's obstruction. She wanted a good view of the street. Even then, she got out of the car and nervously scanned the vehicles parked along the block. Caution in abundance was a good thing. Though she reasoned the stranger was long gone, scared away, the conversation with Michael had unnerved her, a feeling underscored by the distant, mournful wail of the fire siren.

No old Chevy lurked in the shadows. In fact, the only car in sight was Rikki's black Jeep which crept to a standstill at the foot of the driveway.

The girl waved. Clea approached and responded in kind, although puzzled by Rikki's presence this early in the morning.

"Get your days mixed up?" Clea asked. "The Jenkins shoot isn't until two."

"Well, I'm the bearer of either good news or bad news depending on how you feel about a cancellation. Mrs. Jenkins tried to reach you yesterday afternoon, but the line was busy every time she called. Finally gave up and dialed me. Of course, I couldn't get a hold of you either. What's the scoop? New boyfriend burning up the land lines between your mother's house and yours?" Playfully, Rikki punched Clea's arm through the open window. "Or is it the other way around?"

"Stuff that wild imagination of yours back into its leather thong, Rik. Addy was connected to the Internet is all. Now what's this about Mrs. Jenkins?"

"Twins're sick. Noses running non-stop. She'll reschedule later."

"That means the whole day is free."

"Yeah, want to ride around town in search of that green car? I know you're worried about it. Saw you checking out the street before I pulled up."

"Concerned yes, but that man's gone into deep hiding."

"Or changed cars."

"Oh, thanks for the reassurance. In either case, there's nothing much anyone can do. However, if you don't mind getting dirty, there *is* something else. If you're game."

"Wow! Killer outfit." Rikki whistled, her neck craned to spy over Clea's shoulder as Addy rounded the van.

"I second that," said Clea, thankful Rikki had the good sense to shelter Addy from talk of sinister strangers and their cars.

Addy twirled for inspection. Her outfit was obviously new and obviously expensive, but stylish and in good taste. The sight of her daughter all grown up tugged at Clea's heart, though she praised the girl for her winning selection.

"Daddy knew you'd like it. He was right, wasn't he, Mom?"

Well, she'd blindly stepped into that trap. "Yes, Addy, your father was right. But, hey, where's that present you promised me?"

Addy's shoulders slumped, regression into teenhood. "Oh, Mom. I'm sorry. I ran out of money."

"Honey, I was only joshing. Hop in the car." To Rikki she said, "If you're up to grubbing through the dust of ages, meet me by Mike's Car Wash." She extracted several containers of film from her pocket. "On your way, drop these at Walgreens Express Photo."

"Walgreens? What about Mitz? She does quick turnaround too."

"Not this time, okay?"

"You're da boss. See you in a bit."

Rikki blew Addy a kiss, executed a tight U-turn and sped off toward town.

"What's at the car wash?" asked Addy.

"A needle in a haystack, and, if all goes well, maybe a clean car in the bargain."

"Are you trying to be funny? You are, aren't you?"

Clea laughed. "And failing miserably. Let's go before you're late."

Once on their way, to Clea's relief, Addy dropped the subject of the car wash in favor of chiding her mother about her total lack of computer savvy. Clea pretended insult, but didn't mind the insinuation she was teetering on the brink of old age, for they were teasing like friends. She even came to peaceful terms with the absence of a good-bye kiss, which Addy was surely far too grown up to deliver on the steps to the high school.

She settled for a wave, threw the car into gear, and rolled toward Mike's Car Wash and the impending task of sifting through cartons of ancient receipts. Good thing Rikki had volunteered to help. No doubt Ren had requisitioned Paul's two hands. With four able bodies on the job, the chances of finding anything useful improved from one in a million to just shy of impossible.

Of course, there was always that glimmer of hope. And the thought of spending a day with Ren was....

The extension of that thought was interrupted by lights flashing red and white. Dead ahead. Hurriedly Clea mapped out in her mind a route around the emergency, then realized a detour wouldn't matter. Fire trucks and squad cars not only blocked the way *to* her destination, they were *at* her destination.

She stared in disbelief at the lot behind the car wash where a raging fire engulfed an old wooden shed. It was the only structure in the open area, and no amount of wishful thinking could convince her it was anything but David Murray's costly storage unit.

Cautiously she inched forward as far as she dared. Bits of ash trickled from the sky onto her windshield. One larger piece stuck at eye level. Through the glass Clea read "FTD 2 dozen." Two dozen what, destined for whom, to commemorate what special occasion would forever remain unknown, for the rest of the order was an unreadable, blackened scrap.

The spectacle of the fire had drawn dozens of curious, who congregated in the parkway, there separated into a number of small, tight cells where they shook their collective heads and watched streams of water arc toward the burning structure.

Hungry tongues of flame lapped at billows of thick, gray smoke. The fire had a voice of its own, a low, angry growl which was interrupted suddenly by the sharp report of overstrained lumber giving way. A side wall buckled. The roof collapsed, sending wads of fiery material spewing from the interior like lava from a volcano. The onlookers snapped to attention. Policemen lunged forward and shouted: "Get back! Get back!"

The shrill blast of a whistle broke Clea's absorption with the fire, and she was conscious of a baton pointed directly at her car. The officer flicked the nightstick to the side like one would dispose of a dead fly. She got the idea. Move out of the emergency zone...or else. No sooner had she shifted into reverse than Rikki appeared from between two parked cars and flagged her toward a strip of grass, out of the way and next to the Wrangler.

"What happened?" shouted Clea.

Rikki shrugged. "I've only been here a minute or two. It was already burning like crazy."

"We were supposed to meet Ren here. Have you seen him?"

"No. Wait, yes. There he is."

Clea's gaze followed the dagger of Rikki's finger, past the red pumper and into a clutch of police vehicles. Ren was deep in heads-together conversation with Frank Peterson. She didn't relish another meeting with that particular policeman, yet Ren was over there and as well as anyone he would know why their morning's project now resembled a pep rally bonfire.

"Let's go," she said to Rikki.

The two elbowed passage through the crowd only to encounter a flimsy yellow tape. Though the ribbon drooped sadly between two hastily-planted sticks, its authority stopped them in their tracks.

"Now what?" said Rikki. "Even if we yell, he won't hear us from here."

Clea was still shaking her head when someone tapped her shoulder.

"Paul!"

"Finally," he said. "I've been looking all over for you. Don't move. I'll tell Davis where you are." He pulled identification from his pocket and stepped over the tape.

Clea turned and found Rikki who, with obvious appreciation, watched the back end of Paul Francesco as he marched steadily away.

"Uh-oh. Guess I should have introduced you."

"You think?"

"That was Paul. Ren's friend from New York."

"Well, they're coming back. Mind your manners this time, Clea."

Formal introductions, however, would have to wait. As soon as the men arrived, Ren launched into an explanation. "Peterson there was first on the scene, but already too late to save anything. Damn curious, wouldn't you say? Just when we're about to tackle what might have become a possible lead, the whole thing goes up in smoke."

That's what bothered Clea most. The rotten timing. Weren't the Irish supposed to be lucky? What good was hauling around a name like Reilly if it didn't cut slack with the Wee People once in awhile.

"And," said Paul, "did you catch a whiff of the air closer up?"

Clea abandoned her train of thought and searched his face for a meaning.

Ren scraped a hand along his jawbone and nodded. "Gasoline."

"Arson?" Despite the ambient heat generated by the blaze, Clea shivered.

"Most likely. Peterson'll be questioning people in the neighborhood. He'll want to talk to us too, Clea."

"I was at home all morning."

"Makes no difference. I had to tell him we were planning on going through the contents. He'd find that out soon enough, so no use pretending otherwise. Paul, you're clear to go."

"Good. My time would be better spent at PFO. Let the SAC know I'm in the area. See if anyone there owes me favors."

"Paul, there isn't a field office in the country that doesn't somehow owe you a favor, but I'm afraid you'll have to arrange your own transportation into Portland."

"Need a lift?"

Three sets of eyes zeroed in on Rikki as she invaded their triangle and made it a square. "Fire just cleared *my* schedule for the day. Right, Clea?" Without waiting for confirmation, she went on. "By the way, my name's Rikki…even though my employer here seems to have forgotten it. I'd be glad to drive you to wherever or whatever PFO is."

"Portland Field Office. And I'm Paul." He offered his hand and a full-blown smile.

"All settled," said Ren. He placed a foot on the police line and pressed downward so Clea could more easily pass. She hesitated long enough to glance at Rikki, who looked as though she'd just pulled off a coup in a small South American country.

Ren's fingers encircled Clea's upper arm. He guided her across the field, his grip firming protectively when they encountered scattered equipment or hoses crisscrossing the ground. Halfway to Peterson, he slowed and spoke directly into her ear.

"Unless you're point blank asked a question, this time I *will* do the talking."

"I don't see what…?"

"Until I learn more about the origin of the fire, I want to control what information finds its way into public record."

"Is that our new motto? Trust no one."

Ren squeezed her arm and flashed his teeth. "Now you're catching on."

Peterson looked up when they approached.

"Ms. Reilly. We meet again." He touched the peak of his cap.

She opened her mouth to greet him, but, remembering Ren's words, let a second of indecision slide by and in the end only bobbed her head in salutation.

Ren edged forward. "Deliberate?" he said, tilting his head toward the fire and speaking with just enough inflection to allow Peterson to voice the official determination.

The officer first inhaled deeply as if to double check with his nose what he was about to say. "Oh, yes. Insurance man was already here too. Surprise, surprise. Claim denied. Place was a firetrap anyway, stuffed to the eaves with paper like it was."

"You know," said Ren. "I've some experience with this sort of thing. Be happy to join the investigating task force."

"That right, huh?" Peterson removed his hat and swiped an ashy sleeve over a sheen of perspiration on his forehead, making a bigger mess than the sweat alone had been. "Maybe in the 'big city' task forces come a dime a dozen, but we out here in the country mostly go by the seat of our pants. Fits the budget better."

"Have your trousers drawn any conclusions?"

"As a matter of fact, yeah. Halloween's around the corner. I figure some of the local kids let an early prank get out of hand. And I imagine by now they've sworn their buds to secrecy. That Murray fellow's not hollering about his loss either, though it's a damn shame about the building."

"So that's it?"

"Pretty much. I been talkin' to the folks standing around. No one seen or heard so much as a damn squirrel around the place. Evidence is toast, and frankly Lady Summers won't take kindly to throwing good money at a dead end."

"You were right, Peterson. We don't do it this way in New York."

The men stared at one another while a viperous hiss behind them indicated the fire had been reduced to a sodden, smoking heap of embers. Clea looked around. The crowd had thinned since first she arrived, and those left were now departing by twos and threes.

Finally the hometown officer broke the stand off.

"Why was it exactly you and Ms. Reilly showed up this morning?"

"Taking care of the business Sheriff Summers sent me to do."

Peterson shook with a burst of laughter. "In that case, I'll tell you what I'll do. Soon as the lab boys are through, I'll give you a call before the clean-up crew moves in. You're welcome to have a go at what's left."

"Thanks. I fully intend to take you up on the offer."

Chapter Sixteen

"*Please,* say you have Plan B worked out," said Clea the moment Frank Peterson was out of earshot.

"Not yet," Ren said, "but I don't believe for one minute that less than twenty-four hours after we get a key to go inside, a couple of bored teenagers target this exact place to strike a match to."

Another setback. A big one too. Clearly learning who sent roses to Josephine would have been a tremendous boon to Clea's search for answers. Might even have led to Barbara, and another window would have opened.

Clea was not alone in her frustration at losing the opportunity, but while she had nothing to take it out on, Ren held a small spiral notebook in which he made entries with sharp, brutal jabs of a pencil. Soon, though, any pretense of note-taking ceased, while the urgent tump-tump-tump of lead on paper continued, its beat as rousing as a drummer's call to arms.

In a war pitting two against the world, Clea was glad she and Ren wore the same uniform, but his anger erupted from a situation impossible to undo, and they needed to get back on track. No amount of consolation would lessen the impact of the fire. A sharing of the moment would have to suffice. Her hand capped his and held until the muscles in his fist relaxed.

She mustered a calming tone to her voice, difficult because what she had to offer was more bad news. "Unfortunately, Officer Peterson has a valid point. What happened this morning is not so outlandish at all. Every Halloween it's something. Last year, rowboats."

"Set on fire?"

"No, no. *Borrowed* from backyards and hauled up onto the roofs of every church in town. God only knows how the kids pulled that one off."

"Unsolved?"

"No one ever ratted, if that's what you mean. It's one of those annual things. We all expect it, hold our breaths waiting for it to happen, then look the other way when it's over. Call it a town tradition."

Ren eyed her with interest. She also saw what looked like amusement flicker in his eyes. "Does this tradition date to the adolescent years of a certain Clea Reilly?" he asked.

She blushed. "A little tamer then, but yes." She threw her hands in the air. "I confess to a cover-up in the matter of toilet paper streamers as it pertains to Mountain Ash Street."

"The whole street?"

The flush deepened on Clea's cheeks as she nodded.

Ren's lip curled, though not enough to be called an actual smile. A second later seriousness returned.

"Still, those were pranks." He gestured toward the burnt-out shed. "This is malicious. I see no connection. At least not to Halloween."

"But I take it you do see a link to us, what we're doing?"

"Don't you? There were only five people who knew we had that key. Myself and Paul, you...and I presume you told Rikki...and David Murray. I think our friendly neighborhood florist has some explaining to do."

"So, to the flower shop?"

"Step One of Plan B. Then it's back to your mother's house to sift through the odds and ends. We found a break once, we'll find another. I can work alone if you don't have the time."

"Like Rikki said, the fire cleared my schedule. This time of year is slow anyway. It'll be a few weeks before it dawns on most people that Christmas is only two months away. Then, if history repeats itself, I'll be swamped for family portraits. So my answer is yes. New day, fresh look. I'm all for it."

A return to the offensive boosted Clea's spirits, and she gladly fell in step when Ren hooked her arm and led her across the field. It was a light touch this time. The need for caution gone with the departure of the heavier fire trucks and squad cars. Equipment had been stowed. Only a few firemen remained to slog through the water-drenched debris and poke long-handled rakes at the ash. Two policemen—one of them Peterson—sipped at styrofoam coffee cups, their body language attesting to their boredom now that the morning's excitement had died away.

For Ren and Clea new possibilities beckoned, and the reason to stay had gone up in smoke.

Together they reached her vehicle, where he held open the door and she climbed aboard. He had already started to walk away as she turned the key, but stopped when the engine responded with a single, worn-out chug.

"Darn thing sounds worse than I remember," he said. "Here, let me try."

They exchanged places. He floored the gas pedal, forced the ignition, and for good measure thumped the heel of his hand on the steering wheel. Finally the engine turned over.

"Thanks," she said, but he made no move to relinquish his position in the driver's seat. Instead, he handed her his own set of keys.

"Beats me how this piece of crap hasn't imploded a long time ago. It's going to get fixed today. No argument. My sedan's parked right over there, under the car wash sign. Pull it here, then lead the way to your mechanic. Murray's on hold for now."

Clea did as she was told, at one and the same time flattered Ren had taken charge but also irritated she had so meekly complied. She placated herself with the rationale she was going to have the SUV looked at anyway and the only thing to change was the timeline—sooner rather than later.

It was only a short distance to his car. The second key she tried unlocked it. Both seat and mirror needed adjustment, and doing so struck Clea as an invasion of Ren's space, but then again the switch of vehicles had been his idea. She took that idea one step further and looked into the back seat, as innocent as a peek into the medicine cabinet of a neighbor's bathroom.

As expected, order reigned—at least in respect to those items associated with his professional life. Three identical piles were lined up in a row like walnuts in a shell game. No doubt they represented tools deemed necessary for the job they'd expected to do. In each group was a legal pad, packet of ordinary white envelopes, pen, and latex gloves. He hadn't expected Rikki or surely the kits would have numbered four.

Of greater interest was the hodge-podge of personal articles lying on the cushions: a small book on sports statistics half obscured under a rumpled police academy sweatshirt, four CDs and a brown paper sack. She eyed the bag, curious, nosy even. But no sooner had she reached through the gap between the front seats when the skin on her arms gathered into nubs.

Quickly she pulled back, glanced toward her car, not fooled that Ren didn't appear to be watching, for she had felt intensely observed. Embarrassed he had caught her rifling through his belongings, she fired up the engine and pulled parallel to the Explorer, smiling wanly as she motioned him to follow her up the street.

In order to buy time to regain her composure, Clea led Ren to the garage via a roundabout route and hoped his newcomer status prevented him from noticing. Finally she signaled a turn and braked in front of one of a pair of roll-up doors, allowing him to occupy the other space where the bay door was half-raised and identified with a lopsided "Service Here" sign.

A hulking cube of a building, the shop's cinder block walls resembled a canvas of peeling white paint brushed from top to bottom with dirt and rust-colored watermarks. A fifty-five gallon drum, overflowing with the color of candy wrappers and fast food cartons, put to shame a flower planter where long-dead stalks clawed from the barren soil like a hand from the grave.

From the outside, Robert Randall & Son's Auto Shop failed miserably to inspire the sort of confidence one preferred in a mechanic.

"You sure about this?" asked Ren as he stepped from the SUV and met Clea at the entrance.

"Absolutely. Mom's used the Randalls since God grew a beard. Never a complaint. Can't argue with years of satisfaction."

"If you say so."

The door scraped on a raised crack in the concrete sidewalk. Ren muscled it open.

"By the way," Clea added with a mischievous smile, "don't let Junior scare you. He's really quite sweet."

"Junior" was the *Randall* not the *Son* in the shop's name. He emerged from the work area, trailing an air of exhaust fumes and the blare of Christian rock from an unseen radio. Despite a head of graying hair, at six foot three and three hundred pounds, Junior looked as if he could lift a car to view its undercarriage without benefit of a hoist. Tattoos of raptors and snakes, and the occasional Latin motto, spiraled up both arms where they disappeared under the sleeves of a black t-shirt.

"Clea, Clea. How you be?" he said, genuine pleasure expressed in both face and voice. "Truck giving you trouble?" When he spotted Ren, he wiped his hand on an oily cloth and extended it across the counter. "Welcome, sir. What can we do for you?"

Clea sucked her lower lip at the comic sight of Ren's hand buried deep in the man's grimy paw, though Ren didn't seem to notice. He just pointed out the window. "Explorer there's in desperate need of a tune-up."

"No kiddin'." Junior wagged a finger at Clea. "Same thing I told her back in June."

"Wouldn't be surprised if the battery was on its way out too."

"Gotcha. What you want is a good lookin' over, bumper to bumper."

The two men swaggered out of the shop, popped the hood on the Explorer, and bent like surgeons over a comatose patient. Ren knowingly plucked at his chin while Junior tugged his beard. The underlying innuendo of unspoken language seemed to reinforce a joint belief in the clueless nature of women when it came to machines. Male bonding at its finest. Clea recognized a lost cause when she saw it and opted to stay inside. She was leafing through a long outdated *Home & Garden* when the examination ended and the men returned.

"Kenny!" Junior yelled above the music. "Get in here and write up this man's order." To Ren he said, "I'll have it on the rack today. No guarantees you'll have it tomorrow. Do my best, though."

"Take your time. Make it safe."

"Gotcha."

Then, as if the customer area couldn't accommodate more than one Randall at a time, Junior withdrew the moment Kenny showed his face. An underinflated version of his grandfather, the seventeen-year-old pulled a form from a hidden recess and began to fill it in.

Clea hauled out her checkbook. "Same as last time?"

Kenny nodded. "Seventy-five up front."

Out of habit Clea left writing the date till last. Precise scheduling was a must when it came to setting appointments, so she never relied on her memory alone. After signing her name, she glanced at a prominent wall calendar.

"You have to use this one," said the boy, tapping a small stand-up calendar with the side of his ballpoint.

"Right. I make that mistake every time. Someday, Kenny, I'm going to buy you a new one."

The kid grinned. "Won't do you no good, Mrs. Reilly. Gramp'd skin me alive for sure if I tried to take away his old calendar."

They shared knowing looks, for it wasn't the first time Clea had made the offer, and Kenny's response was always the same.

Then, check and receipt changed hands. Kenny mumbled "We'll call you" and retreated along the same path as his grandfather. Immediately a compressor roared to life, spilled its noise through the adjoining entryway, and rendered the waiting room an unbearable place in which to wait.

The couple left, though once in the car and on their way Clea realized she had walked off with one of Junior's magazines. "We have to go back." She lifted both magazine and her shoulders in a form of apology for the inconvenience.

"Never mind that. Did you notice the calendar?"

"On the wall?" She laughed. "The one firmly lodged in the last century?"

"May of '67."

"Been like that since I came here with my first old clunker."

"Why do you suppose?"

"Afraid to ask then. Not so sure I want to ask now. Junior is a little intimidating, in case that slipped by you. I always assumed it had something to do with his divorce which happened ages ago. You know, a hallmark in his life. Positive or negative is anyone's guess. He never remarried."

"That's all very interesting but what about the picture on it?"

"Let me think. Big old mansion...villa or maybe a castle."

"Surrounded by a garden. Of roses."

"Not everything spells conspiracy. People around here tend to like roses. Portland *is*, after all, the City of Roses."

If Clea expected an admission of his ignorance about the area's claim to fame, none came. Instead the hum of the engine filled the sedan's interior while he appeared to mentally digest this most recent piece of information. Clea waited, absently fanning the pages of the magazine in her lap.

"I still feel we must at least consider the possibility that here is a connection. Is there any way to determine if May in 1967 held significance to your mother? Didn't you say she kept stacks of old calendars? Maybe she jotted something on the pages."

"Maybe, but I threw them all...." Her voice trailed off.

"What did you say?"

"Uh...away. I...threw them away."

By the time Ren turned and faced her, eyes slitted in a quizzical look, Clea had closed the magazine. Both hands tightly pressed its cover as if a layer of flesh and bones was enough to negate what she had seen inside.

Chapter Seventeen

The front door slammed shut, rattling the windows and setting the curtains aflutter like sheet-draped trick-or-treaters. Clea cringed. Not only had she violated her mother's number one rule of decorum, but the heavy-handed entry into her childhood home hadn't made her feel one jot better.

Ren had preceded her inside, but at the resounding blast he whirled abruptly, so they almost collided, chin to nose.

"You've been as quiet as a clam from the moment we left the repair shop," he said. "Now you're playing wham-bang with the doors. What the devil is wrong?"

"This."

The *House & Garden* flopped like a dying pigeon when Clea waved it in the air.

"So we didn't return the damned magazine. We'll do it tomorrow."

"Not the problem, Ren."

Clea stepped around him to the dining room table. File folders she hadn't seen before were spread out next to the twin laptops. She pushed them all aside, squared the magazine, then thumbed it open to a Dutch Boy ad. She pivoted out of the way and gestured him forward. Pointed.

Someone had scissored a small window in the page so the can of paint now read "Dutch oy."

Without another word Ren shuffled through the manila folders until he found the one he was looking for and removed the plastic page which held the anonymous letter Clea had received two days earlier. The capital "B" in the word *Belong*, set against a powdery blue background, matched for size, shape and color the piece missing from the ad.

Ren slid two chairs close to the table, patted the seat of one. "Sit," he said. Together they leafed through the magazine from masthead to back cover.

The *House & Garden* had been raped twice. An article on terraced flower beds contained a similar void where three letters had been neatly excised as one—the *fac* in the word *facade.*

When they were through, Clea shoved out of the chair and circled the room. Her palms itched, and her feet wouldn't stay planted in one place. For all its wide openness, the great room closed in, a vicious hand at her throat squeezing off the air.

"Good Lord, Ren. Junior sent me that letter?"

"Or Kenny. Or anybody with access to that waiting area of his. Was this the only magazine there?"

"No. There was a stack on the table." Blood drained from Clea's face. "And today's *Sun*, now that I think of it."

"A public place. Every sort of publication. Impossible to lay a finger on who might have helped themselves. Could have been a regular customer, a walk-in, someone who simply strayed in and out without notice."

Clea refused Ren's efforts to coax her back to the table. She needed to move, if only metaphorically—and unsuccessfully, she admitted—to keep her distance from a mushrooming sense of foreboding.

A touch at her waist made her shudder until she realized Ren had risen and crossed the room, fallen into step with her restless pacing, and was now leading her to the sofa. He shoveled it clear of bachelor clutter and forced her to sit.

"Freaking out's not an option." He stuffed a pillow behind her neck. "I'm going to get you a glass of water, then we're going to put our two heads together and figure out a few things." In a quieter voice he added, "You're not alone, Clea. You came to me for help and, by God, you're going to get it."

She downed the water he brought, ignored the fact that, despite what he'd just said, she had not actually gone to him for help. He had been foisted upon her. And for his part, he'd done a fair measure of kicking and screaming. However, when he joined her on the couch, the weight of his body dug deeper into the cushions than hers, forcing her toward him at an angle. Here was someone to lean on, the motion seemed to tell her, someone willing to share the burden.

"Now," he said, "down to the brass tacks. Does Junior have any other employees?"

"None that I'm aware of."

"The mailing label has been ripped off." He showed her where the glue had stubbornly clung to the ragged remnants of a white strip. None of the address remained. "Two things come to mind. One, Junior's magazines were used. However, until that's confirmed by going through the rest of them and actually finding holes to match cutouts from the note, we can't rule out the possibility someone randomly clipped parts of the message from a dozen different waiting rooms."

Clea pushed herself straight. "Or snipped out those letters and dropped off the magazines, a few here, a few there."

"Good. Now you're thinking." Ren bounced to his feet. "Let me enter this into the computer."

"Don't bother." Clea slumped back into the curve of the couch. "What sense does it make to go through all that trouble? Why wouldn't the writer just burn the magazines or toss them in the trash? All incriminating evidence gone in a poof."

"Exactly. That's why your idea is so intriguing. It's a deliberate act. That is, of course, unless we discover the remainder of the cut-outs at the auto shop."

"And the reason behind marching all over town with an armload of books would be...?"

"To confuse."

"Well, I say mission accomplished."

"Or to spread the blame. Anyplace where these things show up would throw suspicion over a wider and wider circle of people."

Slowly Clea nodded understanding. "This guy is either very clever or spends way too much time watching TV crime shows."

Clicking of the keyboard ceased. Ren pressed the save button before he rewarded her with a chuckle. "Glad to see you haven't lost your sense of humor. It'll help keep you sane in the long run, believe me."

"I get it. When all around you is falling apart, a joke is as good as a Valium."

"There you go."

"If only it were so easy." She vacated the sofa and reclaimed her chair at the table next to Ren. "Okay, explain the letters *fac*. They weren't in the note."

"Another excellent observation." Beyond that Ren offered only a shrug.

They fell into silence as each pondered the new development. Clea found it difficult to concentrate here in her mother's house, for the surroundings were so at odds with her memories. Transformed. Alien even. No Mozart or Liszt played in the background, no scented rose petals mounded in baskets soothed the senses. The tidy homeyness, so characteristic of her mother's imprint on the home, had been supplanted by the careless chaos of two males sharing space.

The clock loudly counted off the minutes, dragged the hands forward, to, then past eleven. Clea hadn't come up with a single idea other than to lament the irrevocable passing of a hallowed period of her life. She hugged herself then, an embrace which took in more than her arms, but clutched at her safe, familiar world, attempting to hold together that which seemed ready to crumble like a dried-up ball of clay.

A muffled chirp put an end to the troubling thoughts. Just as well. It did no good to surrender to an unruly gang of *whys* and *what-ifs* instead of sticking to the facts.

Automatically Clea dipped a hand into her pocket for the phone. Ren did the same.

"I win." He brandished a small flip phone and pointed to its display. "It's Paul. I'll see what he wants. You keep coming up with ideas."

Clea blew out a sigh. Ideas. Easily said, not so easily accomplished. She couldn't just whip up motives and suspects like a batch of oatmeal cookies.

And Ren wasn't helping either. He had slipped around the far corner of the fireplace, out of sight, yet snatches of his conversation spilled from the kitchen. Not loud enough to produce actual, intelligible words; not muted enough to discourage Clea from straining to hear.

She drummed her nails on the table. The folders she'd earlier brushed aside offered a distraction. Idly she opened one and glanced inside. The brown wrapping paper from the rosebud pin had been smoothed flat and clipped to a page of handwritten notes. She ruled out Ren as the author. The precise, accountantlike penmanship must be Paul's.

The final entry read: Submit for scan.

What that meant she had no idea. She closed the file and opened another.

Her name rushed up at her like a meadowlark scared from its nest. A second later she wondered why it should have surprised her. After all, she had initiated the investigation. Of course her name would be all over his notes. Even so, it roused her curiosity. What about her had Ren found noteworthy enough to merit a place in his files? A thrill of danger slithered down her arm as she reached out and removed the top sheet.

The tap of soles on hardwood floors warned of Ren's imminent return. "Paul's tied up for another hour or two," he called. Clea responded to her first instinct and quickly shoved the page into her pocket. She lunged at the files on the table, closing the one and shuffling it with the others into a single neat stack.

"Just cleaning up," she said, a little breathlessly when he came in sight. "Sorry I made such a mess before."

She averted her eyes, afraid one of the Bureau's training courses might have armed Ren with the ability to detect the lie and link it to her bit of larceny. When Ren caught her hand, she shivered, but all he said was, "Leave it. I'll deal with it later. Right now I'm going to use those two hours to see if anything helpful survived the fire...or the firemen."

"Weren't you supposed to wait for a call from Officer Peterson?"

"So he said, but I assure you, Clea, his good ol' boy manner didn't fool me one bit. That scene was open to anyone with a badge, including mine. I'm certainly aware no one's happy to be saddled with an out-of-favor agent. New York didn't know what to do with me. Your Sheriff Summers sure as hell doesn't know what to do with me. I don't fit into the established pecking order. But Peterson's trying to yank my chain, which only makes me want to yank back."

"You do seem to be a square peg in a place with a lot of round holes."

Ren's voice softened as if a knot of festering irritation had been swept from his system. "I consider that a compliment. So you see, his *allowing* me a look at evidence is something I chose to accept at the moment...and now I've changed my mind."

All this time his hand had remained on hers. When he removed it, cool air rushed over the warm spot on her skin. The back of her hand felt strangely naked and alone. If she'd had more time, this reaction would have been something to mull over. As it was, Ren produced the car keys and asked, "Ready to plow through piles of soot?"

Clea experienced a moment of panic. She knew if she went with him, there'd be no opportunity to replace the sheet of paper she'd foolishly crammed into her pocket, so she lied.

"Newly dry-cleaned," she told him, plucking at her sweater. "I'll pass... this time...but only because I believe your sole purpose in going back there is to administer a hefty dose of comeuppance."

"And that isn't more than enough?"

"For you, maybe."

"In that case, I'll drive you home."

"Thanks, but...um, a walk is what I need. It's not far. Besides, solitude and fresh air usually clear away the cobwebs. Any earth-shattering revelations will be duly reported. That's a promise."

To seal the pact, she raised three fingers in a Girl Scout oath. To hurry him along, she unlatched the door, flung it open and stepped onto the porch, sure he would have no choice but to follow.

Together they descended the double step and padded through the still-green lawn. Clea stopped at the pavement while Ren continued across the parkway to his car. Again he offered a ride. She waved him off and began to stroll in the opposite direction. With eyes to the sidewalk she listened for the ignition to kick in and tires to roll. She counted the cracks until they numbered three, thought that might not be enough time and suffered till she passed the fourth before she dared peek over her shoulder.

The dark Ford had taken off, turned the corner. The street behind her was quiet. Abruptly Clea executed an about-face and marched back to the house. Being landlady had its advantages, she thought, namely she still possessed a key which she used to let herself inside.

Despite having left only moments before, the house seemed different now, so very quiet, like an animal crouched and waiting for its prey. To lend substance to the feeling, Ren's Yankee cap lay on the small foyer table, its embroidered face asquint with concentration and the peak cocked into a smirk as if to say "I see you."

It gave her a good case of the jitters.

She tiptoed past, giving the animal-cap wide berth.

Her intention? Replace the page and get out.

But her name on the file—on Ren's file—well, who could blame her for being the tiniest bit inquisitive? Before a sense of propriety crept in and waylaid her desire to know, Clea tipped open the folder, fanned the contents over the slick surface of the table, and began to pick through the offerings.

Here were copies of school records, a business loan, her last income tax return, credit card balances, that speeding ticket of five years ago which she'd mentioned to no one, not even her mother, and a clipping of the *Sun's* opinion column where her one and only letter to the editor had been printed. The page which had originally caught her interest turned out to be a standard reply form on stationery of a state security division to the effect she was not considered a dangerous felon or registered sex offender.

Thank God for small favors.

Well, Mr. Ren Davis, she thought, rocking back on her heels. We're not one bit closer to the identity of the woman in the photo or tracing the roses or discovering who wrote that menacing letter, but I see you've done a thorough job investigating *me*.

At the back of the dossier was a fax. It curled into a tube when she lifted it out. She finger-pressed it flat and saw it bore the letterhead of Good Samaritan Hospital and its mission statement: We Care. The message, though, seemed cold and decidedly uncaring. In miserly language it informed To Whom It May Concern that no female child named Clea Catherine Worth had ever been born in their facility. A grotesquely huge question mark in red ink streaked across the lower portion of the memo.

Clea scowled. That's impossible. Of course, she'd been born at Good Samaritan. How often had her mother pointed there and said so? Just because some inept clerk lost her birth certificate didn't alter that fact.

And she would prove it. Her mother was meticulous about details and records, a habit accrued over a lifetime career of teaching. Clea would find that damned certificate, and Ren could take his big red question mark and have it for lunch.

But when Clea glanced around the room, she remembered she'd already been through everything, had cleaned and sorted, had emptied drawers and cabinets, had packed anything of value—twice if the search with Ren counted.

There wasn't a square inch of the house she hadn't....

The thought trailed off as her eyes fell on the fireplace and her mind filled in the room behind it.

There were indeed a few square inches she hadn't scoured.

As if drawn by an invisible cord, Clea slowly made her way around toward the kitchen. Ren had obviously cleaned since she'd been there last—all traces of the plaster disposed of and the floor mopped clean. The canned goods and plastic storage containers that once lined the pantry shelves were out of sight, and the shelves themselves neatly stacked against the wall.

Clea balked at the doorway, a part of her loath to enter. The little room was spooky with its gray pall of dust and lattice work of cobwebs, a macabre decoration for an infant's crib and the delicate bloom of roses.

She continued the argument with herself against exploration. What reason would her mother have to leave such an important document in so improbable a place? However, Clea knew she would never be satisfied with an outcome that didn't include her actually checking out the possibility.

Before her resolve evaporated, she drew a long breath and yanked open the pantry door. Light filtered in but more was needed if she hoped to find something that had been overlooked earlier. She returned for a flashlight, then let the room swallow her whole.

The narrow beam exposed dark corners and crevices. Ren's warning not to disturb—How did he put it? The scene?—rang in her ears. She ignored the voice. Instead she crouched by the diminutive table with the flowers on it, reached underneath and swiped her hand back and forth. The only thing it yielded was the grime of neglect.

Next she lifted the vase and felt along its bottom, then dipped her fingers in among the stems, trying not to dislodge too many of the fragile petals. Those that fell she brushed to the floor.

When she came up empty-handed, Clea abandoned that corner of the room and moved toward the crib itself. Here too she dropped to her knees and shone the light up into the slats beneath the mattress. Stuffing protruded from a gash in the ticking. A mouse perhaps had borrowed a bit of softness to line a nest. Or worse, this was the nest. She cringed at the thought but grit her teeth and probed the opening.

Nothing.

She straightened and examined the coverlet and pillow, purposefully sliding her hand under and over, doing the same along the space between the bumper and side rails.

More of the same nothing, and there was no place else to search.

Clea relaxed, as much for the fact she could now leave the dreadful room as for the exoneration the fruitless exercise brought to her mother.

I told you so, passed briefly through her mind. That and it's the hospital's error. She was already planning her next move, a visit to their records department, when she paused at the side of the crib and realized her intent had been to search every square inch. And she hadn't. Not yet.

Again, she knelt and aimed the flashlight. This time she shoved the cottony fluff upward into the tear so she could see beyond. There, partially concealed by a wooden slat, the corner of an envelope swam in the circle of yellow light. Clea tugged it out and, with the spoils of her hunt locked firmly in her hand, sought the sanctuary of the kitchen.

Once away from the suffocating air of the hidden room, Clea was able to think more clearly. She should wait for Ren's return.

No, she argued, impatient and apprehensive at the same time. She had to know what this thing was and it couldn't wait.

The envelope was plain, with no indication it was the missing hospital document. It was worn and the flap merely tucked in as if the contents had been accessed often. She rubbed the pad of her thumb over the back, clearly heard Ren's admonition not to touch, yet reached in anyway and pulled out a sheet of white paper. If it upset Ren she had broken one of his rules, she didn't care. He'd just have to be satisfied with her explanation—whatever that was going to be.

She shook the page open, startled at first to recognize her mother's handwriting.

But what had been written jolted her even more. It was a numbered list. Of names. Beginning with Josh. Followed by Ashley. Then David and Stephanie.

On and on. Name after name.

Until it ended at number 29.

Barbara.

Chapter Eighteen

Clea rode an intoxicating wave of euphoria.

Bless her mother. At last, a breakthrough.

The feeling, however, quickly died, and her elation hissed like air from a pricked balloon. Neither had she found the elusive birth certificate nor the actual identity of Barbara. Instead, it was as if she'd reached into a rabbit warren and discovered her brood of questions had multiplied like Flopsy.

Chief among the flock: Who were Josh and Thomas, Kate, Stephanie and the two dozen plus other people, each one—judging by the correspondence of numbers—commemorated with a carefully preserved rose? And why had her mother inscribed their names, then secreted the list, hidden the room, mentioned nothing?

Blood thudded through her veins, a grisly, ragged accompaniment to the almost-forgotten words of the bookseller in Reedsport:

Josephine's in trouble, I suppose, and wants to drag me into it.

"Oh, Mom," Clea moaned, the plea one of despair. "What kind of trouble are you in?"

A hush settled like a shroud, allowing space for answers to trickle in, answers she knew in her heart would not be forthcoming. What she *did* hear in just that instant, though, caused her to shrink against the cabinet doors. A board creaked on the wooden porch. A second later the doorknob rattled.

What was Ren doing back so soon?

Clea panicked. Here she was, red-faced and red-handed, caught in the lie that she intended to walk straight home, and no ride needed, thank you very much.

The rear entrance beckoned a scant few feet away, offering a fast track through a neighbor's yard and escape on the other side. But how would she explain the files, left open and scattered? And what of the roster of names that would then have to be smuggled back inside?

As if the details of her foiled stint as detective weren't bad enough, Clea's feet had developed twin taproots, binding her to the floor when in truth she was itching to flee.

"Yoo hoo!"

The eager call filtered through the solid oak of the front door and was followed by an equally earnest rap of knuckles. "Anybody home?"

Clea wilted in relief. "Rikki!" she shouted. "I'm coming. Be right there."

Arboreal bonds severed, she raced through the house and unlocked the door.

"Yikes," said Rikki. "You look like you've just had an encounter with Casper—or maybe one of his not-so-friendly pals."

"What do you expect? You scared the wits out of me. But forget that. What are you doing on the doorstep?"

"Swung by your house first. Not a soul in sight. Paul thought you might—"

"Paul's here?" Up on tiptoe Clea peered over Rikki's shoulder to the curb.

"No. I came alone. He's going to be in Portland awhile. I wasn't allowed in the inner sanctorum, so came on home. But...." She held up a cell phone with obvious delight. "He did land me one of these at the FBI office. Said we all had to keep in touch. Neat, huh? Anyway, he had talked to Ren and said you might still be with him. Is he in there? And where's your car? I didn't see it out front."

"Long story. Right now I've got a dilemma. Get in here and help me."

After a glance along the street, assurance Rikki was indeed sole guest to the party, Clea hustled her into the house. With what amounted to tunnel vision, she set to the task of squaring up Ren's file folders, carefully reinserting papers she had tossed about. Rikki chattered at her back.

"Paul wrangled a Bureau car. It's pretty boring, black on black, four doors, doesn't even have a CD player. It's all they had to spare. *I* wouldn't have minded being his chauffeur, if you know what I mean, but he wanted to be able to come and go as he pleased. Didn't want to inconvenience me. Nice of him, huh? To think about me. I didn't mention there'd be no problem since my social life is so pathetic. Oh, did I tell you I was fingerprinted? How exciting. Look." She held out her hands, palms up. "There's still ink on my fingers."

"Rikki. Please. Take a breath." Clea faced her friend.

"He's bringing along a kit to do you, too."

"Rikki." This time a hint of warning in Clea's voice. "Focus. There's something I have to show you."

She dragged the girl to the kitchen and passed her the handwritten list, explaining how she'd come upon it.

"I'm positive it's hugely important, but I don't dare just hand it over. Ren'll know I came back after I made such a big deal about walking home. What'll I do?"

"Come clean."

"I can't do that. He's paying rent. It's probably not even legal to use my key and waltz right on in."

"Ren won't care. You know he's got the hots for you."

"Don't make jokes. What if I put it back? Show you where. Then tonight or tomorrow you bat your eyes at Paul and ask to see the fireplace room. Be a little cagey, though. Poke around a bit before you accidentally find this thing."

"Overkill, but okay. We'll play Cagney and Lacey. Anything you want. But don't underestimate my reading of your Special Agent."

"Let's do it then."

"Not so fast." With a wink Rikki relieved Clea of the sheet of paper. "Copy first. They do it all the time in the movies. I saw a machine on the table."

As soon as the duplicate fed out into Clea's ready hands, Rikki reset the buttons and the two women replaced the envelope exactly as Clea had found it. When Rikki started to look at other things, Clea steered her from the room. "Later. Save the genuine surprise for Paul. I don't know when Ren will be back. Best if we're long gone. Oh, and if anyone asks, you ran into me on the street."

Ignoring Rikki's tsk and head shake, Clea hurried out the door. The Jeep roared to life. They sped toward the business district, turning down the street where the fire had been. The place reeked of wet paper and burnt ash. Only limp strands of yellow police tape guarded the premises, for the emergency vehicles and patrol cars had all departed. Ren was nowhere in sight.

Clea directed Rikki to park off the road, under trees, the same spot she'd occupied earlier in the morning then brought her friend up to date on what had transpired after she and Paul had left the scene: the face-off with

Frank Peterson, the tiresome car trouble, the trip to Junior's where the *House & Garden* had been innocently acquired.

The relatively few hours since breakfast had stretched like an over-used rubberband, distorting Clea's concept of time until the retelling jogged it back into proper order. So much had happened in so few hours. She paused, wagged her head as if it required physical motion to reorient herself to a world of sixty-second minutes. Only then did she pick up her tale at the description of the clipped-out letters and how they matched the anonymous note she'd received. She began to enumerate Ren's surplus of theories as to their origin, and as she did it struck her she could reduce the number by one with a quick visit to Junior's.

It seemed the thing to do since it was so handy and, she rationalized, a suitable trade-off to her troubled conscience. One lead followed through to conclusion balanced quite nicely a minor deception, the performance of which still loomed hazily in the future.

If Junior questioned Clea's reappearance in his waiting room, he didn't share it, just nodded blandly at the explanation that she thought Ren might drop by to check progress and she hoped to meet up with him. With a wave toward the assortment of plastic chairs and a hearty "Make yourself to home," Junior disappeared into the work bay. The radio's volume ratcheted higher. The deafening onslaught of a power tool followed. The noise encouraged haste, not that Clea had any intention to dawdle.

Immediately she divvied the magazines, whacking off the upper portion of the stack and plopping it in front of Rikki. She claimed the remainder for herself. In rapid succession the two plowed through the pages of *Road and Track, Car and Driver, Motor Trend,* automotive flyers and sports car publications of all description. When the last had been set aside and not a single additional cut-out found, Clea wasn't sure whether that spelled good news or bad. Let Ren decide. For now it was plenty to put one question to bed: Other than one lonely magazine, the source of raw material for the mystery note was not the auto shop.

Their mission accomplished, the music and mechanical racket, which had been background noise while they worked, now took on T-rex proportions and threatened to devour, if not their bodies most certainly their sanity. A shout into the bowels of the work area failed to penetrate the din, for Junior's head remained firmly buried in the gaping jaws of an ancient pickup. A sign above the door warned *Employees Only Beyond This Point,* stranding Clea on the customer side.

She'd leave a note. To that end she slipped behind the counter, located a pen, and jotted a few words on a scrap of paper to explain their sudden departure. When she tacked it to the log-in sheet, it surprised her to see her Explorer penciled in at the bottom. They'd had no appointment, were an unannounced drop-in but had been duly recorded under the column designated for Monday.

And, despite the vehicle being Clea's, as well as the check, and she the loyal patron for a decade and a half, Ren's name had been affixed to the work order, her involvement summarily dismissed in favor of a fellow male. Any remorse Clea felt at having remotely and ever so briefly suspected Junior of a late-night clip fest vanished. She dusted her hands together. Absolution. A clear conscience.

With Rikki at her heels, they scurried to the sanctuary of the Jeep, there to exchange high-fives and giggle, giddy over the success of their clandestine escapade.

When excitement abated, Clea heard a small-animal growl from the seat beside her.

"Oops, sorry." Rikki's hand gently massaged her mid-section. "I skipped breakfast."

"That settles it. Lunch is next on the agenda. We eat. We plan."

"My stomach thanks you."

They decided on Sandy's Sidewalk Café. During the summer months lunch-goers crowded the outdoor tables. At this time of year, however, most of the furniture had been hauled inside. A few all-weather tables and plastic chairs remained to accommodate the more stalwart customers, those loath to yield quite so soon to the passing season. Clea and Rikki braved the chill and opted for soup and hot chocolate in the relative privacy of the open-air, smack-in-the-middle-of-downtown arena.

While they sipped and ladled, Rikki prattled on about her adventure in Portland. At first Clea paid dutiful attention, but the conversation was largely one-sided, and she drifted into a half-listening state, then lost track altogether. On a storefront opposite the café an hypnotic glare of sunlight bounced off the plate glass window. It blurred her vision, played tricks with her mind. The gaily-carved jack-o-lantern faces of Halloween advertisements turned malicious and snarled.

Though Rikki sat across a table no bigger than a pizza, Clea felt isolated. A breath later, hauntingly observed.

Heeding a sense outside her five, she turned sharply, but black and white geometric shapes, the quirky aftermath of staring into the light, took too long to blink away. When normal eyesight returned, there was nothing to see. Not behind her. Not on the sidewalk, nor across the avenue. What lingered was like a draft of air where none belonged, a feathery touch when one was completely alone.

Paranoia.

Clea almost smiled at the diagnosis, then wondered if this was akin to her mother's existence, trapped by Alzheimer's in a shrinking world to be feared and distrusted. Increasingly her mother shied away from contact, but at this moment Clea wanted company, wanted to empty herself of the confusion and growing unease to a sympathetic soul, wanted a strong hand, a cocksure voice telling her everything was going to be all right. She sighed, not terribly surprised to admit Ren could fit that bill just fine.

"Quarter for your thoughts." Rikki's words soaked through the layers of her consciousness, forcing to the surface the here and the now, while impossible fantasies settled to the bottom.

"Quarter?" she quipped in return. "What happened to a penny?"

"Inflation." The punch line came with a playful jab. "And now that the monster in my belly has been appeased, what's next?"

Rikki looked far too perky to have been bothered by whatever had raised Clea's arm hair. Just as well. No need for the both of them to jump at shadows. "Hmm. Right. The plan of attack. My mind's a blank. How are you fixed for ideas?"

A shy glance at her watch, a deep suck of air and Rikki leaped to her feet. "Paul's probably back from the city. We should go see him and tell him about those magazines at Junior's." Not waiting for a reply, she shepherded the dirty dishes onto a tray and bussed them into the café. The newly-acquired cell phone, the easy way to "keep in touch," was forgotten. Clea let it pass in favor of amusement over Rikki's obvious infatuation with Agent Paul Francesco.

Truth be told, she too was anxious to depart. The chill of being watched had not entirely dissipated. Spidery threads of wariness teased her skin, though she could scarcely prove that what prodded her apprehension was anything more than an overactive case of nerves. After all, she hadn't seen a thing. A confirming glance over her shoulder and Clea followed Rikki through the restaurant.

In the car, on the move, a goal in mind, a sense of doing instead of being done to, proved therapeutic. Clea relaxed, brushed off the heebie-jeebies. It helped to poke fun at Rikki and her Saran-wrap transparent excuse to hook up with Paul again. But when a rosy glow of embarrassment colored the girl's face, Clea broke off and took to looking out the window.

"That's odd," she said as they passed through town. "There's a closed sign hanging in Mitz's window, and it's only one-thirty on a Monday. Monday's the busiest day for people dropping off film."

"Late lunch?"

"Have you ever known Mitz to close for lunch? She eats at the counter if she eats at all. Now what do you suppose she's up to?"

"Bank heist, maybe?"

"What?" The absurdity of Rikki's statement, delivered with deadpan seriousness, brought Clea up short. She spun away from the window and riveted attention on the driver, only to catch a sly smile upturning the corner of Rikki's mouth. "Oh, I see. A joke."

The Jeep rattled by the photo shop, a tad above the speed limit. "Of course, it's a joke. Honestly, Clea, move away from the pool before you do a header into the deep end. Granted, this week has been full of weird stuff, but not every little thing is suspicious."

"If I recall, my choice of words was *odd*. What's really suspicious is how you cleverly circumvented the stop I wanted to make to check it out."

"Pretty darn smart of me, don't you think? The way I figure it, Paul's bound to be back at your mom's house by now, and the more he sees of me...well, who knows?"

Clea chuckled, but that didn't mean she was happy. Her fingers thrummed the dashboard as Rikki turned off Sixth Street with only five short blocks to go. The talk of Paul led inevitably to thoughts of Ren.

She smiled. An involuntary reflex, she told herself, for Special Agent Davis presented a complication in the fabric of her life, a life she preferred simple and wrinkle-free. But there he was. A contradiction. Supportive yet uncompromising. Concerned about her safety while pushing her to greater involvement. For a single, childless man he'd even put up with Addy's pigheadedness. For that alone Clea felt she owed him.

No, it wasn't difficult to admit he threw her off guard. What was hard was the tantalizing notion she liked it.

"What happens, happens." The words came on a sigh. Clea didn't intend to speak out loud, in fact, wasn't sure she had until Rikki delivered her own sigh and responded.

"Exactly."

Clea doubted they were speaking about the same thing.

A minute later they rolled to a stop in the driveway behind two unremarkable cars, one of which belonged to Ren. Before Rikki had a chance to move, Clea touched her arm.

"Remember how we planned to stumble across the envelope by chance? Well, forget it. I'm having a vicious attack of guilty conscience, so I'm going to go in there and fess up...like the good little Catholic I am."

Whoever insinuated confession was good for the soul never had to face one of Uncle Sam's agents and blurt out the truth. More than once Clea drew a deep breath only to gratefully find reprieve with a sudden shift in conversation.

She bided her time while Ren explained he skipped the fire scene after one look at the rubble, which had been shoveled into worthless piles. He then revisited Dave Murray who added nothing new or helpful, and body language convinced Ren the florist was telling the truth.

Next up was Paul. Although he directed his comments to Ren, the boyish flair of his delivery seemed to have another audience in mind. He had succeeded in bartering future goodwill with the New York office in return for immediate technical assistance from Portland. They agreed to begin with an analysis of the warning letter, which gave Rikki the opening she needed to step up with an enthusiastic recounting of their afternoon trip to the auto body shop. Her description relied heavily on details. The noise. The magazines. The intrigue. Clea rolled her eyes at the overblown performance. If Oscars were dished out for embellishment, Rikki would be thanking the Academy.

Eventually she finished and talk dribbled away into silence.

The four remained standing just inside the front door, but no one made a move to disperse. All eyes turned toward Clea, a drumroll implicit. It was her turn.

Rikki bobbed her head in encouragement. Clea swallowed hard.

"If you promise not to lead me off in handcuffs," she finally said, "I have a confession to make. When you left here earlier, Ren, I said I was going home, but that wasn't quite the truth. I came back, used my key to let myself in because I wanted to look through your files. I'm sorry. It was an inexcusable thing to do."

"No secrets in any of my notes," said Ren. "In fact, most of it came from you in the first place. As for breaking and entering…." He shrugged, a grin plastered on his face. "So what? Your house. Your right to—"

Clea shushed him. "Please. It's hard enough to own up without your being so reasonable."

Ren laughed outright. "If you don't like reason, I'm sure Paul here can trade something off for a nice cozy jail cell."

"Why can't you show some old-fashioned righteous indignation, so I can make up for it all with a very interesting piece of paper that's been overlooked till now."

At last she'd captured the attention of the two men.

Rikki bounced from one foot to the other. "Show 'em. Show 'em, Clea."

They followed her crooked finger and moved as one solid mass through the house, to the room behind the pantry, where they lined up like judges at a county fair. Clea broke ranks, stepped forward and knelt in the dust at the side of the crib. Her hand disappeared underneath.

The expression on Clea's face immediately melted from irrepressible triumph to one of utter disbelief.

"It's…it's gone," she whispered.

Chapter Nineteen

The Law Enforcement Center.

The first time Clea passed through these doors, she had naively believed a simple request would generate a simple result, like a penny in an arcade machine assured five minutes of chewing enjoyment.

The gumball, however, had long since lost its taste.

She didn't particularly want a second go at it, yet wasn't altogether certain why. After all, it was the logical course of action. A crime is committed. A crime is reported. Yet the cold and final stamp of officialdom was scary, an admission things had spiraled out of hand.

She thought too of the tiny modicum of control she enjoyed with Ren in charge which would vanish like smoke in a hurricane with the entire police department involved. And then there was the admittedly irrational notion that to seek help would only compound her trouble. It had happened before, and Clea didn't like the arithmetic.

No matter what the reason for resisting, resistance was moot. Ren insisted. Paul backed him up, and once the band wagon pulled into the station, Rikki climbed on board.

Three against one. It didn't seem quite fair.

And now they were at the Law Enforcement Center, on a beeline to the fishtank office of Sheriff Beatrice Summers.

With Ren in the lead, the foursome barreled ahead like Sherman's army on its way to the sea. The march raised a few eyebrows, but generally the squad room took the disturbance in stride, whether because a commotion was commonplace or to acknowledge it might result in extra work, Clea could only guess.

The glassed office door hung open. The sheriff stood behind her desk, partially turned away as she struggled to cram manila folders into an overstuffed cabinet. She didn't appear to be in a good mood.

"Ever think of knocking?" Summers slammed the drawer shut and faced her intruders, looking pointedly at Ren. "Or is this an example of those New York manners we hear so much about?"

Ren ignored the barb. "We've got a problem."

The room, now crowded with five people and the manly-sized office furniture, closed in on itself. The sheriff didn't bother to sit, nor did she offer the option to anyone else. Instead she crossed her arms and waited. Her no-nonsense gaze ranged over the assembled group, pausing briefly on Clea before returning to Ren.

"This have anything to do with that itty-bitty assignment I handed you?" At Ren's nod, she continued. "You *do* realize that was largely unofficial."

"Not anymore." He launched an explanation.

Clea's breath went ragged as she relived the events he described. While he'd been gallantly cavalier about her unauthorized reentry into the house, when he had learned someone else had violated the space, he exploded. The two women were ordered to retreat. He and Paul sobered fast. Their Bureau training kicked into high gear. In the end it mattered little. The back door lock had been expertly picked, care taken to leave not so much as an eyelash of evidence.

To mitigate the loss of the original list of names, Clea and Rikki offered the photocopy, but the fact remained someone had been watching, waiting, then broken in and helped themselves.

Ren's story wound down. His closing line involved a wish list of rotating patrols outside Clea's house and manpower to comb the neighborhood surrounding the break-in. The sheriff stifled a grin while she listened to Davis's final request. It was clear she thought he was out of his mind. Mobilization on that scale was reserved for serial murderers, not a missing piece of paper.

When Ren finished, Summers spoke through steepled fingertips. "Too bad the family jewels weren't swiped. If so, I might be able to spare—"

Ren cut her off. "There's more going on than simple breaking and entering."

"So it appears, but I need more than your word for it to loosen the county's purse strings. My hands are tied."

Ren waded forward until his thighs bumped the edge of the desk. The two glared at one another while an overhead fluorescent buzzed and flickered. No one dared intervene.

Clea composed a mental prayer and released it like a dove, to wing its way to receptive ears before the stare-down escalated into pointless rounds of demands and refusals.

It embarrassed her to see so much energy expended both for and against her case when even she herself was unsure which side of the argument she favored. In the futile hope escape was possible, she glanced out the office, only to see a huge planet in regulation blue orbit by, near to the door but not overly so.

Either the sheriff noticed the man too or the recipient of Clea's prayer mistook the catch in her throat as gratitude. The unfortunate result was the same. Summers shifted her weight for a better view.

"Frank," she barked. "Get in here."

Frank Peterson hoisted his bulk over the threshold, displacing cubic meters of air in the rapidly shrinking room.

"The B and E deserves some attention," the sheriff told Ren. "Frank here has been jumping around shifts to help fill in. As luck would have it, the vacation schedule has let up until the holidays. He's your man. Take him or leave him."

On that note Summers scooped an armload of folders from the corner of her desk and walked them to the filing cabinet.

The meeting was obviously over.

Clea moped around the foyer of her mother's house. Even though the rest of the great room was in full view, she confined herself to the tiled area just inside the door, a small island of self-imposed exile. She argued the reason was to stay out of the way while Ren brought Peterson up to speed. The truth was not so kind.

Her eardrums twanged like wire in the wind each time the policeman unleashed his vocal chords. The volume transformed even the most inane of his comments into accusations to be shouted to the world. In alternating waves, Clea despised his manner, then forgave him as easily. What did it matter, she told herself. Just because he had a loud voice was no excuse to dislike the man. She vowed to be more charitable. After all, he was only doing his job. His lung capacity was Mother Nature's doing.

Then, he callously poked and pawed at her mother's cherished knickknacks. Clea's charity fled the building and slammed the door in its wake.

The briefing concluded, Ren escorted the newest team member to the front door. Passing Clea, Frank paused long enough to acknowledge her with a tip of his cap.

"Ain't this a stitch. Our paths are crisscrossing all over the place lately." He laughed at his own joke—a boomer—then added in all seriousness, "You've no cause to worry about a thing, Ms. Reilly...Clea. Me and Davis here are taking care of business."

Clea managed the weakest of smiles.

As soon as Peterson departed, the house sighed, or maybe it was only the rush of her own breath expressing relief at a return to normalcy. She rubbed the back of her neck where a dull ache had formed.

Ren lifted his shoulders and let them drop, a sheepish I-couldn't-help-it look on his face.

Clea knew he was right. At this point an extra set of hands and ears and eyes would be invaluable. It was the mouth she could do without. To prove she was okay with the direction things had taken, Clea interlocked elbows with Ren and steered him center room.

"C'mon. Let's make some hay. The sheriff says she needs more, let's bring her more."

Whereas the previous hour had dragged leaden minutes laboriously around the dial, the next hour took flight. Still they failed to shake any meaningful headway from the cache of evidence.

A frustrated Ren called a break and opened the fingerprint kit procured by Paul. He recorded Clea's loops and whorls on a strip of white cardboard. The experience wasn't nearly as exciting as Rikki implied. The handholding was awkward. The ink stubborn to remove.

Rikki and Paul secluded themselves in a corner nook. He, engrossed in the list of names, furiously pecked the keyboard on his laptop. From the vantage point of six inches off his left shoulder, Rikki adored his every move.

Once Ren stowed the kit and rejoined Clea at the table, he leaned back in the chair. "That'll take awhile," he said, nodding toward his partner. "Once Paul gets his teeth into something, he's a bulldog."

For the sake of conversation, Clea asked, "What's he doing?" Anything requiring more than the most rudimentary computer skill was out of her league.

"From the looks of it, he's accessing databases. See if those names fall into any patterns, set off any bells."

"Seems unlikely. They were pretty ordinary. Catherines and Thomases. There must be millions. Zillions."

"Paul does like a good challenge."

They lapsed into silence, a pair of unoccupied observers of work actually being performed. The respite lasted barely a minute. Ren latched onto a pencil. Like an oft-repeated ritual he rolled it slowly between his palms. Soon he had one of his many lists in hand, trailing the pencil from item to item until he came upon one that caused him to stop and tap it thoughtfully.

"The MIA status of your birth certificate still puzzles me. Even the hospital has no record of it."

Clea squirmed in her seat. The Good Samaritan fax was precisely the thing that had ticked her off earlier when she'd rifled through his files. "An oversight," she said somewhat miffed.

"You've said your father was out of the picture while you were growing up, but his name would be on the certificate. Locating and questioning him might fill in some gaps. For instance, who Barbara is. Give us a toehold to get this investigation going."

"Impossible."

"You don't know that."

"Oh, yes I do."

Even though Clea tried to concentrate on counting bricks in the fireplace, she could feel Ren's scrutiny. An explanation was called for. "I know because…."

"Yes?"

"Because…." A deep breath. "My mother was in her forties, unmarried, with no Mr. Right conveniently waiting on the corner of Sixth and Elm. She'd devoted her life to children and wanted one of her own."

As a youngster Clea had asked why all the other kids had fathers at home and she didn't. In answer to her questions, her mother had talked of maternal longings, of donor sperm and a clinic. She heard the story only once. After that the subject was closed. A child's imagination filled in the details until the line between fact and fiction fuzzed beyond recall.

"I was too young to really understand. Always pictured her in a secluded cubbyhole somewhere, flipping through a Dad Catalog, like placing an order at JC Penney. 'Give me one of number 246. And rush the order, please.' Of course, she would consider the contributor's height and coloring, though her final selection would be weighted heavily in favor of IQ scores. Mom was a teacher, you know. Probably wanted a little Rhodes scholar to come out of the deal." Clea laughed. "Which proves genetics is not an exact science. So, you won't be finding a father, only wasting time as a result of the hospital's deplorable recordkeeping."

The telling done, Clea watched Ren for a reaction. It wasn't what she expected.

"Two forty-six, huh?" He bent over his lists, selected one and wrote the number down.

Clea wrinkled her brow. "You *do* know I just made that up."

A crooked grin served as his answer, and Clea shook her head, for the umpteenth time not quite sure what to make of Ren Davis.

A slash of yellow light, alive with dust motes, angled through the west facing window, a reminder of the lateness of the day, and with it concern Michael would prove less than dependable in his resurrected role of parent.

Clea tried to think back to the morning. Had she extracted a solid promise from him or had she, under the pressure of a time crunch, read more into his grunts and groans than he meant to deliver? School let out at 3:30. It had to be close to that hour now. Addy would be home soon, and Clea didn't want her alone.

Though she hadn't moved a muscle, all this ran through Clea's mind as she watched the spear of sunlight spread bright across the table.

"It appears you've tired of my company." Ren dug into his pants pocket and jangled a set of keys. "You need a ride but don't think you can pry Rikki away with a crowbar."

"You moonlight as a psychic?"

"Only on Mondays."

"Well, you're partly right. About the ride, not about the company. I'm just—"

"I know. Worried about Addison. But you're in luck. I run a mean taxi service on the side."

"A man of many talents, I see."

He seemed a moment lost in thought before he answered. "Many… many talents."

Michael had parked his truck halfway up the driveway, leaving no doubt to nosy neighbors which house the rusting eyesore called home.

Deprived of the opportunity to find fault with her ex's responsibility, Clea remained seated in Ren's car, not certain what to do. She debated going in but knew it would start a row. Michael would cry foul, accuse her of checking up, peace shattered once again. Ren left the engine idle, discreetly offering her an option.

"Guess I'm not needed here," she sighed. "Would you mind dropping me at Green Haven?"

"Yes, I would. Dropping's out of the question. I'll drive you, wait, and see you home."

"Thank you. I'll make it a quick visit."

"You take as long as you want."

By the time they reached the nursing home, late afternoon sunshine bathed its outer walls in an other-worldly glow. Bold strokes of purple shadow, easily the work of a crazed artist, streamed across a brick and stucco canvas. To a photographer's eye, the lights and darks begged lens and film, but to a daughter the harsh contrast was unsettling, as cold and heartless as her decision to confine her mother within.

Clea started up the walk, but soon slowed to a stop. Several visitors emerged from the home. An elderly gentleman held the door for her, but let it swing shut when Clea failed to move. A smaller path branched to the right. It promised seclusion, and Clea followed it as it wound through a stand of maples into a quiet courtyard formed by the U-shaped building.

Here a family named Cassidy had honored their patriarch with a memorial bench nestled near a bed of black-eyed Susans. From the window of her mother's room, the seat always looked inviting. Up close, Clea changed her opinion. Pigeons had clearly laid a superior claim. She moved on.

In the grassy courtyard, solitude was complete. Trees and shrubs mopped up sound and softened the institutional effect. Clea spotted her mother's third floor room by the small ivy plant on the sill. The empty glass drew her gaze, but she couldn't bring herself to go inside, up the elevator, into that room.

Today should have been no different from any other, yet it was. Today there was doubt where a week ago faith had existed. What had seemed commonplace before was commonplace no more, and flaws marred what was once pristine. Something dark and a little sinister had drawn a shade over Clea's heart. She squeezed her eyelids shut against the hot tears forming there, for she recognized the specter of loss and knew it had found her again. If sadness had a voice, it would be the sound that broke from Clea's lips at just that moment.

She lowered her eyes. Only then did she realize Ren was at her side. So steeped in concentration, she'd missed his approach.

He stood quite still, seeming to study her. "Penny for your thoughts," he finally said.

Ah, a penny. At least someone had managed to keep the cost of brooding in check. However, her thoughts stung too much to share.

"They're nothing worth quite so much," she replied instead, hoping to end that line of talk. She might have guessed Ren wouldn't be dissuaded, but hardly expected him to place his hand on the small of her back and gently yet firmly ease her around till they faced head on.

"I'll bet in high school you were voted Most Likely to Avoid."

"Avoid? What do you mean?" A nervous chuckle spiced her words, for he'd struck dangerously close to the truth.

She started to pull away, but Ren held fast. A faint, ashy odor still clung to his clothes. It made him seem outdoorsy, perhaps even a little wild.

His eyes had deepened from steely blue to the color of the ocean embracing a storm. But unlike a tempest, they harbored no threat. The hand on Clea's back softened, meandered up her spine, caressed her neck. Before she could catch a breath, fingers laced into her hair and grabbed a fistful of curls, then reversed the process until the hand was again at her waist.

"Avoid this." He whispered low. His breath, so near, warmed her skin, but the kiss that followed burned hot, a fire as intense as the morning's blaze.

Wrong, Clea thought in a panic. On so many levels this was wrong. What did she really know about Ren Davis, or he about her for that matter, but—God help her—she kissed him back.

Chapter Twenty

Clea's head spun. Though October was in the air, an inner fire warmed her from head to toe. Thankfully, Ren's arms were still around her. She'd have fallen were she stood if they weren't. Never in her life had she been so soundly and expertly kissed. It took a moment to regain composure and for breathing to return to normal. And another to place herself in the courtyard of the nursing home.

Awkwardly Ren and Clea pulled apart. A blush rose to her cheeks, as heated as the still-smoldering imprint of his lips on hers. The shock of his advance should have left her speechless, but didn't.

"Not bad for an FBI agent," she blurted, then winced. What an idiotic thing to say.

Had she really uttered it aloud? Please, not out loud, she prayed, but a peek at Ren's face left no doubt.

He wagged an eyebrow. "That's *special* agent, if you don't mind."

In spite of the circumstances, Clea giggled. The tension broke.

Ren cupped her chin in his hand and leaned in to brush an airy, almost brotherly kiss on her forehead, then stepped back. "Shall I wait for you in the car?"

Wait in the car? He kissed her within an inch of her life and was going to waltz off like nothing happened? She wanted to grab him for a repeat performance, just to prove to herself she hadn't dreamed up the whole incident. A second thought convinced her that would rank on the stupid meter right up there with her mindless comment, so instead she packed the experience away in a corner of her mind to be recalled at a later time. The pleasure relived. The emotions sorted through and assigned their rightful places. She took a deep breath. "I thought that's what you were supposed to be doing in the first place."

"And you were supposed to go *into* the nursing home, not vanish behind a clump of bushes. At police academy one of the first things you learn is to watch your partner's back. And as good as I am, I don't have X-ray vision."

"I needed to think a bit."

"Next time do it in plain view."

Clea didn't answer. The highs and ordinaries of the last few minutes had minced her brain cells, so try as she might she couldn't immediately remember what had made her shy from going inside.

Deliberately then, as if someone might have taken the trouble to scribe the reason on Green Haven's broad façade, Clea peered over Ren's head, up three levels and two windows to the right.

"That's odd." She pointed toward the sill that was sadly bare except for one tiny ivy plant, and remained silent until Ren followed the imaginary line from her finger to her mother's room.

Three figures stood side by side. Though they faced inward, their identities were unmistakable. To the far left, the ample uniform topped with a nappy frizz of hair was certainly Lydia. A tightly-wound, snow-white bun gave away the much smaller woman on the right, Mitz Maguire. Hunched in the middle, arms spread and resting on very different shoulders as if gathering two cohorts under conspiratorial wings, was Delbert Sheznesky.

"Your mother has visitors. What's strange about that?"

"They seem an unlikely threesome. A few days ago Mitz confided she'd given up coming here altogether. Mr. S was a colleague, true, but not a close friend. At least not so close as to visit a sick old lady who's bound not to recognize him. And they're looking pretty cozy. What do you think they're up to?"

"Are you always this suspicious? You're probably reading more into it than necessary."

"Or not enough."

While Ren appeared to consider the possibility, the figures moved away from the window and the blinds were drawn. Once they were out of sight, Clea's certainty something was amiss wavered. Perhaps she *was* overreacting, but who wouldn't given everything that had happened this past week.

"I should go up to say goodnight, but with Mitz and Delbert there, Mom's already had enough disruption to her routine. I think I'll just go on home."

"It's your call, Clea. Whatever you decide. It's been a rough day all around."

Ren offered his arm which rekindled Clea's awkwardness. Was he merely being a gentleman? Or would accepting his arm somehow acknowledge a change in their relationship? Which, of course, *had* changed, but was she ready to admit it?

Her mental debate must have exceeded Ren's patience quota, for without warning he physically lifted her hand from her side, lodged it securely in the crook of his elbow, and proceeded to guide her along the path to the parking lot.

The ride home was short and mercifully uneventful. Now Clea stood on her doorstep and listened to the engine sounds recede into the distance. In her hand was a brown paper bag, the same bag that had invited curiosity when she first saw it lying in Ren's car. Ren had pulled it from the back seat and passed it through the window.

"I'll see to it first thing in the morning," he said before taking off down the street.

Clea clutched the bag. A deadbolt hardly qualified as a romantic token, but the gesture meant he had gone out of his way for her, a fact which pleased her very much.

The sun, a fat, red ball set low among the trees, bled crimson into the fast-approaching evening. *Red sky at night*, thought Clea, dredging up from childhood the sailor's mantra which promised fair skies and calm seas on the morrow. It seemed a good omen. With a lighter heart she extended a hand, but just as she grabbed the door handle it twisted away and the door flew open in her face.

Fred Astaire footwork prevented a collision with a young woman Clea had never seen before. The girl was about seventeen, tall and thin, sun-streaked blond hair tamed into a ponytail. She wore a high school sweatshirt blazoned on the front with the team mascot and hugged a load of school books to her hip. Multi-ringed fingers fluttered a greeting.

"Ooh, you must be Mrs. Reilly. I'm Cynthia." As if that cleared up the mystery of who she was and why she was coming out of Clea's house. "Didn't mean to startle you. Gotta go. G'night."

The girl jiggled keys. Long legs carried her past a gaping Clea to a small, sporty car that quickly roared to life and sprang from the curb like a captive animal freed from its cage.

When the shock wore off, Clea tried again to go inside only to be jolted a second time.

"That's Cynthia." Addy blocked the doorway, bouncing from foot to foot, as animated as a wind-up toy. Her eyes sparkled like crystal. "Isn't she the coolest?"

"I seem to have missed something. Why don't you fill me in."

Linking arms, mother and daughter entered the kitchen. Clea reheated coffee in the microwave and spread Oreos on a plate to share while Addy explained the school's new mentoring program.

"It's for the seniors and freshmen. Seniors team up with the new kids. You know, show 'em the ropes, study together, stuff like that. Cynthia's going to graduate next year. She's almost eighteen. Anyway, at assembly today the principal lined up the freshmen and let the seniors decide who to ask. Can you believe it, Mom? Out of all the kids, she picked *me*."

Motherly words of pride formed in Clea's head. Of course this Cynthia chose her daughter. Why wouldn't she? Addy was bright and funny and, once the black dye washed out of her hair, as cute as a button.

But to speak held risk. In the short flight from her side of the table to the other, what took off as reassurance might land as something entirely different. Clea bit into a cookie instead.

"Cynthia's going to help me with midterms. And once a month we get together and do something really fabulous, like get our hair done or have a sleepover. It's okay with you, isn't it, Mom? You have to sign."

"Sure thing, honey."

A waiver form materialized. Then a pen. Clea had barely scribbled her name next to a big red "X" than the paper disappeared as if a moment's hesitation might undo the deed. Addy shoved away from the table and planted a kiss on Clea's cheek.

Happiness swelled like bread dough on a warm oven and remained in place even after Addy had skipped down the hall to her bedroom. Much of the joy still prevalent in the kitchen belonged to Clea. She was glad her daughter had found a friend, even if Cynthia was only fulfilling a class assignment. It was a healthy nudge in the right direction for Addy, away from the oppressive weight of loneliness, of being an outsider at a new school.

This too was an omen.

And on a totally selfish note, Clea hoped Addy's newfound self-esteem and sense of belonging would lessen the girl's need to somehow mend the impossible wreck that was her parents' marriage. Reconciliation was out of the question, and if not for Addy, Michael's ass would be on the curb.

Which would be another very good omen.

Clea dumped the coffee in the sink, humming a tune as she did. On the floor near the refrigerator sat the bright blue dish with the stenciled cat paws. The bowl was full. The Kitten Chow untouched. With arms akimbo and a wrinkled brow, she tried to recall if she'd seen Kitty-Face yet that day or not.

She was still piecing together the morning when Michael stormed in from the living room. She hadn't realized he was in there, although where else would he have been?

Angry strides ate up the distance between them. His face was dark and menacing. Even before he thrust the double-folded sheet of paper at her and demanded "What the hell is this?" Clea's stomach lurched.

Cut-out letters arranged in three arrow-straight lines leaped from the page.

She snatched the note from Michael's grip. "Where did you get this?"

"With the mail."

"You didn't let Addy see it?"

"Hell no, but you'd better start explaining."

Only then did Clea see he also held an envelope. "You opened my mail?"

"That's beside the point. I see this kind of stuff on TV all the time. The words don't make a whole hell of a lot of sense, but no one takes all this trouble for nothing. Answer me. What's been going on around here?"

"What goes on in this house is none of your business."

"You're not the only one who lives here."

"Meaning what? You?"

He growled at that. "Social Services won't take kindly to crap like this."

Michael backed off then, triumph stenciled in the lines of his face. Clea's hands curled into fists, but his mention of Social Services had already hit its mark, and hit it hard.

Fear was a strange emotion. Sometimes it incapacitated. Sometimes it roused one to action. For Clea, her mind wheeled through a hundred ways to defuse the situation, coming back time and again to settle stubbornly on Ren. Of course. The problem was already being handled. She steeled her spine, braced to deliver a slightly-enhanced version of the truth.

"There's nothing to get excited about, Michael. After the first note like this showed up, I called in the Federal Bureau of Investigation. It's all but taken care of."

She hoped to calm him, but his eyes only narrowed into slits. A feral sound rumbled in his throat. "The frickin' FBI's in on this and you say not to worry."

"It might well be a simple case of a Halloween prank. I asked you to stay home this afternoon as a precaution only. I'm honestly moved by your concern, and as long as you and I keep a sharp watch out for Addy when she's not in school, everything will be all right. There's been nothing overtly dangerous."

Michael quieted. He seemed mollified, though one could never tell with him, and the minute Clea shut her mouth, she thought of the stranger who had followed her and Rikki to Reedsport and the intruder who'd stolen the list. Did stalkers and thieves qualify as "overt danger"? Best not to mention them and rile Michael up again.

For a moment neither of them spoke. Michael plucked at his lower lip. Suddenly he tossed the envelope on the counter and jabbed a finger to within inches of Clea's nose, reviving the panic that he might yet act on his words. "This is by no means the end of the conversation."

But Clea held her ground, locked eyes with his. "Do you need me to spell it out? Everything is under control."

He backed away, his accusing digit still poking the widening space between them. The door flew open and he stormed through.

For someone who a week ago had barely given his daughter a second thought, the sudden eruption of parental concern on Michael's part was suspicious, and more dangerous than any pasted-up note would ever be. Clea shuddered.

The door was still wide open. A spatter of swollen raindrops hit the kitchen floor. With a vehemence she had not anticipated, she reached out and slammed it shut.

So much for the wisdom of sailors.

So much for the theory of omens.

Chapter Twenty One

"**What's** wrong with this mirror, anyway?"

Clea squinted above her vanity into the oval illuminated by four tiny globes, barely recognizing the face that stared back. She inched closer until the flesh and blood nose bumped the one of glass. When she reached out and flicked the wall switch, a burst of light from the overhead fixture chased shadow from the buttery yellow bathroom.

"Oh, God."

The half-circles beneath her eyes did not disappear. If anything, they darkened and leaped from her reflection like savage, purple monsters. Gingerly, Clea dabbed at the discoloration with a wet hand towel, but the damage of a fitful night of unrest would not be so easily undone.

She blamed the lack of sleep totally on Michael, on the scare he'd put into her. For the hundredth time she told herself the bastard was only bluffing. He wouldn't dare file a report, and Clea would rocket Addy to the moon before she'd let Social Services disrupt their lives.

Then a voice inside her head whispered. Her fingers trailed from puffy eyes, over pale cheekbones, to lips that yet bore the memory of Ren's kiss. Reluctantly she admitted someone else shared guilt with her erstwhile husband for her sorry state this morning.

She made a face at her image and sighed, yearning for the simple life of a mere week ago when juggling a rebellious teen, disabled mother and mounting debt was all that faced her at dawn each day. She doused the lights and staggered toward her bedroom in search of ten minutes of uninterrupted sleep. But that too was not to be. The voice of KKRZ's deejay blared a way-too-cheery greeting through her daughter's alarm clock radio. Very soon Addy would be up and about.

The aftermath of the scene with Michael returned like a thunderclap and jarred Clea full awake. She lit out for the kitchen.

Once Michael had left—good riddance—dinner over and Addy abed, Clea had emphatically locked the back door. If she'd had a hammer and chisel she'd have installed the deadbolt herself, but settled for wedging a chair firmly under the doorknob. Michael had no right to threaten her as he did. Let him spend a cold night in his damned truck.

But morning had a way of sifting through the chaff of personal vendetta. Clea would not lightly dampen her daughter's "Cynthia-high" with this glaring display of acrimony aimed at her father. She dislodged the chair, smugly satisfied, for while the lock had been sprung, entry had been denied. Hmph, she crowed. Who needed a deadbolt with kitchen furniture about?

As an afterthought, Clea went to the dining room window and teased apart the wispy sheers. Outside, driveways and curbs were deserted, their cars long departed for the daily commute into the city. Not a truck to be seen, red or otherwise. A puddle had formed at the foot of Clea's drive, giving testimony to the overnight rain. Now and again its glassy surface rippled with a single drop wrung from the gray rag of sky.

"Watcha looking at, Mom?"

Clea whirled, surprised to see Addy in front of the open refrigerator, arms laden with milk, fresh oranges and two kinds of jelly. She was already fully dressed, a small miracle in itself.

"Are you ready early or am I running late? Give me a few minutes to—"

"No need, Mom. Don't you remember? Cynthia's picking me up today. You said it was all right."

That part of last night's conversation had dropped off the scope of Clea's memory, if indeed it had ever been fact. There had been a consent form and a call to Cynthia's mother, ostensibly to introduce herself, but realistically Clea needed to fill in gaps left wanting by the oh-so-brief encounter with the senior mentor. She had been suitably reassured; and if she was then, nothing had changed overnight.

"Okay. Anything else I may have forgotten?"

"Duh!" Addy rolled her eyes and lolled her head. "The meeting? For all participants? After school?" She dumped her burden on the table and went back for bread and utensils. "Afterwards Cynthia and me are going to grab something to eat and study at the library. She'll drive me home. Before ten, so don't worry."

"I'm not worried a bit, sweetie." Clea wondered if her assurance came across as believable. She tore a corner from a slice of bread and nibbled. "By the way, where's that kitten of yours? Her food dish hasn't been touched."

"She cried to go out yesterday morning. Maybe she found a boy cat to hang around with."

"Hmm. I think Kitty-Face is a little young for that just yet. Anyway, put her bowl on the stoop in case she gets hungry."

The rest of breakfast passed with nary a word between them. Clea twirled a blond curl that hung limp at her neck. With the other hand she held a glass of juice to her lips—untasted. Unaware she did either. Her thoughts were like broken glass, shattered and scattered. Soon the rumble of a powerful engine neared the house and sent Addy into a frenzy of activity—snatching up books, gym clothes, sweatshirt, lunch. She kissed the air in the vicinity of her mother's cheek and bounded out the door.

Left alone, with no distractions other than the intermittent hum of the refrigerator, Clea slouched over the table. A host of worries settled onto her like a swarm of hungry mosquitoes. While there was plenty to think about, she found herself incapable of concentrating clearly on any one thing. Her body was leaden from lack of sleep, her mind dull as an old razor.

But sitting at the kitchen table would accomplish nothing either, so she rose, determined to tackle a single item, and from there she'd just have to wait and see. Remembering the care Ren had taken to protect the previous anonymous note, she decided slapping the latest message between two sheets of plastic was a good start. It required minimal brainwork, though it was probably a waste of effort since Michael had manhandled it. And she, by also touching the letter, had added or smudged or wiped out completely whatever might have clung to its surface and provided Ren with a clue. The only thing she could do was protect it from this point on.

A report cover served the purpose the first time, so Clea picked up one from Addy's desk and then moved on to her own room. The sheets, heaped on the bed and twisted like jungle vines, reminded her of the fretful hours she'd passed there. A cheerless day seeped through the window and veiled the room in mourning, laying a pall over everything including the letter and envelope sitting on the dresser top.

Ah, the letter. Of course she had read the message, and reread it many times throughout the night until the words were burned into her memory like a brand on leather. In itself the note wasn't threatening and under ordinary circumstances might sound dry and scholarly. It was the manner in which it had been prepared and delivered that rendered it menacing. Someone was out to scare her and doing a mighty fine job of it.

More than anything she had wanted to call Ren last night, had been on the verge of doing so, picked up the phone even and punched in numbers, although never to the full count. Mostly she stopped because of Addy, who would question Ren's late-night appearance and be frightened if she learned the reason why. To run to Ren was equally unacceptable. She wouldn't leave Addy by herself in an empty house simply because she lacked the fortitude to tough out a few hours on her own. She had swallowed the hard knot of fear and waited, but now she would wait no longer.

Taking care to touch only the corners, Clea slid the articles behind plastic. The message drew her gaze as sure as a vampire draws blood. Paper squares formed three lines, a triple row of ghoulish teeth, opened wide, ready to bite.

As she slowly worked her way back toward the kitchen, she studied the page, mouthing the words over and over:

Not every truth is better
for showing its face...
silence is the wisest thing

Not your everyday language—at least not in the twenty-first century—which begged the question, Why couch the warning in old-fashioned rhetoric? Clea was quick to note the letters *fac* were scissored out as part of a single block, a match to the hole she and Ren had discovered in the magazine from Junior's waiting room. One thing was for certain, both notes had been assembled by the same person. Who that person might be...?

The thought dangled unfinished as Clea reached the end of the hallway, looked up and screamed.

"Good Lord, Ren." She clutched at her throat. "Is it your mission to scare me half to death? This is the second time you've sneaked into my kitchen. I swear, you must've been a cat burglar in a former life." Her fingers dropped to her chest, forming a little tent over her rapidly beating heart.

Ren's eyebrows arched in mock surprise. "Not sneaking. Door was wide open...just like the last time."

"You know what I mean." The pique in her voice reflected as much the alarm at his sudden appearance as for his far too chipper mood. He was dressed for manual labor in jeans and navy shirt with the sleeves already rolled. Under his arm he carried a small toolbox which Clea recognized as coming from her mother's garage.

"I came to put in the new lock," he said, responding to her unspoken question. "I can't force you to use it, but I strongly recommend you do. Addision as well."

The warning omitted Michael, his place in the household left unacknowledged.

"Well, as long as you're shopping for reasons to make your point, here's one more." Anticipating his reaction, Clea deposited the note on the counter and snapped on a light. "It arrived yesterday in with the mail. Obviously hand delivered. No stamp."

Immediately Ren's expression dimmed. He pored over the latest communication, examining both sides. All business. Concentration boldly written across his face.

"Anything here strike you as personal?" he finally asked.

"I guess I consider the whole darn affair personal."

"Familiar then. Could the sender have slipped up and inadvertently used a phrase or turn of words that might be unique, identifiable?"

Though totally unnecessary, Clea carefully read the sentence one more time. "Nothing."

"Why don't you give it some more thought." A roguish smile nudged at the corners of his mouth. "Perhaps while you're changing clothes."

Color drained from Clea's cheeks as it dawned on her she still wore what served as pajamas—a ragged T-shirt and faded flannel bottoms. She spun on her heels and fled down the hall, chased by "I'll take care of the lock" and what she was sure was the sound of laughter.

A narrow rivulet of muddy water raced along the gutter and splashed the underside of the car when Ren wheeled into his driveway. Raindrops still hung from trees like prisms on a chandelier, though the sky had already made up its mind about the day and was swiftly scrubbing itself free of clouds.

At the sight of Rikki's black Wrangler, Clea blew out her breath. "Here already, is she?"

"At the door before I rolled out of the sack. A few challenging moments, I have to admit. Paul has the bedroom and I'm camping out on the couch. You know that whole first floor is one big room with windows all around. A guy has to be quick as well as inventive."

"And did you succeed?"

"Honestly, I think I could have been buck naked and she wouldn't have noticed."

"Ooh. Sorry."

"What for? That I had to scramble or that Rikki didn't give me a second glance?"

Clea laughed. "Both, I guess."

A wink from Ren caused a visual of the two scenarios to pop unbidden into Clea's head, followed closely by a blush that warmed her ears and threatened to spread. Embarrassed, she flung open the car door and clambered out.

The playful mood immediately died. Parked opposite the house and unnoticed till this moment was a black and white cruiser. Apparently Officer Peterson was an early riser too. Clea looked to Ren for confirmation. His scowl was all the answer she needed.

Rikki met them at the door, her face aglow. Clea detected a touch of makeup, enhancing eyes and lips, and that Rikki's ponytail, usually carelessly wrapped with an elastic scrunchie, had been abandoned in favor of meticulous French braiding.

Clea nodded approval and delivered a poke of the elbow. "Big plans in the offing?"

"Not yet, but the day is young."

"Aren't you being somewhat transparent?"

Rikki grinned. Her voice dropped to a whisper. "I'll let you know if it works. Then you can try a little of the same stuff on your own Bureau man."

Too late for that, thought Clea, though the insinuation that she could use some primping made her self-conscious about the khakis and years-old blouse she had thrown on and the quick finger-comb she'd given her hair.

A shout from across the room cut short her mental inspection. "Come on in. Come on in. We've been waiting for you two." Peterson's stance was largely territorial, a thing which bristled Clea since Ren was the tenant of record. His tone suggested he was the one running the show. The man rubbed Clea the wrong way, but such feelings had no place in what must be a group effort, so she forced a smile.

"Ren installed a stronger lock at my house. Then we stopped by Junior's shop to see about my car."

"Still out of commission, huh?" asked Rikki.

"The brakes. Waiting on a part. Ready tomorrow...maybe...." With a flourish Clea dug into the tote bag she carried and produced a wadded ball of paper. "While Ren and Junior were deep in discussion about drums and shoes and whatnot, I acquired this."

"Wow!" said Rikki. "Garbage."

Clea pitched the girl a withering look, then marched to the table where she methodically ironed wrinkles out of the paper until the sheet lay relatively flat. Roughly the size of a desk blotter, it was divided vertically by thick black lines, each column representing a different day of the week. Penciled in and around oily smudges were names and phone numbers. Clea took a step backward to allow everyone an unobstructed view.

"Ta-da!" she sang, waving an arm toward her find, but no one moved a muscle. Well, she hadn't expected high fives, but a little enthusiasm would have been nice. She prompted Rikki.

"C'mon, girl. Get with the program. Remember how we wondered who had access to the magazines in the waiting room? Customers, right? This is last week's schedule of all the people who had their cars serviced." She looked at Peterson and added defensively. "I didn't steal it...actually. It was in the wastebasket. Junior doesn't rank housekeeping high on his list of priorities, but it was obviously ready for the trash bin. If we'd put it off till Wednesday, it would have been gone. Garbage pick-up day, you know."

"You waited until now to spring this on me?" asked Ren.

"I was going to tell you but wanted to make a big splash with a bit of good news. It *is*, isn't it? Good news? Helpful?"

"Excellent," said Ren. "Anything that makes this job easier is a boon. Let's give a look."

His comment jump-started the others. As if coming out of a trance, they shuffled into a tight knot at the table to inspect the work log.

Clea recognized a number of the names. Junior's reputation was more widespread than she had given him credit for.

Paul spoke first. "What are these?"

The letters *LEC* followed by various four-digit numbers appeared twice on Monday, three times on Wednesday and once on Thursday.

Peterson explained. "Law Enforcement Center. Police department has a contract for work on their squad cars. Mayor's too, I think. And some of the smaller city trucks. In fact...." He thumped a stubby finger down on the paper. "...that's me. Eleven-thirty Monday. Lube job and a worn hose."

"Can you find out who the others belong to?"

Frank draped an arm over Clea's shoulder, almost knocking her off her feet with a heavy-handed pat. "Honey, they're all police cars, but if it makes you feel better, I'll check it out." He rolled the sheet like a pirate's map and tucked it under his arm.

"As long as you're working on the names," said Ren, "separate those who dropped their cars from those who waited for the work to be done."

"Gotcha."

"And for now, Frank, let's keep it between us that you have that weekly schedule."

"Sure thing. And while I'm at it, I'll knock on a few doors in the neighborhood. Maybe smoke out some info on our prowler."

Nods all around.

However, despite his apparent interest and the enormity of the project he'd laid out for himself, Peterson failed to act the least bit in a hurry to get started. Instead he plopped a huge buttock on the corner of the table. "What else is cookin'?"

Paul reported no luck as yet connecting any of the twenty-nine names. He wanted to confer with the Portland office, and if he and Rikki weren't needed for a few hours, would drive into the city, taking with them the brown wrapper with its partial postmark for analysis which was beyond the scope of his computer.

"I'll pick up those photos at Walgreens along the way," offered Rikki. "It totally slipped my mind yesterday."

How quickly and easily Rikki and Paul had become the "dynamic duo." Clea covered a grin, amused at the girl's obvious infatuation and secretly pleased the attraction traveled both ways. Rikki was a sweet girl and a hard worker, and it was about time some young man noticed it.

When she again focused on the here and now, it was to a lull, edgy and uncomfortable, in which only the tick of the clock marked the progression of time. Ren didn't bring up the subject of the second warning note. As soon as they had entered the house, he placed it, face down, on the foyer table, slipping it under the Yankees cap. She wondered about it at the time and now followed his lead and kept mute.

Finally Ren shifted his body weight and rubbed his hands together, effectively ending what felt to Clea like a face-off at high noon.

"Everyone has an assignment," he said. "Paul and Rikki to Portland. Frank to track down the auto shop lead. Clea and I will review what's here. We'll all meet up about two. Let's get to work."

The house cleared, some leaving more reluctantly than others. As soon as the door clicked shut, Clea rounded on Ren to ask why he had chosen to keep everyone in the dark about something as significant as the second note. The opportunity to quiz him was lost in the singlemindedness with which he grabbed the plastic folder off the foyer table, led her into the great room, and settled her on the couch. Plunking himself so close their hips touched, he pulled the computer onto his knees and powered it on.

"Okay," he said. "Let's you and I get busy. Since you already have petty theft down pat, no reason why you can't learn to use one of these."

Before Clea could protest, she found the intimidating piece of equipment resting squarely on her lap.

Ren guided her through the basics. Skimming her finger over the built-in mouse pad took some getting used to, as well as the unfounded fear of breaking the darn thing every time she made a mistake. As the newness wore off, though, Clea relaxed, found herself with a screen name and password, and an admittedly limited idea of what a search engine was and how to log onto it.

"The more specific the information you feed in, the more likely you are to come up with exactly what you're looking for. If that doesn't work, you can always broaden the search, but that would mean culling through a lot of unwanted results. Ready?"

"As much as I'll ever be."

"Hang on. I'll get those two letters. You enter the text word for word, and we'll see what pops."

"Okay." But Clea chose not to wait. As soon as Ren's back was turned, she typed a few strokes and hit the enter key. If the Internet was the "wonder-tool" Ren touted it to be, why not utilize its powers for some research of her own. For sure, response was fast. In the few seconds it took him to fetch the evidence, the screen filled.

"My, my." Clea clucked her tongue. "You certainly are quite the popular fellow, aren't you? You're listed here as writer, photographer *and* accomplished hiker through the wilds of Georgia."

"What are you talking about?"

She swiveled the computer until the page of references to *Ren Davis* faced him head on.

"Checking up on me?"

"As they say, turnabout is fair play. Thought I might be rewarded with the full, unedited version of your name."

He chuckled. "That's not me."

"Internet's not all it's cracked up to be, is it?"

"On the other hand, it speaks well to the thoroughness of my deep cover."

He reached over, refreshed the screen, and passed her the two sheets. "Try these."

Their fingers brushed as lightly as butterfly wings, and a current rippled up Clea's arm. When she typed in the words, she hoped the tremor was not obvious.

Secret things belong unto the Lord

Immediately the computer spat out seventy-eight listings. Most appeared to be religious sites. Selecting the top ranked link produced the citation and its source: Deuteronomy 29:29.

"That was easy." Clea asked for paper and wrote it down. "From the very start I thought there was a biblical feel to that message."

"Unfortunately, the only thing we've learned is where the words came from, not what they mean. What about context? Before and after?"

Clea pushed off the couch and headed for the bookshelf where she hefted into her arms one of the few books remaining there, the Bible. After consulting the table of contents she flipped to chapter and verse.

"It comes at the end of a chapter dealing with adhering to the covenants of God, but the wording is different. Of course, this is only one translation."

"What's another?"

"King James version."

Ren typed. "Here it is. The second part of the verse has to do with obeying the commandments down through the generations. I see no correlation to warning you into silence."

"Try the other message."

His fingers sped over the keys.

Not every truth is better
for showing its face...
silence is the wisest thing

Twenty-six sites flashed on the screen, the one most closely matching their input referenced Pindar.

"What or who the hell is Pindar?"

Clea's shoulders bounced in a shrug. "Ptth. Beats me."

The link uploaded and revealed the full quote as:

Not every truth is better for showing its
face undisguised; and often silence is the
wisest thing for a man to heed.

Pindar proved to be a lyric poet of ancient Greece.

"Some poet," said Ren. "It doesn't even rhyme."

"Not all poetry needs to rhyme, and maybe it does in the original text."

"Is this where I say 'It's Greek to me'?"

She ignored him, more interested in wringing some sense out of the note. "Here's a curious thing. See where words have been omitted and an ellipsis—those three dots—inserted? How well versed in proper punctuation is your average criminal?"

"I hate to disillusion you, Clea, but prisons are full of well-schooled, highly-intelligent inmates."

He was right. That wasn't what she wanted to hear. She continued to theorize out loud. "I'll bet it's been shortened for two reasons. First, to eliminate the word *man* since it was sent to me. And dropping a few unnecessary words emphasizes the one coming right after the ellipsis—*silence.*"

"The first note," said Ren, "cautions you to lay off things that are or have been for a long time a secret and the second one's a warning to keep quiet."

"Someone went to a lot of trouble to find quotes that relayed those messages precisely."

"Someone with a knowledge of both scripture and dead Greek poets."

"Someone like a teacher." The scene in her mother's room the evening before replayed clearly in her mind. "Someone exactly like Delbert Sheznesky."

Chapter Twenty Two

"I can't arrest him."

"Why not?" Clea chucked the Bible onto the sofa cushion she had vacated moments before. Ren jumped. The book came close to hitting him, though she hadn't aimed, not exactly. At any rate, she knew she had his full attention now and pointed to the papers in his hand. "This stuff's second nature to him. He's been quoting obscure authors forever. Ask anybody."

"Just because the man spouts literary passages and happens to be a teacher you despised in high school doesn't make him guilty of a single thing."

"Why are you sticking up for him? You were at Green Haven last night. Go ahead. Explain away his sudden interest in my mom."

Ren got to his feet. "Well, that cinches it. I'll haul his ass downtown on the charge of aiding and abetting a hospital visit."

"Stop it, Ren."

"No, Clea. You stop...and consider for a moment."

"Wait. He was also at the library the first night I tried to find out who Barbara was. I showed him the picture. Told him all about where I'd found it." Clea paced as she spoke. Nervous fingers plowed through her hair until Ren seized them and held them to his chest.

"What I'm failing to do—miserably I might add—is to get you to see you're missing a little item called proof. Not to mention motive, means and opportunity."

"So, what do I do? Turn the other cheek?"

"He's not off the hook. Right now my hands are tied, but that doesn't mean we don't keep a close eye on Mr. Delbert Sheznesky and figure out why he would threaten you and why do it in such a manner that would make his involvement obvious."

Clea scowled, hating the logic and the dead end that came with it. Short of beating a confession out of the old man, how did one breach the fortress of another's inner intentions and come up with motive?

She broke free, gathered her things, certain she would go crazy if she stayed shut up in the house one more minute staring at a computer screen. Ren let her go with a look of resignation and the words "Back at two." He said it in such a way as to allow her to interpret the remark as either a request or an admonition. Knowing Ren left her this option somewhat appeased her annoyance at his insistence on sticking to the rules. It wasn't until she was on the front porch, greeted by a slap of cold air, that she woke to the fact her truck was still in the shop. Reluctantly she turned around, only to find Ren in the doorway, keys to his car extended like a peace offering to an angry goddess.

Clea steered the car up and down the side streets that skirted the business district. The drive was therapeutic more than productive, for she had no clear destination in mind. It did give her a chance to mull the three gaping holes—motive, means and opportunity—which Ren said needed to be plugged with irrefutable fact. She was unaware her attention had strayed until the front tire hit the curb and the resultant jolt rocked her back to her senses. Shuddering at how near she'd come to crumpling a government fender, she turned the next corner and rolled to a stop across a series of diagonal yellow lines. Since the no parking zone was obvious, she left the engine idle and kept a vigilant eye for patrol cars while she calmed her nerves.

Almost immediately her thoughts circled back to the three requirements of guilt. She felt certain she had a lock on *means*. Delbert was a gifted teacher, his knowledge of world literature almost a legend in this town. After decades in the school system, he probably had a store of source material that would choke a whole barnful of horses. Clea recalled he was at the library that night doing research. Far from vegetating in retirement, he apparently worked hard at keeping his mind acute. No, Delbert Sheznesky would have no more trouble plucking quotes from the air than a magician would pulling scarves from his sleeve.

Next Clea turned to the issue of *motive*, a much more difficult thing to prove. After pondering the question of why from as many angles as she could muster, she gave up, no closer to an answer than she had been before.

That left *opportunity*.

The warnings had arrived with her mail, but both had been unstamped. Someone—Delbert, she corrected herself—had brazenly come to her door and slipped the envelopes through the mail slot.

Clea inhaled deeply, sucking in fresh determination with the lungful of oxygen. She shifted out of park and spun into the street. With a little luck she would nail him on this one too.

No sooner had she pulled ahead a car length or two than she noticed the police vehicle in the opposite lane. Automatically her foot let up on the gas. She crept forward, wondering if a ticket for illegal parking was in her future. She was surprised to see a hand emerge from the driver's side window and Frank Peterson offer up a salute. The seemingly serendipitous encounter caused her to question what he was doing in this part of town, especially since his self-proclaimed assignment this morning should have placed him several miles away.

Then it dawned. Ren, worried about her safety and perhaps even her state of mind, had contacted Peterson and asked him to keep an eye on her. As much as she hated to admit it, there was a portion of her that welcomed his presence. She felt less vulnerable, less exposed. She raised her hand in a feeble attempt at a wave and passed on by.

Seeing Frank, though, reminded her of his intent to canvass her mother's neighborhood in search of someone who might have glimpsed the thief. The idea stuck with her and took shape into a plan as she backtracked through town to her own street. Once there she found it quiet as usual, although several neighbors were in evidence, taking advantage of the improving day to sweep leaves from a sidewalk or set out decorations in advance of Halloween.

Clea pulled up in front of her house but didn't go in. Across the street and kitty-corner in a green-shuttered Cape Cod, Lucille Roper attempted to roll a gigantic jack-o-lantern from one end of her porch to the other.

"Mrs. Roper!" Clea sprinted up the wooden steps. "Here. Let me help you. I swear every year you manage to find a bigger pumpkin than the year before. This one's a whopper."

"It's for the children, dear. They come trick-or-treating just to see it."

"Are you sure it's not the monster-sized Hershey bars you give out that brings them calling?"

The woman laid an arthritic finger against her lips. "Can't blame an old lady for trying. I do so much like to see the little ones in their costumes."

"You like to see the kids no matter what they're wearing. I know you keep a sharp look out for them all summer and afternoons now that school's in session."

"My, my. Here I thought I was being quite the clever one."

"Well, don't let me discourage you. All the mothers love you for the extra pair of eyes."

While Lucille basked in the compliment, Clea cleared her throat and continued. "By the way, you didn't happen to see a man around here on Saturday and again on Monday? Late sixties, fully gray, even his beard?"

"No." Lucille tensed. "Should we be concerned?"

"Nothing to worry about, Mrs. Roper. I was…uh, expecting a visitor but he never showed. I thought he might have come when I wasn't home."

Lucille lifted her shoulders in a helpless shrug. Clea bid the woman farewell and moved on up the street. She interviewed the leaf-sweeper, knocked on doors, talked to stay-at-home moms and senior citizens, but in the end learned nothing. The fruitless task was discouraging, though not exonerating. Just because none of the handful of people remembered seeing Sheznesky, by no means meant he hadn't been there.

The setback weighed heavily and Clea slumped visibly as she headed toward the car. If Delbert hadn't been spotted in the area, how was she to convince Ren her suspicions were based on more than sour grapes over a few lousy grades when she was a teen? She rehashed that meeting in the library, trying to recall if Delbert had mentioned the subject of his research project. Was he working on a paper or article even remotely related to Pindar? Was he checking out the Bible? She pictured him in the reference room—empty-handed, she was sure. A reconstruction of their conversation failed to enlighten her either. Dead end.

Suddenly Clea jerked upright as something even better struck her with the force of a club. She bolted for the car. The tires squealed as she tore away from the curb and sped in the direction of the high school.

She waited in the parking lot until a bell inside the building sounded once and again five minutes later. The hallways would be empty now, kids in class for another full period, and the Student Services secretary more likely to have the time to assist her.

Her request to see the school's archive of old yearbooks raised no alarms with the young woman behind the counter. Indeed the secretary displayed not a scintilla of curiosity as to why Clea wanted to see them, just mumbled "Follow me" and led the way to an alcove on the second floor.

Team trophies on shelves behind glass lined one entire wall. Opposite, group pictures of boys in uniform, many of which Clea recognized as her own work, added to the school's Hall of Fame. The yearbooks were locked in a cabinet.

"When you're done," said the long-suffering secretary, "just return all materials and push this button to relock the drawers."

"Sure thing."

Clea stacked a dozen or more books—most before the year 1970, though some after as well—and retired to a scarred and uncomfortable wooden bench.

How had she let something like this slip by her before? Delbert steadfastly maintained Barbara had been a former student of his, and Clea had failed to follow up. Now she would correct the glaring oversight.

The old books were relatively thin, the town and school much smaller then. Clea paged through them all, squinting over grainy head shots, the assembled English Club and other social groups, the casts of plays, the athletic teams. Although there were Barbaras, none resembled the girl in the photo. No student of any name bore a likeness to the elusive woman.

Done, she returned the books. Though the search had been futile, it was less of a disappointment today than it would have been a week ago. Clea brushed the dust from her hands and smiled smugly.

Delbert Sheznesky had lied.

A bell clanged. Doors flew open, disgorging a wave of teenagers into the corridors. Clea struggled against the tide of students as she descended the stairs. A clock on the wall reminded her of the lateness of the morning, and Ren expected them all to gather at two. The revelation about Delbert's misinformation stoked a growing curiosity about who else might have developed a sudden interest in visiting her mother. As well, she wanted to experiment with Addy's computer before she reported in. To do all this, she'd have to hurry.

She bulldozed through the packed hallways. Once outside and free of the crowd, she joined a field of skittering leaves and raced them across the parking lot to her car.

The halls of Green Haven bore a resemblance to the corridors of the high school...busy, though at a considerably slower pace and lower volume. Clea's work schedule did not allow late morning visits, so the bustle at this hour surprised her. Doctors made their rounds. Aides trundled patients to physical therapy and other destinations unknown. A floral cart, parked askew, blocked access to the nurse's pod. Clea shoved it aside. At the moment, the station was unmanned.

For a few minutes she watched the activity around her. Her fingers thrummed the Formica counter and her foot tapped the tiled floor. Outward signs of impatience were clear yet failed to summon a duty nurse.

Her mother's room was immediately around the corner. Clea opted not to go in and felt miserable for the decision, but she remembered all too vividly her own reticence of the night before. The reason behind that feeling largely escaped her, now as it had then, though the same numbing sense of loss and emotional distance pressed heavily on her heart. Neither wishful thinking nor bare-bones calculation could snap her out of it. She refused to believe she loved her mother less, yet something *had* changed. True, the last few years had been rough. That enemy at least had a name. Recent events proved equally troubling. The ravages of Alzheimer's had stolen the future, and now secrets and lies threatened to rob her of the past.

She was about to abandon the mission that brought her to the nursing home in the first place when a voice she had never heard before interrupted her reverie.

"Sorry. Have you been waiting long?" The harried nurse plunked an armload of white binders onto an existing mountain of more of the same. She pulled a vending-machine sized bag of chips from her pocket. "Lunch," she added as she tried to tear the foil packet open.

"Is this a bad time?"

"When isn't a bad time?"

"I only came by to ask if I could look through the visitor's log for my mother. Josephine Worth. Room 303."

"You're free to come and go whenever you please."

"I don't mean for me." Lydia had been quite clear she was exempt from the sign-in process. "I'd like to check who—outside of family—has been to see her."

"Then you've wasted a trip."

"Why's that?"

The nurse paused in her battle with the uncooperative package and cocked her head toward the stack of patient histories. "We've got enough paperwork that's important without generating more that's not. There's no such thing as a visitor's log."

The new deadbolt stuck when Clea tried to open it. After jamming the key in and out several times it freed, but she made a mental note to tell Ren.

The house felt hollow when she stepped inside, an emptiness that bespoke more than the absence of people. The air was palpably dense, devoid of sound and movement. Briefly Clea feared she'd blundered into a stranger's house instead of her own. The feeling quickly subsided, and she tossed her bag and keys on the table.

In Addy's room she powered on the computer and walked among her daughter's possessions while the system cycled through its upload commands. On the dresser, a newly-acquired photo of Michael now lay face down. Did this signify a fall from grace or merely reflect the less-than-tidy housekeeping evident throughout the rest of the room? Clea righted the photo and studied his face, noting with mild chagrin the similarities in cheekbone structure between Addy and her father. She puffed out a sigh and returned the photo to its prone position.

The clicks and beeps of the computer ceased. Clea settled in the chair in front of the screen and tapped a few keys, relieved to find Addy hadn't changed the access code to the Internet without telling her. Thanks to Ren's instruction she was able to connect to Google and place the cursor in the proper box to initiate a global search.

Paul had concentrated his efforts on the twenty-nine names, but Clea wanted to try a different approach. She typed in the word *roses*, dumbfounded when over ten million possible sites were suggested. Then she remembered Ren's caution about narrowing the field. Precise was better.

She tried again, this time adding *children*. Still too many returns. Changed it to *infants*, for the crib in the secret nursery implied occupants much younger than toddler age. Next she plugged in a range of years that predated her own birth because she had no memory of the room's existence.

Each time she entered her request, the Internet spat out fewer choices. She continued in this manner, adding words, subtracting others, shuffling the delineators, all to the end of reducing the list of possibilities to a manageable few. Finally—reluctantly—she typed in the word *crime*.

The vast repository of knowledge and information available through the magic of technology suddenly shrunk to a bite-sized morsel.

Chapter Twenty Three

First instincts aren't always the best. Clea learned that lesson the hard way.

She clicked on the link and waited while several pages of simple, double-spaced typing appeared. A quick read of the initial sentences, and the gist of the writing became painfully clear. Her eyes watered, causing the words to bob like corks on the ocean. But Clea had already seen more than enough to convince her she didn't want to read any further. She reached out and slammed her hand on the power switch, relieved when the screen flickered and went dark.

Then came second thoughts.

She should have at least saved the information, or read it through to the end, if only to satisfy herself that an admittedly amateurish computer search had led her far afield. The problem now became one of finding the necessary sequence of keywords to relocate the same reference. And time was running short.

She consulted her watch. It was already too late to cover the distance from her house to her mother's and beat Ren's two o'clock deadline. She might as well stay and play the game of hit and miss here, without the added pressure of an audience. Her wrestling match with the Internet was still fresh in her mind. If she succeeded in stumbling across the site again, at least she would have the opportunity to cope with it in solitude.

And reject its implication. Reject it completely.

Her pocket chirped. The cell phone demanded attention, but Clea ignored its persistence, opting instead to focus on the keyboard and the process of signing on. She'd not trust her memory this time, rather use old-fashioned paper and pencil to record the string of words used to launch the search.

Addy always kept a notebook next to the computer for this exact purpose, but Clea couldn't find it. Not in the desk drawers, not on the floor, not buried among the sheets and blankets of the unmade bed. In fact, the room seemed to be devoid of any spare paper. Frustration rumbled in her throat as she hurried to the kitchen and back. She checked her watch again. The simple task of finding paper had eaten away minutes with the ravenous appetite of a locust.

Once more the phone interrupted. This time Clea acknowledged it long enough to hit the disconnect button, then sat down to the laborious process of unraveling the code. An unnerving inability to recall work completed a mere half hour ago picked away at her patience. The specter of Alzheimer's made a brief appearance, and she was on the verge of admitting defeat when she struck upon the correct combination of words and found herself presented with the same, single entry.

Unlike her previous cursory scan, Clea now took careful note. The article appeared to be a draft, for remarks and reminders were set off in parentheses within the body of the text. The author's name was Kevin Warner and he a sometimes investigative reporter for the *Los Angeles Register-Star*. How the piece happened to become immortalized on the Internet was left to the imagination. It bore the date of April, 1969 and a working title: The Rose Society. As it had before, the requisite newspaper hook firmly reeled her in:

Children are disappearing. Without a trace.

Clea finished the article, shaken to the core by the cold, impartial voice of Kevin Warner that spanned the gap of thirty plus years to describe things she'd newly discovered, things she was at a loss to explain and fervently wished to deny.

If one was to accept the truth of Kevin Warner's observations, this Rose Society's existence was surely restricted to places like LA, New York or Chicago, huge cities with dark underbellies capable of supporting any number of questionable activities. Sleepy little towns, where churches outnumbered the bars, were miles off the radar. And Clea's mother? Her involvement was ludicrous.

Not knowing how to mark the site, Clea saved the handwritten stream of search words to use in accessing Warner's page in the future. She dashed from the room and was at the back door when she heard the furnace kick on, accompanied by a funny noise—very faint, a pitiful-sounding squeal that boded ill. Great. Mechanical trouble at the onset of winter was all she needed. Cupping an ear, Clea listened more intently but detected only a reassuring steady hum and felt a kiss of warm, dry air from the heating vent at her feet.

Thank God, she thought. False alarm, nothing more.

She closed the door, locked the new deadbolt, and flew to the car. The dash clock flashed on with the ignition and taunted her with the time. She was so late, but it made little sense to call and apologize. She'd be at the house in ten minutes tops. Best simply to get under way.

She navigated the maze of streets until St. Gerard's Catholic Church and school loomed like twin gargoyles on the corner. Classes were through for the day, the grounds, with their empty jungle gyms and dangling swings, forlorn. The rear parking lot stretched between Chestnut and Alder and had entrances on each of the two parallel streets. A detour through the lot would bypass several stop signs and bring her closer to the library and a straight shot to her mother's house.

Speed bumps slowed her a bit but soon enough she was at the far exit, checking both lanes for traffic. She had started to pull forward when movement caught her eye, not in the street but on the sidewalk. Clea gasped. Unbelievable! Right in front of her was Delbert Sheznesky, strolling casually toward the library as if he had not a care, as if he wasn't an underhanded, lying, threat-writing predator.

The afternoon's agenda crumbled. Clea rammed the brake and, without thinking, rolled down the window and shouted, "Mr. Sheznesky. Stop! I want some answers from you."

The man paused, confusion animated by the jerk of his shoulders and his swiveling head. Their eyes met then…and held. An instant later he reversed directions and urgently took off up the walk. Clea's reaction was almost as fast. She maneuvered the car through an awkward, two-part turn that brought her back to the church's entrance. She pulled in and ground to a halt, but by the time she jumped from the car and rushed to the sidewalk, it was empty.

Her jaw dropped in astonishment. How could he be nowhere in sight when he was afoot and she had been so close on his heels?

A sharp, metallic click shattered the stillness. Though Clea turned full circle and still saw no one, she did identify the source of the noise—the sacristy door. Save for that one side door, the entire length of the church wall facing Chestnut was unbroken. An Olympic sprinter would have failed to clear the corner in so short a time. Certainly an old man, looking to make himself scarce, would have opted for a different route.

Clea mounted the step and dragged the door open. The cavernous interior was dim, relying on two altar candles and daylight filtering through massive stained-glass windows for its illumination. The pews were devoid of parishioners. The neighborhood outside had seemed quiet, but in comparison the inside of the church was a deaf man's world. Not a sound disturbed the peace.

She had been mistaken. There was no one here.

Even so, she tiptoed down the side aisle, unconsciously preserving the sacred silence. As she passed the confessional, she noticed the small light above the curtained booth glowed red, a sign someone had entered and tripped the signal that the space was occupied. On the other hand, the indicator above the adjacent paneled stall, the one reserved for the parish priest, remained unlit.

Anyone who attended St. Gerard's knew confessions were a Saturday rite. It was Tuesday. No need for divine inspiration. Clea knew she had found Delbert Sheznesky.

She hesitated for a whispered prayer that Father Leo would forgive her invasion of his space then gently turned the knob and entered the pastor's cubicle. She waited until her eyes adjusted to the absence of light to sit on the padded bench and faced the small connecting window.

She drew a deep breath, slid aside the partition. Behind the grille a shadowy figure huddled against the far wall.

"I know you're in there, Mr. Sheznesky." Clea spoke in undertones, a totally unnecessary thing given the vacant church. "You might as well answer my questions. Why did you lie about Barbara?"

A muffled stirring confirmed he'd heard, was aware of her presence, and perhaps even now weighed his options. She feared he would bolt, but there was no scramble to exit.

"Barbara who?" he finally asked.

"That's what I want to know. Barbara is the woman whose picture I showed you and who you claimed had been a former student. She wasn't. I checked."

"A mere oversight. You can't expect me to remember every student who ever snoozed through one of my classes. It was unimportant. A throw-away response."

Clea's nerve wavered, for this explanation had originally been her own. She decided it best to move on to what really alarmed her.

"Those letters. Dropped off at my house. They're from you."

"Letters?" A nervous laugh. "I assure you I don't know what you're referring to."

"Of course you do. The one citing Pindar. The passage from the Bible."

"I know of no such communication." The humph apparent in his voice remained unspoken.

"The quotes, Mr. Sheznesky. Threatening me if I didn't watch my step."

"Good God, young lady. What are you accusing me of?"

"Why were you with my mother last night?"

"You don't understand at all. We have your best interests at heart."

At this answer, Clea rocked back in the seat. What did he mean by her *interests* and just how many people did *we* encompass?

Baffled, distracted, she realized too late the scrape and shuffle coming from the adjoining room signaled Sheznesky's getaway. She leaped to her feet only to be stymied by the doorknob which had automatically locked when she entered. The latch eventually succumbed to her fumbling, but by the time she gained her freedom, she was once again alone and the main entrance door within inches of swinging shut.

"Damn!" The curse echoed back to her, magnified beyond belief. "Oops, sorry!"

She aimed a hurried sign of the cross at the altar, executed an abbreviated genuflection and raced to follow him outside. There she spotted Delbert with a good head start and adding to the distance between them with a gusto surprising for someone his age.

She could have caught up, but what was the use? The old guy was disclosing nothing.

As she stood on the corner, her heart rate settled back to normal. Though her thoughts had been scattered by the encounter with Delbert, now the bits and pieces of new information slowly blended with the old, herded home like cows at milking time. She had much to consider.

Clea's thoughts turned to Ren. His experience at analyzing fragmented details and half-solidified theories would be invaluable. At this juncture, just his presence would be of immense comfort. No sooner had Clea taken heart than she cringed, equally certain Ren would be nursing a foul mood stemming from the fact she blew off the two o'clock gathering.

On the way to the car she extracted the phone and turned it on but vetoed a call. Just show up, she told herself. Let the others form a buffer until Ren's annoyance dissipated. With luck, it would be all but forgotten before the end of an hour.

Minutes later Clea pulled in front of the house. What struck her as most unusual was the absence of vehicles, either at the curb or in the driveway, followed close behind by the sight of Rikki pacing the wooden porch with unfettered irritation. Clea honked. Rikki started, threw her arms in the air, and stomped down the stairs. They met halfway across the lawn.

"Where is everybody?" Clea asked.

"Where do you think? Out looking for you. When you didn't come at two, Ren called your phone."

"I suspected that was him, but I was busy and didn't bother to answer."

"Well, by quarter after he was all antsy-pantsy. This time your phone cut out mid-ring."

"Uh-oh. That's when I shut it off."

"Nice plan, Clea. Since when is ignoring a guy like him a good idea?"

"Okay, okay. I owe apologies all around."

"Start with me. While they got to go out and play FBI, I'm stuck here like some nervous-mervous mom waiting for you to get home from prom. Ren took my car, and Paul and him split up. You'd better give a call pronto."

"I will, but let's go inside. I found out a few things. It'll make it easier to tell the men if I tell you first."

Together they entered the house. "I'm all ears," said Rikki. "C'mon, spill."

"For one, I know about Barbara."

Rikki dropped into a chair with obvious relief. "Thank goodness. I was worried how you'd take it when Paul broke the news."

A chill washed down Clea's spine. Clearly she and Rikki were tuned to different channels. Paul hadn't been investigating Mr. Sheznesky nor the high school records of girls named Barbara. Clea approached the chair and looked down at her friend. "What news?"

"About the kidnappings."

It was Clea's turn to collapse into a chair. "Then you already know about the Rose Society?"

"The *what* society?"

"Rose. Rikki, maybe you should tell me exactly what you're talking about."

"No. You first."

Clea hunched over, elbows on her thighs. "I used Addy's computer. Ren taught me the fundamentals of searching the Internet, and I lumped together topics like roses and infants and a bunch of the strange events and behaviors I've come across in the past week. After a lot of trial and error, it spat out an article about something called the Rose Society. It is—or was—a network of conspirators that facilitated kidnappings by non-custodial parents. The piece highlighted cases involving the famous, the rich and famous, and the rich and infamous. It worked something like a modern-day Underground Railroad. The reporter, this Kevin Warner fellow, apparently gave it the name. A long-stemmed rose served as a signal. It meant: Expect a *delivery*. They shuffled babies along a chain of so-called stations until it was impossible for anyone, the police too I guess, to trace a path from beginning to end. The children disappeared. Without a trace. That's how Warner began his article. Even now it gives me chills."

"What does this have to do with your mom? Or that?" Rikki glanced toward the fireplace.

Clea shook her head, afraid to give voice to a growing suspicion that the Rose Society had very much to do with that little room, this house, Josephine Worth and...who else? Who else knew the truth? Clea fixed her eyes on Rikki. "Your turn."

The girl's face turned ashen. "Can't you wait for Paul? He can explain it so much better than me."

"No way. At least give me the *Readers Digest* version."

"Remember the list of first names you found? Paul did some fancy fingerwork on the FBI database in Portland. All twenty-nine names corresponded to kidnap victims. Children. Lots of other names showed up too, but if you eliminate the ones that didn't count.... I mean, they all counted, of course. Those poor kids."

"Stay on track, Rik."

"The names appeared in exactly the same order as those on the list, spread out over a period of years in the fifties and sixties. Some of the names were pretty common and appeared more than once. Paul said by simple ex...ex...—whatever word he used—he was certain the names belonged to kidnapped kids. It was...." Rikki shivered and said no more.

Clea prompted. "Did the kidnappings end with Barbara?"

"No, and Josh wasn't the first by a long shot. It was like a section was chopped out of the middle and made into a smaller list."

"In mom's handwriting."

"I'm so sorry."

"Yeah, me too." Clea buried her face in her hands. Pain, as physical as it comes, threatened to defeat her. It was becoming harder and harder to escape a bitter truth. Her mother's near obsession for roses made more sense, the purpose of the tiny, dusty crib room sadly clear.

The Warner article had described the society as subrosa yet enumerated specifics of its methods and secrets, one of which could still be verified years after the fact. This single detail separated conjecture from absolute certainty. Weighted by despair, Clea heaved herself to her feet, trudged to the kitchen and entered the pantry. She did so as a ghost, a spirit beyond feeling, numb to the finality of what she would learn. What was, was.

Despite Ren's oft-repeated warning to leave the room untouched, she went to the glass vase, lifted the bouquet with two hands and bore the roses to the kitchen counter. The dried petals and leaves crackled as she spread them out, side by side.

Rikki, who had followed her in silent amazement, found her tongue. "What are you doing?" she whispered.

"The roses used by the group were to have all the thorns removed—all but one."

Clea picked up a flower by its stem and examined the shaft. Her fingers probed, starting at the bottom and working up, over the bumpy ridges where thorns had been snipped off until they neared the calyx. Suddenly a sharp projection pricked her thumb.

She barely flinched, threw the offending rose into the sink and grabbed another. Same inspection. Same result. The rose joined its mate.

One by one, twenty-nine nicks stung Clea's fingers while Rikki stood by, tears of empathy streaming down her cheeks.

Chapter Twenty Four

The two women sat opposite each other at the dining room table. The clutter of what Ren had accumulated on Clea's behalf lay between them. Its very existence gave credence to the awful truth of the Rose Society and what Clea now could not deny—that her mother had played a part in it, an indisputable, active part.

"I wished I'd never found that picture, Rikki."

"I know. It's led to nothing but grief. And your mom's in no condition to explain." From the kitchen the teakettle sounded an incongruously cheery note. Rikki held out a hand. "Stay put. I'll fetch a couple mugs and teabags. Earl Grey to the rescue, I say. The old boy'll do us both some good right about now."

Rikki returned with the fixings for tea and two paper napkins folded around a handful of sugar cookies.

"How can I eat knowing my whole life's been a lie?" Food held no interest. Clea poked at the sweets. When her cell phone rang, she pulled the instrument from her pocket and frowned at the Caller ID. "It's my neighbor, Lucille Roper."

"Ignore it," said Rikki.

"She hardly ever calls. The last time was when Addy sprained her wrist trying out a skateboard." Despite Rikki's protest, Clea punched the button. Her half-uttered "hello" was cut off by a frantic voice.

"Mom, Mom. You gotta come home. Right away. Please! It's terrible. It's so terrible."

Clea leaped to her feet, bumping the table and sending hot water splattering all around. "What is it, Addy? What's wrong?"

"Just come home. Now."

The line went dead. The logical act of redialing to get more information completely escaped her. Clea bolted for the door.

Rikki had heard the entire exchange. "You're going nowhere without me," she called as they raced to the street and clambered into the sedan, Clea behind the wheel. "Give me that phone. I'm calling the boys to meet us at your house."

The scene that greeted them wasn't nearly as horrific as Clea had painted in her imagination on the whirlwind drive home. Addy circled the giant, grinning pumpkin on Mrs. Roper's porch. She hugged her arms, distraught for sure, but Clea detected no spurting blood and nothing led her to believe broken bones figured into the emergency. Lucille stood by, wringing her hands, but otherwise calm.

The minute Addy spotted them, the girl flew down the steps and flung herself into her mother's arms. Immediately Clea modified her first read of the situation, for her daughter trembled uncontrollably and tears flooded her eyes.

"She's dead. Oh, Mom, she's dead," sobbed Addy.

"Who? Who's dead?"

"Kitty-Face."

"What happened?"

"Cynthia couldn't hang out today after all and dropped me home. There's something wrong with my key. It didn't work in the door, so I looked in the flowers for the spare. That's when I saw her. Just laying there, Mom, not moving at all. Dead." The last was a wail.

While Clea stroked her daughter's hair, Mrs. Roper took up the story. "Addy pounded on my door, wanting to use the phone. At first the poor dear was so upset I couldn't make heads or tails of the problem. I didn't realize you had a cat."

Clea was about to explain when two cars screamed to a halt, and an agitated special agent spilled from each. Thank God they didn't come with weapons drawn, thought Clea. It was bad enough Mrs. Roper had frozen in the classic deer-in-headlights pose at their arrival. Clea didn't want to be responsible for the old lady having a coronary. After a deep breath, she quickly introduced the newcomers and related to all what she had pieced together.

"Let's have a look," said Ren. "Addison, would you show me where?"

"That's really not a good—" Ren cut short Clea's remark.

"I can do it, Mom." Addy's voice was barely audible, but she wiped her sleeve over her eyes and headed across the street. All but the neighbor trailed behind. Halfway up the driveway, Addy slowed and at the concrete stoop stopped altogether and pointed.

Ren continued forward, the rest shrinking back in the knowledge of what he was bound to find. He knelt on the cement slab next to the little blue food dish. A piece of white paper had been folded in two and tucked under the base. He slid it out, gave a quick glance and pocketed it. Then he reached into the flower bed, tearing away at the withered petunias.

The tiny kitten lay stretched out in the dirt, its gray fur matted, its skin showing blue beneath. Ren eased a hand under the body and gently rolled her onto his open palm. The kitten looked so much smaller than Clea remembered. She choked back her own tears as Ren got to his feet. He faced the group, but when he spoke, it was to Addy alone.

"Addison, your kitten's not dead. I can feel a heartbeat. It's very faint. We need to get her to a vet."

Great gasps of relief broke from Addy's throat. "I know where the clinic is," she managed. "I can show you."

"We'll take my car. Clea, you drive. Paul, Rikki, you two wait here for us."

Hurriedly Clea tossed Rikki the house keys. Ren moved on ahead, still cradling the kitten with Addy all but glued to his hip. Clea rounded to the driver's side door while Ren and Addy piled into the back seat. Once in motion, she chanced a look in the rearview mirror. Her passengers huddled close, their hands—two big and two smaller—melded into a cocoon of warmth and comfort for the stricken animal.

Judging by the few remaining spaces in the parking lot, the Pioneer Animal Clinic enjoyed a brisk business. The fact was driven home when the three entered to a chirping-barking-mewling menagerie in the waiting room.

Addy groaned. "We'll never get to see the doctor."

"Don't you worry." Carefully Ren transferred the kitten to the cradle of Addy's arms and strode to the reception counter where he exchanged a few words with the attendant. Clea saw the woman shake her head emphatically until Ren produced a leather bifold and flipped it open. The woman reacted to the gold shield the same as Clea did, by snapping to attention. Addy too perked up in amazement at the power of Ren's badge, for the woman hustled behind a closed door and returned in seconds to usher the newest and most-deserving patient into an examination room. Once there, Addy tenderly laid Kitty-Face on the table. She cooed softly, petted lightly, held back her tears.

"Not exactly SOP," Ren whispered to Clea, "but the occasion warranted a nudge from Uncle Sam."

"Then putting a kink in the rules isn't entirely out of the question with you."

A wry smile tweaked the corner of his mouth. "I supposed you could say they didn't kick me out of New York without a *little* justification."

Just then the door burst open, and a man in a white lab coat charged in. "What's this all about?" His manner was harsh, a sure sign he had been apprised of and was indeed put upon by Ren's method of gaining access ahead of regular patients.

"Are you the vet?" asked Ren.

The man glared and tapped a finger to a plastic lapel tag.

"Sorry to pull rank out there, Dr. Benedict, but this animal is evidence in an ongoing investigation and needs immediate attention."

The doctor's attitude softened considerably as he probed Kitty-Face's limp body. "Hmm. Point well taken. Is this your kitten, young lady?" he asked Addy in a much-altered voice.

She nodded.

"Very sick. And if I'm to help her, you—all of you—must return to the waiting room and let me do the doctoring."

Addy's eyes pleaded against separation from her pet, but she allowed Ren's arm around her shoulder and conceded to being led through the door. Clea was about to follow when Dr. Benedict held up his hand.

"Are you the girl's mother?"

"I am."

"There are papers you'll need to fill out, but if this is what I think it is, we'll be keeping the cat for a day or two. You might as well go on home. The office will call when we have a better grip on a prognosis."

"You mean whether she lives or dies?"

The vet didn't commit to an answer, rather turned abruptly and began to minister to his patient. Clea feared the worse and wondered how best to prepare Addy. She almost missed the doctor's final comment.

"If you have other small pets around, don't let them anywhere near this one's food supply. It's very probably been poisoned."

On the way home Ren drove. Addy insisted on riding shotgun, relegating Clea to the back seat. Her heart labored in the grip of desperate sorrow for her child and overwhelming guilt. It was she, after all, who had told Addy to place the little blue dinner dish by the back door, outside in the open. And worse. Could it be the noise she'd heard earlier and attributed to an aging furnace had actually been a plaintive cry for help—and she'd ignored it?

Eventually the conversation from up front sifted into her consciousness. Over and over Addy grilled Ren: "Kitty-Face wasn't too sick, was she?" "The doctor's good, isn't he?" "Kittens are strong, right? Nine lives. That means she's got eight more to go."

To his credit, Ren offered encouragement but made no promises. Clea remembered he'd had a dog killed by an automobile and knew he would handle Addy with a compassion molded out of personal experience.

Perhaps it was the steadiness of Ren's voice or that a male's assessment of a situation like this trumped that of a mother's, but Addy seemed marginally comforted. As they rolled up to the house, the girl whispered "Thank you" and gifted Ren with a sincere, if weak smile.

Once inside, Clea suggested Addy help Rikki heat milk for hot chocolate—not that cocoa was high on any list of priorities, but the activity would serve to occupy her daughter's mind, at least for the moment. Addy obeyed, though with an obvious lack of enthusiasm.

As pans clattered and cabinet doors banged open and shut, Clea motioned Ren outside and related Dr. Benedict's remark about poison.

He stooped to pick up the food dish, sniffed it warily and frowned. "Is this what the cat ate?"

"I can't be certain, but yes, most likely."

"We'll bag the contents. I'll send Paul to a lab for analysis. Be sure to wash the bowl thoroughly."

"How could that man be so cruel to a defenseless animal?"

"If by *that man* you mean Mr. Sheznesky, it's a bit premature to point fingers."

"C'mon, Ren. Who else? Delbert was a teacher, for God's sake. Always around children. How was it no one recognized this dark side to his character?" Clea shivered in disgust.

"Chilly?"

Even as she shook her head no, Ren folded her in his arms—a Kitty-Face of a different species to be rocked and consoled. He seemed in no hurry to release her, and Clea willingly remained locked in the embrace, her cheek nestled against his shoulder.

The door swung open and Addy's head appeared. Surely she hadn't missed the closeness of her mother and Ren, or the awkward shuffle to quickly put a foot of space between them, but Addy only asked, "Do you want hot chocolate now? It's ready." The remark seemed directed solely at Ren.

"In a minute, honey," said Clea. The door slid shut. "My daughter's either in shock or you've miraculously attained hero status."

Ren chuckled. "Why miraculous? I'd prefer to think Addison merely recognizes my own true self. You know, the Clark Kent type, without a cape under his clothes, of course."

"Oh, brother. We'd better go in while your head still fits through the doorway."

"First, I want to show you something. I found this sticking out from under the food dish on your stoop." All levity vanished as Ren produced a scrap of paper and unfolded it for her to see.

The page had a ragged top edge as if hastily ripped from a small-sized writing pad. Letters had been cut from newspaper stock and affixed to form a sentence:

Keep quiet or else

Clea ground her teeth. "Then it *was* Sheznesky who poisoned the cat. He almost killed Addy's pet, and he did it just to drive home the point he wasn't playing games with the first two notes."

"Whoa. Take a real good look, Clea, and tell me what you see."

She studied the note again, rereading the threat and examining the cut-out letters. Finally she understood what Ren referred to. "It's not like the others, is it?"

"Uh-uh. Not by a long shot."

Chapter Twenty Five

The smell of onions permeated the kitchen. Empty take-out wrappers, wadded into greasy yellow balls, lay scattered over the countertop. At six-thirty the Animal Clinic called and pronounced Kitty-Face out of the woods and resting comfortably. Thus assuaged, an exhausted Addy migrated to her bedroom, and the four adults left behind heaved a collective sigh. One by one their faces recast from masks of support and encouragement for Addy to more somber reflections of the situation at hand. They adjourned to the dining room table where Ren introduced the latest knot in an already convoluted chain of events. He produced the third note, passed it around and directed Clea to itemize what set it apart from the first two.

"Okay," she said. "The paper's different. Smaller in size and lined. And the message is placed up toward the top, whereas before it was neatly centered."

"Here's one," Rikki chimed in. "The letters are all cut from newspaper, not a combination of newsprint and magazines." Clea opened her mouth to speak, only to shut it again as Rikki continued. "The wording sounds like a line straight out of a Bruce Willis flick—a not-so-good one at that. *Keep quiet or else.* How lame."

"Excellent observation," said Paul. "You'd make one heck of an agent."

Clea jumped in again. "The first two notes were delivered through the mail slot, not left outside the back door. And the other quotes simply implied a threat. You had to read a warning into the words, and given the circumstances, that's exactly what we did. This, on the other hand, is blatant. So, Paul, what do you think? Am I agent material too?"

Paul lowered his head, but the tips of his ears burned red, beacons for all to see.

To divert attention and obviously rescue his friend from embarrassment, Ren thumped the table. "New development. We're dealing with at least two people now, one of whom is connected somehow to the auto repair shop, if only as a customer. We should run through those names and see what pops."

The four agreed. Clea's acquisition of Junior's work log would prove invaluable. Unfortunately, the list had not been duplicated, and Frank Peterson had taken the only copy with him.

"Speaking of Frank…." Ren looked around as if expecting the officer to squeeze out from behind a kitchen cupboard. "Has anyone seen him?"

"Wasn't he supposed to be at your two o'clock meeting?"

"To be truthful, Clea," said Ren, "when you failed to show, I completely forgot. Paul? Did he contact you or you him?"

"Nope."

"I held down the fort till Clea showed and Addy called," said Rikki, "so he wasn't just late, he was AWOL."

"I'll see what I can find out." Paul stepped into Clea's workroom to use his cell phone, reappearing moments later with the news. "Said he'd bitten off a lot, what with interviewing neighbors and running down those LEC numbers. His schedule fell apart. He lost track of time, and the house was empty when he finally got there. He's on his way here now."

Clea knew Peterson hadn't spent all his time chasing down leads. She had encountered him on the street and assumed Ren had sent him, a thing Ren would not have forgotten he'd done. No, Peterson had not acted on Ren's instructions, and Clea intended to ask him why.

While they waited for the officer's arrival, discussion centered on a course of action. The two professionals waved aside any suggestion to interrogate Junior directly. If he was involved—and at this juncture, no name had been crossed from the list of suspects—a confrontation would be a sure tip-off they were narrowing in.

"In that case," said Clea, "I have a confession to make." She related cornering Delbert in the church. The details, when retold, sounded ludicrous and might have elicited laughter if not for the gravity of the third warning letter and the subsequent cost to Addy's kitten. "So if you're worried about clueing in anyone to what we're doing, I suppose you could say I managed to single-handedly spill *all* the beans. I think it's way too late to keep a low profile."

While Clea spoke Ren's hand traced the line of his jaw. He eyed her with a look that vacillated between admiration and concern. But it was Paul who spoke next.

He reported using Bureau equipment to study the postmark from the package containing the rose pin that had been mailed to Clea's mother. Though not one hundred percent successful, enough of the zip code had been reconstructed to indicate posting from the Philadelphia area, a hunk of real estate so densely populated the chance of tracking down the sender catapulted out of the range of possibility. Unless Clea knew of a Philadelphia connection, that clue had brought them to an impasse. The mysterious Gift Giver #21 would remain just that, a mystery.

"Thought I'd get the bad news out of the way first," Paul said, then continued with what he considered—to Clea's dismay—the *good* news: how he had correlated the twenty-nine names on the list to children kidnapped years ago.

Ren clapped Paul on the back. "Good work, Francesco."

Their jubilation dragged Clea's spirits even lower. The investigation seemed to have picked up speed and was now hurtling forward like a sled on an icy hill, hell bent for disaster. Circumstances, however, left her no choice but to wax the runners. After all, she'd already told Rikki. The men would have to know.

She fretted at a wayward thread along the hem of her blouse and hesitantly related her own Internet search which culminated in Kevin Warner's portrayal and indictment of the Rose Society. As her account unfolded, it scored a captive audience.

The Society's beginnings, like everything else about it, were shrouded in secrecy. Kevin Warner, a now-and-again reporter looking for a big break, had stumbled across its existence. He had been doing background research on prominent LA families with the power and resources to wield unusual influence in the city. Those legitimately wealthy and politically successful were scrutinized side by side with those of questionable repute or who had ties with organized crime.

Information on one particularly troubled marriage caught his interest. The interest soon warped into obsession. As he delved beneath the outer layers of respectability, a new drama emerged, and his original story fell by the wayside.

A divorce had led to a custody battle. The war between parents escalated. Just as power, money and influence—aided by a dose of back-alley persuasion—claimed victory in the tug-of-war for a 14-month-old son, the toddler disappeared.

Snatched.

The mother—possessing little clout within the legal system—vanished too.

No ransom note was received and, despite Herculean efforts, neither child nor mother ever resurfaced. Over time the case grew cold and worked its way to the back burner.

Intrigued by elements of the police investigation, Kevin Warner probed deeper and wider, discovering similar cases in which heated exchanges, charges of abuse, anger and threats, peppered the proceedings until a child and mother disappeared—gone, like dust in a hurricane. Without proof of anything, Warner pieced together components of a number of like cases into one scenario.

The losing parent—most always the mother—went to ground, kidnapped her own baby, and placed it under the protection of a stranger, whose sole purpose was to pass the child secretly into the care of another stranger, on and on, over a wide-spread web of safe houses. Each hand-off obscured the trail. The mother too fled, cast off her identity, and took up another, perhaps a third or fourth, until her former self no longer existed. Only then did the circle of flight close and mother and child reunited.

Help came in many forms. Sympathetic people opened their hearts to clear the way through overwhelming odds to a new life. The illegality of the entire operation was ignored. Dedication to the cause was absolute. No one quit. No one told.

An anonymously delivered rose, marked by the removal of its thorns—all but one—triggered the machine. Each person executed one small service, a wafer-thin slice of an overall plan. Secrecy was paramount. When a child was received into a home, it was hidden until a predetermined date and time when the caretaker, after sending ahead another signal rose, moved the child further along the chain.

So many details were frightfully familiar. A concealed room. Roses. The tight network of close-mouthed co-conspirators. Only one conclusion awaited at the end of Clea's tale—her mother's deep involvement. Tears threatened, and her fingertips throbbed with the phantom pain of twenty-nine thorn pricks.

A sharp rap on the door never registered until Ren shoved back his chair, disappeared for a moment, and returned with Frank Peterson in tow. His ill-fitting uniform emphasized his abundant frame. Despite the warmth of the kitchen, he tugged the sleeves lower as he joined the group.

To Clea's relief, Ren paraphrased her story.

"Did you make a copy?" Paul wanted to know.

"No. I have only this." She handed him the small sheet of paper on which she'd saved the path to the website.

Paul perked up. "Outstanding. I want to see the thing in whole. I'd better get myself on over to the house and pick up a laptop."

"I have a computer."

Everyone jumped, for Addy had entered the room on stockinged feet. Clea searched her daughter's face. At what point during the conversation had she come in? How much had she heard? What required explaining and what could be withheld?

An edgy silence enveloped the table, for the idea of including Addy in their confidence had never been broached. Even Frank Peterson seemed intimidated by the teenaged girl who planted hands on her hips and stared down the room.

Paul wriggled in his seat. "No good without a printer," he said weakly.

"I have a printer."

"Oh." He shot Clea a hopeless glance then cast his eyes downward and proceeded to chase a wayward crumb across the tabletop with his thumbnail.

"It can wait, hon." Clea reached out for her daughter but caught only air as Addy maneuvered out of range.

"You always treat me like such a kid, Mom. Is this about Daddy?"

"No. Why would you think that?"

"Then grandma. Tell me. I can take it. Is she dead or something?"

"No, of course not. I'd never keep *that* from you."

"Then you *are* hiding something."

Clea flinched. It had been her mistake to underestimate Addy's quick mind, but to burden a child with the implications inherent in the Rose Society was untenable. Clea would protect her from that truth at the risk of heaping one more lie onto the pile.

"Remember last week when I showed you an old photo and said I was curious who the woman in it was? She may be a long-lost relative. We're trying to find her. That's all."

"It takes five people to do that?"

"Well, it became a bit sticky. I called in the cavalry and here they are." The gallant attempt at humor nose-dived when Addy didn't budge.

"If it's got to do with you, it's got to do with me. That makes it more my business than any of theirs."

"True...but you have schoolwork and they don't. Best you get at it, too. Soon as I put a name to that face, I'll tell you."

"Swear?" Addy flashed defiant eyes on Ren. "Make her swear."

He raised both hands as if confronted by a mugger in a dark and deserted park.

"I promise, sweetie," said Clea. "Okay?"

Addy's indignation deflated into slumped shoulders. She mumbled "okay" and headed back to her room.

Once the girl was out of earshot, Ren tapped his palms together in muffled applause, fanfare to Clea's handling of the matter. However, further discussion now seemed unwise. The meeting broke up.

Paul and Rikki departed first. "We almost slipped up big time, didn't we? I feel terrible," said Rikki on her way out the door. "Here." She pressed a thin wad of singles into Clea's hand. "Don't know how else to make up for it. The least I can do is contribute to her stereo fund."

Frank followed. Once he wedged himself through the doorway, he gestured Clea outside. In a downright normal voice, he confided. "People tell me I come across a little too strong—oh, hell, pain in the ass is what they really say—but I'm on your side, Clea. A blind man could see you were suffering in there. If you want to put the brakes on this whole thing, I'll do my damnedest to shut down the investigation. Davis doesn't have the last word, you know, even though he may think he does."

"Thank you, Officer Peterson."

"Frank. It's just plain Frank to you."

"I appreciate your offer. I'll keep it in mind."

"Think about it. You have a little girl to worry about."

He turned and was halfway down the flagstone walk when Clea softly called his name. "Frank, tell me honestly. If you learned a secret like this about *your* parents, what would you do?"

It was a moment before he haltingly faced her, cheeks and brow chiseled deep with lines of concern. "I…I ain't never been married, never had kids, but my ol' man's still kickin'. Family is family. By what I mean…well, it's human nature to look out for one's own." He drove all ten fingers through his hair. "Everyone's situation is different. It's a decision only you can make."

On that perplexing note, he lumbered off.

Clea stared after him until he was out of sight. His car door slammed, the engine rumbled to life, and still she hadn't moved.

Could Peterson really put an end to all this pain? Her heart skipped at the chance to undo the mess she'd created. But true, blessed ignorance was no longer possible. She couldn't erase memory. Doubt would forever cloud her horizon, and she would always wonder what the final picture would be with all the pieces snuggly fit together.

"You planning to camp out here all night?"

Heat coursed through Clea's body when Ren came from behind and stood next to her, so close his hips and arms molded with hers and sealed off the cold night air.

"You've been worrying again," he said.

"Does it show?"

"Yeah, it does. Right here." Warm lips brushed her temple. Smoothly he turned her. "And a little bit here." His mouth closed over hers.

When the kiss deepened, Clea forgot to breathe. Every prudent cell in her body warned her away, and had she the good sense to listen, she wouldn't have gone on tip-toe to beg for more.

Delicious, forbidden stirrings threatened to drown her in their sweetness. "Mmm," rolled from the back of her throat.

"Ah," said Ren, releasing her. "At a loss for words, I see."

As Clea settled onto her heels, she sucked the taste of him from her lips. Was she losing her mind or just plain foolish? She needed to think so stepped away. Once apart, a damp chill reminded her they were still outside.

"It's cold…and late too. I'd better get inside."

Ren held the door open as Clea entered the kitchen and savored its inviting warmth. She turned to say "Good night," surprised when he followed her inside. Immediately she spied a leather bomber hung on the back of a chair. Of course, he wanted his coat. She crossed the room, lifted the jacket by the shoulders and held it out for him, surprised a second time when he walked by, on course for the living room.

There he wandered the length of the room, stopping first at a curio cabinet then on to a bookcase, where he inspected titles. From there he drifted to the coffeetable which held a small collection of sculpted angels and what was easily identifiable as a pair of men's undershorts.

Clea choked. Damn that Michael. Gone, and still a royal pain.

Devilish crinkles spidered from the corners of Ren's eyes, but when he started to pick up the offending item, Clea rushed forward and thrust his coat at him.

"Like I said before, it's getting late. There'll be a lot to do tomorrow. I'd like to get to bed. You better get on home too."

The jacket dropped in a heap on the floor. "You don't think I'm leaving you and Addison alone?"

"Ren, we'll be all right. We have a brand new lock, remember? Besides it's far too cold for you to be sitting out in your car all night just to keep an eye on the house."

"The car isn't exactly what I had in mind." A blush spread over Clea's cheeks when Ren plumped a throw pillow and tossed it on the couch. "This'll do…unless, of course, it's already been reserved."

"You can't be serious."

"Dead serious."

"I won't allow it."

Ren picked up the green and white afghan that lay on a nearby chair, and with one dramatic flick spread it over the sofa cushions. "You've been outvoted."

"For God's sake, Ren, my daughter's not twenty feet away."

"All the more reason I'm staying."

Clea's temper soared like mercury to heated indignation, but she knew she was defeated. To physically extract him from the premises was beyond her strength, and she could come up with no challenge to which his answer wouldn't be the same.

She stalked across the hallway to her bedroom. "Lights out at eleven," she growled and slammed the door.

Self-imposed confinement did little to bring calm. She paced the room until spent, then gave up and went to bed.

Sleep did not follow.

The hush of the house as well as a pale crescent moon that softened the darkness paved the way for thoughts of other nights and other times. Her mother's presence loomed large. Idyllic scenes of years past butted images conjured by recent events. Control fell away, replaced by a sob.

And then another.

And then another.

Once the tears began, she was lost in the terrible knowledge that nothing would be the same again. No matter how many good intentions might be tallied for the Rose Society, it was wrong. It was illegal. And worse, it was her mother's legacy.

Clea didn't hear the door open nor see the figure cross the room. She was only aware of his presence when he sat on the bed and wrapped her in a protective embrace. He said things like, "It'll be all right" and other things that really had no words, but comforted nonetheless. He settled next to her, separated by a blanket, united by something more. Soon the hysteria drained away...and the fear...and the bone-crushing sadness.

Clea slept then, glad, after all, she had lost the argument with Ren.

Chapter Twenty Six

Strident cries of gulls and the rush and ebb of waves pierced the mantle of fog that had descended over Cannon Beach. The great hulk of Haystack Rock, for all its size, was virtually invisible. Ren and Clea sought the high tide mark and spread a blanket, sitting on a narrow swath of its hem while the rest they tented over their shoulders and snugged tightly around their necks. For awhile they watched a smattering of hardy souls walk the shore, one indistinguishable from the other, ghostlike blurs gliding over the sand.

Earlier Ren had seen Addy safely to school. If the girl noticed his car had not moved from where it sat the evening before, she never let on. Upon his return he called a day off—at least a morning—and he and Clea had driven to the coast. Good weather or bad, Cannon Beach was Clea's favorite spot.

"That first time I called you," he said, "you were here."

"A wonderful place to sit and think, wouldn't you say?"

He swallowed a groan. "Actually I prefer doing my sitting as well as my thinking in a nice cozy room—"

"This isn't cozy?"

"…with a glass of Kentucky's finest firmly in hand."

"Well, you're out of luck in the whiskey department. Coffee'll have to do." She pulled a silver thermos from her carry-all bag and twisted off the lid. "We'll have to share. I forgot to pack a second cup. Black okay?"

"I don't care if it's green as long as it's hot."

"I see New York produced its fair share of wimpy boys."

"And I suppose Bigfoot runs more to your taste."

Last night Clea thought she'd never smile again, much less laugh, so when she did, she stopped pouring to listen and appreciate the sound. It penetrated the fog bank, then rang back at her like the bell on a lightship. She corked the thermos and stowed it. "Now to work."

"Wait a minute. What happened to a few hours' R and R?"

"Don't worry. No heavy lifting involved."

Clea tipped her bag on its side. Two thick envelopes tumbled out, the print order Rikki had finally liberated from Walgreens. She broke the seal on the first packet and fingered through the shots while Ren looked on.

"These are good," he said. "Dunes, right?"

"Uh-huh."

"And yet you're frowning."

"Color balance is way off. Mitz always fine tunes my photos. And see, dirty solution." Her thumbnail scraped across a dark smudge that marred an otherwise well-composed scene of land and sea.

Ren took the picture from her and held it up, angling it this way and that in the limited light. "Not a flaw...a face."

"What?" She squinted at the photo. "My God, you're right."

Heads together, they searched the remainder of the prints, but only one had captured the distant image of a man staring through blades of beach grass. Breath hissed between Clea's teeth at the memory of the stranger who had followed her and Rikki into the preserve. Her skin gathered into knots.

"With everything that's happened since, I'd almost forgotten about him. I also haven't seen him. Could that mean he's been scared off?"

"That's one possibility."

She wanted to ask him what another was, but the stony look on Ren's face warned her to keep the question to herself. Instead, she tried to be helpful. "If I were to enlarge the—"

"Good idea. I want to see for myself what that bastard looks like."

Now their attention zeroed in on the second package which contained Clea's photographic inventory of all the rose-related memorabilia scoured from Josephine's possessions. In hindsight, the effort to catalog the items proved a waste of time. The knickknacks and cheap trinkets were unremarkable, impossible to trace, difficult even to determine if they had been gifts or Josephine's own purchases.

The oil paintings, though unique, had also led to a dead end. Ren related his inquiries into the auction houses listed on the backs of the canvases. One no longer existed. The other offered minimal help other than to educate him in the practice of allowing anonymous bidding and purchases through agents. In either case, divulging the identity of a buyer was easily circumvented. To prove the point, a search of their records turned up nothing.

While the trail of the rose-shaped pin suggested a Philadelphia connection, that too could be bogus—a package dropped off on a business trip or mailed through a friend.

The Rose Society had indoctrinated its members well. They obviously guarded their anonymity with ferocious single-mindedness.

"I blame myself," Clea said on a sigh.

"Don't beat yourself up."

"If I'd only been smart enough to recognize Mom's fascination with roses as something more than a simple hobby, I might have asked the right questions, pressed harder when it was possible to get answers."

Ren leaned forward so he could face her straight on. "Martha…that's my Aunt Martha…had this passion for fish…glass ones that she parked all over her house. Of course, if Paul digs up some dirt on a Fish Society somewhere, this analogy won't be worth a damn, but what I'm trying to get across is one thing doesn't necessarily lead to the other. There's no logical connection. Your mother certainly didn't assume one, otherwise she wouldn't have allowed a rose within a hundred yards of your house."

"Thanks for trying to make me feel better, even though I'm not sure it has. I'm torn between what I've lived all these years and what I'm finding out."

"Could be worse."

"How worse? No, don't even try to answer that one. Mom…whom I always considered my soulmate…a criminal. She may not have smuggled diamonds or been a drug dealer—as bad as either of those are—but, good Lord, Ren, she ferried innocent children around the country for the express purpose of keeping them from one parent or another."

"Abusive parent."

"You don't know that for sure. Maybe just a well-connected parent."

"Do you really believe that?"

"Right now, I don't know. It's all so new…and appalling. I try to imagine how those fathers felt. If I lost Addy…like that…into thin air…I'd go insane."

"We've yet to pull together the entire story."

"How much more bad news can there be?"

Ren's arm slid around her waist and tugged her nearer, though they already sat hip to hip. He glanced out over the still-heavily-shrouded beach. "Eventually," he said, "the fog lifts."

"I'm scared of what's behind the mist."

"The truth, Clea. Whatever the truth might be."

It was a moment before she spoke again. "Then the only course of action is full speed ahead."

Ren snagged her hand and pulled her to her feet, stooped to gather their belongings, and set out for the lot where they'd left the car. So much for R and R.

During the ride home Clea speculated on her mother's roses. Aunt Martha's obsession notwithstanding, what if the roses actually did have meaning? Not exactly the same as a secret handshake, more like a badge of honor or a covert sign of participation or approval.

She recalled Mitz's behavior upon seeing the picture of Barbara and the fact she displayed in her shop a large framed photo of a rose which she'd always refused to sell. Was that a giveaway of the society? Junior too. Was he eccentric or suspicious with his calendar firmly stuck on a date long past? Was it there because the picture, as Ren had pointed out, featured a rose garden?

Who else?

Clea admitted she'd never given any thought to a tie-in. As a kid, what decorated other people's homes held no interest. Later, preoccupied with her own life, she never bothered to notice. And now, so many of her mother's contemporaries had passed on or moved away, there was no way to be sure if a connection existed.

She thought about Lydia at the nursing home. Did the unusual threesome of Lydia, Mitz and Delbert in her mother's room that night imply an alliance? Here Clea's theory broke apart. She was acutely aware of Lydia's work station on the third floor and had never seen it adorned with flowers of any sort.

When she voiced her exasperation, Ren offered encouragement. "Not everyone's inclined the same. Some might be scared for themselves or their families, others of exposing the society's existence, if indeed it still exists. That nurse might not have a clue. On the other hand, her house could be plastered ceiling to floor with roses. You've never been there, right?"

"No."

"Keep thinking. In the meantime when we get back to town, we'll hook up with Frank and run through Junior's work log. I'm more concerned about these notes that keep cropping up, and his customer list promises the solidest lead yet."

It was shortly after noon when Clea and Ren arrived at her home, and she had no sooner stepped from his car when a voice called her name.

"Hey! Mrs. Reilly."

A slickly-polished gem of an old car rumbled to a halt at the curb. Its chassis rocked as if engaged in battle between gas pedal and brake. An arm dangling out the window looked vaguely familiar, but Clea had to bend and peer inside to recognize Tommy Aberlane, her neighbor's son.

"Hi, Tommy. New set of wheels?"

"Yeah. Eighty-eight Fleetwood. Ain't she a beaut? Drove by to show the folks." A hamper on the front seat indicated he'd also picked up a load of clothes, freshly laundered by his mother.

"Congratulations! You're moving up in the world."

"Yep, and I'm showing this baby off to everybody."

Clea signaled a thumb's up and backed away from the car, expecting him to rev and run. Although he shifted into drive, Tommy held the car in check. "Oh, by the way, Mrs. Reilly, Mom said you stopped over asking about a man who might've come to your house when you weren't home."

"I did." Clea's hopes soared. "Did she remember somebody?"

"No. I was just thinking it's too bad you weren't looking for a woman."

"She saw a woman?"

"No, but I did."

"Who?"

"Dunno. Some old lady. Was at your front door."

"What did she look like?"

"Couldn't see her face, but if it helps, she was wearing a blue coat. One of those loose hanging jobs with fringe on the bottom."

"You mean a poncho?"

"Yeah, one of those."

Before Clea could question the boy further, Tommy tossed her a wave and rocketed off. She joined Ren on the driveway, noting his frown and the narrowed eyes that followed the old Caddy as it disappeared around the corner.

"What was that all about?" he asked.

"Tommy. Neighbor kid."

"What did he want?"

"Just stopped to say hello and serve up a new complication."

"Huh?"

"Unless Mr. Sheznesky leads a secret life as a drag queen, I may owe him an apology." She filled in the details. "A woman," she continued, talking now only to herself. "But what woman?"

Still deep in thought, Clea unlocked the door. The house had a dreary, unoccupied feel to it. Quiet too, until a watery plop hit the sink. Clea crossed to the faucet and adjusted the taps, scowling at the orange circlet that had blossomed at the bottom of the basin. It struck her how closely recent events resembled the rusty blotch, forming slowly and relentlessly building into an ugly stain. She turned her back on it.

She heard Ren's voice, realized he wasn't talking to her but on the phone. He said, "Bring the log," and she knew it wouldn't be long before Frank Peterson appeared at her doorstep.

An eleven-note melody rang out as Ren dialed again. This time it was impossible to identify who was on the other end because he listened more, his own comments few and generally one syllable.

Trying to walk off a restive, what-do-I-do-now feeling, Clea wandered the room. She heard Ren say, "Got paper?" but dismissed it as more of his phone conversation. When the words were repeated, a little louder and more insistent, Clea snapped out of her daze.

"Sorry. I was somewhere else for a minute."

"Deserted island in the Caribbean?"

"Don't I wish. What was it you wanted?"

"Paper."

She pointed to a counter drawer where Ren found a notepad and ballpoint pen. He sat at the dining room table and beckoned her to join him, then proceeded to tear off three sheets and mark them *Note 1*, *Note 2* and *Note 3*. These he arranged in order and began to jot down every known fact about each one, duplicating information that overlapped so each sheet was in itself complete. Clea added what she could, reminding him that while the four of them—she, Ren, Rikki and Paul—had been privy to all three communiques, Frank Peterson had seen the first but had not been present for discussion of the second or third, while her ex-husband had found and read the second one and been told about the first.

"Of course," said Clea, "the writer was none of these people, but an unidentified, older woman."

Ren corrected her. "Possible writer. And don't forget the third note was composed and compiled by someone entirely different, perhaps an accomplice."

Clea rested her chin on the open palm of her right hand and stared straight ahead with vacant eyes. "A woman," she mused. "One educated enough to quote ancient poets. Here I was so positive it could only be Delbert."

"Maybe the mystery lady's only a courier."

"Ren, if you keep twisting everything around, we'll never get anywhere."

"Only a suggestion."

"But what if that *is* the case? We're back to square one."

"For now. Say, where's Peterson with that worksheet?"

As if on cue a car door banged. In unison Ren and Clea looked up and out the window as Frank dislodged his body from a black and white and labored up the drive.

Once inside, his presence seemed too big for the house, and even though he hadn't uttered more than "howdy-doody" and "Got here as fast as I could," his voice reverberated into every nook and corner.

Clea chastised herself. This aversion to the man's personality had to stop. He was on her side, for heaven's sake, working all hours and producing results. Sympathetic. Kind even. When he spread out the repair log on the table along with several pages of handwritten notes, she found an opportunity for redemption. His uniform sleeve hiked up an inch or two, uncloaking an angry scratch the width of his wrist.

"Frank, that's a nasty cut." She laid a hand gently on his arm. "Looks infected. You stop right there while I go get something for it."

"This?" Frank tugged at his cuff. "It's nothing."

Clea insisted and wasted no time running to the medicine cabinet. She looked for the hydrocortisone and, not seeing it, feared she was out. Then she noticed the bottle of Tylenol on the wrong shelf. Setting right the errant pain reliever revealed the missing ointment.

"Here we go, Frank." She returned, waving the tube like a trophy, and smoothed the salve on his arm. "Lady friend giving you a hard time?"

At first Frank looked bewildered, then laughter burst forth. "No, no, nothing like that. Was bundling brush the other day. Must have happened then. You've no cause to fuss over me, Clea, but thanks." Though he quickly turned aside, Clea was certain she detected a filmy shine to his eyes.

"Okay, okay," said Ren. "If Florence Nightingale here is done, let's move on."

The auto shop list was long which attested to Junior's reputation as a reliable mechanic. Clea marveled how he managed to accommodate a thriving business with only his grandson, Kenny, as help, but popularity had its down side too as she was finding out. Work on her SUV had been delayed yet another day.

Frank had taken the week's worth of entries and revamped them into a single listing with repeat customers eliminated, addresses and phone numbers filled in where none had been, and the patrol cars identified by officers. He had personally spoken to each policeman about repairs and learned that none had waited at the shop but partnered with another officer until the work was done.

He refrained from contacting anyone else, for an official visit had not been Ren's instruction. Instead, he had performed a preliminary check with the state DMV on roughly fifty vehicle owners but turned up nothing. Law-abiding citizens, one and all.

As Clea perused the list, many of the names were quite recognizable—people from church, former classmates, shop clerks, her own clients, there probably because she had recommended Junior's services. Other names were familiar, though it was difficult to pair them with faces. Still others she didn't know at all.

They argued over which end of the spectrum to focus on. Clea voted for the unknowns, disbelieving her friends and acquaintances could be involved. Ren tried to persuade her strangers had no motive. Frank made the whole thing moot when he told them Sheriff Summers had pulled him off the job beginning this afternoon and on through Halloween night.

"She's looking to head off the major pranksters. And there'll be a lot of kids on the streets come Friday. Safety first, you know. I'm yours again on Saturday. Sorry."

Without Frank's extra pair of legs, a thorough follow-up would be physically impossible.

Clea said, "Not your fault."

Ren growled. He pushed off the chair and stomped a lap around the room, muttering about priorities and voicing rather pointed opinions that Clea hoped wouldn't find their way back to the sheriff.

Peterson bounced his shoulders up and down. Orders were orders. What was he supposed to do?

Before Peterson left, Ren calmed long enough to apprise him there had been, in actuality, three threatening letters. He shared the facts, directed Frank to contact him if he had any thoughts on the originators of the notes, and ignored the man's obvious affront at having been left out of the loop till now.

Not long after Frank departed, car doors again announced an arrival. Paul lugged a utility box toward the house—loaded, judging from the way he carried it—while a laptop computer was slung over Rikki's shoulder by its case strap. They'd obviously come prepared for work.

Soon file folders spilled their contents over the tabletop, the papers restrained from cascading to the floor by constant prodding and reshuffling. The session—a handball game of ideas tossed against a wall of four different perspectives to see what bounced back—lasted an hour and ended only when Rikki tapped her watch to indicate the time and volunteered to pick up Addy from school. Clea dug out the negative of the dunes photo.

"On your way," she said, "drop this at Walgreens and order the biggest blow-up they can do on site. Tell them it needs to be done before dinner."

"Wait a sec." Paul intercepted the strip of film. "Isn't your daughter's computer hooked up to a scanner?"

"Sure."

"Then I'll make the copy here. It'll save a trip. Take only a minute or two."

Clea pointed down the hall and gestured left toward Addy's room. "It's a mine field in there," she warned. "Step carefully. And make it fast." She began stacking folders and dumping them into the box. "I want all of this stuff out of sight before my daughter sets foot in this house."

"A need for speed. Got it." Paul saluted with a smile. However, as he walked by the table, a puzzled frown clouded his features. He laid a finger on the photo of Clea as a child, letting it drag slowly from the image of the infant to rest on the young woman called Barbara. "Something bothers me about this picture. I wish I knew what."

Chapter Twenty Seven

"**No,** Mom. Don't do that."

Addy rushed through the door. School books cascaded to the floor, and in a burst of energy she covered the ten feet of kitchen to where Clea stood with the cookie jar in her hands. She grabbed it and tried to wrest it from her mother's grip. Clea pulled back, more in surprise than anything else, the perfect cartoon of a bizarre tug-of-war over a ceramic pig.

Until a minute ago Clea had all but forgotten the little pile of bills Rikki had given her the previous evening. Outside contributions to Addy's babysitting money had always been made on the sly, so, adding four dollars of her own, Clea had hurriedly hauled down the pig. In another few seconds she would have stashed the cash, Addy none the wiser. Unfortunately, her timing was a bit slow.

The girl's reaction troubled her more than being caught. Surely Addy didn't think she was taking money out. With an expression that gouged her eyebrows into a tight "V," Clea wrenched the jar free and yanked off its lid. Her mouth dropped open.

"It's empty. Where's all your money?"

"That's my business."

"Watch your tongue, young lady, and answer the question."

Addy hung her head and mumbled.

"I can't hear you."

"I said…"—now defiant—"…Daddy needed it. He couldn't find his wallet when we went shopping at the mall, so I let him borrow some of my money."

"*You* gave him close to two hundred bucks, so *he* could buy you new clothes?"

"He said he'd give it back."

"And you believed him."

With a fist Clea dug at the hurt between her eyes, a sorrow bordering on pain that Michael would pull a stunt like this on his own flesh and blood. The cash was gone, of that she was sure. Some in a splash to play the big shot. Anything over and above into his pocket. What a jackass!

Clea set the cookie jar aside and folded Addy into her arms. "Don't worry, honey." What else could she say?

Teardrops dampened her blouse where Addy sobbed into her shoulder. Eventually the sounds quieted. Addy stepped away and dried her cheeks with the backs of her hands.

"He's not going to pay me back, is he?"

While Clea searched for the proper words—those that would not judge Michael too harshly yet break the news the savings were indeed gone for good—Addy's face settled into one of knowing. Her eyes aged even as Clea looked on, leaving no doubt Addy knew the truth about the money, and bigger truths about her father.

The girl shrugged. "No big deal."

But to Clea it was a big deal, a very big deal. Addy had flung open a door into the world of adults, an alien land peopled not only with those who loved, but those who disappointed and deceived, who raised hopes then walked away. How would the experience change her daughter? Make her stronger or break her spirit? It felt as though a hangman's noose encircled her heart and someone had tightened it with a mighty yank.

Although Ren and Paul wisely turned their backs on the scene, and Rikki pretended to pick lint from the dining room draperies, Clea sensed Addy's embarrassment at having an audience. She hooked an arm around her daughter and steered her toward the back of the house.

In the quiet of the bedroom, Clea expected Addy would settle down to the business of hashing through her feelings, so she sat on the edge of her bed, inviting her daughter to do likewise with a hand-pat on the daisy-festooned spread. But Addy was restless. She wandered first to the window, then plopped in a chair only to bounce up, jack-in-the-box fashion, and on to her mother's dressing table. There she shuffled perfume bottles and pill boxes like rooks in a game of chess.

Clea welcomed the reprieve, in truth, petrified of the moment her daughter would turn, anticipating pearls of motherly wisdom when all she had to offer were clichés.

Eventually their eyes met in the mirror.

"Come and sit down, honey."

The girl complied.

With featherlike strokes Clea brushed an unruly curl from Addy's forehead. "People aren't always what they seem at first. It's a terrible thing. We can wish them to be something they're not. And for awhile we can even trick ourselves into believing they've become what we want them to be. But in the end, a leopard is a leopard. His spots aren't going to change. Not for me. Not for you."

"Daddy's a leopard, isn't he?"

Clea nodded solemnly.

"I just thought if we all could spend time together...."

"I know."

The room grew heavy. The silence palpable. Other than a storm of dust motes whirling through a shaft of failing light, the only movement was Addy's hands, clasping and unclasping like the beat of a troubled heart.

Finally Addy said, "If I could make the days go backwards, I don't think I would email him again."

"Sometimes it's good to make a mistake, sweetie, if only for the lesson you learn."

"He's not coming back." A statement, not a question.

"No. I don't think so."

"I was so wrong. I feel stupid."

"Shh. You weren't the only one fooled."

"He didn't even say goodbye."

At this point Addy took a deep breath, sucked from the bottom of her soul and expelled in a long and cleansing sigh. In that one whoosh of air, Michael Patrick Reilly made a final exit.

They hugged then, Addy and Clea. Closer for sharing. Bound by this common understanding: As Clea and her mother had been over a lifetime, now Clea and Addy would find their strength in one another.

"But...," said Addy, "don't you ever wish it was more than just you, me and grandma?"

"Aren't we enough? The three Musketeers?" Clea brandished an imaginary sword. "Besides, Rikki's like family. And we have friends. You've a new friend at school and more will come along, you wait and see."

"Not the same, Mom."

"No, but it'll have to do."

"I suppose." After a pause Addy sneaked a sidelong glance and coyly added, "What about Mr. Davis?"

The question caught Clea completely off guard. Although an intriguing premise, she didn't know herself when or if or how Ren fit into the future. It had been a long time since someone had wanted her and even longer since she had wanted someone to want her. To sort it all out was near impossible, even if she'd had a moment's peace in the last few days to attempt it.

When a soft rap on the door afforded a way out of answering, Clea grabbed it and leaped to her feet. "Come in."

The door cracked open.

"Everything okay in here?" asked Rikki.

"We're having one of them heart to hearts." Addy rolled her eyes and giggled, signaling the Reilly household was well on its way to a return to normal.

"Then you've *got* to come see this." Rikki held out a hand to Addy and winked at Clea. The three filed into the hallway. A heady bouquet of Italian spices drifted from the kitchen. They followed the aroma until a good view of the stove revealed Paul, outfitted in one of Clea's frilly aprons, waving wooden spoons over pots aboil like Maestro conducting a symphony.

Rikki ribbed Clea with an elbow and whispered, "And. He. Cooks."

Simultaneously the three girls burst into laughter, prompting Paul to set aside the utensils, clutch the hem of the apron and execute a grand if awkward curtsy.

Ren sat apart on a chair isolated from the activity, engaged in animated conversation on his cell phone. At their arrival he looked up and shifted the receiver to his other ear, the one further from the group. He barely acknowledged their presence. After a moment he rose and made for the back door, pulled it open, and disappeared on the other side.

Strange. Clea stared at the blank slab of door. The sudden vanishing act seemed so un-Renlike. Her second thought was a reminder she truly didn't know the man well enough to separate unusual behavior from the quirks that defined his personality. No wonder Addy's probing question had so unsettled her.

Ren Davis had been a bundle of contradictions from the get-go. Closer scrutiny, however, would have to wait. As Clea looked on, the door again swung wide. It struck her how Ren's presence filled a room, and this before he'd even crossed the threshold.

"Paul," he called, though his eyes and a broad grin seemed reserved for Clea. "Francesco's *ristorante* open for business yet? I know it's early,"—this to all occupants of the room—"but we skipped lunch. How about it, Addison? Hungry? Paul's whipping up a mean mostaccioli."

"Sure. It almost smells good enough to eat."

"Hey!" Paul complained. He balled up a dish towel and tossed it at Addy. "I'll have you know I'm a fantastic cook. Learned from hanging around my mama's kitchen."

"Yeah," said Ren, "and it's a good thing he got transferred to the downtown office when he did. If he'd stayed living at home any longer, wolfing down his mother's cooking...well, let's say Paul would give Frank Peterson a run for his money when it comes to pant size."

After a chorus of laughter, Addy volunteered to set the table. The jovial mood continued throughout dinner. Topics tainted by unpleasantness were scrupulously avoided in favor of lighter fare. Addy pelted them all with questions.

Had Ren and Paul ever been to the Statue of Liberty?

Where did Rikki learn to French braid her hair?

What was the difference between virgin olive oil and extra virgin olive oil?

To Clea's amusement Addy brought up the subject of Ren's name, insisting Ren had to be a nickname and grilling him on what it was *really* short for. He protested loudly though good-naturedly. A Reilly conspiracy he called it. Paul pleaded the Fifth.

The only bump in an otherwise convivial dinner was when Ren's phone rang and he stepped aside to answer it. If he returned wearing a thoughtful expression, it soon vanished in the wake of lively table talk.

When the pasta bowl had been ladled clean and the last of the garlic bread disappeared in a pass among five eager diners, conversation finally petered out. The silence stretched on. It wasn't strained, rather a comfortable lull in which to savor not only a delicious meal but excellent company.

Addy's voice eventually broke the silence and like a period marked the end of dinner. "I have to go to the library," she said. "Mom, can you give me a lift? Cynthia's helping me with a project. I'll see if she can meet me there and then drive me home. Even if she can't, I still need to go."

Necessary arrangements were made, and the men relegated to sink-and-towel duty. Rikki insisted on staying behind while Addy impatiently urged her mother to hurry. Clea rushed about grabbing coat and phone, purse and keys. She was only seconds slower than Addy, yet the girl was already in the car, buckled up and leaning on the horn.

In sharp contrast to Clea's previous excursion, when a proper library hush enveloped the rooms, this evening the building bustled with students and other patrons. Addy deserted her mother in the lobby and headed for the reference area.

Clea followed, but at a measured pace. The unexpected meeting that night last week with Delbert Sheznesky, as well as his peculiar behavior then and now, left her with a sense of foreboding. She stopped outside the reading room for a peek at its occupants, hoping against hope he would not be there.

Several men pored over various newspapers, but otherwise the room was empty, as was Merriam's desk when Clea entered the library proper.

Here activity was a different story. Memories of her own high school days reared like dragons aroused from slumber. A paper due. A project put off till the last minute. She remembered the panic well and could see it in these students' frantic eyes. Some parents, enlisted to the task, removed books from shelves or fingered through encyclopedias. Others stood by like dour-faced generals commanding the troops against the twin enemies of time and the paucity of materials.

So as not to disturb her daughter, Clea stayed clear of the work table where Addy sat dwarfed behind a stack of what looked like phone directories but could have been almost anything. Instead she wandered crowded aisles.

Her daughter approached her once. "Mom, you don't have to stay. Cynthia's on her way."

But Clea wanted to be sure.

Not ten minutes later she happened to round an end cap display of atlases just in time to see the blond and pony-tailed mentor arrive. They exchanged queenly waves. Clea pointed to the table Addy had commandeered. Her job was done, but still she ambled through the stacks, worried to leave Addy alone even with the crowd about...or perhaps because of it.

To while away the time, she absently pulled a random volume from the rack and read the title. *Computers For Dummies.* She chuckled. Talk about serendipity. She had just reshelved the book when an urgent tweedling sound escaped her pocket. A cellular phone. The ring was foreign. The instrument, when brought to light, was definitely not hers. She'd picked up Ren's phone in error. But mistake or not, it demanded attention and left Clea to wonder what she was to do with his incoming call?

Several women registered their opinion of the disruption with blistering frowns. Clea hurried toward the outer doors, accumulating additional scowls along the way, still not sure what to do as the fourth ring, then the fifth disturbed the peace. She had gotten no farther than the librarian's desk when, decision made, she jabbed the talk button.

It was disorienting at first to hear a stranger's voice, interrupted mid-sentence. The caller, a woman, was in the process of recording a message. Through some glitch in the system, perhaps the timing of Clea's connection, the voicemail remained open and functioning and the caller unaware someone shamelessly listened in.

"...arrange for the transfer once the information is all in. Good show, Ren. This is great news. Call me when the details are nailed down."

The line went dead, leaving Clea halfway between regret at having eavesdropped and unabashed curiosity at the cryptic message.

The first thing to pop into her mind was Ren's ex-wife. Had there been a reconciliation? Experience told her marital harmony wasn't so easily or quickly restored. Ren had spoken dispassionately about his marriage as if it was one of life's chapters, written and later discarded as unworkable. Besides, outside the use of Ren's first name, the message struck a more official, businesslike note.

So who had called?

The woman spoke with an East Coast accent, New York if one relied on Hollywood for authenticity. Propriety flew out the window. A single push of a button and the incoming call history filled the cell phone's viewing screen. The last number received bore a 212 area code and the designation "office." The word "office" altered the script. Cross out the former Mrs. Davis.

Clea knew 212 wasn't a Portland area code nor that of the local sheriff's department. What office could this mean besides the one Ren had recently vacated in New York City? It fit. From the moment she'd met him, he'd scarcely concealed his opinion the Northwest trailed a sorry second to the Northeast. The oh-so-private phone calls this evening graduated from odd to suspicious. Ren was communicating with the New York office of the FBI, not with good news, but *great* news. There was only one way he could have managed to worm his way into the Bureau's good graces—the promise of a breakthrough in twenty-nine longstanding kidnapping cases, the only *anything* Ren was working on at the moment.

Bitter resentment dug a hole, reached out with bony fingers, and dragged Clea to its miserable depths. Ren had used her, betrayed her confidence. He was willing to throw her mother to the federal dogs, all so he could return to New York the conquering hero. And do it with honeyed words and a smile on his face.

Savage nails dug into her palms. First Michael. Now Ren. Her own stupidity when it came to men surpassed by bounds what Addy felt in regards to her father. Clea wasn't an impressionable teenager. She had read Davis's signals correctly the first time she'd laid eyes on him. Why had she so foolishly allowed herself to be swayed?

Well, as of this minute that was history.

Her mind made up, Clea shoved away from the librarian's station, glad Merriam was out of sight and therefore not witness to what Clea considered her public humiliation. However, she had been leaning heavily against the sturdy desk a good length of time, cutting off circulation to her leg, so on her first step she wobbled and on her second dashed a toe into a soft-sided bag propped alongside the corner of the desk.

The pouch tumbled over. Its contents spewed onto the carpeting. Clea took one look and bit her lip—hard. If she hadn't, she might have screamed.

Chapter Twenty Eight

The objects at her feet were in themselves nothing extraordinary, nothing menacing, yet Clea backed away as from a nest of vipers.

It can't be, she kept telling herself, but *can't be* and what she had seen were one and the same.

She stumbled a little. Regained her footing. Spun around and collided head-on with a book-laden student.

"Hey!" he protested as volume after volume hit the floor like gunshot.

Clea mumbled an apology, but left him standing while she skirted the mess and hurried down a row of new releases, around the end of the aisle into the A through C's where she pulled up sharp. There was Merriam, ever so intimidating from the height of a twelve-inch step stool. The older woman opened her mouth, may have even uttered a greeting. Clea didn't hear. She'd already fled in the direction she'd come from.

Never had the library seemed so large and convoluted, nor the fluorescents so mind-numbingly bright. Clea searched the stacks, a frantic Alice lost in a Wonderland maze, looking for the island of study tables that contained her daughter.

Finally the way cleared. "Oh my God, Addy. There you are." Addy and her friend had been heads down, deep into a four-inch tome. At Clea's voice they raised anxious faces. "Quick. Collect your stuff. We're leaving."

"Mom, I just got here. You can go on—"

"Listen up, Addy. You're coming with me. No ifs, ands or buts."

"But—"

"I said no buts." Clea slammed books into a pile, rounded up papers and colored marker pens. "Check out what you need. Leave the rest."

"Mo-om. You're embarrassing me. A couple hours at the most, and Cynthia's promised to take me home."

Although the two girls sat shoulder to shoulder, Clea had focused a narrow channel of vision on Addy. That changed with the mention of Cynthia's name. Now she earned Clea's full attention, and paranoia kicked in. Who was this Cynthia? And why had she—out of the blue—befriended her daughter? A slimy layer of distrust coated her every thought until she was hopelessly mired in uncertainty.

In the end she merely said, "We're leaving."

Reluctantly Addy shuffled to her feet, mumbled something about her mother having gone berserk, and trailed behind, at the requisite number of paces to properly quantify the injustice of the whole affair.

The short ride home went as expected. Addy slumped in the passenger seat, arms locked across her chest, the look on her face one capable of warning off an entire battalion of irrational parents. When she spoke, the hurt was obvious.

"Why are you acting like such a nut case?"

"I have my reasons."

"You are so unfair."

The accusation stung, mostly because it was true. But what did Addy expect her to say? Someone poisoned your kitten, honey. A strange man has taken up following your mom around town. It's impossible to tell friend from foe. Oh, and by the way, grandma's a felon.

Addy was not prepared for such a conversation. Hell, who was? Though she knew she owed her daughter something, precisely *what* was harder to come by.

While Clea debated, they reached their destination. Home. How she longed for the refuge promised in that single word. She pulled even with the house. Rectangles of warm, inviting light spilled from the windows and checkered the lawn. Cars aplenty lined the street. It appeared Frank Peterson had made a showing too, for a police squad blocked the end of the driveway, effectively trapping Rikki's Jeep and Paul's loaner in while keeping her out.

She parked on the street and shut the engine, grateful when the dash lights blinked off and plunged the interior into a darkness that mercifully concealed Addy's contempt. Hesitantly she slid an arm around her daughter's rigid shoulder. Now or never, she told herself.

"It's difficult to explain what's been going on lately."

"Try."

Clea cringed at the challenge in Addy's voice.

"Well...what I mean is...it's difficult to explain because I can't make sense out of most of it myself." She went on, careful to tiptoe around the particulars. "It's like…like when you have one of those story problems in math and you don't understand the question. How do you answer it? I guess everything began with that baby picture of mine…when I first realized there was a woman in it who I didn't know. You remember the one."

"Yeah."

"As it turned out, I had considerably more questions about it than answers."

"You mean like who took the picture? And why we'd never seen it before? And who sent the pretty pin to grandma?"

Though Addy's curiosity had already branched out from Clea's simple explanation, the now-pliant shoulder under her fingers was encouraging. "Exactly," said Clea.

"What else?"

"Yes, what else? Let's see." Clea mentally checked off that which she didn't want to mention, only to realize the exercise left her with nothing more to tell. "Those things are for me to worry about—not you."

"There you go again."

"Well, I *am* the mom and that's the way it's going to be."

"So why are Mr. Davis and Mr. Francesco always hanging around?"

"They were here to help for awhile, but…not so much anymore."

"Oh." Addy seemed puzzled. "They weren't at the library. What happened there?"

"Sorry about that, hon. I simply overreacted to something I saw."

"What was it?"

Wanting more than anything to put the conversation to bed, Clea forced a laugh. "Would you believe a silly piece of needlework?"

"C'mon, Mom."

"It's the truth." In the dark she raised a hand in oath—her left hand as it turned out, appropriate, she reasoned, for she had, in fact, not told the whole truth—only half. Beyond that, Addy would just have to stew. She opened the car door. "No more talk. Let's say we get inside."

The click of her shoes on the asphalt drive outpaced Addy's, the lengthening distance between them reassurance against a second, more trenchant barrage of questions. As explanations go, Clea's had fallen miles short of its mark. She conveyed neither the gravity of recent occurrences nor the depth of her anxiety about them. Also left unsaid were the square of linen lavishly embroidered with roses which had fallen from Merriam's sewing bag, the pair of tiny Stork scissors that followed, along with an issue of *House & Garden* magazine.

Whether protecting Addy from the stark reality of the Rose Society and all its ramifications was good or bad, Clea wasn't sure. She only knew it was exactly what she was going to do. Her daughter wasn't stupid, and if she allowed Addy to nibble around the edges, before long the girl would be at center target. For now, the less Addy knew, the better.

Convinced she'd dodged the worst of it, Clea waited at the back door with a modicum of relief.

She entered first, Addy having caught up and now at her heels. The spotless kitchen welcomed, though the empty dining room table seemed mildly out of place. This was where the group congregated, but no one was in sight. They *were* here. Evidence was lined up in the driveway, and every light in the house seemed to be adding to her utility bill.

Where were they then?

The answer took the shape of Rikki, who rushed in from the seldom-used living room, her eyes huge and face the color of bleached sheets. A cold trickle of dread stayed Clea's feet. Words formed on both sides of the room but remained unspoken, the language of fear all too well articulated without them. Immediately behind Rikki the doorway filled with strangers—a thin-lipped woman and two police officers, neither of whom Clea recognized.

The civilian seemed to be in charge and identified herself as Ms. Stevens. It was the woman's title that chilled Clea to the bone—social worker from the Department of Human Services. Instinct prompted action. Clea stepped in front of Addy.

"What do you want?" she said, her tone frostier than a Wyoming winter.

Stevens opened a file Clea hadn't noticed before and pulled from it an official-looking document. With half-spectacles riding a face worthy of Madam Toussad's, the woman droned through her canned speech. Occasionally she referred to the page in her hand. A complaint. The need for investigation. A hearing date. Temporary placement.

Immobilized till now by shock, Clea practically spat in the woman's face. "What did you just say?"

"The complainant has alleged members in this household have been threatened by anonymous communications..."

"Who told you...?"

"...constituting a dangerous environment..."

"How dare you...."

"...for a minor child."

"Are you talking about Addy? She's fourteen."

"It's in the best interests of all concerned that said minor child be removed pending—"

"Pending my ass. No one's touching my daughter. Who is this complainant anyhow?"

"Mrs. Reilly, if you would stop interrupting."

On impulse Clea whipped the page out of Stevens' grasp. The two policemen startled to attention and, in unison, took a giant step forward. The social worker waved them back with an upraised hand.

The stare-down between Clea and the woman lasted only a moment and ended with the return of the page. Clea, however, had held it long enough to confirm her suspicion.

She stabbed a finger at the document. "My ex-husband's a Grade A bastard. He doesn't even pay the child support he owes. Why don't you go ask *him* about *that*?"

"Regardless. His concern is for his daughter's safety."

Clea snarled. "That's *my* daughter."

"A hearing will make determination regarding any transfer of custody."

From behind, Addy asked, "What's happening, Mom? Who are these people? What's Daddy told them to do?"

"No one's doing anything, sweetie. A mistake has been made—a big one."

"Mrs. Reilly, I have a court order."

"Let me see that." At this point Ren stepped forward, shield and ID leading the way. Despite Clea's earlier misgivings over Ren's motives relative to the case, the magic of FBI credentials, raining like fairy dust on an Orcian world, gave her hope.

While Ren scanned the page he'd been handed, Stevens scratched a note in her folder. If Clea's confidence had been raised, it was now dashed to cinders, for the woman merely said, "Duly noted, Mr. Davis. But I assure you that piece of cardboard in your wallet carries no weight whatsoever with DHS. Addison Reilly will be coming with me. Today. Right now."

"No!" Clea launched the word like a brick of ice, only to see it fall without effect. The woman had far more practice in tearing families apart than Clea had in holding them together.

"You have no choice, Mrs. Reilly. And these officers are here to help effect a smooth transition."

"Sorry, Clea," said Ren, still scanning the paper. "She has a temporary order of protection, all right. Legal and properly executed. There's nothing we can do."

"Mom?" A terrified Addy stepped into view, but Clea's arm shot out from her side, a protective reflex, as if Stevens were a windshield and Clea had just slammed on the car brakes. She pushed the girl back.

"Like hell there isn't," Clea said. And even though it wasn't fair to expect of Ren the same degree of outrage she felt, she fixed him with an icy glare. "If you won't do something, I will."

What Clea had in mind involved fingers around the woman's throat. It surprised her when Ren seemed to read her thoughts. Calmly and evenly, he admonished her to do nothing foolish. "You'll only make matters far worse."

"You'd be well advised to heed those words," said Stevens. "Now, Addison, go pack a bag with school clothes and such."

"I don't want to go. Do I have to, Mom?"

How could Clea tell her yes? How could she tell her no?

Clea was painfully aware of the odds stacking up against her. Ren was right. An outburst would not help. With one stroke of a cheap ballpoint pen, Stevens would make it part of the official record and play right into Michael's hands. She ground her teeth, willing herself to keep her mouth shut, though her eyes blazed with unbridled hatred.

The brittle moment, which began in silence, ended with Rikki taking Addy's hand. "I'll help you, sweetie," she said softly and led the girl down the hallway.

A nightmare followed.

With Addy out of earshot, Clea's vow fell by the wayside and she unleashed a burst of invective. Refusing to be consoled, she circled the room challenging Stevens repeatedly. What contained her anger and prevented her from physically assaulting the woman were the two large policemen hovering in the background.

That and a wall of muscle. Each time she worked herself into a frenzy, Ren stepped in with a stern warning. If he told her one more time to remain calm, she'd give Mount St. Helens a run for the money and explode. In her frustration, she picked up a tumbler and flung it hard against the wall. The impact crystallized in time as the sound of glass shards hitting the floor seemed to go on forever.

The social worker registered no outward sign of distress, as if such behavior defined the normal course of a day's work. If anything, the self-righteous look on her face became more pronounced. However, the officers, whose hands had been behind their backs, let them slide into view, in close proximity to their gunbelts.

Ren's arms clamped around Clea in an iron grip. "Get a hold of yourself, Clea, or you'll end up in a jail cell."

"So what's your point?"

"You want Addison to see her mother hauled off in cuffs?"

Clea twisted free of his grasp, but the threat had its intended effect.

Addy emerged from her bedroom, bent under the weight of a heavy book bag, a carry-on suitcase bumping her leg with each hesitant step. Red-rimmed eyes testified she'd been crying.

Rikki kissed the girl's cheek. "You'll be home before you can unpack."

"Promise?"

Unable to do any such thing, Rikki made do with a second kiss, then looked helplessly at Clea, who scooped her daughter into a frantic hug. "Be strong, baby. I won't stop until this is all straightened out. And *that's* a promise."

"I hate this," Addy whined. "I hate *him*."

"Shh. Just remember, I love you."

With starched efficiency, Ms. Stevens intruded on the good-bye, and, as Clea watched, the social worker left with her unwilling charge sandwiched between the uniformed guards. A few steps away, Addy turned toward her mother one last time. The porch light reflected eyes moist with tears and a look that reminded her of a wild, trapped animal.

A silver mini van swallowed Addy and Stevens while the cops folded themselves into the squad. For some ridiculous reason they turned on their red and blue bar lights, and the sad parade of two, its grotesquely-lighted drum major in the lead, rolled slowly forward and down the otherwise darkened street.

Clea didn't move. She couldn't bear to close the door. The night air still held a connection, still throbbed with the essence of her daughter. Instead she stared at the curb, her soul as empty as the parking space where the van had been.

Eventually gentle hands eased her into the house and toward the sofa. Clea rubbed her arms, the cold only now seeping through her skin.

Rikki sat beside her. "What are we going to do?"

"We're going to make a stink about this, for damn sure," Ren said. "I'll get the sheriff to intercede. Addison'll be home before you know it. A couple days—"

"Days? I want her back five minutes ago." Clea buried her face in her hands. "She looked so frightened. I was crazy to start poking around in the past. All it's brought is trouble."

"Not so," said Ren. "Knowing the truth is important."

"Maybe for you," she said. "Not for me."

"Now you *are* talking crazy. This thing with Social Services isn't going to fizzle out by itself. It calls for serious damage control. Which means explaining away a lot of things. Which means knowing the facts."

He laid a hand on her arm, but Clea shrugged him off.

"I want my daughter. Beyond that, nothing matters."

"Of course, you do. We *all* want the same."

His comment triggered a chorus of assent, but when he tried a second time to draw her close, Clea shied further away. The mistrust nurtured in the library flooded back. Certain his agenda was heavily one-sided, she didn't want him around. Slowly Clea rose to her feet, the better to face him head on.

"The way I see it, our priorities are at odds." Dipping into her pocket, she produced his cell phone and slapped it into his hands. "Right now, I can't think straight and more than anything I want to be left alone."

"Bad idea, Clea," said Ren.

"Maybe so, but it's *my* bad idea."

She ordered them all out—Rikki, Paul, Ren—and stubbornly refused to listen to any attempt to change her mind. In the end her wishes prevailed.

Once they'd departed, she wandered aimlessly through the house, pausing briefly at her daughter's bedroom door, unable to make herself go inside. The space would be too full of Addy's things, too empty of Addy herself. Returning to the kitchen, Clea slumped against the counter, her eyes awash, her spirit flattened. She didn't see the figure emerge from the living room.

"You don't get rid of me so easily," said Rikki.

One look at her friend and Clea knew, no matter what she'd said before, she was glad Rikki had a stubborn streak of her own. Their tears began to flow. The friends fell into an embrace and hung on tight, wringing from each other a comfort neither could have found alone. Behind them, a sympathetic faucet wept into the kitchen sink, its noisy, swollen drops, plopping furiously onto the ever-widening stain.

Chapter Twenty Nine

Her back ached. Twenty ounce hammers pounded her skull from the inside out, and when slitted open, Clea's eyes burned like acid. At the sound of subdued voices she forced her lids to half staff, only to find a TV news anchor reporting on political unrest in some Third World country.

Clea groaned as memory returned. After she and Rikki had cried themselves dry, they'd migrated to the living room and turned on the television. Volume low, for they weren't interested in entertainment, only mindless, senseless background noise.

They talked quietly about Addy and not so quietly about the soullessness of government in general and Ms. Stevens in particular. At some point, they succumbed to emotional exhaustion and had fallen asleep. Slowly Clea hoisted herself on an elbow and glanced toward the other end of the couch. Rikki looked as uncomfortable as Clea felt. She arched her back until the bones cracked. The disturbance woke Rikki, who shifted position and opened her eyes.

"Good Lord! It's bright in here. Kill some of those lights, will you?" Rikki grabbed a throw pillow and held it to her face.

Stretching the kinks from uncooperative joints, Clea extinguished a table lamp and dragged to her feet, her mind now fully awake and raging against a body slower to respond. "How could I have possibly slept at a time like this? Like Addy doesn't exist. God, I'm the worst kind of mother."

"Don't be silly. You're the perfect mother."

"I don't even know where my daughter is and I take a damned nap."

"News flash! You're human like the rest of us. You needed a dose of Nature's narcotic. Me too, I guess." Rikki sat up straight and scrubbed at her eyes. "What time is it anyway?"

"Nine o'clock news," said Clea, pointing at weather maps on the TV screen.

"Good. It's not too late. Paul and Ren'll still be awake. All we have to do is call."

"No," said Clea. Hostility flared to her cheeks, warming them to a feverish pitch. Why was she forever cursed with deceitful men? Ones who crashed over her like a wave, teeming with life and promise, only to ebb away at the turn of the tide, leaving her high and dry. "No," she said again.

"They'll come right over. I'm sure they will." Pushing herself off the couch, Rikki headed toward the phone. Clea caught her arm.

"Rikki, I may not have been thinking clearly on all accounts tonight, but I meant what I said about that." She briefed her friend on the message she'd heard over Ren's cell phone at the library and the conclusions she'd drawn. "I admit he's been a real charmer. Had me all softened up, but apparently I was only part of the Master Plan." She drove home the point with a sarcastic, mid-air hook of her index fingers around her sum-up of Ren's motives. "I'm wasting no energy helping him anymore. I've far more serious things on my mind."

"Oh, Clea. You're wrong. He likes you, and you're blind if you don't see it. Besides, even if what you say is true…that he wants to crack a big old case…so what? He wouldn't put it ahead of getting Addy home."

"It's not something I'll gamble on. Besides, this is family business."

Rikki wrinkled her nose.

"Don't make those faces. You heard Witch Stevens. His being FBI doesn't amount to a hill of beans. So, there's not much he can do anyway."

"But—"

"Rikki, please. This war is between Michael and me. I can't be distracted, and I've got to handle it on my own."

"You want me out of here, too?"

Clea's tone softened. "You're as close to a sister as I have. *You* I need." Another bout of tears threatened. Clea dug around in her pockets for a handkerchief, without success. It was Rikki who came to the rescue with a crumpled tissue. "See what I mean? What would I do without you?"

"Then you ought to listen to me. Ren made perfect sense when he said you needed facts to fight this thing with Michael."

"What makes you think I have no facts?"

Wide-eyed, Rikki dropped to the sofa and pulled Clea next to her. "Why didn't you say so. C'mon, out with it." She silenced the TV with a click of the remote.

Absent the murmur of voices from the television and with Rikki intent on an explanation, a deadened, cavelike quiet overwhelmed the room.

Clea faltered. For all her talk and certainty a moment before, the void that waited to be filled seemed vast and unforgiving. To speak her theory out loud committed it to scrutiny.

What if it didn't hold up? What if, instead of flooding a spotlight into the darkness, it shone as a feeble pinpoint, easily swallowed by the gloom? What if she was wrong?

"Tell me, Clea."

"Perhaps saying *facts* was a bit ambitious. More like suspicions—but solid ones."

"Stop playing word games. Do I have to pry it out of you?"

Clea drew a deep breath and revisited the evening's excursion, culminating in an inventory of the contents of Merriam's sewing bag.

"I should have realized from the start it wasn't Mr. Sheznesky actually writing up those notes. He wouldn't quote even the most obscure author without giving proper attribution. He was the butt of a lot of jokes in high school for doing just that. And last week when I ran into him at the library, he was still giving credit where credit was due. A habit so ingrained it was automatic, even after being retired for years."

"But Merriam? The librarian? She's...she's...."

"A mouse. I know. On the surface it doesn't seem plausible, does it? But think. She's surrounded by books and newspapers. At the click of a button or flip of a page, any quote imaginable is hers for the taking. And once magazines are converted to microfiche, the old paper copies are discarded, becoming a mountain of raw material for Merriam to snip and paste her way through."

"I get it. The gardening magazine. But the one with the holes chopped out of it... that you found at the car shop. What does it have to do with Junior?"

Clea shrugged. "Perhaps nothing. Merriam's name showed up on the service log. She had her car worked on. Most probably left the magazine there. Why doesn't matter. I was so focused on Delbert at the time, I dismissed any other explanation. Now it all makes sense."

"Sense to you. I don't get it. Why all the cloak and dagger?"

"A question I'll deal with later—after I drop this little bomb on Social Services and get Addy back home."

"Whoa! Slow down."

Though spoken in earnest, Rikki's caution failed to rein in Clea's enthusiasm. She dashed from the room. Pieces of the broken glass still strewn on the floor scrunched underfoot as she crossed into the kitchen, but she paid no heed. Shards embedded into the soles of her shoes and resounded on the tile with every step—a determined click-click-click—giving voice to her state of mind.

"Clea, I said whoa." Rikki ran after her. "What you're planning will only prove Michael's claim valid, that threats *were* made. The so-called danger *is* real."

"Then I'll go to the sheriff first and have Merriam arrested."

"On what grounds? I've read about a zillion detective stories. There's a big difference between flimsy circumstantial evidence and stone hard proof."

Clea stopped dead in her tracks. As compelled as she was by the need to act, to feel she was working towards Addy's homecoming, she could summon no logical contradiction to her friend's argument. In her heart she knew Rikki was right.

"I can't sit here and do nothing at all."

"Then get your coat."

"And leave? What if Addy calls?"

"She'll call your cell. We're going for a drive."

"A drive? Where? It's almost ten o'clock."

"Trust me."

The drive turned out to be a short hop that ended at Green Haven. Rikki eased the Wrangler into a parking stall in the mostly-vacant lot, opposite the pedestrian pathway leading to the nursing home. Twin alpine firs stood sentinel, one on either side of the walk. Not a breath of air stirred their branches. The building itself lay like an etherized giant.

A dim light shone through the glass entrance doors. As Clea stared into the lobby, a dust mop with a plaid-shirted man at the helm, silently crossed into her line of sight and seconds later just as mutely out.

"What good is coming here? Besides, it's late."

"Go on in."

"You haven't seen how Mom's condition has spiraled downhill. And at this hour, she's bound to be asleep."

"Trust me." This was getting to be Rikki's pat answer.

Clea balked. "To be perfectly honest, with all the secrets and lies that have surfaced lately, I'm having trouble coming to terms with who she really is...or was."

"Have you run out of excuses yet?" Rikki nudged her from the passenger seat. "Take as long as you want."

Reluctant feet carried Clea inside. After greeting the first floor receptionist, she encountered not another soul. Even the janitor had steered his broom to parts unknown. Corridors echoed. The elevator waited, door agape.

Clea took her time, torn between warring emotions. On the one hand, she missed the routine of visitation and the sense of normalcy that came with it. The daily contact had always rewarded Clea with the comfort of knowing her small family remained intact. Though Alzheimer's had plowed into their lives like a killer wave, thirty-some years of feeling safe and cherished counted for a great deal.

The innocent discovery of Barbara's photo had changed all that. Had raised the awful specters of kidnapped children, underground societies, dishonesty and betrayal. Her life had become a seismic field of special agents, stalkers, threats and, above all, the loss of Addy. How did she deny her mother's past had been largely instrumental in making this the new norm?

Hesitantly she entered the elevator and pushed the button. The door glided shut, sealing Clea within. The shiny steel panels in front of her were mesmerizing. Thought drained from her head, feeling from her heart, until only a sad emptiness remained. It barely registered when the car bumped to a stop on the third floor. Habit drew her out and past the Georgia O'Keeffe's.

Though it was mid-shift, Lydia was not at the nurse's station. At the sight of the empty chair, a different emotion swept over Clea—that of relief. She could turn and bolt with no questions asked, without having to endure judgmental glances meted out if she chose not to continue on.

For awhile she stood at the juncture of hallways, undecided. Rikki's words made the decision for her. *Trust me.* Clea had nothing to lose with a quick in and out, yet gained deliverance from having to excuse her action—or inaction—to a close and sympathetic friend.

She covered the last few steps. Turned the knob. A bump of the hip cast the die. The door to Room 303 opened. Despite the lateness of the hour and the abundance of bedcovers tucked around Josephine's sleeping form, the room temperature launched an all-out assault. The sickly glow from the over-bed light spread only so far, shrinking the room to a tight little box. The light encompassed her mother, the night stand and windowsill where the long-suffering ivy plant made an heroic stab at life.

The unused rocking chair had been relegated to a shadowy corner. Clea dragged it near the bed and sat. The rhythm of her mother's breathing had an hypnotic effect. Clea's mind skipped back to times when a day's worth of worries disintegrated over a pot of chamomile tea and easy, mother-daughter chatter.

Little by little Clea scooted the rocker closer, palmed her mother's hand like an injured sparrow and pressed her forehead against the heated skin.

It wasn't long before a flood of questions burst free. Previously unasked why's and when's and who's spilled like spring melt down a mountain slope. There would be no answers. Her mother was beyond explaining, yet, surprisingly, Clea felt better. The Rose Society didn't really matter. It was ancient history. It was the stuff of novels and paled in significance when weighed against the true nature of the woman who had raised her. Clea thought of the tiny bulbs she and her mother had once planted in beds around the house. Each spring they battled their way through frozen soil to thumb their noses at winter. Tough little flowers, those crocuses. And not unlike the sense of peace that now shoved into the room…along with something else, something that felt very much like forgiveness.

Once again Rikki's intuition had proved on target. The visit had been cleansing and, in turn, empowering.

Clea released her grip on her mother's fingers only to feel a desperate squeeze in return. Her eyes darted upward and met the one thing she had given up hoping for—recognition.

"Hi, Mom." She said it as if they had come upon each other by happenstance, then quickly, while there was still time, added, "You know I love you."

Josephine's lips parted. "B…B…."

The smile faded from Clea's face. How fleeting the moment of coherence had been. She prayed her words had somehow gotten through.

"Yes," she murmured. "Barbara. I haven't found her yet, Mom. I'm sorry. And…well, I haven't the time to look right now."

Her thoughts shaped around Addy's removal to foster care, but a verbal explanation was stillborn, for Josephine's hand went slack. The deep, steady breathing of sleep was so like when Clea first entered, the intervening period could easily have been a dream.

Rising, she hauled the chair to its corner and tiptoed out the door. From this vantage point, the nurse's pod was visible. Lydia had returned. Beefy forearms rested on the countertop as the woman leaned into conversation with someone just out of view.

Clea hadn't yet taken a step when Lydia's head swiveled ninety degrees. The nurse's mouth dropped open. The fingers of her right hand twitched in a manner Clea often used to brush an uninvited bug from the lens of her Nikon.

Abruptly Lydia vacated her post with a speed reserved for someone younger and slimmer. She quickly approached Clea and planted herself mid-corridor, squarely blocking passage.

"Evenin', Miz Reilly," she said in a voice overly loud, considering the proximity of sleeping patients. "Josie's resting easy tonight."

"So I see. I always hate to find her agitated, as if what's left of life is so burdensome."

"Amen, amen."

"Well," said Clea. "I won't keep you from your work." She offered up a weary smile and attempted to bypass the woman, but Lydia shifted her bulk, again barricading the way out.

"Tain't no bother. Shall we go in?"

"She's fine. Really. I just left. Good night now."

Clea stepped to the side, expecting Lydia would move in the opposite direction, thus facilitating her departure. Instead the nurse repositioned herself, and the path again closed.

"Miz Josie be mighty appreciative of a tuck-in." Lydia spread her arms and shuffled forward, the very picture of a mother hen scooting along a brood of chicks.

A solitary ding traveled along the cross corridor, signaling the elevator's arrival on the third floor. Clea was in no mood for the nurse's persistence and further annoyed that Lydia seemed to deliberately counter her attempts to leave. Besides, Rikki was waiting in the car and Clea wanted to go. She feinted right, and the instant Lydia shifted to follow, she ducked under the outstretched arm and sprinted past without a backward glance.

She hurried around the corner. Too late. A good thirty feet ahead of her, the heavy elevator door slid shut, not, however, before Clea saw a flash of color. She sucked in a gasp. The passenger had been wearing a coat of blue, one that floated loosely and sported a swish of fringe along the bottom hem.

Long-legged strides gobbled the remaining distance. It was Merriam for sure, dressed as she had when delivering the anonymous threats to Clea's door. To catch the woman would physically and finally put the coat and its owner together. The picture, once complete, would be incriminating: blue poncho, roses, books and magazines, a scissors, quotes in abundance, eye witness placing her on the front porch. Means and opportunity. All that was missing was motive. And Clea fully intended to find out about that.

"Wait!" With the heel of her palm, she hammered the call buttons. To no effect. A soft whir grew ever fainter as the car descended in the shaft. Clea reeled back, searched with her eyes for another means of getting downstairs. It took but an instant to pick out a red-lighted exit sign, race toward it, and muscle open the door marked *Stairwell*.

When she burst into the lobby, the receptionist leaped to her feet, setting the swivel chair into a wild spin. The woman's hand flew to her mouth.

"Where is she?" demanded Clea. A glance at the elevators showed both doors open, their chambers empty. "Where did she go?"

The woman shook her head, too flabbergasted to speak.

Clea knew better than to dally. The receptionist was worthless, and trying to calm her enough to respond would waste precious time. A low growl squeezed from the back of her throat as she headed for the entrance doors and out onto the sidewalk.

The Jeep was still parked immediately at the head of the walkway, though the engine idled and the passenger side window had been lowered half way. Rikki was a shadow, slouched low behind the steering wheel as though the extended wait had left her hungry for sleep and she had hunkered down to nap.

"Rikki! Wake up. Did you see her? Merriam. Did you see her come out?" Clea rushed forward, grabbed the door handle and yanked. "Rikki!" One foot cleared the doorwell. Clea's head disappeared into the dark interior. Momentum committed her body to follow. The figure in the driver's seat stirred, unfolded, and bloomed to a size much too large to be Rikki.

Chapter Thirty

"*Paul?*" Except for the stretching, yawning young man—and now Clea—the Jeep's interior was empty. "What are you doing here? Never mind. Did you see a woman dressed in a blue poncho come out that door over there?" Clea twisted in the seat to face the nursing home and stabbed a finger along the concrete walk.

"Sorry, Clea. My eyes must have dropped shut for a second."

"Damn. I missed her by a minute—less than a minute."

In answer to Paul's quizzical look, she rattled off an abbreviated version of the narrowly-missed confrontation with Merriam. The information sparked a great deal of interest. Paul straightened into Bureau-esque attention. Rapid-fire questions followed until Clea could offer nothing he didn't already know. By mutual, unspoken understanding, they fell silent and each began a visual, if unrewarded, scan of the parking lot and lawns.

When nothing and no one materialized, Clea slumped against the seat, body language plainly scaling from heightened anticipation into resignation, bottoming out with a sigh. That's when she gave him the once-over.

"What's going on here, Paul?" Irritation colored her voice. "I distinctly remember arriving with a driver of a different gender."

Paul's professional manner morphed into a sheepish squirm. "Rikki's idea, not mine."

"How come that doesn't surprise me?"

When prodded, he recounted Rikki's phone call laying out the scheme she'd hatched that would put Clea and Ren on working terms again.

"So, why are *you* here?" she asked.

"The word *abduction* comes to mind—but only because Rikki insisted." Paul raised his hands in defense. "She thought it best her idea be executed in stages."

"Hmm. The man's a real chicken."

"Huh?"

"Oh, nothing. What if I resist?"

"Are you planning to?"

Clea threw her hands in the air and let them fall limply to her lap. "Doesn't seem to matter to anyone anymore what I think."

"That girl is pretty persuasive," Paul said with an approving smile.

"Then we'd better not keep *that girl* waiting."

To exit required maneuvering through a maze of grassy islands, each with its own shade tree, some posted with warnings to "Lock your doors." Clea stared out the window, eyes still keen to blue-frocked shadows. She saw nothing, though a sense of being observed prickled her skin like an itchy sweater and hung on until they'd cleared the parking lot and were a full block and a half away.

If Paul had an opinion on all that had transpired over the previous eight hours, he didn't share it. In fact, he refrained from speaking altogether until a faint yellow glow appeared in the roadway ahead.

His foot tapped the brake. "What's that?" he said.

The object was round as if a harvest moon had slipped from its moorings and lay on the ground; though as they slowly approached, it formed more clearly into a candlelit jack-o-lantern planted squarely in the center of the intersection. Paul cut around it. Two blocks along another scraggle-toothed harbinger of Halloween mischief stood mid-street. Their headlights sliced the darkness. Black-clad figures scurried out of the wash, scrambling for invisibility behind hedges and tree boles. The pranksters were out early this year, portending spectacular things to come.

Clea paid no mind. Once a year the kids had their fun. The pranks were never malicious. The townspeople turned a blind eye, most tacitly enjoying the annual spectacle that marked the run-up to the Day of the Dead. Though the town's borders had spread over the years and the population multiplied, it struck Clea how firmly entrenched was this holiday tradition. And the more she thought about it, she realized the notion of village-wide collusion encompassed more than just Halloween. The Rose Society had relied on the very same bonding of people to a singular, conspiratorial goal.

She paused at her unconscious usage of the past tense. *Was* this society truly a thing of the past or yet a living, breathing brotherhood...sisterhood... with secret rooms still regularly dusted off and kept at the ready? She grimaced at the notion of an unseen colony of workers operating as busily and efficiently as ants in a subterranean nest. When her innocent inquiry into a woman named Barbara had upset the order, guardians of the secret had swarmed to set it right. Everything that had happened of late was clearly interconnected. To answer one question would shed light on another. A single key could unlock many doors. The question was, did Barbara hold that key?

The car stopped in front of her house and roused her from these musings. She turned to Paul. "Is Ren in there?"

Paul reached up and massaged the back of his neck, his face screwed out of shape by a frown. "If I say yes, will I have to throw you over my shoulder and carry you inside?"

Though his words sounded like a joke, the look on his face was dead serious. Clea started to laugh. "Don't worry. I'll come peaceably." But not without designs of my own, she added to herself. Since Ren harbored no qualms about exploiting her, it seemed only fair to return the favor. Oh, yes, she'd work with him. Make use of his inside track. His badge. His skill. Take advantage of every last bit of expertise he had to offer and blast into oblivion any and all of Michael's arguments. DHS was in for a shock wave the likes of which they'd never seen.

Driven now, Clea popped the door and climbed from the Jeep. "What are you waiting for?" she called behind her. Then, like a soldier marching into battle, she strode up to the house and disappeared inside.

The inviting aroma of fresh-brewed coffee laced with hazelnut wafted in the air set aswirl by the opening and closing of the door. A coffee pot gurgled noisily in the background. Rikki had engaged the big guns to see her plan through, obviously taking advantage of Clea's weakness for richly-flavored coffee to pave the way. All signs of the splintered glass had been swept from the kitchen floor. Ren was nowhere to be seen.

Hovering near the stove, Rikki nervously wrung her hands. For a moment their eyes made contact, Clea's rife with desperate hope.

"Addy?" she said around a lump in her throat.

Rikki shook her head. "Not a peep. I was hoping she'd called you on your cell."

Clea swallowed a sob, then with effort rearranged her features more affably and glanced around the kitchen. "You've been busy, I see."

"You're not mad, are you?"

Clea avoided an answer. "Break out the cups," she said, "and collect Mr. FBI from wherever it is you have him hidden. We've things to do."

As she said this, Paul slipped in through the back door. Giving Clea wide berth, he shed his coat and without a word headed straight to the cupboard in which Clea kept an assortment of mugs. Apparently for him the night's order of business was unquestioned obedience.

"Where's that box of stuff?" said Clea.

Earlier in the afternoon the bulk of their work in progress had been hastily thrown together and dumped into a cardboard container to be stashed out of sight when Addy was due home from school. Clea remembered seeing it last under Ren's arm and him on course to the living room. Not bothering to wait for Rikki's response, Clea hurried in that direction.

Subdued light from a small reading lamp on the far side of the living room barely chased shadows, yet it was enough to outline the six foot frame of a man. Obviously Ren had overheard the exchange with Rikki, for the box in question was at his feet.

Without acknowledging his presence, Clea bent down, pried her fingers under the carton and hoisted it waist high. Ren matched her movements with the result their hands overlapped, the box cradled precariously between them, and Clea and Ren trapped face to face. The dearth of light made reading his eyes impossible, but heat from his touch raced up Clea's arms. She forced cooler thoughts, reminding herself he had fully earned his new status as enemy, to be treated as means to an end and nothing more. She wished he'd let go of the box, but he didn't. She tightened her grip and tugged. He did too.

"Just trying to be the gentleman here," he said dryly.

"I lug around heavy camera equipment all day long," countered Clea. "I can certainly tackle a half-empty box of knickknacks."

The challenge hovered in the narrow space that separated them—as ominous as the blade of a guillotine. Despite his claim, Ren's tone had a decided bite to it, and Clea's response was anything but accurate. The box was solidly packed and gaining weight by the minute. Yet neither backed down. Finally, they duck-walked in tandem into the brighter light of the kitchen and wrangled the load onto the dining room table.

"As I always say," murmured Ren so only Clea could hear. "Half a gentleman is better than none."

His flip remark merited no outward reaction, nor did Clea give one. Inside, though, she rankled at his manner which suggested nothing had changed between them when, in fact, nothing had remained the same. Of course, she was operating from the enviable position of knowing his ulterior motives while he continued to read from a well-prepared script. Whether his acting ability reflected favorably on Bureau training or Ren was an incredibly good liar, Clea didn't know. And frankly, she didn't want to waste the effort it would take to decide which.

Means to an end.

Deliberately she turned away from him, tipped the lid off the box, and selected from the contents photocopies of the warning notes she'd received. Paul had appropriated the originals and done with them whatever an FBI agent does with such things. Next came the three lists she and Ren had compiled earlier—a single sheet devoted to each note. Despite a haphazard appearance caused by the blend of handwriting—his scribble, her Palmer-perfect script—the lists were a fairly complete catalog of what they knew for sure and what conclusions they'd drawn.

When Ren dipped back into the box and lifted out Josephine's well-worn address book, Clea took it from his grasp and dropped it back inside. She then replaced the box's cover, resolutely tamping it shut with the palm of her hand. There would be no diversions tonight. Only the messages had been referred to in Michael's complaint to Social Services, so only those messages held relevance to springing Addy from DHS's bear-claw grip.

She arranged the notes neatly in the center of the table, each with its corresponding work sheet directly beneath. For awhile the four of them quietly studied the six pages, sipping the coffee Rikki passed around and refreshing their memories.

"One and two are the work of Merriam," said Clea at last. Her tone brooked no objections, yet Ren interrupted.

"Two days ago you said the same about Delbert Sheznesky."

"That was two days ago. Before a pair of scissors and magazine landed on my shoes at the library." Firmly-crossed arms measured the depth of her conviction. "I saw what I saw."

"No one's doubting you on that point," answered Ren.

"Then exactly which point *is* bugging you?"

"Your persistent habit of premature finger pointing."

Clea whirled away from him, but after two steps circled back and poked a belligerent finger at his chest. "Who else had the resources and opportunity? Who else came bold as brass to my front door?"

"A judge would laugh himself right under the bench if you tried to offer that as proof."

Rikki jumped between them. "Waving a white flag here," she said, flagless arm in motion. "What do you say we skip to the end?"

Clea knew bickering would get them nowhere. "Fine," she said, pleased at being the first to concede, at least verbally, while Ren remained frozen in a combative stance. She busied herself realigning the papers on the table top so the final note and its accompanying itemized listing now occupied center stage.

This note contrasted sharply with the others, both visually and in its message. Most of what they knew about it had to do with its looks: the sloppy cut-and-paste job, the exclusive use of newsprint, the oddball placement of the letters, notebook paper in a size much smaller than its predecessors.

Ren threw out the first question. "What does all this tell us about the sender?"

They spent the next few minutes offering impressions while Rikki penned their remarks at the bottom of the sheet: *Crude, in a hurry, vindictive, angry, not up on old Greek poets.*

In other words, a different writer altogether. But they already knew that.

Now Ren posed a second question and looked pointedly at Clea as he did. "Anyone you know come to mind?"

It didn't take much thinking on her part for a very familiar face to rise to the surface. Pure disgust stiffened her spine.

"Michael." She spat out the name, knowing without a doubt he fit the profile like jeans on a cowboy. "He was aware of the first two messages," she said, "although not their literary connection—which, by the way, he couldn't duplicate if he burned up every brain cell in the trying. But what better way for him to make a case for custody than to manufacture a third anonymous warning that screamed danger and then run to DHS with his accusations."

"One of us should have picked up on this sooner," said Ren. "The timing is so obvious."

"In hindsight, yes, but, as I recall, the complaint didn't specify the number of threats I'd received, only that the situation was more serious than a single, isolated incident."

"What possible reason could Michael have for wanting to take Addy from you when he's ignored her most of her life?" A moment later Rikki answered her own question. "Ah…money."

"Of course money," said Clea. "He doesn't have any and thinks I do. And if I was the one who had to mail a monthly check for Addy's welfare, he knows I'd make damned sure it got done. He could apply for support from the state, too."

Remembering the latest note had shown up under a dish of poisoned cat food was even more loathsome. Had Michael done that too? The coffee, which moments before had been so welcomed, turned to acid in her stomach. Clea bit back comment. It didn't cast a very favorable light on her judgment that she'd shared a marriage with the man, however brief and unhappy it may have been. Yet Michael had been the one who'd encouraged Addy in the first place to elevate Kitty-Face from stray to cherished pet. The cold-hearted act of poisoning the kitten's food, to the end of easing his current financial woes, was more than Clea felt comfortable assigning to him. Michael was a lot of things—mostly unpleasant—but killing small animals? Or coming darn close? Was he really capable of that?

A glance at the others left no doubt they had all asked themselves the very same question and answered in the affirmative.

Weakly and uncharacteristically, Clea rose to Michael's defense. "He wouldn't. Besides, I don't keep any poisons in the house."

"He didn't have to obtain it here," offered Paul. "Nor does it have to be something exotic. Easy to check out too."

He produced a cell phone and used it to call the lab where he'd FedExed the sample of cat food. An expectant hush loaded the room with tension. After much nodding and uh-huhing, Paul signed off and faced the anxiously-waiting group. "Acetaminophen."

It took Clea only a second to make the connection. The small red and white bottle of Tylenol in her medicine cabinet had been disturbed. Addy never used Tylenol, preferring plain aspirin instead. And even if she'd made an exception would know which shelf to return it to.

Michael had frequently been alone in the house and never one to shy away from helping himself to other people's belongings.

Motive, means *and* opportunity. It all came down to that. And a dead cat on the premises would be just the frosting to decorate his argument for custody.

When she relayed the information, Ren asked, "Is the Tylenol still there?"

"Sure."

He eyed Paul knowingly. "Find an envelope, would you? Or a paper sack. We'll have the bottle dusted for prints. It's circumstantial, I know, yet if we're to build a case every brick counts."

"But, Ren," said Clea. "I put it back where it's supposed to be. I probably smudged out all traces of his fingerprints and replaced them with my own."

"Not necessarily the case. We can exclude any that belong to you. Remember, as of a couple days ago, your prints are in the system. And if your ex's aren't, we'll demand a sample...or get them some other way."

From his tone of voice, what Ren suggested didn't sound quite legal, but Clea had long since left the land of caring. She directed Paul to a kitchen drawer where she stored small sacks for packing Addy's school lunches. He took one and snapped it open. The crisp, new paper crackled smartly. He led the way to the bathroom. They all crowded into the confined space and watched as he extracted a ballpoint pen from his pocket and nudged the bottle to the edge of the shelf. A final flick sent it tumbling into the sack, landing with a pop.

Despite the lateness of the hour, Paul shrugged into his coat, mumbling something that sounded like "The Bureau never sleeps." He declared his destination to be Portland and a session with the tech who would lift the prints and utilize AFIS—the FBI's Automated Fingerprint Identification System—to search for match-ups. Clea strongly suspected he was glad for the excuse to slip out and take Rikki with him, for he and Rikki had barely exchanged surreptitious nods when she joined him at the door and they hustled out. Clea wondered too if this was part of the master plan, for the end result was she and Ren alone together.

The sound of their car speeding away faded. Paul's drowsiness in Green Haven's parking lot may have been gone in a puff of exhaust, but not so for those left behind. Ren yawned. Even Clea's eyelids drooped heavily, victim of too much worry and too little sleep.

"Shall we call it a night?" he said. "You want to be fresh for the custody hearing tomorrow afternoon."

Clea acknowledged the wisdom of his words by picking up the white and green afghan and tossing it to the couch, leaving no question as to where Ren would be spending this night. Then she crossed the hall to her own room. Once inside, with the door firmly shut, she kicked off her shoes. Without bothering to undress or to fold back the covers, she flopped, bone weary, onto the bed.

Sleep wrapped around her easily but refused to stick. Demons prowled her dreams and chased her into wakefulness. By the clock it was two-thirty when Clea's eyes tore open. She could not force them closed again except to the same hellish scene: Addy screaming frantically. Her young voice ricocheted from the depths of a murky maze of corridors and seemed to emanate from all directions at once until Clea was hopelessly muddled as to which path to follow to her daughter. To make matters worse, black, vaporous shapes, humanlike but not entirely so, repelled her efforts to even try by enveloping her in a soupy, malodorous presence and dragging her inexorably away. Clea feared the maze would soon be out of sight, the pleas for help so weak, so far, she would begin to doubt their existence and in that moment Addy would be lost forever.

The digital clock face provided the room's only illumination, the soft whir of its innards the only sound. Clea rolled to the edge of the bed and sat upright, her body chilled by sweat and panic. Gradually her muscles relaxed as the real-world feel of chenille under her fingertips and carpet under her toes forced the nightmare to recede. She slipped on her shoes, felt her way to the door and opened it a slit.

Ren had doused the lights, for the darkness of her bedroom met the darkness of the hallway. She cocked her head and listened. The refrigerator hummed, a drip let loose from the kitchen tap and fell into the sink, the house creaked as it struck a balance between interior warmth and exterior cold. Familiar sounds all. When Clea blocked them out, what remained was a measured drawing in and exhaling of breath. Ren slept, untormented, it seemed, by anything coming close to the spirits which peopled her dreams and personified her abysmal inadequacy in protecting her child.

Well-oiled hinges made not a sound as the door arced all the way open. Clea eased into the hall and sidestepped toward the kitchen, guided first by the feel of her spine against the wall, then fingertips skating over the backs of chairs and the edge of the countertop. When she reached the sink, she stopped and listened again but heard no stirring from the other room.

A new problem faced her. Turning on the light risked waking Ren. They'd be alone in the house, together, in the middle of a very dark night. Not that they weren't technically in that situation already, but it was simpler with only one of them awake. Nor could she reheat a cup of coffee without making noise, and sitting idly in the pitch black seemed ridiculous as well. A drive would help. Give her a chance to think, away from distraction, away from Ren.

She felt around for her coat and the carry-all she'd abandoned earlier at the back door, even had her hand on the knob when it dawned the Explorer was still parked at Junior's and she had returned Ren's car keys. She cut a path towards the room where he slept, but never made it over the threshold, stalled by the image of his waking at an inopportune moment and catching her with a hand in his pocket.

A walk then. Maybe a walk as far as the auto shop. She'd reclaim her vehicle. Those unobtainable parts began to seem mighty suspicious, one more facet of some grand conspiracy—perpetrated for a reason beyond comprehension—with Junior the newest player among the ranks of many—Delbert, Merriam, Mitz, Lydia and God knew who else.

The late October nip cleared her head the moment she stepped outside. Purpose and a destination carried her with determined footsteps along the avenue and steadily toward town. What had been a mere idea evolved into a goal. Once in possession of her truck, she would canvass the streets in search of Michael's pickup. An ambush was fitting. She wanted a piece of his ass. Couldn't wait to see the look on his face when she informed him they were on to his scheme and could prove it—just as soon as Paul returned from Portland with word Michael'd left a forensic trail six lanes wide. He might as well drop his complaint. Not even Addy was an ally. He'd torched *that* bridge when he walked off with her money.

Clenching a fist and trying on a satisfied smile, Clea said, "Take that, you bastard."

No one was around to hear. The streets were deserted. The highschoolers had abided by curfew and long since headed home. The smell of burnt pumpkin was strong in places, and occasionally mounds of orange, fibrous mush gave evidence of a run-in with a not-so-alert driver. Soon, though, what had begun as a harmless walk through the neighborhood, took on another dimension, where every innocent and unexplained sound magnified her vulnerability and perhaps the hastiness of her decision to venture out alone. Clea hurried along.

Within this altered state of mind, the hum of rubber on asphalt coming from behind sent a charge of electricity streaking down her arms. She moved to the inside of the sidewalk, picked up her pace, wondered which house would afford a safe haven should she need one.

When the car didn't pass but slowly lagged in her wake, Clea dug into her bag for the cell phone. She came up empty-handed, the missing phone a by-product of the earlier mix-up with Ren's. Knowing the reason offered little comfort. Muscles gathered in anticipation of her next move—an all-out sprint through a stranger's backyard. Before she had a chance to bolt, a familiar voice shattered the night.

"Clea Reilly! It *is* you. What in God's name, girl, are you doing out and about at this hour?"

Never mind the bellow, Frank's appearance was like salve on a wound. She sucked in a lungful of relief and turned. "One could ask the same of you, officer."

By way of explanation, Peterson jerked a thumb over his right shoulder at the load filling to capacity the back seat of the cruiser. "Pumpkin patrol," he said. "A pure waste of my time if you ask me. Most are pancakes already." His shoulders bounced as he chuckled. "Now, let's hear your excuse."

Clea shrugged. "Couldn't sleep. I'm on my way to the repair shop to pick up my truck. I've been long enough without transportation of my own."

"Well, climb aboard then. Flat or round, I'd hate to have you trip over one of these suckers in the dark."

Clea wasn't sure she wanted the company. Maybe it was just *his* company she didn't want, but he seemed so earnest she crossed the parkway into the street and opened the door. To make room for her on the seat, Frank swept aside an array of printed forms, maps and work gloves. An empty can of soda clunked to the floor, pills rattled in a plastic bottle. He nestled a large bag of sugar cookies protectively to his side. Clea shook her head. Little wonder the man's belly crowded the steering wheel.

Frank needed no directions, and five minutes later he pulled in front of Junior's second bay. From the looks of it, Clea's SUV hadn't moved an inch in its three days of residence.

Clea's appreciation of the lift turned quickly to annoyance. She wanted to launch the hunt-for-Michael Reilly plan free of scrutiny or a law officer's second guessing. Frank, though, ignored a pleasant "Thanks and good-night" and seemed incapable of comprehending her send-off wave. Instead he waited, motor running, while she fired up the Ford, scribbled a note to Junior, folded the paper into a tight square and stuffed it through the key drop-off slot. Clea ran out of things to do, and still Frank waited.

Finally he rolled the window down and called. "I'll follow you home."

"I'm not going straight there."

"It's the dead of night."

"I'll be fine. Really."

"Does Davis know you're out prowling the streets?"

Clea's jaw locked. "He's not my babysitter," she said through her teeth.

Without a ready comeback, Frank sat, stumped. "S'pose you know best." His accompanying look said he believed anything but, yet he shifted into gear and drove away.

Once the squad car was out of sight, Clea too departed.

Most of the bars in town were closed, but she made the circuit anyway. When a canvass of parking lots turned up no sign of Michael's old pickup, she headed closer to the expressway where the diners and taverns kept ungodly hours.

Nothing. If Michael was in hiding, it was the first smart move he'd made since hitting town. For Clea, though, the repeated dead ends sapped her enthusiasm. Late night was rapidly becoming early morning. Canada geese honked noisily overhead. Clea encountered the first traffic of the day, including a car that followed her for several blocks before turning south toward the high school. She threaded the side streets, in and out, up and down. When St. Gerard's twin spires pierced the ashen predawn gray, it struck her that all along she'd unconsciously called it quits and been on a slow migration home.

At the church she slowed the car. A small sacristy window emitted filtered light. Clea imagined Father Leo on his knees, reciting his Office in advance of the five-thirty Mass. Thoughts of Mass and prayers led on to remembered sermons, then to hymns and, at the end of the string, to the choir and its soloist, Merriam.

An idea took shape.

Clea knew the frustration experienced by both Paul and Ren when all three of the notes she'd received yielded fingerprints but nothing to match them to. Needed were exemplars which was why the Tylenol bottle was so important in the case against Michael. Lacking was something of Merriam's.

Clea parked the Explorer at the base of the steps leading to the main entrance. Instead of getting out of the vehicle, though, she spent a long moment staring at the heavy oaken doors on which a skilled woodcarver had depicted the saint to whom the parish had been dedicated. The young monk held a Paschal lily in his right hand and stood in a garden surrounded by more of his beloved flowers. With his other hand he reached out to a woman in the advanced stages of pregnancy. Gerard...guardian saint of expectant mothers and the falsely accused. Interesting combination of patronage. She wondered what Gerard would think of her predicament—desperate mother seeking to accuse another.

Minutes passed into history while Clea vacillated whether to press forward with her scheme or wait for the legal system to wend its slow and grinding way to the same end.

She decided, in a roundabout manner, to let Father Leo do the deciding for her. If he'd left the door locked, she'd drive away. On the other hand, an unlocked door would signal a go-ahead. Permission, as it were, to carry out her plan.

From the car it was a short walk to the church which Clea covered in seconds. She wrapped fingers around the brass handle and tugged, but the door didn't budge. Whether the catch in her throat was one of disappointment or relief would remain unknown, for after a moment's hesitation, and with her continued pressure, the huge door cracked open and Clea slipped inside.

A hint of dawn dribbled through the stained glass, enough to dilute the darkness of the interior while mosaiced saints parading from window to window were still garbed in murky grays. A pale aura silhouetted the altar, its source no doubt the vestry room with its entrance behind the ornate reredo. Clea avoided the main aisle, choosing instead the one on the far right which, if followed, would land her near the sanctuary where a section of pews, cordoned off and turned to face the congregation, delineated the choir "loft." A temperamental organ as well as the presence of personally annotated hymnals rendered this area "off limits" to parishioners. As soloist, Merriam maintained a separate chair with a sturdy music stand on which Clea could see several songbooks. Drawing nearer, she noted with satisfaction their high gloss covers—fertile ground for Merriam's fingerprints.

With a watchful eye on the sacristy, Clea stepped over the braided cord and moved quickly to the music stand. She wanted to duplicate the caution displayed by Paul when he handled the Tylenol bottle, but when she looked through her tote bag for a pen or pencil, discovered she had none. Her ignition key would have been a fine substitute, but she'd left it in the car. She looked around. A candle rack offered the next best thing—a cup holding wooden matches, each about six inches long.

Over the rope a second time and on to the votives display. Clea snatched up several of the matchsticks, examining their suitability, returning one weakened by a crack.

"One should be sufficient."

"Oh my God!" Clea spun on her heels, her breath in rags, the purloined matches flying out of her hand. "Father Leo! What are you doing here? I mean, I knew you were here. You belong here. I just didn't see you…here…by the candles."

Recognition registered on the priest's face. "Ah, Mrs. Reilly, you're out early today." He consulted his watch. "Mass doesn't begin for another… well…." Father laughed. "For a good long time."

"I'm…uh…lighting a candle for my Mom."

Clea scrambled to recover the scattered matches, grateful for a reason not to have to look him in the eyes and have him read her deception. The pastor, however, patiently waited for her to finish, a thing which she couldn't prolong much longer. There *were* only four matches. When she gave up and stood, he plucked one from her hand.

"Lovely person, your mother. Devoted to the church. Let me help you." A trace of carbon flavored the air as he raked the head across the striker and touched flame to wick. "There. And now I'll leave you to say your prayers in peace."

"Uh…thank you, Father."

As frozen as one of the statues looming over her, Clea watched the priest disappear into the sacristy. She willed her heartbeat to a slower pace, but it refused to obey. The moment he closed the door, she sprinted to the choir and as quickly and quietly as possible used the matchsticks to maneuver one of Merriam's songbooks to the lip of the music stand, over it and into her bag.

Mission accomplished.

She hurried to the back of the church. Once outside she slumped, breathless, against the door's façade, cataloging in her mind what she'd just done. In the very shadow of the crucifix, she'd taken the Lord's name in vain, told an outright lie, stolen a piece of someone else's property, and neglected to pay for the candle offering.

So many sins. And the day had yet to dawn.

Chapter Thirty One

The promise of a rising sun poured blood red between the trees, spilling crimson into the coming day, and rouging the clapboard siding of her house like a Mardi Gras whore. The photo-worthy view barely registered as Clea sat behind the Explorer's wheel and waited for the engine to shudder to a stop. Movement caught her attention instead, a shadow passing behind the gauzy curtains of her dining room window.

Ren's awake, she thought. What am I going to do now?

She needn't have asked herself. She'd go in, of course. It *was* her house. As much as she'd rather return the same way she'd left—undetected—a smugly condescending entrance held its own special satisfaction. She'd been up and out, committing crimes in the name of justice, while he slept like a baby.

Clea hooked an arm through the straps of her tote, careful not to hold the bag too close to her body. Whether rubbing its canvas material against the songbook within would smear Merriam's fingerprints was outside the realm of her limited knowledge of such things. She *was* familiar with guilt, though, and it was guilt over her early-morning sacrilege that engendered the caution. No way was she going back to St. Gerard's for a repeat performance.

The back door yielded at a twist of the knob, reminding Clea she'd forgotten to engage the deadbolt on her way out. At the sound of the opening door, Ren spun around from the kitchen counter. He faced her with an overly-browned piece of toast in either hand. He'd been whistling when she entered, but the tune died on puckered lips while his expression turned to one of alarm or confusion or fury—a whirly-gig of all three if Clea was reading it right.

"Morning," she said, as if her appearance was nothing out of the ordinary. With suppressed humor she watched his glance flick back and forth between her position just inside the back door and down the hallway to the room where she should have been and where Ren obviously thought she still was.

"Where were you?" he finally demanded.

"Out doing your work for you, it would appear." She laid the bag on the table. "Nice to see you've made a stab at filling my shoes while I was gone." She moved in closer to snatch a blackened slice from his fingers, regretting it the minute she took a bite.

"I asked you a question," he repeated.

"Which I'm not required to answer, mind you, but I will. I walked to Junior's."

"In the middle of the night?"

"I simply wanted my car."

Ren frowned. "I'd have taken you. All you had to do was ask. Besides, the engine in that clunker still needs work." He tossed the ruined toast into the sink. "And the brakes. Junior said—"

"Junior's diddling around for no good reason. When he works himself into a fixing mood instead of a let-the-car-sit-doing-nothing mood, I'll bring it back. Until then...well, I want my car."

"Driving it could be dangerous."

"My car. My risk."

"Clea, you're as stubborn as a mule."

"As if an East Coast city boy like you knows anything about mules."

He was on the verge of a reply when Clea stopped him with a raised hand. "It's only to get me from here to there around town." She bristled at having to justify her decision, and the whole discussion watered down her envisioned unveiling of the pilfered songbook. Resentment took over, and absent the speech she'd had in mind, Clea upended the tote bag. Keys and pocketbook, tissues, sunglasses and loose change spilled onto the table. A few embarrassing items followed. Last and most prominent, though, came the thick volume of hymns—glossy green, gold-lettered and, she expected and hoped, covered in fingerprints.

To Ren's quizzical look and cocked head, she replied with a curt, "Merriam's."

Again, Ren appeared about to speak. She hushed him. "Don't ask how I got it. Let it suffice I need to return it by Sunday morning. Does that allow you sufficient time to obtain prints?"

A nod.

"And compare them to those on the notes?"

A second, thoughtful nod.

Clea turned from him then. A proper container had been important for other pieces of evidence, so she opened a cabinet door and withdrew a large paper bag from a local grocery. "Here to serve all your food and sundry needs," it read. This was definitely in the sundry category.

As she produced the bag, a smile flickered at the corner of Ren's mouth. His aggravation evaporated, exposing eyes that sparked with undisguised respect. The look would have puffed her with pleasure at the acknowledgement of her contribution to the investigation were it not for an overriding ire that his uppermost interest had all along been not to help her but to feather his own cap. Clea forced rigidity into her facial muscles as she carefully transferred the ill-gotten hymnal into the sack. Ren marked it with the date and several numbers that meant nothing to her.

"This is a tremendous assist, Clea. We'll get all we can from it first." He paused for a final, speculative glance into the bag before he folded the ends closed. "I'll arrest you later."

A wink signaled he was only teasing, but at that moment something inside Clea broke. Any space not already glutted with grief or loss or frustration filled with an anguish bearing little relation to his innocent remark; and while others might deserve equal shares of her wrath, Ren was the only one present. Her words spewed on him like hot beads of lava.

"You heartless son of a bitch. How dare you crack jokes at a time like this? Addy's gone. I'm near insane with worry. My life is ass over ears. For God's sake, I actually went out and stole from the church." The outburst ended with a sob and a fist to his chest.

"Calm down, Clea. I appreciate you're upset, but—" He fended off another blow.

"Upset? I'm a thousand miles beyond upset. Just get out of here, will you. Leave me alone."

"I won't."

"Yes you will. Do your job. Impress the almighty FBI." She picked up the evidence bag and heaved it at him. "God knows nothing's more important to you than a closed case. Unless it's two, or twenty-nine to be exact. Go on. Rustle up all the clues and ride your white horse all the way back to New York City."

By this time Clea herself knew she wasn't making sense, but she couldn't seem to stop. Everything was so mixed up. Her brain was a ticking bomb. Any minute—boom!

"What's this about New York?" Confusion blurred his voice.

She ignored his question. Rattled on. "Looking to get yourself a commendation, are you? A promotion maybe? Put on a nice show while you're at it. Had *me* snowed."

Ren took a giant step backward, the paper sack hugged in his arms. "Where'd this stuff about my going back to New York come from? You think that's why I'm involved now?"

Sarcasm laced her reply. "No, Ren. I think so much more."

"Well, you're wrong. And you know what else? You *are* crazy." He stared at her, his eyes storm clouds, his mouth a tight line of threat on the brink of something he struggled to contain. "You need my help, Clea, and, by God, help you I will, whether you want it or not, whether you like it or not." With that he strode across the tile floor, threw open the door and was gone.

After he left, Clea continued to steam. He was right. She did need him. He was right again. She didn't like it. He was wrong, though, so wrong if he thought she'd come around to being happy about it.

Roughly she corralled the articles scattered across the table, added her Nikon and phone, and shoved them all into the tote. That done, she surveyed the kitchen. In evidence everywhere were Ren's attempts at breakfast—a breakfast obviously meant for two. Coffee cups side by side. Two small glasses of orange juice. Eggs whipped into a froth. Pan on the stove. Toast.

Clea set about undoing the damage. She refrigerated a milk carton, shut utility drawers, wiped the counter, fed the garbage disposal. Inexplicably the task did not stoke further hostility. Instead, when she touched the still-dripping wire whisk, a sudden emptiness overwhelmed her. The waiting pair of cups evoked a sting of regret. The feelings were unwanted yet refused to go away, despite much head-shaking and self-reproach. Damn! Why was it so impossible to shut her mind down when it came to that man? She balled the towel she'd been holding and dumped it on the counter. The dishes could wait.

The wall clock read quarter to seven. If she hurried, she could get to the high school before first bell, find Addy and reassure her the ordeal would soon be over. Perhaps doing so would reassure herself.

Fifteen minutes later Clea pulled into the one-way drive and up to the curb opposite the school parking lot. Starbucks in styrofoam cooled untouched as she scrutinized the flow of arriving students. A strawberry smoothie for Addy dripped with condensation.

Not knowing DHS policies, Clea agonized the agency might segregate her from her daughter by temporarily enrolling Addy in a different district. The worry etched lines across her forehead as minutes ticked by without a sign of her girl.

Cars came, dropped their charges and rolled away. Yellow buses unloaded streams of kids. Had she already missed Addy? Clea watched a handful of students mount the school steps and disappear inside. Most, however, congregated in knots of four and five on the campus lawn. Their laughter penetrated the Explorer's closed windows but not Clea's consciousness. Her focus was solidly directed to searching out among them that one familiar, sorely-missed face.

Almost by accident, she spotted Cynthia coming from the direction of the student parking area. The girl's ponytail bounced in time to sprightly steps and whipped smartly about as she chatted with friends on either side. Instantly Clea resented Cynthia's carefree behavior. Seconds later, though, she was sorry for her rush to judgment. Cynthia certainly had no idea what had happened to Addy the night before. And as Clea looked on, the girl became distracted, worried even, as if looking for someone and not finding that person there. A boyfriend? Or was Addy on her mind too?

Just then a mini van crossed Clea's field of vision, stopped at the crosswalk and emptied its back seats. Three boys, two girls. The last to emerge was Addy.

Clea grabbed the door handle, ready to spring out when it struck her there might be rules against making contact, an infraction to be duly reported to Ms. Stevens. She pressed into interior shadows until the van moved forward, and it was impossible for the driver to see her. She then flung open the door and raced across the street. The sight of her daughter, head slung low, eyes to the concrete, plodding, feet dragging, tore at Clea's heart.

"Addy!" she called.

"Mom!" The girl came running. "Can I come home now?"

"Not just yet, I'm afraid."

"When?"

"I'm…I'm not sure. Soon, though. Is the foster home so bad?"

"I hate it. The other kids are mean. And the people wouldn't let me call you."

Tears threatened on both sides, so Clea steered Addy off the walk and behind a gaudy lawn ornament, a sculpted tangle of metal ten feet tall. Here mother and daughter hugged in private.

"Honey, I'm doing all I can to counteract your father's objections."

"If they'd let me talk to him, I'll bet I could get Daddy to stop. You know, tell him I made a mistake. That I don't want to live with him—or have him live with us."

"Unfortunately, it's not simply between your father and you anymore. Or between him and me for that matter. Now we have to prove to the State you're not in any danger."

"Danger?"

Clea drew in an anxious breath. She hadn't meant to reveal quite so much about the reasons leading to her daughter's removal, but Addy latched onto the word and wouldn't let go. Fourteen years of mothering had educated

Clea in the dogged persistence of one Addison Reilly. That nature—passionate though not always well thought out—had most recently culminated in the arrival of a better-left-disinterested father and an orphaned cat.

"What danger, Mom?" brought Clea back to the moment. She bit her lip but slowly and carefully tried to explain.

"I found that photograph. You know the one. Ever since, there've been some...well, unusual things going on. For a while there was a man following my car. And that fire in town last week. But mostly letters I've received. Your father saw one of them and picked that precise moment to act like an involved parent. In his own way, I suppose, he thought he was protecting you because the letters were warnings to stop asking about the photograph and the woman named Barbara."

Clea thought it best to say nothing of the poisoning of Kitty-Face and remained mute as well about what she'd learned of the Rose Society.

"What's so important about an old woman in an old picture?"

"Honey, if I knew that, I don't think we'd be in the mess we are today. But you're not to worry about any of this, hear?"

"But Mr. Davis will take care of it. Paul too. The FBI's big time stuff, right?"

"This isn't a TV show, Addy. Not everything gets wrapped up in sixty minutes."

"But he *is* helping."

Clea sighed. She tried to keep a lightness in her voice for Addy. "In the end, it's just you and me. We're a regular country western song. Whatever it takes, I'll find out what we need to know to get past this setback."

"Let me help."

"No, Addy, your job is not to worry."

"But I've been—"

"No, sweetie. Say, isn't that Cynthia on the other side of this monstrosity?" Clea thunked a steely corkscrew on the sculpture. "Bet she's looking for you." Clea cupped a hand under Addy's chin for encouragement then took her shoulder and gave a gentle shove. "Go on now. Visit with your friend."

Reluctantly Addy ducked under the art piece and set off. The noisy scrunch of fall-crisp leaves trailed off in her wake. No sooner had the two teens linked up than a bell sounded through an outdoor speaker. Like giant lips the school doors flapped open and sucked in the mass of students until Clea found herself alone, the fruit smoothie still clasped in her hand.

Cheerless, Clea picked her way across the grass, her mind crowded with *what ifs*, her heart rejecting all the answers. Though reluctant to sever the tenuous connection with Addy the school grounds afforded, she could come up with no real excuse to stay. Soon enough someone would see her and report a loitering adult. She headed to the Explorer. As she neared it, a curious spot of white on the vehicle caught her eye. It was a tag, dangling from the passenger side mirror which had escaped notice until just this moment. Upon inspection the small piece of cardboard turned out to be a work order identifier of some sort, for the card bore the auto shop's name and a handwritten number. Seeing no need to allow the thing to thrash about in the wind, Clea gave it a yank. It clung on tight, anchored as it was by a twisted wire. To reach and unravel the ends required she swing the mirror out and away.

At that moment she saw it. In the reflection.

Her hand froze in its task. Her breath followed suit.

An old green Chevy, bumpers rusted over, skulked at the curb a half dozen vehicles to the rear. Exhaust rose from its tailpipe like a genie from a bottle. Could it possibly be the same car, the same driver, the same mysterious stalker?

Briefly Clea toyed with the idea of marching back and demanding to know who he was and what he was doing. Threaten to call the police. Even as she pumped herself up for a bold confrontation, the risk of such a foolhardy act coated her hands with sweat and chased her into the SUV.

Her mind swelled with thoughts of Ren. He would know what to do. Before she realized it, the cell phone was open and in her hand. But, no. She mustn't think of him. She'd pushed him away for a reason and choked at the prospect of giving him the satisfaction of coming to the rescue. Besides, when she punched a button on the phone, she discovered the battery was dead.

She tossed the instrument aside and checked the mirrors. Each provided a slightly different view, but all confirmed the same thing. The Chevy was conspicuous. There had been no attempt to conceal it. Perhaps she'd been mistaken. The car might easily belong to a hapless parent or a teacher grabbing a cigarette and a final few minutes of respite before a long work day.

That was it. Nothing to worry about. She was on home turf. If help was needed, she knew where to go and how best to get there. She worked up a laugh over the whole ridiculous idea and pulled the keys from her pocket.

The noise of the Ford awakening at the turn of the key masked the sound of another engine, so Clea was startled when the green car moved by on its way toward the school's entrance drive. It traveled faster than the posted fifteen miles per hour, and the driver was in and out of her sight within a second. Yet that's all she needed to identify him. His swarthy skin and thick, dark mustache gave him away. This was no parent. Nor was he a teacher.

Not five minutes had passed since Clea had sought refuge in the SUV, cowering at a *possible* reappearance of the man who had followed her. Now that she knew for sure, she rejected caution in favor of a half-hatched plan, one that had materialized without thought. She threw the car into gear, but was held in place by a sedan with tinted windows moving along the narrow lane and after that another vehicle, this time a pickup.

Impatient now, Clea worried over losing sight of him. Where would the man lead her? What clue to his purpose would his destination provide?

When finally in pursuit, Clea found switching roles—playing the part of stalker—was not as easy as Hollywood made it appear. Stop signs must be heeded, speed limits obeyed. Additional traffic shoehorned its way into the queue. As the Chevy zigzagged aimlessly through the business district, then headed toward the neighborhoods, Clea's foot pressed harder on the gas pedal. She rolled through stops.

Five cars separated them now. Clea was certain the man knew she followed him, as surely as she knew she had the upper hand here in town. Take the upcoming "T" in the roadway. A right hand turn brought them into a construction zone where barricades would confuse and slow. A left would lead toward an elementary school with crossing guards at every corner.

The man chose right. Only one other driver made that same decision. With luck she could quickly close the gap between them.

Clea didn't actually see the dog. She swerved to avoid a brown and white blur that instinct warned didn't belong in the middle of the street.

She'd been traveling too fast and misjudged her brakes, or braking too fast as she misjudged her speed. The SUV skidded. Tires squealed on the asphalt. A wheel cover flew off and sailed against the curb like a wannabe frisbee. Clea's ears filled with the sound of her scream.

Chapter Thirty Two

Clea opened her eyes, not quite certain when they had closed. An exploratory probe of the bridge of her nose reaped a yelp of pain and a finger tipped in red. She stared at the small, round spot, a bloodshot eye that stared back with intense accusation. A glance in the mirror assured her the cut was superficial, though promised to soon darken into a nasty bruise.

The accident flashed through her mind in a spurt of vivid images. The dog. What had happened to the dog? She reached for the door handle, afraid of what might lie beneath her wheels, yet compelled to look. Legs rubbery, she stepped from the driver's seat, relieved when the brown and white dog appeared, not as a crumpled mess, but indignant and telling her so from a nearby lawn. Once he'd said his piece, he presented his backside and, obviously uninjured, loped away.

Inspection of the car was equally reassuring. It had struck the curb and skidded in an arc, coming to rest inches from a fire hydrant with its rear end swung outward. She could find no damage outside a missing wheel cover.

She peered up and down the street. Not a single car had passed since the accident. The construction zone ahead could explain the lack of traffic. Of more concern was the fact she'd lost sight of her quarry.

A door squeaked open. Clea looked toward the nearest house. Behind a lumpy screen a woman fisted closed the lapels of her pink bathrobe. "Are you all right, young lady?" she called.

Clea waved. "Yes, thank you."

"I could call the police, if you want. Or an ambulance."

"Not necessary. I'm fine, though I'm pretty sure I scared the spots off someone's dog. Hope it wasn't yours."

The woman shook her head and ducked inside.

There was nothing left for Clea to do but remove her vehicle from the middle of the road. That and dab between her eyes with a tissue moistened with spit.

The thought of returning home briefly crossed her mind, but what a moment ago had been a dull ache at the front of her skull had gathered steam. The saving bottle of Tylenol no longer occupied a shelf in her medicine cabinet. Too, an empty house would only magnify her growing apprehension over the pending meeting with DHS. She needed aspirin, something to do, a place to go, someone to talk to. She thought of Rikki as she started the Explorer, but even with a working phone, she probably wouldn't make the call. Let Rikki have her time with Paul. Ren flitted in and out of her mind. She didn't know what to do with the image nor the hollow feeling that came with it, so shoved it aside to concentrate on moving the car.

A lopsided maneuver placed her in the proper lane. Slowly she drove away. No particular destination. No plan.

The coffee she had bought earlier was not only cold but victim to the impact with the curb. It streamed in latte-colored streaks down the side of the cup and dribbled onto the carpeting. As good a plan as any, she thought, as she righted the container and set out in search of replacement caffeine.

She passed several small diners but continued on, drawn as if by magnet toward the heart of town. The accident, as well as the encounter with the green Chevy, had affected her far more than even she had realized and didn't let up until her windshield framed the concrete hulk of the Law Enforcement Center. The sidewalk out front was well-populated despite the early hour. A clutch of black and whites, though driverless, elevated her comfort level. A building full of men with guns was exactly what she needed.

Directly opposite the Center, Clark's Café offered Clea a good place to sit. Besides, she was hungry and could order up breakfast with two capsules of pain reliever on the side. She entered to find the café in full swing, catering not only to policemen changing shifts but Center office workers and strays like her. Couples and threesomes occupied the booths nearest the door, leaving no choice but to cut through the ragged line of beat cops at the register. The cash box dinged constantly as officers paid and left, yet the line never seemed to grow shorter. The abundance of uniforms reinforced the sense of security she'd felt outside.

The counter stools were full, and other patrons bumped her as she negotiated the narrow aisle. The first empty booth was well to the rear. She slid in, aware it was the same one she and Ren had shared little more than a week ago. Strangely, that too was a comfort.

Her weary head sunk against the cushioned seat and with closed eyes she replayed the morning's pursuit. It was a brash act. Whatever would she have done had she caught up with the other car? Her lips curved into a smile, partially out of relief the chase was over, but mostly out of pride at the bold thing she'd done. Of course, it was easy to be brave surrounded by half the town's police force, but nevertheless the smile remained.

The chink and rattle of earthenware startled Clea alert, eyes wide. A waitress zeroed in on her upturned cup with an oversized coffee pot. The woman poured without asking.

"I'll get back to you in a few minutes," she said, then hastened on to the next booth to repeat the routine.

Clea had already decided on a bagel but couldn't fault the frazzled woman for her brusqueness. Traffic in and out of the café was non-stop.

The bustle made Clea woefully aware of her own business which, in contrast, had come to a grinding standstill. Very soon she would have to deal with her flow of income—now a trickle—and aggressively drum up Christmas orders. In the meantime, the proofs from the Homecoming shoot had surely arrived from the lab. The task of logging in the material and arranging for student pick-up needed attention. Let activity be her Novacaine and dull the pain in her head as well as the one gripping her heart.

Although Mitz didn't open shop until nine, the backed-up service here at the café showed little sign of abating. She'd skip breakfast instead of waiting and bet on being able to catch Mitz ahead of her stream of morning customers. Decision made, Clea hurriedly downed the coffee, tucked two singles under a corner of the napkin, and, for the second time in minutes, squeezed through the crush of people in the take-out line.

In the short time she'd been inside the restaurant, the cars parked to either side of her SUV had been replaced by different ones. She peered down the row of painted diagonal slots. Not that she really expected the guy in the green car to flip-flop roles and again become the stalker, but it was a relief to find no car resembling the Chevy parked anywhere in sight.

Across the street was a different story. A familiar figure sat in a department cruiser. Frank Peterson touched the peak of his cap in salute when Clea glanced his way. She responded with a half-hearted smile and quickly climbed into her vehicle. Motivated with purpose and a destination, she didn't want to be trapped in conversation with Peterson. He had been temporarily pulled from aiding the investigation, so she felt no need to bring him up to date on Ren's trip into Portland, tests being run on the Tylenol bottle, her suspicions of Merriam, or her recent, ill-fated stint as hound dog. Hurriedly she backed up, then relented as she shifted into drive, enough to raise a hand in friendly farewell.

The retail district in the older part of town showed signs of coming alive. Shopkeepers were in the process of preparing for the day. Here and there interior lights blinked on, though the stores themselves remained closed to customers.

Mitz Maguire sat on a low step stool on the sidewalk outside the photo shop, engaged in taping a poster to the front of her building. More of the same lay like a blanket across her knees. Ghosts and pumpkins grinned from a black background. Multi-colored text announced: Chamber of Commerce Approved Trick-or-Treat Site. With everything going on, Clea had almost forgotten the next day was Halloween.

She tooted the horn as she pulled into a parking space. Mitz turned. Though the woman had been smiling, her rosy color bleached into gray and her mouth suddenly went slack. As chilly a greeting as Clea could remember.

For sure, their last conversation had ended badly. Mitz had denied knowledge of a connection between Barbara and Josephine Worth. Clea hadn't believed her claim of ignorance then…and she didn't believe it now. But this morning a new element entered the picture. In Mitz's split-second transformation from amiable to downright frosty, Clea thought she detected a fleeting glimmer of fear. While yesterday she might have explored reasons for the change, today all she wanted were her pictures.

With forced cheer and words carefully scrubbed of any hint she'd noticed the frigid reception, Clea rolled open the window and called, "'Morning, Mitz. I know it's early, but has that order I dropped awhile back come in? You know, the really big one."

The tactic worked. A tentative smile eased the lines of tension in the older woman's face. In fact, she seemed flustered at Clea's pleasant attitude. "Oh…my…. Is that all you want?"

"That's all." For now, Clea added to herself.

"The day's bundle has already been delivered. It was much larger than usual, so, yes, I'm certain your order is among them. But it's not sorted yet, and…" She indicated the pile warming her lap and shrugged. "I'm block chairman."

"If it's okay with you, I'll pull out the packets that are mine and be on my way," said Clea as she emerged from the SUV.

"My, my. What's happened to you?"

Gingerly Clea touched the bridge of her nose. "A little fender bender. Nothing serious, though sooner or later it's bound to turn an ugly shade of black and blue. But…about the order?"

"If you don't mind serving yourself, as they say, it would save me a lot of work."

"Not a problem."

A lime-green, coiled plastic bracelet encircled Mitz's wrist. On it several keys hung like ornaments. She selected one and rocked herself to her feet. "I'll just let you in and lock the door behind you. All you have to do on your way out is close it tight."

"Are the pouches on the counter?"

"No, you'll find them on a table in the back room."

"I appreciate this, Mitz. Really, I do."

They met at the door, brittlely polite. The woman eyed Clea's injury, and although Mitz made no further comment, her hand trembled as she inserted the key.

The back room was less of a room than an area separated from the sales floor and pay counter by a half wall. Here were cluttered work stations, overflowing bins of office supplies, and every size and shape box containing inventory for the shop. Clea located the large plastic bags from the developer, unsnapped the flaps and emptied the contents onto a table. One by one she collected those envelopes bearing her name. She pulled a memo pad close and copied down individual order numbers. As each was carefully recorded, the envelope disappeared into her tote. The task took fifteen minutes. Mitz had yet to return.

Job done, Clea sat back in the chair and let her eyes carry over the room. She'd never seen the shop from this back-to-front perspective. Controlled chaos seemed an apt description. A saver's paradise. Two large banks of files took up most of one wall. A gap a foot or so wide divided the cabinets into two groups—one organized alphabetically, the other numerically. Out of curiosity Clea rolled the chair a few feet away from the table and peered into the recess. Filling the space was a coat tree on which a tan raincoat hung from the uppermost peg. The garment had a bloated look. Clearly it was not the only thing hanging on the rack, yet its length and spread effectively hid what lay beneath—all but one small detail. The sight brought Clea out of the chair. She crossed the room, brushed aside the raincoat, and gasped.

The poncho was unmistakable. Exact blue color. Saucy tassels at the hem. Clea vividly remembered it swirling into the elevator at Green Haven. She pictured it at her own front door.

For a moment her mind blanked. What did this mean? That Mitz Maguire, her mother's long-time friend, had turned on that friend's daughter? It didn't make sense. She tried to organize her thoughts. The trigger of so many things had been the photograph of Barbara. The name Barbara had appeared on the list she'd found in the secret room. What if Mitz knew who Barbara was? What if she didn't want Clea to find out? Motive for the two warning notes and Mitz's decidedly cool behavior became clearer, though the question *Why?* remained a mystery.

If roses linked one to the Rose Society, the large, framed photo on the wall not ten feet away suggested knowledge of, if not actual participation in the underground network. If that were indeed the case, Mitz would want to protect herself from exposure, from consequences. But would the woman concoct a scheme to scare Clea from delving too deep? How did Delbert Sheznesky, Merriam, and Lydia fit into this new picture? The web of intrigue grew. Who else? Chet Martin, the bookseller from Reedsport? Junior? Suddenly the fire which destroyed the flower shop's records evolved from unfortunate coincidence into a deliberate act.

The mental exercise connected some of the dots, but unlike the child's activity, Clea had no numbers to follow. The total picture was incomplete, difficult to understand, possibly wrong.

Clea's spine stiffened. Had she heard the doorknob twitch? She spun toward the front. No. All was quiet. In fact, through the storefront window she could see Mitz across the street chatting with the owner of the hair salon, offering the Chamber poster. Body language gave no clue how long the conversation might last, nor could she determine if Mitz was just beginning or had completed her circuit of the block. Carefully she redraped the raincoat, returning sleeves and tails to their former positions.

Clea's eyes darted into corners and skipped over piles of this and that, not quite certain what she sought or where to start looking or even why it occurred to her Mitz might keep *it* in the back room of her shop. Only the need to hurry seemed clear.

A stack of unmarked boxes held promise, but a search of its contents would eat time. She swept the room for Mitz's purse. It wasn't there. The filing cabinets beckoned. Quickly she found the drawer marked "R" and located her own name. The folder was crammed, but a rapid shuffle of paper revealed copies of her monthly statements from the photo shop and nothing more. Shoving them back into place she moved from "Re" to "Ro." A folder dedicated to the Rose Society seemed highly unlikely, but she looked anyway.

Then she turned to the cabinet drawer labeled "W." *Worth, Josephine.* Excitement mounted at the sight of her mother's name, for why would Josie Worth have an account at a photo shop? Her mother had never owned a camera. Had been particularly creative in eluding the camera's eye.

At first glance the Worth folder appeared empty. Clea freed it from the drawer and let it fall open in her hands. A small brown envelope was the lone enclosure. Clea plucked it out, surprised to hear a muted patter, like seeds rattling inside a gourd. On the reverse side the name Josephine was penciled across a firmly sealed flap. The envelope weighed but a whisker more than the paper it consisted of. Clea's fingers kneaded the surface, tracing the shape of seven tiny spheres within.

She should have put the envelope back immediately and maybe would have except at that very moment the silver bell above the front door tinkled.

Clea's mouth dried to cotton and, in a rush to replace the file and shut the incriminating cabinet drawer, she ended up with the envelope clasped in her hand.

"Yoo hoo. Clea? Are you still here?" Mitz's keys jingled. Comfortable shoes padded across the floor.

Clea bolted upright. "Just finishing," she called.

A flush of heated panic raced over her skin. Had Mitz detected the movement of her hand, however slight, for what it really was? Or had the artifice worked, the envelope now residing, secure and concealed, up the sleeve of her jacket?

Chapter Thirty Three

The envelope lay in two pieces. Seven pearl-pink beads contrasted sharply against the dark mahogany surface of Clea's dining room table. A tiny black letter had been inscribed on each bead, and a through-and-through hole attested they had once been strung together.

Clea recognized them immediately. Not these exact beads, of course, but ones remarkably similar. Ones that spelled *Reilly*. She kept hers safe in a drawer with other cherished mementos, with Addy's birth certificate, with the pink, knit cap her daughter had worn home from the hospital.

Clea poked the beads with the tip of her finger until they formed a straight line.

N S I D A E T

The mix of letters reminded her of the jumble word puzzle found in the Sunday paper. She gathered the spheres into a cluster and lined them up again.

E D I N A T S

And again.

S T A N D I E

If what she suspected were true—that the letters spelled a name—how would she ever know if she hit upon the proper combination? This name wasn't as simple as Jones or Smith.

And what did it have to do with her mother, Josephine Worth, anyway?

At a loss, Clea shoveled them into one half of the torn envelope, crimped the ends and tucked it into the pocket of her jeans.

The answer had to be somewhere, she told herself, though endless shuffling and reshuffling of seven letters did not seem an efficient way to find it.

That's what computers are for.

The idea materialized like a shiny coin in a magician's hand. Thanks to Ren's instructions, she knew how to log on and perform an Internet search. Maybe she could find a site that would enable her to concoct meaningful names out of a string of mixed-up letters.

She hurried to Addy's bedroom but stopped shy of the door. Since Addy had been removed from the house, that door had remained firmly shut. She hadn't expected turning the knob on her daughter's domain would be so difficult and steeled herself with several deep, oxygen-filled breaths before venturing inside. The constant messiness of the room—in the past a sore spot between them—bothered her not in the least. And never would again, she swore. As difficult as it was to place herself among Addy's things, Clea picked her way to the desk. Her last encounter with the computer netted an important find, knowledge of the Rose Society. Would her luck hold up a second time?

Smiley faces floated across the screen like bubbles in an aquarium, but disappeared the instant she touched the mouse. She took a seat, entered her password and signed on, then wasted ten minutes trying unsuccessfully to locate help in unscrambling the letters of the hospital nursery bracelet. Frustration took its toll and she was about to sign off when it dawned on her the name she sought—a name somehow connected to her mother—might also relate to the Rose Society and, by extension, to the reporter whose notes on the group had struck so close to home.

Beads forgotten, Clea faced the computer again. This time around there was no need for the complex stream of prompts to find what she was looking for. She simply typed in *Kevin Warner*. The search engine spat out numerous entries. Clea clicked on the first, surprised when a death notice appeared:

> Eleven o'clock service at Church of the Holy Cross. In lieu of flowers please make donations to a scholarship fund at the School of Journalism, UCLA.

The year was 1970.

His byline accounted for many of the entries—mostly features about housing developments in his home state of California. The bread and butter of his trade it appeared, at least early on. Later his articles took on an investigative nature, though nothing as momentous as the baby transport business of the Rose Society. It appeared Warner perished just as his career might have taken a Woodward-and-Bernstein-sized leap into the limelight.

More telling were the stories *about* him, rather than *by* him. Kevin Warner had been engaged, enjoyed basketball, had a Beagle named Ted. He'd died young, shy of twenty-six by a month, his journalistic aspirations ground out under the wheels of a hit-and-run driver. Case unsolved.

Though details were sketchy, the manner of his death had sparked a firestorm of accusation—from faulty police work to blatant cries of cover-up and payoff. However, as the case cooled, editors lost interest. Front page columns shrank to page six blurbs. There was no mention of Warner's efforts to expose the Rose Society. That apparently had been yet in the planning stages.

As Clea scanned the various entries, she made mental notes. The accident had taken place in a part of town far from Warner's usual haunts, though for a reporter, this fact was not entirely out of the ordinary. The Friday night had been summer-weather ideal for drawing people from their apartments, yet not a single eyewitness came forward. Again, this was not unusual. Then as now, people were reluctant to get involved.

More suspect in the deadly impact was the paucity of physical evidence. It was as if the area had been vacuumed clean. No shattered plastic from headlights, no telltale tire marks, no flecks of paint. At least no official disclosure of any such evidence. This in itself gave credence to the short-lived blitz of outrage in the media.

Clea pushed the mouse away.

Was it only paranoia at work or was Kevin Warner's death a logical consequence of a dangerous, fact-finding mission into the inner workings of an underground society? The overpowering sense that this particular hit and run was no accident screwed tighter the muscles of Clea's shoulders. Warner's previous investigations had been benign, targeting government agencies, huge conglomerates, political parties. Nothing that hadn't been done and overdone a thousand times before. The Rose Society seemed much more personal.

His demise occurred as the background and research phase of his work had reached a fairly sophisticated level but before actual publication. Would someone go as far as murder to insure his silence? And if so, who?

More than once Clea shook her head trying to prevent a niggling impression from worming into her consciousness and becoming an actual thought. Eventually she lost the battle and in flooded the image of her mother, of Mitz Maguire and others in town for whom an exposé would spell disaster. Her palms moistened. A tie-in seemed self-evident, but she refused to believe any one of them would—or could—orchestrate something of this magnitude a full two states away.

Upset now, she flipped the off switch and watched the damning information became a small white dot on a very black screen. The air in the bedroom was stifling, difficult to breathe. Harder still was getting out, for tears filled her eyes. She stumbled over books and clothes, out the door and along a hallway made alien by watered-down vision until finally she was in the kitchen. By painful degrees composure returned. She dug in her pocket for a tissue, blotted her eyes, blew her nose.

A knock on the back door was as startling as it was unexpected. If she hadn't been reading about Warner's questionable accident or thinking about the illicit Rose Society and the recent upheaval it had caused in her life, Clea might have crossed to the door and opened it without a second thought. As it was, she hung back and called, "Who's there?"

An attempt to roughen her voice with menace failed. The words faltered. When no one responded, Clea pressed her spine against the edge of the countertop. Her hand groped over the smooth surface.

An instant later the door flew open. "Ta-da!" Rikki breezed in. Her grand, Garbo-like entrance collapsed when she caught sight of the upraised pancake turner. "Whoa! You making a late breakfast or mad at me for taking off with Paul last night?"

The utensil clattered on the Formica. "Neither. I'm jumpy, is all. Didn't know who was at the door."

"So you pick up the nearest kitchen tool and start flailing?"

"Lame, huh?"

"More than lame—downright paraplegic. But forget about that. See what I brought you." Rikki peeled open her coat and lifted out a small, gray bundle. The mound stirred, flashed a tiny pink tongue and squeaked.

"Kitty-Face!"

"In the flesh—or, in this case, fur. I stopped by the clinic to see how she was doing and was told she was ready to be released. I thought it would be nice for when Addy...you know...gets home. Did I do the right thing?"

"Of course."

The two women fussed over the kitten, but the distraction was brief and eventually Clea settled into a more contemplative mood. She told Rikki about meeting Addy and the girl's misery. She related spotting the green car in the school parking lot and didn't stop talking until she pulled the little brown envelope from the pocket of her jeans and spilled the beads onto the table.

"Wow," said Rikki. "What does Ren make of this?"

"He doesn't know."

At the question mark on her friend's face, Clea recounted the part of last evening she'd avoided in her earlier rendition.

Uncharacteristically, Rikki did not pursue the subject, rather focused instead on the small pile of beads and said, "You think these have something to do with your Mom?"

"Don't you? This envelope has her name written on it. Everything that's happened lately began with her. First a long-hidden picture of Barbara comes to light. Next we discover a plastered-up, secret room in her house with twenty-nine dead roses and a list in her handwriting of an equal number of names, Barbara being the last one."

"And the list turns out to be a catalog of abducted kids."

"Correct. Moving children into hiding from abusive parents happens to be the mission of the Rose Society. Once I started asking around about Barbara's identity, instead of answers, I got anonymous notes strongly suggesting I mind my own business."

Rikki picked up a bead and examined it. "Not anonymous anymore."

"Precisely. And those beads came straight out of Mitz's filing cabinet."

They fell silent for a time. Absently Rikki stroked Kitty-Face until the kitten purred herself to sleep.

The box with the accumulated items from her mother's house and elsewhere was still on the table. Clea lifted the lid. "It all started with Barbara," she murmured as she peered inside. After a moment she added, "I don't see the printout of all those kidnappings in here."

"Paul had it. Maybe he still does. Why?"

"I'm wondering if any of the children's last names is seven letters long... Barbara's especially."

"Hmm. A match-up to the beads. I'm on it." A cell phone appeared and Rikki dialed. "If Paul doesn't answer, I'll call Ren at the house and tell him what we need."

"Ren is probably still in Portland. He was on his way to the FBI office."

"I don't think he was going there."

"Sure he was. He had the book with Merriam's fingerprints on it. He was supposed to take it in for analysis."

"Actually, while we were there, Paul got word the prints had been received, but not by Ren personally. Faxed or something."

"They can do that?"

"I guess. What I'm trying to say is, if Ren were on his way, Paul would have stayed in the city, or at least mentioned it. But he didn't."

Clea tapped her front tooth with a fingernail. Interesting, but not her concern.

The box again drew her full attention, and she unearthed a ceramic mug with yellow roses painted around the rim. Gently she lifted it out and set it on the table. Resurrected next was the photo of Barbara and herself as a child. How appropriate it would have been if Clea's mother had named her Pandora, for her damned curiosity had unleashed a world of trouble. She wished the gods had kept their so-called gift and left her in blissful ignorance of everything ever having to do with roses.

The picture fell open at a touch. One thumb traced the bumpy ridge that folding and time had etched down the center.

Something about it had struck Paul as peculiar. Clea remembered his look of puzzlement. Was that yesterday or a lifetime ago? It didn't matter, for now she felt it too.

Thoughtful concentration furrowed her brow. Her lower lip disappeared, sucked in as Clea stared at the young woman's face and her own, months-old, toothless grin.

Like midnight fog rolling off the ocean, understanding whispered in and thickened to strangling certainty. A chill shivered down Clea's arms.

"Oh my God."

Her voice barely cut the silence, yet had the strength to compel Rikki to come alongside and watch as Clea's finger trailed from the left half of the picture—the Barbara half—and settled on the baby.

Chapter Thirty Four

"*Oh* my God is right." A quick grab and the photo was in Rikki's hand. "Are you saying what I think you are?"

Clea sank into a chair. "She was trying to tell me."

"Who? Tell you what?"

"Mom. That morning at the nursing home. She said, 'It's not mine.' I thought it was the Alzheimer's talking, but she really meant it. The picture. Not hers. The child. Not hers."

"How can that be, Clea? It *is* a picture of you."

"Yes me…and yet in some strangely discrepant way, not me. At least not what I've thought was me."

The room dimmed as purple-bellied clouds hid the sun and fulfilled the omen of the morning's scarlet glow. Clea glanced at the filmy window curtains, vaguely aware they'd grown dingy in the failing light. Her heartbeat marked the passing time. The weight of a sympathetic hand warmed her shoulder.

All along she had wanted only the truth, little expecting it to be a bitter pill—one that would choke in the swallowing.

"I need that list of Paul's," she finally said.

"And I don't think that's such a good idea. Drop this, Clea. It's only bound to lead you somewhere you don't want to go."

"Rikki, if I'm…Barbara…."

"You're Clea."

"…it would explain why no birth record exists for me."

On her feet now, Clea pointed sharply at Rikki's phone. "Try Paul again."

"Convince me first."

Clea sucked in a breath and made a slow circuit of the kitchen and dining area, time to organize her thoughts before rejoining Rikki.

What had once been a skeleton, strung together with nothing more substantial than secrets and lies, took on meaningful shape when fortified with logic and fact. Much flesh was yet needed to fully form the entire story, but Clea was convinced she had a good, solid start. Lines of concentration dug deep in her forehead as she began to explain.

"When I showed the picture to Mom, she uttered the name Barbara. I assumed she meant the young woman on whose lap I was sitting. I've been perpetuating that mistake ever since. Don't you see? Paul's list of kidnapped children contains—among others, of course—the same names in the same order as the handwritten list in Mom's secret room. Twenty-nine names. One rose for each. Each a passenger on the underground railroad of the Society."

"That doesn't mean—"

"Yes, it does, Rikki. Listen. The room must have been boarded up around the time I was born. In my earliest memories I never knew it was there, and the pantry was a favorite hiding place of mine. I remember it smelled of onions and spices and whatever else Mom stored there.

"Mother owned the house less than ten years before I was born, probably closer to six or seven. The woman in this picture is too old to have been an infant occupying that room."

"But if—and I mean just that…*if*—you're the Barbara, this woman…."

"Is my birth mother. At minimum a close relative—one Mom claimed never existed. I was blind not to pick up on the resemblance at first glance. Compare the eyes, Rik. Look at the shape of the faces and how closely their hair color matches. This must be my mother. Mom's story of a sperm bank and an anonymous donor was a horrid lie. She—"

"Don't say it, Clea. Nothing's final until some fat lady somewhere belts out a song."

Clea nodded. "Okay, but I'm not going to sit on my butt and wait for the end of the opera. Paul's list will have names and dates. I want to know Barbara's surname, if it has seven letters, and if unscrambling those beads will match it. Then I'll have a lot of questions for a lot of people."

"One step at a time."

"Step one. Call Paul."

While Rikki dialed, Clea picked up Kitty-Face, who had wakened from her nap on the tabletop, found the pink beads and was batting them playfully from paw to paw. She stroked and nuzzled the kitten, the only way she could think of to apologize for its recent brush with death all because of her personal battle with Michael. The soft, answering purr—forgiveness she hoped—should have been welcomed, yet it only reminded Clea of Addy's situation, the upcoming hearing, and how to explain this new, developing mess to her daughter.

Squeezing shut her eyes solved nothing. On the contrary, it provided more fertile ground for disbelief to grow into conviction, and shock into horror.

Who was she?

The hurt was overwhelming, but Rikki was right. One step at a time.

She nailed her friend with a questioning glance.

"Nada." Rikki shrugged, the phone held aloft. "Ren's cell doesn't ring either, and nobody answers at your Mom's house."

"Great. Where's the FBI when you really need it?"

Clea handed over the cat and proceeded to repack the box and secure the beads. By the time the table was cleared and she'd pocketed the little brown envelope, the ghost of a smile played along her lips. "You know, we're not entirely without resources of our own," she said.

Rikki mirrored the grin. "You've got something up your sleeve."

"If computers in Portland can spit out a list, why not the ones at the police department here in town? Our tax dollars at work, right?"

"And since you're buds with the sheriff...."

"Well, that's a tad optimistic, but asking is worth a try."

Clea drove. She had refused to leave the kitten alone in the house, so Kitty-Face sat poised in Rikki's lap, ears perked, eyes restive and searching. The ride seemed to take forever.

When the gray brick edifice of the station finally came into view, visuals of the first time she'd been there and spoken with Sheriff Summers rose like specters. The difference between today and a handful of days ago was her lack of hesitation. She parked and boldly led the way across the street, engrossed in rehearsal of a winning appeal for cooperation. She never noticed the black and white brake alongside.

Frank Peterson filled the driver's seat. "Clea Reilly. We meet yet again." His deafening greeting accompanied a snappy salute.

Clea likened him to a bad penny—always showing up when least expected, or wanted. This time, however, she could actually use his services to pave the way for her request and was about to speak when Rikki yelped.

"Ow! Naughty kitty."

Hair on end, claws unsheathed, Kitty-Face squirmed in Rikki's grasp. A mini-hiss would have been laughable if not for Rikki's cries of pain. "You little monster. What's gotten into you?"

There was nothing to do but stop and soothe the frightened animal. A chipmunk, equally on edge, scuttled beneath the dying salvia.

"Did that big ol' rodent scare you?" Rikki scowled after the now-departed chipmunk. She pushed up a sleeve and held out her wrist for Clea to see.

"Ouch."

"Tell me about it. Glad this little one was only frightened and not seriously mad."

"One way or the other we'd better calm her down and take care of those scratches."

The process ate up minutes. By the time peace was restored and two bandaids applied, Clea realized Peterson had driven off and no way to know where. Of course, she hadn't arrived with any expectation of help, so his abrupt departure hardly mattered. Still, she admitted, a go-between would have been nice. Hopefully Bea Summers had a softer spot for cats and desperate women than she might have had for overweight, aging police officers.

She pulled at Rikki's arm. "C'mon, let's see what we can wrangle out of the sheriff."

The energy in the squad room paralleled a busy hill of ants marching to a symphony of electronic noise and human voice. Once buzzed into the area, she and Rikki became merely two more in the colony. They cut a path to the glassed-in office of the sheriff, unimpeded until the moment they reached her open door.

A crisply-uniformed rookie seated at a desk outside leaped awkwardly to his feet. A memo pad and several ballpoint pens went flying.

"Sorry, ma'am. You can't—"

Too late. While Rikki lingered on the threshold, Clea tapped the glass and walked on in.

"What now?" Summers snapped without lifting her gaze from a thick binder squared on the desk.

Clea's optimism plummeted. The sheriff, for all her outward, matronly appearance, nursed a surly mood. Clea stammered out an apology. "I'm sorry. I should have made an appointment instead of barging in. I had such a small request, but it was silly of me to presume. I should have gone through the proper channels."

"Oh." Summers looked up. Her expression softened one anemic degree. "Ms…."

"Reilly. Clea."

"Of course. The missing person. Found?"

"No, not yet."

A head tilt took the place of a second question, so Clea blundered on. "Getting closer. There's a database list of old and unsolved kidnapping cases that must be available on your computers. It would be a big help if I could have a copy."

Summers rolled her eyes. "Where're Davis and Peterson? I've a meeting with the mayor in a few minutes and—" She waved an impatient hand over the book she'd been studying.

"At the moment, I can't seem to locate either one of them," Clea explained.

"Hell, that's why I.... Oh, never mind. No harm in your seeing what they'd show you anyway...if they were here and doing their jobs, that is. Carter!" The young officer shot out of his seat. "This woman here wants something out of archives. If it's cleared for detective or below, pull a copy and give it to her." Summers sighed and struggled out of the depths of her chair. "Sorry to be so short with you, Ms. Reilly. I'm in a hurry and generally not in the habit of running interference, especially when I've assigned two perfectly capable men to handle such things. You understand, I'm sure."

"Yes, ma'am. It's very gracious of you to—"

"I'm off." The woman rounded her desk. As she passed Clea, she paused long enough to add, "Good luck."

Whether Clea's muttered "Thank you" carried beyond the empty door to the woman's rapidly receding back was impossible to tell. Clea didn't care. She'd achieved her objective. As soon as Carter assembled his wits, she'd have the list in her hands. Itchy fingers traced the slight bulge of the small, brown envelope in her pocket.

Leveling her voice toward Rikki, she said, "On to step two."

Clea didn't need the beads to confirm her worst fears. She knew the letters, and it wasn't difficult to mentally shuffle them into the name.

In August of 1970, at age four months, Barbara DeSanti had become, depending on one's point of view, an innocent victim or a rescued child. Her birthdate was given as April 17th. Clea snorted softly. It wasn't the same as hers, but then what about her life was real anymore?

Rikki cut into her thoughts. "Where the devil is Paul? And Ren?" She tossed the phone onto the dashboard and sagged wearily in the front seat of Clea's SUV. "My head is doing a disco dance, and I don't understand any of this."

"Neither do I really," said Clea, "other than something is terribly out of whack. According to that reporter's notes, the Rose Society was well-intentioned even if illegal. Their purpose was to protect children, move them out of harm's reach then reunite them with a protective parent, not separate them for good. The big question is: How did Mom end up with someone else's baby? And why?"

"Could we be taking a giant leap in the wrong direction? I mean, Clea, it's a stretch to imagine your mother just grabbing a kid…or that it would even be possible to keep something like that quiet considering how many people seem to be in on it."

"A well-kept secret, for sure, but where better than in this town? Think of Halloween, Rikki. Year after year of pranks. Everyone feigning ignorance, whether they've lived here fifty years or five."

Traffic droned by their parked vehicle while the two women settled into an uneasy silence. The pressure at Clea's temples rose and fell like a cathedral bell clanging painfully inside her head. Without asking, she reached into Rikki's purse, found aspirin, and swallowed two without water. No amount of pain reliever, however, could lessen the torment in her heart.

The envelope containing the beads had been scribed with her mother's name. The letters spelled DeSanti. A Barbara DeSanti disappeared within a four-month window of Clea's own birth, making for a hauntingly plausible argument they were one and the same.

Barbara on a list, Barbara in a photo, Barbara in a safe and secret room, Barbara on her mother's sometimes lucid tongue. Involuntarily Clea shuddered.

Apparently Rikki had also been knotting the newfound bits of information together with the old. "You don't just invent a nine-month pregnancy," she said and curved her hands around the suggestion of a swollen stomach.

"A few months out of the public's eye would do," said Clea. "Not impossible for a schoolteacher with summers free."

Again a gravid silence filled the space between them. The interlude lasted only long enough for Clea to extract her keys and insert them in the ignition.

"One way or the other, I'm getting to the bottom of this, and I can think of at least one person who has the answers."

By the time they reached the photo shop, a fine moist haze coated the windshield, a cold appetizer of what was in the offing.

At the counter Mitz arbitrated a friendly disagreement between two elderly ladies as to the general merits of white matting over cream-colored. The shop was otherwise empty. When the bell above the door announced them, Mitz raised an offhand glance. Her smile faded.

The arrival of Rikki and Clea clearly disturbed her, yet when she spoke, she could have been addressing any customer. "I'll be with you shortly, dears," she said.

The younger women browsed while the matting dispute wound down and concluded with a purchase. The moment the ladies departed, Clea stepped to the door, turned the deadbolt and flipped the sign in the window so it read *Closed*.

"What are you doing?" Mitz asked, though there was no challenge in her voice.

"Assuring our privacy," said Clea. "You and I are going to have a little talk." She produced the paper envelope and laid it in front of Mitz. The bead marked "D" rolled out and wobbled along the counter.

Mitz blanched, her face as pale as her snow-white hair. "What's that?"

"I think you know."

"You've no right to go through my things. Josie would be so embarrassed at your behavior, Clea."

Clea ignored the accusation and the fact she had indeed stolen the envelope. "This had my mother's name on it."

"All the more reason you should have left it alone."

"You sent those messages to me."

If possible, Mitz's face lost even more color. "I don't know what you're talking about."

"Yes, you do. Fingerprints don't lie, and yours are on every letter pasted to the sheets of paper." Clea didn't know if that was the case or not. Ren had yet to match those prints to any one person.

"That's impossible," gasped Mitz. "I never touched the notes, I only—"

"Delivered them?"

Mitz shut her mouth but nervously wrung her hands. Clea's gamble had paid off. She tried another.

"Threatening a person is a crime. The FBI's involved. Two agents are on their way even as we speak."

"Those notes were harmless. They weren't meant as a threat, just a gentle nudge that some things are best left alone. And it wasn't a crime. They weren't sent through the mail."

"Doesn't matter. I felt threatened when I received them. And because of them my daughter's been taken into foster care. I have until three o'clock today to come up with a damned good explanation and prove she's safe with her own mother."

"Oh dear!" Mitz's fingers fluttered awkwardly to her lips. "We never intended for something like that to happen."

"We? Who are the others? Merriam?"

"She only cut out the letters and pasted them on paper."

"And Delbert?"

"He came up with the wording."

"Lydia?"

"We all love you, Clea."

"Then tell me what's going on."

Mitz shook her head. "I promised Josie. We all did."

"You might as well tell me. You're going to have to explain it to the authorities."

"For years I feared it would come to this." Mitz sucked in her breath then drew herself into a rigid, five foot pillar of resolve. "I've nothing to say, and I'm prepared to be arrested."

"Now you *are* scaring me."

"For once, take advice meant for your own good and let it go."

A low and mournful rumble of thunder accentuated Clea's reply. "I don't think I can, Mitz. I honestly don't think I can." She waited a moment before adding, her voice subdued, "I know all about the Rose Society. I found the room in Mom's house. The one hidden behind the fireplace."

The rod in Mitz's spine disintegrated. She staggered, making contact with a glass shelving unit. Photo frames chattered. An album slid to the floor. Clea hurried behind the counter. Putting an arm around the older woman's waist, she led her into the back room and the relative security of a chair. Strands of white hair had escaped the confines of Mitz's bun and stood in spikes around her head—a ghostly Statue of Liberty. It was the most disheveled Clea had ever seen the woman.

Stooping at Mitz's knees, Clea clasped the woman's trembling hands and gently forced eye-to-eye contact.

"My real name is Barbara DeSanti, isn't it?" When Mitz didn't answer, Clea went on. "Mom was supposed to complete her task for the Society and hand me over to my birth mother, but instead she wanted a child of her own and—"

Vehemently Mitz shook her head, the denial emphasized by eerie gyrations of her flyaway hair.

"—and kept me," continued Clea. "Changed my name. Enlisted her friends to cover up for her."

"You don't understand."

"You're right. I don't. So make me understand."

"I promised Josie."

"Mom may be incapacitated, but I think she finally wanted to set the record straight and lead me to the truth."

"The truth isn't always what you want it to be."

"Am...I...Barbara?"

The slightest of nods confirmed it.

Clea squeezed the fingers entwined with hers. "I love my mother, Mitz, but I have two birth parents out there—somewhere—who love *me*, must have been frantic when I disappeared, and sad beyond belief. They have a grandchild they don't know about. What's been done to them is unbearably cruel."

Pushing herself to her feet, Clea faced a shrunken Mitz. "I intend to find them." At last, a clear objective. One only seconds old, yet already unwavering. She engaged Rikki and turned, bent on departure, when a whisper-thin voice stopped her mid-stride.

"You'd better hear the whole story first."

Chapter Thirty Five

The whole story read like fiction—a horror novel really—chilling in every aspect, yet impossible to put down.

In the early sixties Josephine Worth took a vacation. California sunshine lured her south. United Airlines brought her to Los Angeles. For three days she played the consummate tourist. By the fourth, interest in the canned spiel of tour bus guides lagged. Josephine ventured out on her own, prowling museums, galleries, and used book stores. Quite by accident she ran into a man named Chet Martin whose wife turned out be the former June Springer, a colleague from Josephine's semester as a student teacher. Over the course of the next few days the two women renewed and deepened their friendship. Each confessed a love of children and regret, for one reason or another, over being childless.

June confessed something else.

By the time Josephine boarded her return flight, she was well indoctrinated in the mission of the Rose Society.

"Josie didn't participate immediately," said Mitz. "Several months later, though, she came to me. She was going to buy a house. Had one in mind. Did I know of a handyman with discretion for a small remodeling project inside? I was curious. After all, what could be so hush-hush about a plastering job? As luck would have it, I *did* know someone clever with his hands. In the country illegally, I'm afraid, but in the end that insured his silence, and eventually he returned home."

So, the house was bought. The hidden room constructed. The secret kept.

Quietly Josephine became an integral part of the network, receiving the signal roses, stealing away in the middle of the night to pick up an infant, then off again days later to deliver the child either into the hands of its mother or to another Society member who formed another leg of the infant's journey.

"Josie did it for the better part of six years. These poor little tykes passed through her arms. Dozens, I think."

"Twenty-nine," said Clea.

Mitz merely nodded, resigned, it seemed, to how much Clea had figured out.

The twenty-ninth child was Barbara DeSanti.

From humble roots as a family of tailors, the DeSantis had grown into a dynasty of clothing distributors on both coasts. With money came power, with the power arrogance. The family expected—things, deference, unquestioned compliance.

Young Nicholas DeSanti had been brought up tutored in a ruthless way of life and spent the next thirty years honing it to an art form. As with his father and grandfather before him, no one crossed Nicholas without consequences, quietly and efficiently administered. When he married, it was to a young and unsuspecting college senior named Sarah. Sarah quickly learned the true nature of the man she shared her bed with and came to fear it. The birth of a daughter failed to soften Nicholas. If anything, his autocratic and brutal behavior intensified.

Sarah wanted out. Nicholas wouldn't hear of relinquishing his only offspring.

The Rose Society offered a lifeline, a conduit away from the DeSanti nightmare for both her and her child. Sarah and Barbara would melt into the populace. A new identity in a new part of the country meant hope for better things for the two of them.

Mitz paused. Her eyes misted. "The poor girl had no idea how strongly her husband would react to a wife taking a stand against his authority. Nor of his ability to turn a single-minded fixation into action."

Clea hadn't spoken, stunned speechless by the cold facts of her bloodline. She wanted to deny it all, close herself off from hearing any more, yet when Mitz hesitated, she found herself asking in a very small voice, "Then what happened?"

Sarah complied with every precaution the Society insisted upon. Even aborted the first attempt to reunite with her daughter as she sought one more layer of anonymity. Finally a rendezvous was arranged.

The summer had been unusually hot for Portland, and the night was still warm despite the sun having set two hours before. As Josie drove into the hills far outside the city, the air cooled. The scent of the forest filled the car through an open window. Josie reached toward the towheaded child in the car bed beside her and gently traced her finger along the baby's cheek.

"Don't worry, precious," she cooed. "Soon your Mommy will be with you again. You'll be safe. Your life will be wonderful. I promise."

No sooner had she returned her hand to the steering wheel than the car pulled sharply to the right, and a loud thump-thump-thump confirmed her fears. A flat. Of all the times for Goodyear to fail her. The road was isolated by design, for the meeting was purposely secret. Josie had no choice but to pop the trunk, gather tools and spare, and change the tire herself. By the time she was done, forty-five minutes had elapsed. Darkness and a washboard gravel surface precluded speed. Josie was impossibly late. What if the child's mother had grown skittish over the delay and left?

Concentrate, she told herself.

Caution, which had been drilled into her during training, had heightened over the years. The moment of transfer was crucial—to her charges as well as for her own safety.

With this in mind she pulled well off the roadside and doused the lights. The meeting place was still some distance. She would walk the rest of the way. But first she must wait ten minutes, an excruciatingly long time since she was already so late, but necessary to assure no one had followed her. She marked the hour on her watch, tuned her ears to Nature's chirps and tweedles, straining for any alien sound.

Finally she gathered the child in her arms. She hid Barbara under a black cotton shawl, and snuggled her closely against her own black attire.

"Sleep now, little one," she said and quietly opened the door. She allowed herself only a small flashlight. Its circle of artificial light pooled at her feet to illuminate a barely visible path. She stopped often to listen. When the brush thinned, she clicked off the flashlight and trusted a half-moon to guide her steps.

She hadn't gotten far when she heard voices. Not utter silence, as it should have been. Not even the solitary voice of a distraught mother. Voices. Plural...and male.

This had never happened before. Josie dropped to her knees and pressed herself into the shadows of a berry-laden bush. The jolt awakened the baby who whimpered once, then seemed to sense the urgency telegraphed through Josie's tension-filled muscles and mercifully settled down.

To insure an inadvertent cry would not give them away, she lightly placed a hand over the child's mouth and herself took a slow, shallow breath. She envisioned racing along the path to the shelter of her car, then tearing down the highway home, yet fought the urge to move lest a twig snap underfoot and betray her presence.

A female voice startled her. "Let me go."

Josie's mental image of the unseen hilltop confrontation ballooned from alarm to panic. Her fingers curled around the fabric of the shawl and drew it tighter.

"Where's the kid?" The gruffness of the demand was foreboding.

"Safe. In a place Nick'll never find her."

"You underestimate Mr. DeSanti."

"No. It's he who gives *me* no credit. She's dead to him. He can rot in hell, and I'll tell him so to his face."

"Bringing *you* back wasn't what we were ordered to do."

A scuffle ensued. Grunts and groans told of a violent struggle. The report of a gun pierced the night. Josie gasped but that insignificant sound was drowned out by a scream and the crash of a body falling heavily to the ground.

Muttered curses. A cry of pain. A second shot. Josie swallowed the nausea that rose in her throat. She bargained with God.

It seemed to take forever for the men to leave. Eventually the clomp of boots receded. A car door slammed. And then another. Tires skidded on gravel. Within minutes an ominous silence weighted down the forest. Even the night creatures stilled their voices, themselves afraid or perhaps out of deference to the tragedy that had just occurred.

Josie cowered in her hiding place until convinced the men would not return. Her joints protested when she rose on shaky legs. Barbara fussed but did not cry.

Sarah DeSanti lay on a patch of meadow grass. A ghoulish red stain smeared the front of her blouse, but her face was peaceful as if she'd died firmly trusting that with the intervention of blessed Fate she'd prevented her husband's thugs from finding and taking her daughter. Tears streaked down Josie's cheeks. One dropped from her chin onto the baby's forehead.

What was she to do?

Stooping, she touched the woman's hair, so like that of the baby in her arms. She offered up a prayer. It was the best she could do. Before getting up, Josie felt into the woman's pockets. There was no ID, not a wallet, not a credit card, not so much as a handkerchief. The woman's car was also gone. As she started to rise, the corner of an envelope half-concealed under the body caught her eye. If the men had seen it, they might have taken it with them, but now Josie pulled it out and looked inside. Here was a photo of mother and daughter together, the Society's required proof positive to assure identification. Rattling in the bottom of the envelope was a beaded bracelet. Josie tucked them under the wrap covering the child.

There was nothing more to do for the mother. Protecting the child was now all-important. Quickly Josie stood up and backed away. With the edge of her shoe, she roughed up the grass where she had trod. Then she returned to the bush, tugged and twisted the branches until they filled the depression she'd made while hiding. Some of the berries were squashed. She plucked them all and threw them as far as she could, trusting hungry animals would carry off evidence she'd ever been there.

She made a fast and final assessment of the vicinity then turned and hurried to her car.

The trip home took hours, for Josie deliberately strayed off course, doubled back and around the usual route until she could drive no more. She was bone tired but had a plan.

Once she crossed the threshold into the familiar surroundings of her own house and behind a solidly-locked door, that plan unfolded. The child, Barbara, ceased to exist, and Clea came into being.

Furiously Josie scrubbed the berry juice from her hands, as if sending the purple-stained water down the drain also washed the past into oblivion. She laundered her clothes, tossed out her shoes.

"She called me then," said Mitz. "There was no way we would return you to the Society's network and back to a man capable of having the mother of his child ruthlessly murdered. Josie and I agreed she should leave town with you and not come back until school started and she had to show up for work. She'd already concocted a story about a fertility clinic. She would explain she'd decided not to tell anyone of her pregnancy in case things went awry."

Clea interrupted. "The baby…uh, me…I had to have been a good four months old at the time."

"Thank God for friends, Clea. Those who knew, kept the secret. And those who didn't know, believed the lie. Your mother resigned the Society, boarded up her safe room."

"And began a lifelong deception."

"With reason."

Clea took in the knowledge only to feel it explode behind her temples into a throbbing headache. Of course, Mitz was right. Her mother had acted out of protective instincts, out of love, and certainly within the bounds of reason. But the newness of it all was overwhelming.

"She could have told me," Clea whispered. "You could have told me."

"No, honey. A single wayward remark might have spelled disaster. And now that you know, you must also keep the secret. Danger is ever-present. You mustn't breathe a word. You too, young lady," she added to Rikki.

"Mum's the word," said Rikki. "I never heard a thing. Nothing goes beyond these lips."

Mitz looked to Clea, her eyes clearly communicating the profound gravity of her next request. "Sweetheart, swear to me on your mother's soul."

"Yes, of course," answered Clea. She spread her arms around the trembling woman, invited Rikki to join them, and pulled them both into a tight embrace. "I'm glad I finally know the whole story, though. It explains a lot. I'm only sorry it's too late for Mom to understand how much I love her for it."

"Your safety was all the thanks she ever asked for," said Mitz.

"From what you've told me, it was enough for Sarah DeSanti."

"And for Josephine Worth."

"Mom was so brave. They both were."

Tears winked in every eye, Clea's as much out of love and admiration for her mothers as for knowing she'd finally come to the truth.

"Thank you for opening up, Mitz," said Clea. "Otherwise I might have pursued this until I'd actually found that family." She shuddered, then managed a smile of relief. "All's well."

Abruptly Rikki shoved herself from the triangle, sober urgency written on her face. "There is one problem."

Chapter Thirty Six

Tires squealed as the SUV took the corner above the posted speed limit.

"Slow down," said Rikki, "before we have to talk our way out of a ticket."

"I'm doing the driving," countered Clea. "You keep trying to reach Paul or Ren."

"Neither one of 'em answered thirty seconds ago. They're not going to answer now." The phone slipped from Rikki's grip as she lunged for the kitten who'd lost balance during the swerve and appeared ready to tumble to the floor. "And myself? I'd prefer not to arrive there dead."

Clea relented and eased up on the gas pedal, but only because her mother's house was coming into view and she'd be braking anyway for the swing into the driveway.

"I keep telling you, they're not here."

"Maybe," said Clea, "but I'm going to see for myself. If not, I'll leave a note in case they return. There's always the chance they've left behind a clue as to where they went."

"And just how do you expect to find this clue? X-ray vision?"

"Who said I was going to cool my heels outside?"

"Wait a minute. There're laws against stuff like that."

"Try to stop me."

For sure Clea wasn't going to allow minute technicalities like lessee privileges and privacy issues deter her. Whatever leads Ren and Paul were developing had to be nipped immediately. Avenues of inquiry they'd opened must be turned into dead ends. There wasn't a moment to be wasted, and she intended to take no flak from Ren even if this case *was* his ticket back to the Big Apple.

According to Mitz's telling of the story, Nicholas DeSanti was a man who relentlessly nursed a grudge. Who knew to what proportions his revenge had grown after being massaged for thirty-three years? Clea didn't want to find out. If the gory details failed to convince Ren, if he'd retracted into a hard, self-serving shell, she was fully prepared to beg, to threaten, to do whatever it took.

Gooseflesh nippled her arms at the possibility they were too late. Acid flooded an already nervous stomach. She thought of the green Chevy that had appeared off and on, stalking her from the moment she'd begun inquiries into the past. With this in mind she flicked her eyes to the rearview mirror. There was only one car in the street behind her and that black and far away. As she watched, it turned into a side street and out of sight.

Its disappearance offered no reassurance, for there was still the list of babies' names that had been swiped from her mother's house. As well, the almost-forgotten, yet eerily-timed fire which destroyed the floral shop's delivery records remained unexplained.

Who? What? Why?

If posing unanswerable questions were an Olympic sport, she'd take the gold. What Clea didn't need right now was another mystery, so she cringed when she saw a woman standing on Ren's front porch. An umbrella bobbed and twirled as the woman wrestled with an overlarge envelope which stubbornly rebuffed efforts to shove it through the mail slot.

A slump of shoulders told of growing frustration, but when Clea pulled to a stop in the driveway, the woman perked up and called, "Yoo hoo! You live here? I've got to deliver this, and I hate to leave it out in the rain."

Clea emerged from the SUV, holding aloft her ring of keys. "Sure," she answered.

The sound of Rikki's disapproval mimicked a sagging floorboard, but she tucked Kitty-Face in the curve of her arm and climbed out too.

"Thank goodness." As soon as Clea was close enough, the envelope exchanged hands. The woman raised the umbrella and gave it a shake. "Nasty weather," she added and hurried down the steps.

"Now was that so bad?" Clea said to Rikki as she selected and inserted a key.

To assuage Rikki's obvious reluctance, Clea called Ren's name several times and waited impatiently outside the door for a response. When none came, she walked in. Over her shoulder to Rikki, "Consider it my performing a public service. Saving this valuable package from certain ruin."

The foyer was warm and inviting, packing boxes still in evidence from Ren's recent move-in. Rikki found an empty one and deposited Kitty-Face while Clea studied the envelope in her hand. She had hoped to find herself in possession of case material that would allay her fears, but instead the package was from a local real estate company. Why Ren needed the services of a land broker was beyond her. She was tempted to open the envelope; however, when she turned it over, a sealed flap barred easy entry. She felt the sharp prick of Rikki's eyes on her back, then a tug as the envelope was pulled from her grasp.

"Doesn't look like something a man with a short-term stay on his mind would need," said Rikki.

Clea's expression sagged. She took a moment to sigh and come to the conclusion she might have been hasty in her judgment of Ren. "This does raise a question or two," she said. "I swear, Rik, that man confuses me to no end. One minute I'm panting over him, the next madder than hell."

"Goes with the territory."

"What territory is that?"

"Love."

Clea opened her mouth to object but found all her arguments had vanished. Instead she retrieved the envelope, laid it on the table and returned to the task at hand. She noticed a FedEx box she'd not seen before. It was open and empty. Atop sat a pair of New York Yankees caps wrapped in clear plastic. She glanced over her shoulder toward the front door and the small entry table that held the trophy baseball. An identical cap—Ren's—was still in its honored place. Strange he'd want a second one...and a third.

She shrugged, dismissing the caps to focus on the neatly ordered work space. It appeared Ren had made copies of everything, for she recognized duplicates of documents she knew were in the box on her own kitchen table. Curling faxes decorated the spread of paper like chocolate shavings on a birthday cake. Clea grabbed one and scanned it.

The text yielded unfamiliar names peppered throughout blocks of FBI-speak. It made no sense, so she tossed the page aside and selected another. It too suggested much but gave up little. Clearly Ren was working leads he'd not shared with her. What had he learned? Worse, what had he revealed? And to whom?

She tore into the faxes then, frantically willing into existence a morsel of useful information, a crumb that would bring to light Ren's intentions or perhaps his present whereabouts. Discarded pages resumed their fetal positions. Some rolled to the floor.

"There's nothing here," she finally said, dropping into a chair. "At least nothing I can make heads or tails of. How do I stop Ren from doing what he's trained to do when I can't even find him? Why the hell doesn't he answer his damn phone?"

Rikki plopped onto the couch. "Think his sudden invisibility could have something to do with your heavy-duty suggestion he bug out of your life?"

"Ow! That cut deep. I admit, though, the thought had crossed my mind, but according to the sheriff he's still on the clock. As a professional, isn't he supposed to stay in touch with the client—me—instead of being deterred by…by…."

"What? Rain, sleet, and dark of night? Don't confuse him with a postal worker. You can't have it both ways, Clea. Is he in or is he out? Besides, the reason could be as simple as a dead battery in his phone—just like yours, by the way."

"So why hasn't Paul called you?"

A sigh whispered from Rikki's lips as she stared at a spot midair between her nose and the far wall. "Good question."

"What if they're together, racing to make a huge breakthrough, so Ren can come back and throw it in my face?"

"Give him a break, Clea. He's only trying to help you. Bottom line, he's not such a bad guy, you know."

The truth of what Rikki said triggered a memory of Ren's lips on hers. Clea leaned back into the worn padding of the chair, let her eyelids drift closed, and for a moment, without much control over it, savored the sensation. Good sense stepped in, though, reminding her the path where that kiss might have led had long since been plowed under.

Rikki's next comment brought her fully around to the present. Her eyes snapped open when she heard, "What if they're together and something terrible has happened to them?"

"No," said Clea with a hard shake of the head. "That's not possible."

But once she gave it some thought, anything was possible, especially in light of what she now knew about the DeSanti family. Had the two men investigated their way into dangers they couldn't predict without Mitz's confession? It would be her fault. Had she been too hasty in her criticism of Ren, too harsh? Had she prompted him to act rashly, whether on her behalf or in spite of her? Either way, it would still be her fault.

Her face must have broadcast a growing apprehension, for Rikki reached over and touched her hand. "You're right," she said, though her voice lacked conviction. "They're okay."

"Of course they are." Clea wasn't so sure herself, and the conversation made her acutely aware of the need to hurry. She rose, sidestepped until she could read the wall clock in the kitchen. The amount of time lost here in the house came as a shock. Intercepting Ren fell to second place behind the more-important DHS hearing looming within the half hour.

"It's late. I've got to get to the court. Why don't you stay here and wait for Paul?"

"No way. If I'm alone, I'll just worry in technicolor. Besides, you're going to need backup when it comes to a face-to-face with Michael. We'll write the guys a big note and stick it in a place a blind man couldn't miss."

Together they composed a warning, concise yet complete, and propped it in the center of the table.

As they prepared to leave, a sudden burst of wind threw pellets of rain against the window glass. The house creaked like tired old bones, too arthritic to carry any further the burden of its secrets. A second creak, however, had a far different quality and came from the lee side of the house.

"Did you hear that?" she asked Rikki and cocked her head to listen.

The sound had broken off sharply, as if someone were attempting to quash the noise of an ill-placed footfall. Quietly Clea moved to the front entrance and peeked through a sidelight. There was no one there. Behind her, Kitty-Face whimpered and scratched at the side of the box, begging to be freed. Perhaps Clea had heard the kitten's antics and mistaken it for something more sinister. She tried to dismiss the incident, but the uneasy feeling wouldn't leave her.

Rikki appeared with a saucer of milk. "The wind?" she asked.

"Probably. At any rate, I can't see a thing."

The women buttoned into their coats and pulled lapels to their ears. On the porch, Clea walked a zig-zag across the span from door to steps, testing the floorboards. Their solidity reassured her, but not a hundred percent, and the feeling of eyes boring into her remained strong as they dashed toward the Explorer.

As Clea raced around the car to the driver's side door, she noticed a muddy clump on the wet asphalt. About three feet away, almost at the far edge of the paved surface, was another. Her eyes followed the suggested path into the neighbor's lawn. A depression in the grass had collected rainwater, forming a shoe-sized puddle.

Puzzled, Clea reversed her stance and looked over the hood of the car toward the house. If she drew a line through the three footprints behind her, and continued it in front of her, the other end of the trail led straight to the porch, a flowerbed along the way disturbed. Someone had been suspiciously close to a window. Spying? More than the dampness chilled her. She made a move, but Rikki stopped her with, "Get in, will you? They deduct points for dripping all over a judge's carpet."

Court. Yes. Clea abandoned any thought of investigating further and slid into the car. She needed to concentrate fully on the one thing that had the potential to outweigh hit men and disclosure of who she was and how she came to be, yet when Rikki asked, "What are you going to say when you get there?" she had no ready answer.

"I can't lie to a judge, but I also can't tell him the whole truth."

"He'll want to hear your side."

"Demand's more likely. In my favor, Michael doesn't possess the actual notes to support his allegations. His version's hearsay. He can accuse from now until the second coming, but he has no proof."

"Your word against his."

"That will have to be good enough. If Ren hadn't picked this very moment to drop off the face of the earth, he might have good news to present—Michael's telltale fingerprint on the third note. He can't just make up evidence then use it to persuade a ruling in his favor."

"You don't think that's why Ren's nowhere to be found, do you? There were no prints? Or they turned out to be someone else's?"

Clea blew out a breath of exasperation. "If Michael insists on playing dirty, I can play dirtier. He's in this for one purpose only—the money. A judge with half a brain will see right through it."

"But the notes?"

"A bridge to cross when and if I have to."

They arrived at the Law Enforcement Center with no more concrete a defense—or offense—than mounting anger and a mother's determination to see her child safely home. Clea was fighting for Addy as surely as her mother had fought to keep Barbara safe.

A small parking lot was located off a side street. Juvenile matters, criminal or custody, were handled in a separate wing of the building. Participants in cases involving a minor entered and exited through an unmarked door, ostensibly to assure privacy for the underaged, though in fact the purpose of this particular door was well known and equally as visible as the front entrance.

A narrow hallway led past closed doors of frosted glass. Clea and Rikki hurried to where the corridor hooked left before it widened into a waiting room of sorts. The true nature of the area was lettered on a set of double doors: Juvenile Court. In an alcove to the side, coloring books on tot-sized tables provided diversion for the younger set. For the parents, a pair of wooden benches sat against opposing walls. While they offered plaintiff and defendant a degree of separation, the face-to-face arrangement didn't necessarily discourage adversarial confrontations. At least warring parties were kept at a reasonable distance.

Only one person occupied the area. Clea stiffened at the sight of Michael. He had laid claim to the bench closest to the courtroom. One hand rested lazily on the top rail, a casually crossed leg and smug expression completed the portrait of a cocksure son of a bitch.

"Damn you, Michael," she said, taking up position directly in front of him—within apparent kicking range, though she tried to refrain from actually determining if it was.

"You didn't think I'd show up, did you?" he said.

"On the contrary. The scent of easy money is in the air. Where else would you be?"

Michael's hand dropped to cover a spot on his chest under which, on any normal human being, a heart should have been. "Who could fault a father for protecting his flesh and blood? And you were so helpful, Clea. I couldn't have planned it better. You had the perfect bit of leverage I needed and just left it lying around for me to see."

"As I recall, it was in a sealed envelope."

Michael shrugged, uncrossed his legs and scooched over, inviting Clea to share the bench, his infuriating smile a dare. Before she could rein it in, her foot connected with his shin. He didn't even have the decency to yelp in pain.

She flopped on the other bench then. Rikki followed suit. "Tell him," she urged Clea with a nudge. "Tell him we've got him for coming up with one of his own ridiculous threats to bolster his case. See how far that gets him."

It took a moment for the information to travel across the aisle and sink in, but when it did Michael's smile flattened. He stared at the women, then seemed to relax again. "I get it. A dose of intimidation. To see if I'll turn tail." He chuckled. "Didn't work."

Clea didn't buy his response. She earned a living paying close attention to faces. At each sitting she watched for the nuances that would make an acceptable portrait into a great one. When she read Michael's face, a minute bunching of the flesh above his eyebrows was a telltale sign he wasn't as sure as he sounded. If one accusation produced a wrinkle in his otherwise thick, arrogant skin, what would a second do? She decided to find out.

"A man who poisons his own daughter's defenseless little kitten for the sake of gaining child support is a sicko."

Bang! Instant reaction, though not exactly the one Clea expected. The line of his mouth hardened, yet confusion clouded his eyes.

"What are you talking about?"

"You used the Tylenol from my medicine cabinet. We're getting your fingerprints from the bottle."

"I had a headache. If that's such a crime, sue me for the cost of two pills. Better yet…." He dug into his pocket, the outline of his fingers visible under the fabric as he groped the depths for loose change.

"Cut the act, Michael," she countered. "What galls me more is your claiming I'm an unfit parent and offering as proof a threat you penned yourself? I believe it's called fraud."

Michael bolted to his feet. "That's a lie."

Clea rose too, better to do battle eye to eye than eye to crotch. But Michael wasn't looking at her now. He cast furtive glances up and down the hall as if searching for hidden microphones and the lens of an all-too-candid camera.

"I only found that weird letter of yours and read it. I didn't send it or any other and you can't say I did."

"I can allege anything I want, Michael. You certainly did."

"Keep it down, would you. You'll get me in a heap of trouble saying shit like that."

"I should be so fortunate."

"Listen up." He licked his lips. "I didn't send no letter. I only took what I saw and used it to claim what's mine."

"Yours? You may have fathered her, Michael, but Addy is in no way yours."

"And who says I killed the kid's cat anyway?"

"Attempt."

"Huh?"

"The kitten survived."

"Who cares?"

"I do. I care about anything that involves Addy. And I swear to you, Michael Patrick Reilly, if I have to sell my house and live on the street in order to pay for a truckload of lawyers, you will never get custody of her. And..." She stabbed an accusing finger at his chest. "...seeing you in a jail cell for fraud and filing false reports would be frosting on the cake."

Genuine fear contorted his face. He backed up as far as the bench behind his legs allowed, hands raised in defense as though fending off, not her finger, but the unflinching resolve radiating from the very pores of her body.

"Cool it, will you? I didn't do any of those things you're babbling about."

"Says you."

"Listen." A bead of sweat glistened at his hairline. "Maybe we can work out a little deal."

"No deal. Courts always weigh in favor of the mother, so you lose. Big time."

Clea thought of her own situation. *Always* was far from a given. Her bluster was a bluff and she knew it, but the threat seemed to give her ex-spouse pause. Distress narrowed the blacks of his eyes at the very moment the sound of footsteps echoed down the adjoining hallway. Their three heads turned as one.

Around the corner came Mitz, Delbert Sheznesky and Merriam, boldly marching shoulder to shoulder—the equivalent of the Cavalry charging over a hill—and took up position by Clea's side.

"We're here to help you, dear," said Mitz, the obvious spokesman. "We've discussed the dreadful turn of events our actions caused and we all agree. No matter the cost to us personally, we'll back up anything you say that will result in Addy being returned to you."

Michael blanched, but before he could protest, the door to Juvenile Court opened. Out stormed Ms. Stevens. She wore the same sour-apple expression as on the night she took Addy into the custody of DHS. There was a difference, though. The previously waxen flesh of her face was scarlet with anger, and fury blazed through the thick lenses of her glasses. She dismissed the now-crowded waiting area with a frown, zeroing in on Clea.

"Mrs. Reilly," she spat out. "Your violation of the department's explicit orders will not be tolerated."

Stunned by the accusation and frozen in the rather compromising pose of skewering Michael with her index finger, Clea remained mute. The silence allowed Stevens to rage on.

"It is mandatory she appear. The van driver returned empty handed, and school authorities confirm she has missed all her afternoon classes. The foster family has not seen her since this morning, and there's no sign of life at your house. You must...I repeat *must* produce Addison for this hearing to proceed."

Only then did Clea find her tongue. Words tripped out of her mouth as blood drained from her face.

"Are...you telling me...Addy's missing?"

Chapter Thirty Seven

Inky darkness surrounded a small circle of light. Intriguing. Clea likened it to a peephole in a hotel room door with a distant, oddly-distorted view of Rikki jabbing at the palm of her hand. She crinkled her brow. When had she gone to a hotel? And why was Rikki standing outside?

A hard blink squeezed the fuzziness from her brain and sharper focus into her eyes. The circle widened. The blackness subsided. Rikki grew like Alice in the rabbit hole until, full size, it was clear she held a cell phone and was frantically punching its keypad.

Gradually Clea became aware of other things too. Mitz waved a lace-trimmed hankie at her face while an arm gripped her like a vise and its owner—Delbert—urged her toward the wooden bench.

"Young lady," he growled at Rikki. "Are you getting 9-1-1?"

"I'm trying."

Clea sat, but not before brushing off Delbert's grasp. "What are you doing? I'm okay. And I certainly don't need the rescue squad, so put down that phone, Rik."

With barely two hours sleep in the last twenty-four, and a steady diet of coffee and...well, and nothing...little wonder she'd fainted. But all this fuss over her wasted precious minutes, when one scorching question was all that mattered: Where was Addy?

Rising on wobbly legs, Clea confronted caseworker Stevens. "My daughter's well-being was in your hands, and you're telling me you don't know where she is?"

"We had charge over Addison, yes, but she was not a prisoner."

"Save your word games and find her."

"I'll alert authorities, but you must understand, Mrs. Reilly, with runaways—"

"Addy did not run away." What incredible nerve, thought Clea, to think that, to suggest it, to say it out loud. Bitch. She was about to tell the woman so and had sucked in her breath for just that purpose when Stevens abruptly spun on her heels and reentered the courtroom.

Though five people crowded the corridor, Clea felt suddenly alone. She thought of Ren, a willing oak to lean on. He would know how to proceed. For sure he wouldn't stand around doing absolutely nothing.

Like Michael.

Clea regarded her ex's unmoving form from across the hall. In sharp contrast to the genuine concern for Addy she'd sensed in Ren, Michael's face was a mosaic of second thoughts. Talk of illicit doings had clearly troubled him. Clea could well imagine him balancing the chance of incarceration against the steady stream of income which custody of Addy would allow. What the look on his face lacked was worry about anyone other than Michael, as if he'd chalked up Addy's disappearance to the flighty nature of a teenaged girl and refused to entertain a far more ominous possibility.

Clea's stomach lurched. A spike of pure contempt shot across the room and nailed its intended mark. Bull's-eye. Michael flinched. Their eyes connected. In one fluid motion he closed the gap between them, clasped her upper arm and leaned into her ear.

"You can keep the kid," he said.

With that he hurled a snarl at the rest of the stunned assemblage and brushed past them all.

"Where do you think you're going?" Clea called after him. "Your daughter's whereabouts are unaccounted for, and you're walking out?"

"No, darlin', running. Just like the kid did. You chase 'em all away, don't you? Well, the girl's better off without you. And now I've nothing to stick around for, so *ciao* baby."

Gape-mouthed, Clea stood absolutely immobile as Michael's horrible indictment bounced off the walls and he himself hustled beneath the red-glowing exit sign.

Immediately the others stirred and moved in close, their kindly murmurings as warm and comforting as a soft blanket.

Delbert cleared his throat. "Clea, my dear," he said. "I never knew your former husband, but from the performance I've just witnessed, I'd say he's a cad as well as a cold-hearted bastard…and if I might quote Dickens, 'Good riddance for both.'"

The others nodded agreement. Rikki pumped a fist. "Way to go, Delbert," she said.

Clea felt a weight lifted off her heart.

Michael's departure, though an act of cruel indifference, came as no surprise and actually constituted a godsend. No custody battle meant one less thing to agonize over. She shed him like old, dead skin, straightened her shoulders and faced her covey of friends.

"I'm jumping in the car and driving around," she declared. "Every damn street if I have to. Rikki?"

"I'm in."

"Mr. Sheznesky, do you know of places in town where the kids hang out?"

"Yes, of course. A teacher isn't worth his salt if he doesn't know where his students go and what they do after the final bell. I'll visit each and every one. Ask about your daughter."

"Thank you. And, Merriam," said Clea. "Would you check the library? Addy's been spending a lot of time in the reference room. Perhaps all this is an innocent case of working on an overdue school project."

Merriam nodded enthusiastically.

Mitz took Clea's hand in her own and stroked it lightly. "I'm not too old to help, my dear," she said. "I will be speaking directly with Beatrice. It never hurts to have the sheriff as a bridge partner, you know. I'll see to it a missing person's report has been properly filed and put a bug in her ear about it being more serious than a fourteen-year-old playing hooky."

Even though Mitz had kept secrets and led them far afield with cloak-and-dagger misdirection, the base of it all had been loyalty to Clea's mother. The woman could easily have shut down at Clea's harsh treatment, but here she was, offering to go above and beyond.

Clea's eyes misted. "I appreciate that, Mitz. More than you know."

"And," the older woman added, "I'll give Frank Peterson a call and explain the entire situation."

"That's not necessary. Officer Peterson's already assisting us. He knows just about the whole story and as far as locating him, well, he always seems to pop up when least expected, so he's probably close by."

"Oh no, not little Frankie," said Mitz. "I meant his daddy, Frank Senior."

Clea arched an eyebrow, as much to indicate she knew nothing of a Frank Senior as to express shock that the watermelon-shaped Peterson Junior could ever be described as little.

In answer to the unspoken question, Mitz patted Clea's hand again. "You didn't know? I won't go into all the details, but Frank was sheriff years ago and a valuable asset to the Society. He's been retired for decades. Not in the best of health these days. Frankie takes care of him. He's a good boy, that Frankie."

"I trust you to do what's best," said Clea, though unsure what an elderly, former lawman—a sick one to boot—could possibly accomplish.

The group parted company—Delbert and Merriam out the way they'd come in, Mitz in the opposite direction, ostensibly to negotiate the maze of corridors in search of Sheriff Summers.

When only Rikki remained, Clea's emotions swept to the fore. Her pulse raced.

"Oh, Addy, honey,"—the endearment caught in her throat—"where are you?"

"She's safe. We'll find her."

"If only I could believe you, Rikki. My gut tells me she's in trouble, and I blame myself."

"Nonsense!"

"Oh, yes. I should never have let that DHS woman take her."

"What choice did you have?"

"Michael's right, you know," said Clea, avoiding the question. "I'm good for no one. I've not only failed Addy, but I haven't been fair to Ren either. I had no claim on him. If he wanted to return east, who was I…." Her voice trailed into a sigh. Regret dragged her shoulders lower. "I wish he were here, Rikki. And not just because at the moment I could use an FBI agent."

"That's *special* agent."

Both women startled.

"Ren?" said Clea. "What are you doing here?"

The slight curve to his lips rounded even more. He raised his hands as if in surrender. "Don't shoot. I come in peace. Actually I'm here to give Addy a few words of encouragement, maybe some advice on how to survive a couple days of foster living. So where is she?"

"Then you didn't hear?"

"Hear what? I just arrived."

"Addy hasn't been in school all afternoon. She's…." Clea's voice cracked. "…missing."

Immediately Ren stepped forward. Uninvited, he reached out and pulled Clea into an embrace. She didn't resist. In spite of recent, wildly vacillating feelings about the man, the circle of his arms made her feel whole. "We've got to find her," she sobbed into his shoulder.

"What happened? Tell me all you know."

"Not one damn thing."

Gently he pushed away. "Surely something's been done. What about the school? The police?"

Rikki drew his attention. "The way it looks, everyone dismissed it as skipping school or rebellion against the foster home thing. Clea had a fit. Then the caseworker agreed to file a missing person report, and Mrs. Maguire went to make sure it was done. Merriam's checking the library, and Mr. Sheznesky's off to some of the teen haunts around town. That's in case Addy *did* just skip out on school. Beyond that…." Rikki shook her head as if saying more would take a bad situation and make it worse.

Clea read the words that had been withheld. Her hand fluttered to her mouth. Tears threatened again.

Grasping Clea's upper arms, Ren squared her to him. "Let's back up a step or two. I've only been out of the loop a few hours, but it's obvious I've missed a great deal. What did you learn at that Maguire woman's place this morning?"

"How did you know we were at Mitz's?"

Ren paused, heaved a sigh. "Okay. Complete honesty. I didn't want your poking around in police business landing you in over your head, so I…I've been following you."

"That was you in the green car?"

"No. Though I did latch onto a Chevy of that color, the one you say's been trailing you. Escorted it pretty quickly to the edge of town. I'm pretty confident he'll keep on going."

Clea raised an eyebrow, but didn't question how that might have been accomplished. Instead, she said, "There was a black car near Mom's house and I was afraid…well, my imagination's working overtime."

"Possibly not. If you are referring to a plain, black sedan, that was yours truly."

"Then you've been to the house. You saw our note."

"No. I turned off, doubled back. Watched you two go inside. Figured you'd be safe enough for awhile, so I parked around the corner and made a few phone calls. What note?"

Clea looked at him oddly. "Your phone works? Why didn't you answer when I called?"

He shrugged. "You were pretty clear about how much you wanted my help. And I guess I was pissed enough to want to make you regret it. I shouldn't have let personal feelings taint the way I handled this investigation."

"Then you…?"

He stopped her with a look. "Let's try Bureau protocol. I ask the questions. You supply the answers. And…let's try that complete honesty thing again."

Clea backed up to one of the benches and sat. She told him everything: finding the hospital bracelet, Mitz's confession, the story of Barbara and

Sarah, her own frantic attempt to reach him and silence inquiries into the Rose Society. Stirring up the muck surrounding a years-old kidnapping might alert Nicholas DeSanti. If her birth father was but a fraction of the monster Mitz had described, Clea wanted no part of him. She wanted Addy to have no part of him.

Although Clea had no proof DeSanti figured into all or any of what had been going on lately and Addy's vanishing act could be purely coincidental, the mere possibility a connection existed was enough to drive her mad. With that thought, her hands began to shake.

Immediately strong, reassuring fingers covered hers. "Addison's as good as home," said Ren. "I give you my word."

Clea believed him. Had to.

But sitting here, allowing the minutes to tick away, was unpardonable. She of all people should be out combing the streets. She staggered to her feet, but again Ren restrained her.

"Don't go running off half-cocked," he said. "Tell me. When and where did you see your daughter last?"

"On the school grounds. This morning. I watched her go *into* the building, Ren."

"So we scout up her friends and—"

"Friends? She's new to the crowd in public school, doesn't really have any—" Clea stopped herself. "Of course. Cynthia. The last person I saw Addy with was her senior mentor, Cynthia. If anyone knows what Addy could be up to, it's bound to be that girl."

"Then Cynthia it is."

With a sag of her shoulders, Clea said, "Trouble is, I don't know where she lives. I don't even know her last name."

"I could get around that," said Ren, "but it'll take time. We should look for a quicker way."

"The high school?" offered Rikki. Her eyes shot to a clock on the wall, the movement duplicated by Ren and Clea.

"If we hurry," said Clea. "Classes are done for the day, but maybe the place hasn't completely emptied. Cynthia drives her own car. It's unlikely she's still around, but the girl's popular. Other students will know who she is."

Nodding in agreement, Ren tossed Rikki the keys to his car. The action left no doubt about driving arrangements: he planned to ride with Clea, Rikki was to follow.

The three hurried outside, straight to the vehicles.

A thick soup of moisture-laden air awaited them, though the rain of earlier had ceased. A cold, penetrating dampness raised the flesh on Clea's arms. As they drove, she thought of her daughter, perhaps wandering around exposed to the foul weather. Had Addy been wearing a proper coat that morning? Wretched when she couldn't remember, Clea took one hand from the steering wheel and felt behind her seat for the blanket she kept there for use at outdoor photo sessions. The material was stiff and somewhat scratchy, but it was dry. A warm blanket was a poor substitute for failing to protect Addy against the distresses of the last twenty-four hours, but it was something and having it available and handy eased her mind.

The high school loomed gray and cheerless. Like giant bumble bees, a line of yellow and black buses maneuvered along the drive and onto the road.

"Shoot!" Clea ground to a stop. "Place'll be deserted."

A toot sounded from behind. As if she'd read Clea's mind, Rikki leaned out her window and shouted. "Around behind. Try the gym. It's football season. The jocks'll be practicing."

"In this weather?" Clea called back.

"Don't argue," said Ren. "One way or the other, the school has to be ruled out. Who knows? We might even get lucky."

Unconvinced, Clea nevertheless wheeled away from the front of the building and past a decorative pond, swollen with brownish water that gnawed into the grass at its banks. Adjacent to the student parking lot, a chainlink fence enclosed an oval track. Abandoned. Beyond lay the playing fields, goalposts at either end. They too were empty. Over a side door to the gym a painted gladiator glared menacingly as if to bar their entrance, though the door had been propped open with a cafeteria chair. Inside lights blazed, and the squeal of athletic shoes on a wooden floor raised hopes Rikki's assessment had been correct.

"So, what's she look like, this Cynthia?"

"Good-looking. Giggly."

Ren grunted. "You don't seriously expect me to go in there armed with no better a description than *giggly*, do you?"

Clea felt a smile rise to her lips. "I thought you FBI guys were tough."

"Tough doesn't mean stupid."

"The stereotypical cheerleader then. Blue eyes, blond ponytail."

"Similar to her?" Ren inclined his chin toward the gym door where a girl wearing a short, pleated skirt and Gladiator sweater emerged arm in arm with Uniform No. 24.

"Exactly like her." Clea sounded the horn and clambered out of the SUV just as Rikki ran up beside her.

"Do you see?"

"I do." She flagged an arm over her head and yelled.

At first Cynthia's smile remained in place as she craned her neck toward the gaggle of parked cars, searching for the source of the voice calling her name. Clea tried again.

"Over here!"

Clea watched as Cynthia's focus settled in her direction. She expected the girl to return her greeting or alter course and come closer. Instead the teenager ducked behind the screen of her wide-shouldered friend, then tore down a muddy path between two practice fields.

Clea and Rikki exchanged looks of wide-eyed disbelief. By now Ren had joined them.

"Wait, Cynthia," Clea shouted. "Wait."

The girl hazarded a single glance over her shoulder but did not slow down. Clea took off, sprinting past a startled Mr. Gladiator, Rikki and Ren not far behind.

Though years of student feet had beaten any vegetation from the path, and rain had stirred it into a quagmire, Clea managed to travel a good fifty yards before she lost her footing. One knee slid into the ooze. She flailed about but Ren grabbed her beneath her arms before she hit the ground and hauled her to her feet. When he spun her to face him, lines of concern slashed his forehead.

"I'm okay," she said. "I'm okay. Don't lose sight of Cynthia." However, when they looked around, the girl had disappeared.

"So close," said Rikki.

"Close doesn't count."

"Then it's back to the original plan," said Ren. "That's all we were going to do here in the first place." He reached into his pocket and offered Clea a handkerchief. She took the neatly-folded square of cloth, looked at her ruined slacks, but made no move to wipe them clean.

She blamed herself for blowing the chance to speak directly with Cynthia. She wondered too why the girl had reacted so strangely and jumped to the conclusion Cynthia knew a lot about Addy's disappearance and was not keen on sharing it. That would actually be good news, meaning the two shared a secret. Had a forceful abduction, Clea's worst fear, taken place, surely Cynthia would have reported it. Now Clea wanted more than ever to catch up to the girl and question her. She looked again in the direction they'd been running but conceded it was futile to pursue. The girl could be hiding anywhere—in the outlying equipment shed or under the bleachers or maybe she had made it clear to the service drive and was now cutting through backyards in the neighborhood.

Reluctantly, Clea said to Ren, "You're right."

The three of them headed back toward the school, closely watching their feet to avoid slipping. As they drew closer, a knot of football players gathered outside the gymnasium door taking in the spectacle. An older man, the coach no doubt, stared along the path, his mouth soldered into a hard line. Clea knew an explanation was in order, and she was composing one when a police car, lights flashing, sped into the parking lot and screeched to a stop. Even from this far away, Clea recognized the unmistakable shape of the officer extracting himself from the front seat.

"It's Frank," she whispered to Ren. "I think the coach, or one of the boys, must have called 9-1-1. How else would he be so johnny-on-the-spot?"

"Remember what they say about looking a gift horse in the mouth. Two badges are better than one. His being here might tip the scales and get us what we need in a hurry."

"Hmm. I don't know. Judging from the scowl on the coach's face, I would say anything useful would still have to be pried out of him."

Within a minute the two groups met, the students ordered inside. Ren presented his ID and explained why three otherwise sane adults had been chasing one hapless teenaged girl over school property. The coach relaxed, but said he couldn't help.

"It's against district policy to give out students' personal information. I'd need to see a court order or warrant of some kind. Even with that I'd still feel uncomfortable. These modern times, you know. One can't be too careful." He launched his shoulders upward. "Come back in the morning when the Admin Office is staffed. They have the authority to make a decision. Unfortunately my hands are tied."

Color heightened in Ren's face. He turned away, grabbed Peterson's arm and steered him aside.

"You've been on the force a long time," he said. "Isn't there a way you can get around this guy's objections?"

"This ain't New York City. We do things by the book here, Davis. I know Ms. Reilly's upset about her daughter, but as I see it, there're only three things we can do—go find ourselves a judge to sign some papers, come back tomorrow or—"

"Tomorrow? No. No way!" Clea exploded. "Frank, please. You know me. You know my mother. Is it possible for you to bend the rules a little?"

"Nothin' I'd rather do, but I can't."

"Right. Your hands are tied too."

"It's the way it is, but don't you worry. Lots of people are looking for Addy now. I heard the report go out to all cars over the radio. We'll find her."

If defeated by the legal roadblocks here at the school, at least the police bulletin was a victory or sorts. Clea's gaze drifted toward the coach. She must have presented a pathetic figure, for he responded with a sympathetic gesture but quickly nudged the supporting chair inside and disappeared behind the gym door as it swung shut.

Clea sensed Ren close by. Heard the sharp in and out of his breath and knew he felt the same frustration as she did. She was glad to have him back, even if only temporarily. She toyed with the handkerchief still in her hand, finding it impossible to look Ren in the eye as she offered an apology for her behavior.

"I'm going crazy and you were an easy target. I'm sorry, and so grateful you care enough about Addy to ignore my outburst. I need all the help I can get. So...what now?"

"Let's get away from here," said Ren. "Go where we can think through a few options."

Clea was fairly certain he wanted to distance himself from Frank. She too had been put out by the man's refusal to budge from strict adherence to the letter of the law. Old, mean-spirited impressions from her first encounter with Peterson made an encore appearance. She fought them, arguing the officer had unfailingly offered his support in the past, and chalking the misgivings up to her present state of panic. An exhaled huff got her back on track.

"Where's Rikki?" she said, eager to be on the way, even though a destination had yet to be decided.

Three heads swiveled. Rikki was nowhere in sight. A radio squawked and Frank returned to his vehicle. "I've got to go," he called a minute later. "Accident on Route 12. Car versus canine," he added when Clea caught a worried breath. "I'll be in touch."

He had barely cleared the parking lot when Rikki appeared at the corner of the building.

"I've got it!" Sprinting the rest of the way and landing breathless yet excited at Clea's side, Rikki explained. "While you guys were spinning your wheels out here by the back door, I went in the front. I'd intended to hunt up a student or two languishing in detention but found something better."

"What?"

"Remember those group pictures you take here every year? The ones of football teams, glee clubs...and cheerleading squads?"

Clea nodded, hoping against hope she knew where this conversation was heading.

"There's a slew of them on the wall down the main corridor—framed, and complete with names—first and last."

"Cynthia?"

Clea threw her arms around a grinning Rikki, smothering any reply.

Chapter Thirty Eight

Upon learning Cynthia's last name, the rest had been easy, the girl's address a phone call away. Rikki, Clea and Ren, in two vehicles, sped to the well-spaced neighborhood and rang the proper doorbell. If their luck had momentarily changed for the better, the improvement was short-lived. The teenager had not returned home after her mad dash from the muddy playing fields, and her mother was far from helpful. Though empathetic with Clea's predicament, the woman hadn't a single clue to her own daughter's whereabouts, and knew even less about the recent activities of the two girls.

Clea thanked her anyway. Ren doled out a business card and a "Call me when you hear from her." With spirits at ground level they tramped to the cars. The fruitless chase had cost time. To make up the loss, Ren divvied up the town, east and west, and dispatched Rikki to collect Paul. With him, she was to form a separate search team. A moment later Ren's government-issue peeled away with Rikki at the wheel, followed closely by the SUV.

Ren and Clea switched seats, with Ren now driving and on a course for the high school.

"Cynthia took off on foot," he explained, "but she'll be itching to reclaim her car from the parking lot. It's worth the detour."

Clea stared out the window, half-hearing his words, the passing houses registering as a blur. She pulled the blanket from behind the driver's seat and cradled it in her arms as if its empty folds held her daughter. A muddle of unsupported fears grew by leaps to unbearable proportions, her grip on the blanket ever tightening until her arms ached from the effort. Had it not been for a distant car horn, she might still have been lost in a pit of personal agony and missed it altogether.

"Ren," she called. "Stop! She's there on the side street we just passed."

"Who? Addison?"

"No. Cynthia. Back up."

Instead he braked and swerved toward the row of cars parked along the curb.

"Back up, Ren. Don't let her disappear again."

"Is she coming or going?"

"Coming, but—"

"The minute she sees us, she'll be off in a shot. Think smarter. That's what we have to do."

Faster too seemed on the menu, for Ren's plan was quick in coming, as if its formulation had been well-rehearsed. He deposited Clea on the corner. A bushy, untrimmed yew screened her admirably. The diminished light of late afternoon made gloomier still by overcast skies completed her concealment.

For his part, Ren drove on and around the block, positioning himself to prevent a repeat of Cynthia's earlier escape.

Clea heard the girl rather than saw her—a charm bracelet or key ring acting as metallic informant of her approach. She counted to five and stepped clear of the hiding place and into Cynthia's path. The girl froze. An audible breath of surprise filled the space left empty by the now-silent charms or keys.

Confusion flickered across Cynthia's face. Clea watched the mental process unfold. What to do? Run or stay? To her relief she spotted Ren approaching on foot from behind just as Cynthia reached a decision and opted for flight—a flight that ended abruptly on a collision course with his chest.

The girl could have sprinted, nothing held her save the authority in Ren's stance, and perhaps a guilty conscience. Instead she turned and muttered an insincere greeting.

Clea inhaled deeply. As calmly as her nerves would allow, she said, "I've been wanting to talk to you. I don't know where my daughter is, and I'm pretty concerned about it. You know she never returned to school after lunch break."

The girl bit her lip, but did not respond.

"I have a feeling you could help me out. You won't be in trouble if you tell me, and Addy won't be in trouble when I find her, but not knowing where she is…." In a much more subdued voice, she added, "Or if anything's happened…well, I simply *have* to find her."

Eyes averted, obviously struggling against opposing forces of loyalty and the right thing to do, Cynthia finally said, "She didn't run away, Mrs. Reilly. Really. She just had something to do."

Clea held her tongue, hoping a stretch of silence rather than a string of questions would draw details from the reluctant teen. The wait was interminable but produced the desired result.

"Addy...uh...told me...she'd made a big mistake...the thing with her dad, you know. She wanted to make up to you for the trouble it caused. It was supposed to be a surprise."

More silence from Clea.

"I only helped her a little. She had it mostly worked out by the time we started going to the library. She's such a whiz at figuring stuff out. Like that drawing. She put the whole thing together from two lousy D's. And search? Boy, can she use the computer. I can't believe she actually found who she was looking for. I wanted to go with her but had practice at three, so I only gave her a lift. That's it, Mrs. Reilly. Addy didn't run away or anything. She's not missing at all. I hope she isn't mad at me for giving up her surprise. I promised not to tell anyone."

Cynthia ran out of steam, but Clea had heard enough.

More secrets. More lies.

The girl offered up a ghost of a smile that was either apology or confidence that all had been satisfactorily explained. Ren wore a puzzled expression, yet one totally lacking in the hellish fear that snaked around Clea's heart and held it in a frosty grip. She reached out for Cynthia's shoulder, struggling to control the bite of fingers on the Gladiator sweater as well as the anxiety in her voice, for she knew all too well the significance of the girl's disjointed confession.

"Where did you take her?"

"Uh...the bus station. Out by the big intersection."

Clea glanced at Ren. He snapped to attention, seeming to understand at once the gravity of the situation if not the exact meaning.

"Thank you, Cynthia," Clea said. "You've been a big help. I won't tell Addy how I found out."

"Thanks, Mrs.—"

The rest, if anything, was said to two backs as both Ren and Clea raced to the SUV, climbed in, and, in unison, slammed the doors.

Ren snaked through residential streets on a bead for the highway leading out of town. He pushed the speedometer to five above the speed limit, then ten, while Clea plumped up Cynthia's rambling story with a fistful of details. The partially visible studio mark on the photograph, which she now believed to portray Barbara and the murdered mother, Sarah, had suggested the word *Photography* and what appeared to be two D's. At the time it seemed a dead issue and thus of little importance.

"So much time had passed," she told Ren, "since the portrait had been taken. I didn't bother to mention it to you. There were only the two letters in the name to work with, and studios come and go. When Addy asked to try her hand at solving the riddle, I thought there'd be no harm. She wanted to help. It meant a lot to her. I totally forgot about it."

Clea kneaded her forehead. When she spoke again, her breath came in fits, her voice as dull and dry as powder. "I handed over the picture, gave her my blessing. I exposed her, Ren. If anything...."

He reached for her hand, but they exchanged no words. What could be said, after all?

The light at Sixth Street turned red. Ren braked. The SUV's rear end swished a little sideways before coming to a stop. Ren frowned, but Clea knew they'd been speeding and the streets were still wet in places. She ignored the skid and stared through the windshield. A woman entered the crosswalk, hurried along by a dog at the end of a leash. Two boys on bikes raced by from the opposite direction. People, unconcerned, going about their everyday lives. Clea thought she would scream.

At the green, Ren gunned the engine. The wheels spun, the car lunged forward.

"Nothing's for sure," he said, though doubt peppered his voice and the set of his jaw remained grim.

"If Addy identified the studio, where does it logically lead? To a photographer, to his records, to the DeSanti's. Cynthia specifically said Addy found the person she was searching for."

"You may be one jump too far ahead. Addison might only have located the photographer, not the rest."

Clea chewed her lip while she considered this. She liked the window of possibility it opened. A brief round of mental gymnastics revised her former conclusion, enough to feel encouraged, though not enough to say it out loud. Instead, when she spoke, it was to urge Ren to hurry.

"If you turn right at the next street then left, you'll miss the light up ahead that just turned against us."

Without letting up on the gas, he made the corner. From there a straight shot brought them to the main highway and the gas station/convenience store that doubled as a bus station for the line which carried passengers to Portland one way, Reedsport and beyond the other.

Clea was out the door before the car rocked to a stop. The attendant at the service station pointed her to the store's cashier who gestured to a booth in the rear at which sat a lone man and a cash box amid a scattering of empty plastic chairs. Listless eyes stared at a wall-mounted TV on which actors pantomimed to a scroll at the bottom of the screen. The agent looked askance when Ren and Clea approached, boredom personified. Addy was nowhere in sight.

Ren asked for a schedule.

The man shrugged. "What schedule? There's only the morning bus and the afternoon bus. Take your pick. Both come and gone for the day. If it's tickets you want, you gotta tell me where you're headed."

"Nowhere." Ren produced his wallet ID. "We're looking for a young lady, fourteen, dropped off about noon. Which bus did she get on?"

The man scratched behind his ear. "What she do?"

Ren raised an eyebrow, but didn't offer an explanation.

"FBI on her tail and she ain't done nothing?"

"We'd appreciate your cooperation."

"I'm giving you all I've got since nobody fitting that description's been traveling in or out of here all day."

"That's impossible," said Clea. "I know for a fact she was here, and she's not here now. She's underage, so don't claim you're protecting anyone's privacy. I'm her mother, and I have rights too."

"Lady," he said pulling a small pile of yellow ticket stubs toward himself. He wet a thumb and started to flip. "Here's what we got. Old folks, businessman, woman and two kids, woman and three kids, married couple, black if that's any difference, and Roger from old man Carter's hardware store."

"No," Clea insisted. "That can't be right."

The agent shoved the stack toward her in a help-yourself gesture, but his handwriting proved indecipherable, leaving Clea no choice but to accept both his memory and the honesty of his answer. A long, doleful sigh emptied her soul of optimism. She turned to Ren. "How could we have been so wrong?"

He took her arm. "We're not done yet."

Together they retraced their steps through the aisles of the mini-store. Clea's stomach churned though not from the unappetizing mix of shelf partners—the candy next to motor oil, and chips clipped over a cooler of live bait. They were no further ahead than before. Worse actually, for their one lead was on the verge of evaporation.

At the register they waited while the clerk rang up a sale. She seemed in a better mood than the ticket agent, and Clea forced herself to believe—if only for a moment—the bright spot of the woman's smile boded well. That wasn't to be. Even after Clea produced a photograph, the woman couldn't recall seeing Addy. In fact, she was sure of it.

Last stop, the station attendant, young and male. Discouraged twice, Clea wanted to skip him and hurry back into town to continue on more familiar turf but Ren persisted.

"Cynthia's little sports car," he said, "if not the two attractive girls inside, might have caught his attention, enough to jog a brain cell or two of memory."

He was right.

"Sure I seen it." Obviously the kid meant the car.

"What about the girls?" asked Ren.

"Seen them too. But they didn't buy gas."

"What did they do?"

"Nothin' really. Pulled right past the pumps. The one got out, the other drove off. Purred all the way." The car again.

Clea fixed a malevolent look into the depths of the store, taking in clerk and agent with contempt. "Somebody's lying, Ren. Addy *was* here."

The attendant perked up, and for a reason known only to him, defended his fellow employees. "No, no. If they missed seeing her, it's 'cause she never went inside. Waited a couple minutes over there by the ice machine, until another car came by and picked her up. He didn't buy gas either."

"He?" Panic crept into Clea's voice, dead air settled in her chest at the thought of Addy getting into a car with a stranger.

"What did he look like?" asked Ren.

"I don't know. Old."

"How old?"

"'Bout like you, I guess."

Ren winced but continued the questioning. "What did the *car* look like?"

"Oh. Silver caddy. New. Performance model. Custom wheels."

"Happen to remember the license plate?"

"Sorry. Looked out of state though."

"Hmm." Ren handed over a five dollar bill. "See which way they went?"

The fellow pocketed the money, shook his head and returned to a stool inside the open bay.

A new wave of rain popped against the windshield and dinked the rooftop as a lead-footed Ren steered the SUV toward town. Emotion congealed the air, suiting it more for chewing than breathing.

Clea cut the silence. "Where are we going? There's no way to tell which direction he took her...or how far...or what his—"

"We're not doing anything alone." Ren broke in before she finished the sentence. "Here's what I have in mind. That kid's description of the car was pretty significant. Peterson can take care of an all-points. Have everybody on the road looking for the Cadillac. Get the sheriff involved and up to speed. Meanwhile, Paul and I will run through databases to come up with an owner."

"Start with Nicholas DeSanti."

"You bet." He lapsed into thought, squinting dead ahead as at a screen on which appeared an action plan and all he need do was focus and read.

"I want you to go home," he said.

"And do what? Gnaw my fingernails to the knuckles?"

"An errand."

"Don't humor me with make-do work, Ren. I need to be useful."

"My point exactly. It'll save time if you drop me at my place, so I can get started. You go pick up Addison's computer. Make sure it's turned off before you unplug it, then bring it to me—Paul really—he's better at breaking into computers, unless, of course, you know what her personal password is."

Clea grimaced. "No. No, I don't."

"Then Paul's my man. He can retrieve any communication Addison's had via email as well as her recent searches on the Internet."

"And that will help find her?"

"At this point we grab at any straw in the wind."

Clea wasn't about to argue. She hadn't given the computer a second thought. Besides a task, a simple one, *any* one, would put the brakes on her runaway imagination, at least temporarily. As much as she hated being separated from Ren, particularly now, she would go home, yes she would, and do as told.

When Ren exited the car, it was without a backward glance. A man on a mission. Just as well, Clea thought, as she slid to the driver's seat. Stay on point. Find Addy. That's all she cared about.

In the few minutes it took to drive from one house to the other, the rain kicked up a notch. Clea backed deep into the driveway, parked as close as possible to the door, and sprinted the remaining steps. The deadbolt gave her trouble again. Damn thing. She jiggled the key until it yielded.

Despite her state of mind, the warmth and inviting serenity of the kitchen suggested an island in an ocean of grief. Even though she wouldn't be staying longer than necessary to collect the computer, it was good to be home.

A spot of yellow near her feet caught her eye. A dish towel had fallen to the tile. When she stooped to pick it up, she noticed something else out of place. The telephone receiver dangled from its cord. The absence of a dial tone told her it had been off the hook for awhile.

Her mind blanked. She had no recollection of knocking the phone from its base. The house had been empty all day. How had the phone gotten itself from the counter to the floor? Abandoning the towel, she reached instead for the phone. Her hand never made contact, for a soft glow of illumination spilling from the living room doorway diverted her attention. She knew she had not left a light burning in that seldom-used room.

Had Michael returned and let himself in? He had his nerve, though what else could explain the towel and phone? Why would he come back? A change of heart seemed unlikely, but with him, who knew? She rose and walked toward the door, ready to do battle. She wasn't prepared for what met her.

On the coffeetable a single candle burned, its white-tipped flame transforming the room into a surreal canvas of light and shadow.

In the light, Addy. She sat with her hands folded awkwardly in her lap. All color had been washed from her face. In her eyes, abject horror. Across her mouth a silvery strip of duct tape.

From the shadow, a disembodied voice. "I've been waiting for you... Barbara."

Chapter Thirty Nine

"*Who* are you?" Clea demanded.

The shadow shifted and began to separate, at first peeling apart into an ominous double-headed beast, then along its core until two shapes emerged—one, a silhouetted floor lamp, the other, a man.

Clea gasped. "Who are you?" she repeated, though any hint of former bravado had disappeared.

"You don't recognize me?"

The half-light threw the man's features into stark angles and planes. He was not terribly handsome but also not disgustingly ugly. Neither tall nor well-built, yet by no means short or underpowered. He was, in fact, average-looking. Black hair, his eyes almost so, about Clea's own age and a total stranger.

"Should I?" she finally answered.

"Tsk, tsk, tsk. I expected so much more from you, Barbara."

"My name's not Barbara. You've somehow made a horrible mistake. If you leave right now, that'll be the end of it. I swear."

The man raised his arm. For the first time Clea saw the gun, a grotesque outgrowth of his hand, hard and dangerous, and pointed directly at Addy.

"That's not what the little missie here says."

Clea's voice dried up.

"You don't see the family resemblance?" He turned his face from side to side, posing. "To be quite frank, Barbara, I don't either. But then again, we're only related on papa's side."

Her eyes rounded. Related? Papa? Could this be Nicholas DeSanti's son?

"That's right," he said as if Clea had spoken. "Daddy dearest fathered two children." He tossed a forbidding sneer in her direction. "The fair-haired daughter…and me."

To Clea's immense relief he lowered the weapon, and for a brief moment she relaxed enough to steal a look at Addy and assess her daughter's state of mind. The girl appeared calmer, now that she was no longer alone. How often had Clea's own mother meted out courage with "strength in twos." She had passed the adage down a generation to help Addy over the bumps inherent in a single-parent household. Would the maxim rise above cliché to sustain them in the face of what was likely to come? She summoned an inner force and tried to convey it through her eyes, hoping the energy made it across the room.

The effort was interrupted.

"Where are my manners?" the intruder said with syrupy falseness. "Let me introduce myself—Gabriel Luciano DeSanti, offspring number two, long lost brother, familial outcast. But, please, no formalities. Call me Gabe…." His voice soured into a feral snarl. "…Barbara."

Clea plumbed her imagination for a credible bit of fiction to explain away what was clearly the truth. Finding none, she said, "I tell you I'm not who you think I am."

"This says differently."

He reached into his pocket, withdrew a crinkled sheet of paper, and shook open a poor but distinguishable copy of the once-mysterious photograph.

The revelation was chilling. According to Cynthia, Addy had figured out the studio mark, and the trail had been followed to its natural conclusion. Clea blamed herself. Her anguish deepened.

"Ah," said Gabriel. "I see this girlie of yours failed to mention our pleasant correspondence on the subject of family reunions."

Stoically Clea refused him the satisfaction of an answer.

DeSanti held up the photo. "No need to ask how. I'll tell you. She simply traced these two D's here to Bernard Langford. The old man threw a lot of business Bernie's way—christenings, weddings, graduations, you name it, and Bernie came with tripod and camera. I expected nothing less than he would contact me about an urgent inquiry into his archives. I've been looking for you a long time, Barbara. Never dreamed you'd land so easily in my lap."

Clea slipstepped a little to her left. "What do you want?" The slight movement brought her a few inches closer to Addy, and the question distracted him from her intention. At least it seemed to. In fact, his guard lagged as he began to wander the room, running a critical hand over pieces of furniture and stopping to examine framed enlargements of Clea's work.

He turned back just as she took another, longer step. His expression registered no concern. Instead he answered mildly, "To get to know you." Immediately his attention swept back to the three large prints, each a view of Cannon Beach, which hung on the wall. Rikki called them "prize winners," though they'd never won a thing. DeSanti's interest lingered there.

Clea ventured another step.

With his eyes still on the photos, he said, "Where do you think you're going?"

His tone had escalated from nonchalance to threat. Clea froze. Fear leached through her body. Don't blow it, she told herself.

She glanced his way, trying to read his expression, but he presented only a profile. What might have revealed something of the man was hidden. What made him tick? What would gain a more positive reaction? Whimpering plea? A mother's anxiety? Stoic aloofness?

The moment stretched. Alarmed the opportunity to physically connect with Addy would pass while she debated, Clea opted for a simple, straightforward lie.

"My daughter has asthma. She can't breathe with that thing over her mouth."

DeSanti shifted. The barest tic of his head granted permission. Clea rushed to her daughter's side and carefully peeled away the tape.

Choked on tears and panic, Addy blurted, "Oh, Mom, I'm so sorry. I'm so sorry."

"Shh, honey. None of this is your fault. Shh."

Clea hugged her arms around Addy's shoulders. Only when the embrace wasn't returned did she realize Addy's hands were bound together. Clea reached for the cord. A warning growl stopped her cold.

"Don't test the limits of my good nature, Barbara."

"Why are you doing this?" Clea returned. "What *is* it you want from us?"

"You stole something from me." DeSanti turned full-face. Devil's eyes raked her, and the stench of unspeakable places seemed to fill the room. "Nobody takes from me."

Clea had no answer, no clue what he meant. If anything Gabriel's father—their father—had robbed Clea. He'd taken Sarah's life, depriving Clea of knowing her own mother.

This she kept to herself, for DeSanti's vacant stare and the audible grinding of his teeth told her he had already passed beyond rational thinking.

If not reason, what then? She thought of Ren. Soon he would notice her prolonged absence. With the house phone off the hook and her cell phone dead, would he come looking? She revised the thought without the question mark. Ren *would* come looking. She believed it with all her being.

For the drama to unfold as she envisioned it, she must delay whatever Gabriel had in mind. Calm him. Distract him. Disarm him—well, not literally disarm. No way she could wrestle a gun out of his hand, but with talk, talk about nothing in particular, only to eat up time.

Remembering his scrutiny of her beach photos, she asked tentatively, "You like the ocean?"

"Hmm?"

"That's Cannon Beach and the other, Haystack Rock. Landmarks around here. Famous even."

"Don't take me for an idiot. I know what they are," he answered defensively, though without his previous malice.

"Of course not. It's just you seemed to like the seascapes, so I thought—"

"Don't think."

She retreated into silence, wondering what to do next and mentally calculating the time elapsed. Had it been long enough for her to have driven to the house, disconnect a computer, haul it to the car and make the return trip? How far beyond the minimum time frame would Ren wait until either worry or impatience got the better of him? Until then, Clea would have to find a way to stall, heap on the trivialities to deflect Gabriel from the reason he had taken them captive. She tried anew.

"There are more in the dining room, if you care to see. Cannon Beach. My favorite place."

His face remained as stolid as a clay mask, though for some reason he repeated her final statement. "Favorite place."

This tiny bit of interest provided a springboard to drag out the minutes. "Yes, it is," she said. "Especially from the vantage point of, say, that one."

She pointed to the largest of the three photos which captured Haystack Rock in the distance from a foreground of steep cliffs amid densely forested hills. It appeared dangerous and isolated, though it was neither.

DeSanti gave away nothing in his expression. "Favorite place," he said thoughtfully.

Beach talk exhausted and not understanding his fixation on her offhand remark, Clea was at a loss. Press her luck with another inane comment or change the subject altogether?

And where was Ren? Was it unfair to expect him to miss her so quickly and come bursting through the door? Right now Clea didn't give a fig about the scales of fairness. Where the hell was he?

Addy, who had been quietly sobbing, awkwardly raised her bound hands and wiped her nose on the sleeve of her sweater. Bloodshot eyes sought her mother's.

"Ren'll come get us, won't he? He knows we're here, doesn't he?"

Although she spoke little above a whisper, DeSanti went rigid.

"Let's go, Sis," he said. "And bring the kid."

Go? If they left the house, how was Ren supposed to find them? Rikki's preoccupation with crime novels had been the source of countless conversations on the road to photoshoots. Clea knew about secondary crime scenes and how the odds of rescue plummeted when victims were moved.

"Where are you taking us?" She asked the obvious, wondering if he would slip up and tell her.

"Someplace special." The vague words promised little, but accompanied a deliberate look at the beach photos. He pursed his lips, nodded imperceptibly.

That was it. Cannon Beach. As soon as Clea thought it, though, she doubted. Had she made a valid connection or invented one out of desperate hope? Addy's fate and her own depended on what she did next. Was she right or would she be leading Ren on a goose chase in the wrong direction?

DeSanti had already crossed to Addy's chair and pulled the girl to her feet. He brandished the gun.

"Mom!"

"Shut up!" Roughly Gabriel forced Addy toward the kitchen, obviously knowing Clea had no choice but to follow. In a minute, two at the most, they would reach the back door. Once outside, a chance to leave Ren a message of sorts, a clue to their whereabouts would be gone.

Decide! The thought screamed in her ears. Cannon Beach or nothing—but do something and do it quickly.

The kitchen was as she had found it a nightmare ago. The yellow dish towel still lay in a lump on the floor. Phone off the hook. Tote bag on the counter. Clea kicked the towel, pretending to lose her footing. "Ooh!" she cried and feigned grappling for a handhold on the countertop while she reached inside the bag for her Nikon. Stunned by the commotion, DeSanti hesitated. The barrel of the gun wavered down and away from Addy, just the reaction Clea had prayed for. She aimed the camera at his face and pressed the "test charge" button. The strobe fired. DeSanti recoiled at the blinding burst of light. Clea dropped the camera, sprang forward, grabbed Addy and ran for the door. She twisted the knob and yanked…and yanked…and yanked.

Damn deadbolt! Stuck again.

Iron fingers seized her shoulders and slammed her against the opposite wall. Clea spun. Her head struck one of her framed photos, breaking the glass.

Jagged shards rained onto the floor. A small smudge of blood discolored the silver-gray matting, and the frame hung askew.

"Get over here, bitch!" In control again, DeSanti pinned Addy to his chest. He waved the gun, and Clea obeyed his command. He overrode the lock and forced open the door.

As Clea passed through, she chanced one last, furtive glance at the damage done to the photo of Cannon Beach.

She had done all she could. Would it be enough?

Chapter Forty

As they neared the coast, the rain let up. Patches of fog now lurked in roadside swales, threatening to swell and devour the road. Though the highway itself remained unobscured, Clea drove more slowly than necessary. She counted the delay as seconds and minutes deposited into a bank, from which Ren could withdraw as he followed in hot pursuit. The more she lagged, the more ground he gained. He *was* coming. Only with this thought did she keep a grip on sanity.

They had been an hour on the road.

After DeSanti had herded them out the kitchen door and into her SUV—Addy in back, she in the driver's seat—he'd ordered her to Cannon Beach—a small victory for Clea. She had read his fascination with her photos correctly, and the driving arrangement enabled her to choose slow-going back routes and slack off the gas pedal whenever possible.

Worry gnawed at her insides. It was one thing to direct Ren to the vicinity of Haystack Rock, quite another to fathom DeSanti's exact destination. If luck held, Clea would have the upper hand. She knew the area, DeSanti didn't. But, of course, neither did Ren. What would she do when DeSanti finally realized the seclusion depicted in her photographs was a product of camera angles and clever composition? Cannon Beach was a bustling little town, an unappealing place to someone up to no good, as Gabriel surely was.

Covert glances in the rearview mirror convinced her Addy had detected the circuitous route and her mother's overly-cautious rate of travel. Thank God her daughter was a quick study, having learned a valuable lesson when her mention of Ren's name had prompted DeSanti to move them far from town.

No one had as yet spoken during the drive, but Clea sensed a distinct increase in DeSanti's agitation. It matched her own rising distress level. Was her troubled state feeding his? Or was it the other way around? In her profession she'd spent endless hours manipulating excitable children into cooperative subjects, willing to sit still long enough for a series of poses. Whether her field experience qualified her to distract an adult of questionable mental stability remained in doubt, yet she had to try something. With a gulp of damp, oppressive air, she swallowed her reservations.

"Gabriel?"

She had meant to speak in undertone, and thought she had, but the single word seemed to fill the car. She intentionally dulled the edge in her voice as she went on. "Back at the house you said I stole from you, but you have me at a disadvantage. Until today we've never laid eyes on one another. What could I have possibly taken that belonged to you?"

Clea darted a look his way, but the greedy storm had snatched what light the hour usually offered, leaving only a murky gloom and the dashboard instruments to illuminate her passenger. She couldn't see his face as he peered straight forward. His head swayed as if balanced on a fragile stem, suggesting thoughts far from Oregon. She wondered if he'd even heard her.

Perhaps the better course was not to disturb him at all. Mitz's story of Sarah's heartless execution spilled full-blown into Clea's mind. If Gabriel also knew the story, she would be foolish to draw him back to those distant years. She caught her lower lip between her teeth, unsure what next to do when he suddenly spat out, "Everything."

"I don't understand."

"My childhood. My birthright. My whole life."

A moment passed in agonizing silence before he continued.

"From the cradle on," he snorted, "I heard of nothing but Barbara this and Barbara that. *When he found his precious Barbara* became the guiding rule by which he lived. You were taken from him. He couldn't let a thing like that go, no matter what."

The sound of tires on wet pavement replaced the diatribe. A car swooshed around them, and Clea feared he'd connect the passing traffic with her reduced speed.

Keep him talking, she reminded herself, but "I'm sorry" was all she could think to say.

"Sorry? I was his son." His voice wavered with a rage barely under control. "Yet I counted for nothing. A spot on the carpet. A stone in his shoe. In comparison to the one he'd lost, the one he had was a poor substitute. Try competing with a ghost sometime, Barbara.

"It was worse for my mother. In his eyes she never measured up to the wife who got away. I never understood that one, but he kept Mom around anyway to remind her of it on a regular basis. I was six when it became too much. She lost spirit and decided a lungful of carbon monoxide beat the hell out of another day with dear old dad.

"And you want to know what was stolen from me. Besides my mother? Besides a father? Besides my soul?"

"You're an adult, Gabriel. You can move on. Shed the past. Be free."

A wounded-animal sound escaped his lips. "He let the business slide. Spent hand over fist on private detectives, agencies, reports, surveillance... right up until the day he died."

"Your father's dead?"

"As a doornail. Next to nothing came to me when a final accounting was made. I owe you a lot for that, Barbara. I intend to pay you back...with interest."

Clea's heart lurched in her chest when DeSanti's gaze drifted to the cargo area where Addy sat scrunched between pieces of equipment. Revenge was a powerful motive for the most despicable acts, one that didn't rely on logic, nor beg apology. As much as Gabriel disavowed his father, the two men shared pattern, cloth and tailor. Talk would buy no mercy.

Nor would time.

Cannon Beach came into view. Weather had dulled the once-cheery town sign to a dismal gray, much the same color as Clea's humor.

DeSanti straightened in the seat, taking in a scene obviously far different from what he'd imagined.

He growled. "You tricked me."

"Not at all. This is Cannon Beach, where you told me to go." She gestured toward the fog-enshrouded Pacific. "Haystack Rock is—"

"Shut up! Let me think."

Clea needed to think too. If she could close in on the police station, if she could get Addy out of the car, if.... She crept along the street, trying to implement a weak and hastily-conceived plan, had signaled to turn off Sunset, when DeSanti grabbed the wheel.

"No!" he said. "Turn around in that gas station there and out the way we came. No funny business either." His tone threatened, an emphatic jab of the gun capped the order.

Clea did as told, pulled in, circled the pumps. An attendant appeared briefly at the door, but retreated out of the dank mist when it became apparent the Explorer would not be stopping for gas. The opportunity to catch his eye came and went in a heartbeat. Clea had no choice but to drive on. She rounded the center island and aimed for the exit, but the SUV slid at the curb cut, its rear tire thumping concrete. As she struggled for control, they exploded onto the street dangerously close to an oncoming black sedan.

The near miss gave her another idea, though one she rejected immediately. With Addy in the back and her hands tied, a deliberate accident was too chancy.

She returned to the highway.

A thick, black stain oozed across the sky, rapidly muscling out what little daylight remained. Clea swore silently. Nightfall changed everything. Blind faith in Ren's abilities burst like a dike downstream of a raging torrent. He'd never find them now. Deliverance settled surely and rudely on her own narrow shoulders. She'd find a way, by God…or die trying.

With new resolve, Clea dug her nails into the steering wheel and squeezed. If only it were DeSanti's throat.

The satisfying though imaginary murder ended when the victim waved a pointing finger under her nose, toward the road, and ordered her into the northbound lane. Ironically they approached the very turnout where Clea had shot the pictures of Cannon Beach. Had it been on its way to noon and clear of fog, he would have seen the overview that had compelled him to the ocean in the first place. DeSanti, however, wasn't admiring the scenery, rather scanning the uphill side of the highway.

Without warning, he wrenched the wheel from her grasp. "Here," he yelled. "Turn here."

Clea countered with the brake. The SUV fishtailed violently, bumped into and out of a rock-strewn culvert, and ground onto an old gravel roadbed she never knew existed. The road was rutted and overgrown, and as a result of the recent rain, paved with a layer of sucking mud.

"Where does this go?" he demanded.

Before she could tell him she had no idea, the gnarled fist of a wayward branch slammed the windshield. Fine lines spidered outward in the glass, obscuring her vision above and beyond the tears of panic. Addy's muffled sobs rent her heart as she fought to control the car.

"Keep driving," DeSanti growled when it appeared they were slowing.

Clea punched the gas. The Ford labored up a winding course. Fog and highway retreated. The road deteriorated even more, then surprisingly opened onto a flattened terrace. DeSanti motioned toward the area. She braked, stunned when the pedal gave to the floor. The car slithered to a stop, its headlights washed over a rundown shack near what looked like four upright wooden posts.

Now she understood. The trail they'd followed had been a forest service road, the shed a long-abandoned fire ranger station at the base of a watch tower.

DeSanti pulled the key, doused the lights. "Perfect," he said. "End of the road. Get out."

Reluctantly she did, helped Addy, and with Gabriel's weapon guiding the way, the three of them stumbled toward the cabin.

Clea cast around for anything that offered the slightest pinpoint of hope. The woods were pitch, still as death, empty, dauntingly empty. All she saw, through a break in the downhill tree line, was the hopelessly distant light at Tillamook Rock.

Chapter Forty One

The force of DeSanti's shove propelled Clea over the threshold and landed her on hands and knees. A splinter jammed into the skin of her palm, and a sticky veil dragged across her mouth.

"You son of a bitch!" She clawed at the spider web and scrambled clumsily to her feet. "Don't you dare even think about touching my daughter."

Whether or not DeSanti heeded the warning, Addy walked in without interference. Mother and daughter found each other in the dark and locked into an awkward embrace. Hot tears burned Clea's cheek though she couldn't be sure they were Addy's or her own.

Something had died in the cabin…and recently.

The putrid smell didn't seem to faze Gabriel while Clea gagged and Addy stuffed her face into her mother's shoulder.

"We can't stay in here," Clea said.

"You'll do as told." He kicked the door, splintering a rotten panel, then kicked it again as if the physical damage and sound of violence fed an inner and hungry ogre.

"Let my daughter go, Gabriel," Clea said quietly. "She's just a child."

"I was just a child."

"You've got it all wrong. I picked that picture up at a garage sale," she lied. "I wanted the frame. That's what I do. I restore old frames. Sell them to my customers. It's been sitting around the house forever." What more could she say to convince him?

"You talk too much, Barbara."

"How many different ways can I tell you I'm not your sister?"

"Sister." He ground out the word as one would utter the name Gacy or Manson. Clea knew any appeal would be wasted breath. DeSanti had long since crossed an invisible line and was well into the uncharted territory of madness.

Action. That was the only solution. She must get Addy and herself away, run, hide, do whatever it took.

Addy's hands were still tied. If they were to get past Gabriel and into the woods, the restraints risked slowing them down, or worse, causing Addy to stumble and fall. At the moment the unforgiving blackness inside the shack worked in Clea's favor. She felt for the cords at her daughter's wrists. The ends were shredded. Addy had been at work. Clea added to the frazzle, but dampness had swollen the fibers and the knots refused to budge.

Escape would be more difficult now. She had to think. How could she assure them a head start when, even with eyes adjusted to the dark, obstacles were unseen and everywhere? DeSanti cursed sporadically as he moved about in the small interior and bumped into pieces of furniture.

"There's a flashlight in the glove box," Clea said. While light promised to make it easier for DeSanti to keep an eye on them, she too stood to benefit from knowing a direct and unobstructed path to the door. It would also give her and Addy a moment alone.

DeSanti's noisy pacing stopped. "Stay put," he said.

The instant he stepped out and his footsteps went dead on the sodden pine needles outside, Clea whispered into Addy's ear. "We're going to get away from here, honey. Stay alert. When I grab you, don't panic, just follow. As soon as we're out the door, I want you to run as fast as you can. Aim for the trees. I'll distract him."

"Not without you, Mom."

"Addison Marie Reilly, when I tell you to run, you go like there's no tomorrow and don't look back."

"Oh, Mom. No."

"Yes. Somehow I'll slow him down. I'll find you later."

The car door slammed. Only seconds remained until DeSanti returned. They'd had so little time to prepare.

"Do as I say," Clea said.

Addy whimpered but brushed closer. "Up my sleeve, Mom."

"What?"

"My sweater. The sleeve."

Clea patted Addy's arm, puzzled when she encountered a rigid, splint-like object under the material. She slid it out and concealed it behind her back just as a beam of light flashed through the doorway and shone in their eyes.

Moments later a psychotic cackle and bodyless head full of grotesque shadows materialized as DeSanti reversed the light and aimed it up and under his chin. He let loose a string of hideous ghost sounds which bounced from wall to wall. "Did you forget? Tomorrow's Halloween. Day of the Dead. Fitting, don't you think? Trick or treat. No...trick *and* treat. I get them both. Finally, I get it all. The last laugh. Meet him in hell, Barbara. Give him the finger for me." A demented laugh from distorted features. "A couple more hours, huh? We can wait. It'll be fun." He waved the light in frenetic arcs around the room then killed the power, plunging them once again into darkness.

A savage punch of reality robbed Clea of breath. She shared parentage with a monster. She shuddered, even as a fledgling root of optimism burrowed into hopeful soil, for DeSanti's rant had given her exactly what she wanted—a brief but clearly-illuminated picture of the cabin's interior and her route of escape. She imprinted the image firmly in her mind.

The unnerving darkness now became friend, hiding her movements as fingertips traced the outline of the object from Addy's sleeve. What a girl! Somehow she'd managed to procure a weapon. MacGyverish in its simplicity, but a weapon nonetheless.

Because it was old, the tabletop tripod possessed sturdy metal legs, crowned by heavy adjustment knobs and a sharp-edged mounting platform. Clea turned the instrument in her hands, lining up the business end in a way it would do the most damage. She shouldered the tripod like a baseball bat and prepared to strike. The scuffle of shoe leather, however, told her DeSanti had moved. Clea had lost her advantage.

"Quiet!" The command came from the direction of the door though no one had said a word.

Then Clea heard it too. Swish. Swish. Leaf against leaf. A twig snapped, then all was still. The sounds could have been anything—an animal disturbed by the scent of a predator, a breath of air that funneled from above to rustle through the undergrowth. Or the approach of a savior.

Clea was afraid to call out for fear DeSanti would react with a spray of bullets. At the same time a profound and visceral recollection drove home with ramrod force. At the gas station. The black sedan. Hadn't Ren been driving one earlier in the day?

The surge of hope flashed bright like lightning but died as quickly. A car coming up the trail would have made more noise. No white knight for them. It was up to her.

"Who was that?" she said, banking on the state of Gabriel's nerves. Whether he'd come to the same conclusion or not didn't matter if she planted doubt: Were they alone?

Every muscle tensed as Clea waited for his reaction—an eternity of weighing options or just plain indecision.

"Move and you're dead," he finally said.

Empty words. Who would enforce them once he stepped outside to investigate? Go, dammit. Go!

Clea's ears picked up the moment Gabriel made up his mind and slipped out. Immediately she clamped onto Addy's trembling elbow. "Wait for my signal, honey. Remember, head for the woods. Go downhill. Toward the highway." She stationed Addy off the doorway. "I love you."

"Love you too, Mom."

On tiptoes, Clea crossed the entrance and positioned herself on the opposite side of the opening. Fingers strangled the tripod, while she gauged a strike at a well-calculated distance south of DeSanti's belt buckle.

Now that she was ready, the seconds dragged. How long would he search outside for whatever may or may not be there? Clea feared she'd made a fatal mistake, wasting escape while she waited for his return instead of taking off at once. A bead of cold sweat trailed a slow, torturous path down her spine. The metal legs of the tripod grew cold. Her fingers cramped.

Self-doubt punished even more, muddling her brain and rendering impossible a rational choice between belated flight and sticking to her plan.

Nausea had firmly taken hold when a stream of muttered curses announced DeSanti's return. Clea braced. Felt the stir of air when he passed through the door. Grit her teeth and swung with a strength she hardly knew she possessed.

The tripod connected. DeSanti yowled. Flesh thudded heavily on the wooden planking. The flashlight skittered away.

Clea shoved Addy outside. "Run! Now!"

She herself paused only long enough to rule out going after the light. DeSanti still had the gun, and she couldn't count on his being incapacitated much longer. Instead she raised the tripod over her head and sailed it at the sound of his groans, satisfied when the thing cracked not against the pine floor but human bone.

"God damn! God damn you, bitch!"

A smile briefly replaced the hard, determined slash of Clea's lips, but there was no time to savor the extent of DeSanti's obvious pain. Her plan was not yet complete. She raced to the car and threw open the door. A weak glow from the dome light barely dissolved the darkness. Seconds flew as her hand played along the dashboard then under the seat. What the hell had he done with the keys? She leaned further in and groped behind the brake pedal, aware his moaning had stopped. How long would it take him to regain his footing and tear out of the cabin?

She heard a stumble, a knock against something solid, a vigorous blasphemy. Each and every sound warned she'd stretched her luck to the limit. Despite that she chanced one final swipe over the car mats.

The keys!

Fear quivered through her body, but the key found home in the ignition. She turned the switch, thanking God and Junior Randall when the car started on the first try.

The headlights picked up DeSanti propped unsteadily against the door jamb. He fended off the glare, but his bloodless stare told Clea he was not so much disoriented as collecting strength and tasting the flavor of retaliation.

He drew the gun and aimed.

Panicked, Clea backed out of the car, even as DeSanti took an unsure step forward. She crouched low behind the shield of the door when he fired.

The shot went wild.

Clearly Gabriel was still hurting. Clea turned and ran.

The leather bottoms of her shoes skidded on loose gravel as she bounded down the service drive. Don't fall, she ordered herself, and flailed both arms for balance.

"Stupid, Barbara. Really stupid." DeSanti flung the words as if he had the upper hand. "You're mine now."

"Think again, bastard."

Squeaking springs and shifting gears told Clea Gabriel had taken the bait. The SUV's tires bit into the roadway, followed closely by a sickening crunch as metal met tree.

"Come on, Gabe," said Clea more to herself than the man in her car. "Don't quit on me."

The engine revved. High beams raked across the wall of trees until they landed squarely on her back. A vulnerable target, yes, but now she could see her way. And the best news. He had pursued *her*. Addy was safe within the shelter of the forest.

Clea headed for the dense woods which hugged the edge of the forest service road but stopped short of disappearing into its cover, choosing instead to dash alongside, in the open. Each time they came to a turn she darted to the other side and out of the twin cones of light from the car. She counted on his single-mindedness, that he'd react to losing sight of her, if only momentarily, with added pressure on the gas pedal.

The road snaked. Twists and turns, ruts and holes. DeSanti's relentless pursuit grew wildly erratic. He picked up speed. Another hairpin turn. Mouse and cat were tugged onward and downward by the treacherous slope. The SUV squealed at the brutal treatment, its underbelly clunked over the rock-strewn path.

Inevitably the distance between them halved, then quartered. One curve to go...if she had counted correctly.

So tired. Heat from the headlights and motor stroked her back. An acrid stink scorched the air. He was so close.

When it seemed she could run no farther, Clea leaped sideways, shot between two narrowly-spaced pines and prayed.

The SUV screamed by.

A burst of ghoulish laughter died and the void filled with a series of rapid-fire thunks as DeSanti pumped the useless brakes. Clea drew one anxious breath as he careened around the curve. The initial crash reverberated through the forest. Crunch after agonizing crunch followed, conjuring images of metal and plastic rupturing in a tumble of death.

Clea fell to the ground, flung there by exhaustion, remaining prone while her lungs filled with blessed relief.

The forest floor was damp and cold, but that was not the reason Clea hauled herself to rubbery legs and staggered toward the Explorer. The headlights had remained on, an eerie beacon that guided her through the trees without returning to the road. She approached slowly, adjusting her weight with each step. If the accident hadn't done its job, if the slightest sound or movement suggested Gabriel DeSanti had survived, she was primed to bolt.

Sight of the wreck almost stopped her heart. The windshield was bloody and crazed over like a surreal mosaic. Two wheels hung at improbable angles. The front and rear quarters were severely caved in. DeSanti's badly twisted body seemed trapped in mangled steel. He didn't move, couldn't possibly be alive.

She thought to step closer, make absolutely sure, but the dead silence that enveloped the woods reassured her, and she had something far more important to do. Coldly immune to the violence she had perpetrated on Gabriel, Clea turned her back and began an uphill trek. With the flashlight from the cabin, she would better be able to find Addy and make their way to the highway and help.

"Addy," she called out. "If you can hear me, I'm coming. Everything's okay now. I'm going for the flashlight."

She labored against the grade. Already worn from the downhill sprint, the return climb proved an extraordinary effort. Her lungs burned, and that after managing only a dozen yards. Fatigue forced a halt. Clea slumped against a tree to catch her breath. Off in the distance an owl hooted. Her pulse drummed in her ears.

She had rested only a few moments when into the familiar rhythm of her heart beat, a new sound inserted itself. Faint and muffled. It stood her hair on end. She whirled toward the wrecked car. Nothing appeared to have changed there, but could she be certain without doubling back? While she struggled between come and go, the undefined sound fashioned itself into a distinguishable word: "Mom!"

"Addy, where are you?"

"Mom! Mom!"

Clea shoved into the understory, fighting thorny tentacles and roots designed to trip. She ricocheted off trees. "Keep talking, honey, so I can find you."

"Help! I can't— Oh, Mom!"

The cries escalated from urgency to hysteria, then dissolved into a whimper. Addy's voice seemed closer yet strangely coming from below.

Confused, Clea stopped. "Addy?"

"Mommm."

Dropping to her knees, Clea crawled forward, hands fumbling the ground in front of her. Suddenly the earth dropped off in a shower of pebbles that cascaded to unknown depths. "Oh, my God! Addy, are you down there?"

"Yes. Something's caught me. It hurts so bad."

Clea flopped to her stomach, shifting sideways until she sensed Addy's presence. "Stay still." She squelched her own panic in an effort to encourage while she scooted nearer the edge and draped her body as far over as possible without pitching forward herself. Probing hands explored the precipice's side. Sharp rocks jutted outward. Intertwining snags ended in broken points. The movements triggered a small avalanche, and Clea could hear Addy struggling to avoid the falling rocks.

"Don't move, honey."

She stretched farther into the abyss and finally brushed the tips of Addy's writhing fingers. The connection jolted—electric with relief yet devastating with one agonizing truth. Addy was out of reach.

Clea bit her tongue to avoid crying out. This couldn't be happening. To survive the torment of the last few hours to come to this. Again she touched her daughter.

"Mom, I'm slipping. Get me out of here. I can't hold on."

The child's blind faith in a mother's ability to do all, to solve every problem, heal every wound pierced Clea to the core. In the end she was nothing but helpless.

"I love you, baby," was all she could say through trembling lips and a broken heart. Tears streamed down her cheeks.

In the midst of boundless grief and her own pitiful inadequacy, Clea visualized Gabriel DeSanti. Had he survived the accident, pursued her to this very cliff, and taken his revenge, she would welcome the fate he'd promised. To lose Addy and live was unthinkable.

The crush of persistent footsteps coming up behind fit with her mindset. She braced for the inevitable, even when she heard her name.

An entire second came and went before she realized the name called was not Barbara but Clea, the voice well known.

"Ren! My God, it's you. We're here. Addy's in trouble. I can't reach her."

A pencil-thin beam of light played along the ground. A moment later Ren's body dropped alongside Clea's, and a steadying arm landed across the small of her back. He reached down into the darkness and securely took hold of Addy. "I've got you," he said. "I've got you both."

Chapter Forty Two

Jack-o-lanterns and vases bright with autumn foliage abounded. Walkers and wheelchairs alike sported orange and black streamers. The volunteers at Green Haven Nursing Home had been busy creating a festive atmosphere, and from the smiles on residents' faces, it appeared they'd succeeded.

Josephine Worth's room was no exception. A row of cardboard goblins dangled from strings at the window. Though a smile was missing, Clea sensed her mother was at least peacefully content.

For the second time she introduced Ren, but then went on as if she were alone, quietly opening her heart with words of love for her mother's sacrifices and lifelong protection. While she spoke, she stroked her mother's hair. That Josie allowed the physical contact without overt anxiety was an encouraging sign, one Clea chose to interpret as elemental awareness and relief the long-held secret was finally out in the open. Eventually she and Ren drew away from the bed and watched Addy conduct an animated, if one-sided visit with her grandmother.

"See my costume, grandma?" A full-circle twirl showed off black jacket over white shirt, a narrow black business tie contributed by Paul, slouch hat and dark sunglasses. "All the kids are wearing the same thing. The Blues Brothers. I'm not real sure who they are, but the seniors got to pick the Halloween prank. Anyway, everybody looks like everybody else. It's supposed to drive the teachers nuts." Addy stole a glance her mother's way. "Parents, too," she giggled.

Clea shook her head in amazement at the resilience of her daughter. Not twelve hours had passed since Ren had led them off the wooded hills above Cannon Beach and into a growing phalanx of police and emergency vehicles. Paramedics administered first-aid, wrapping Addy's wrists with gauze. The restraining cords, Gabriel's instruments of intimidation, had proved in the end the saving force. When Addy fell into the chasm, the rope caught on a protruding branch. Though the ties rubbed her wrists raw, they also prevented a disastrous plunge.

After a solemn ride home, Addy received an overdose of TLC not only from Clea but Ren, Rikki and Paul as well. Clea tucked her exhausted daughter under familiar sheets and kissed her goodnight.

For Clea the night progressed on an entirely different note. She and Ren met with Sheriff Summers.

A scowl darkened the sheriff's face, though not from being called to her office in the middle of the night. Summers glared at the lump of humanity occupying one of the pair of interview chairs. Clea had never seen Frank Peterson out of uniform. Wrinkled shirt and equally wrinkled trousers robbed him of dignity on many levels. He looked older, fatter, woebegone, guilt-ridden, defeated.

"Tell me I've got this all wrong, Frank," Summers said, kneading at the furrows on her brow. "You hired some low life to follow Mrs. Reilly here in order to keep yourself informed of her every move."

"So's she wouldn't get into trouble."

"Trouble defined by you as possibly...*possibly* learning the identity of her own birth mother."

Frank shifted uncomfortably.

"Then, for the same reason, you engaged in several felonious acts, namely burning to the ground a piece of property not your own because it *might* assist her in this search *and* breaking into her mother's house to steal and destroy evidence in what ultimately has turned out to be a longstanding, unsolved kidnapping ring. On top of that, you threatened Mrs. Reilly in writing. How am I doing so far, Frank?"

He nodded, a thing not easy to do with his head buried between hunched shoulders.

Summers referred to notes spread out on her desk. "You poisoned a cat."

At this the man winced. He turned toward Clea who sat in the matching chair. "I apologize for that. I had no idea such a little bit of headache pills would do so much damage. Tell your daughter how terribly sorry I am. It was only to scare you into backing off. If it's any consolation, that little bugger scratched the hell out of me."

"And your father," continued Summers, "a former officer of the law—"

"Pop was sheriff. County Sheriff right here, but he's old now and deserves a little peace."

"He covered up circumstances involving an unreported disappearance and homicide, the details of which you knew and also chose to conceal from authorities."

"I know I was in the wrong," said Frank, "but this thing with the photograph came about so fast, I felt I had to move on it."

"And botched the job from beginning to end."

Ren interrupted. "I think we can all agree that Frank—both senior and junior—acted out of the most honorable intentions, even if their methods proved...well, unorthodox."

"Criminal would be my choice of words."

"The bottom line," said Ren, "was protection of an innocent child. Certainly you can concede Nicholas DeSanti was not the type of man who should be allowed around children. He was a murderer. His son no less so. Officer Peterson deserves a break."

"Well, you, Mr. Davis, are not in charge here."

Summers cut off any response with a flick of her hand. An edgy silence dragged on a full minute before she rose, deserted her post and without explanation walked out of the room. Clea watched the sheriff stalk the mostly empty squad room. Up and back. No path or obvious destination. No apparent reason, though formulating an appropriate punishment seemed a good enough guess.

Frank straightened in the chair and heaved a mighty sigh. "I might be a cop, Clea, but I admired your mom and others in the Rose Society and what they did, and my father too for his conviction that what's right ain't always the same as what's legal. Got me in a heap of hot water, but I don't regret none of it. I'd do it all again...except, of course, the thing with the cat."

Clea reached across and patted his knee. "You've been a true friend, even when I didn't know it or believe it. I'm so grateful and blessed...and sad. My stubborn curiosity has wrecked your life, hasn't it?" She swiped at hot tears forming in the corners of her eyes and glanced a second time at Bea Summers. The woman had stopped pacing and was engaged on the phone, but fierce concentration had sculpted her mouth into an intimidating frown. "What do you think's going on in the sheriff's head?"

Shrugging, Frank deflated once more, becoming one with the leather upholstery.

Ren had been leaning against the glass office wall, but now stepped forward to place a hand on Peterson's shoulder. "You'll have plenty of people backing you up," he said. "I personally know of at least a half dozen here in town. Others will come out of the woodwork, you wait and see. I don't have much clout these days, but Paul Francesco does. He's traded favors up and down the East Coast like a kid trading baseball cards. We'll get you help, Frank. Count on it."

Frank mumbled what might have been thanks, but the sullen silence that followed suggested he'd already prepared himself for the worst possible outcome.

Story told, Bea Summers had demanded Peterson's badge and, receiving it, thrown the shield violently into the wastebasket. Whatever the sheriff was doing out among the empty desks did not bode well. And the longer she took, the more ominous the consequences. All too clearly Clea recognized her responsibility for the storm she'd unleashed and the scarred lives scattered in its wake.

She massaged the nape of her neck, combating the knotted muscles there, comforted when Ren's fingers closed over hers. Immediately she berated herself. To derive even the smallest pleasure while others were hurting grated on her sense of what was right, yet the warmth and intimacy of his simple act felt good.

"Don't take it so hard." His lips brushed her ear as he leaned in and whispered.

"I can't help it, Ren. A good man is ruined. Another dead."

"Gabriel DeSanti isn't worth a second thought. He deserved what he got and more."

"What about my friends? Mitz and Merriam and Delbert and probably more people I don't even know about. They might all face charges, and for what? Protecting Mom and me and Addy? It's not fair."

If Ren had an answer, the opportunity to express it was lost, for Sheriff Summers reentered the office and navigated to her desk. All eyes followed as she took a seat, yet no one uttered a word.

The woman regarded her audience, shook her head and said, "This is what's going to happen. Mrs. Reilly will not file charges for the cat, the B&E, the man hired to tail her."

Clea's head bobbed. "If it helps Frank, of course I won't. By all means."

"David Murray has expressed a certain amount of delight in not having to babysit a ton and a half of old bills and orders for pansies, so much so, in fact, he's agreed to rebuild the storage shed for Mrs. Cooke—no insurance claim involved.

"The death of one Mr. Gabriel DeSanti will be deemed a carjacking. Mrs. Reilly will sign paperwork to that effect. Since the perpetrator is dead, the case will be considered closed."

Clea started to speak but was shushed. The sheriff went on. "You, Mr. Davis...you and your sidekick from New York—yes, I know he's more than a mere house guest. The Rose Society thing and the cold cases..." She plucked at her lower lip. "...they're Bureau jurisdiction. I'm dropping that potato in your lap." Her voice softened a bit as she added, "I trust you'll give it the attention it deserves."

Clea couldn't believe what she was hearing. Was Bea Summers actually hinting the long string of secrets remain unbroken? She glanced at Ren whose cat's-got-the-mouse expression confirmed that his feelings about how much scrutiny the Rose Society merited reflected her own.

"Now," said Summers. "Get out of my office. All of you." The harsh order issued from lips curving into a broad smile. "And, Frank...dig out your badge on the way out."

Leaving Peterson to secure his reinstatement over a fully-loaded garbage can, Ren and Clea made their way past the duty officer's desk and out onto the street. Overhead a sprinkling of stars peeked through rapidly-dispersing clouds, prelude to a rain-free morning, though a lingering damp chill chased the two of them to Ren's car.

"Geez, it's cold," said Clea. "Turn on the heater."

Instead Ren folded her into a warm embrace. "How's this?"

She snuggled close. "It'll do in a pinch." He pinched her. "Ow!"

"Speaking of 'ow,' is your head any better?"

Clea had almost forgotten the lump and patch of dried blood on the back of her skull. She probed it and winced.

"Hmm. Touchy, but a small price to pay. If you hadn't gone to my house when you did...." Clea shivered, not from the temperature but from the thought of what might have been.

Twice she'd heard Ren's story, though details had been sparse on both occasions. On the drive in from the coast, his reticence stemmed from Addy's presence in the car. Later, when Sheriff Summers quizzed him about the circumstances leading to Gabriel's death, his rendition was all skeleton and no flesh.

Clea wanted more than bits and pieces. She pressed him for a third account.

Ren had indeed grown concerned when Clea failed to show up with Addy's computer as agreed. Both cell phone and land line proved useless, leaving him no choice but to return to her house and investigate. He had found the broken and bloodied picture of Haystack Rock and come swiftly to the conclusion Clea had not left of her own volition. Heeding a gut instinct as to the meaning of the single damaged item in an otherwise tidy house, he issued an APB and sped toward the coastal town of Cannon Beach. When the park near the shoreline monolith yielded nothing, he headed into the town proper and concentrated on a street by street canvass until a near collision changed everything.

"That *was* you outside the gas station," said Clea. "I didn't recognize Paul's car."

"Which actually worked to my advantage. No reaction to give away my presence, and I was able to follow at a discreet distance, DeSanti none the wiser."

Unfortunately the low-slung sedan could not negotiate the deep swale on the side of the highway, forcing him to abandon the car at the foot of the old forest road and hike.

Clea broke in. "I thought I heard a noise at the cabin, but when nothing came of it, I was sure I'd imagined the whole thing. I felt so alone, Ren, but it didn't mean I had to be helpless."

"Not helpless, Clea. Courageous. The best. Even by Bureau standards." His throat closed around the next words, "But hearing that crash…I…I've never been so afraid." He coughed away the tremor in his voice. "Well, you know the rest."

"I do. And Ren…." Clea struggled with her own emotions. "If I haven't told you yet how—"

"Shh. You have. A dozen times."

"Mom! Mommm!" At the insistent voice, Clea snapped back to the present. "I said show grandma your new hat." Without waiting for reaction or reply, Addy hurried on. "It's a baseball cap. Ren gave me one too. It's only the Yankees, but that's okay. I'll wear it anyway."

Ren playfully grabbed the bill of Clea's cap and tipped it low on her face. "*Only* the Yankees? I see I've got a job ahead of me educating that kid of yours."

"Oh?" Clea was glad the hat hid her face and even more relieved when Rikki pushed into the room and diverted attention.

"Figured I'd find you all here," Rikki said. She seemed to take the Blues Brothers costume in stride, giving one look and saying, "Already ran into a few carbon copies outside. This afternoon ought to be a real stitch."

Her gaze settled on Clea who seemed comfortably at home with Ren's arms draped around her shoulders. "I see you've come to your senses."

Clea blushed. "A bad case of jumping to conclusions."

Rikki went on, gesturing toward the Yankee's cap. "A little traitorous, don't you think, since this is Mariners country?"

Clea blushed again.

"Since Christmas has apparently come early, with presents and all, here." Rikki grinned and handed over a bundle. Under a layer of tissue, Clea discovered a particularly elegant frame, behind the glass the familiar picture of herself as an infant.

"Paul released the photo, and Mitz insisted on giving it a new 'do.'"

Clea extended the easel back and propped the picture on the windowsill. The dazzling morning light made the baby's smile more radiant than she remembered.

"Right where it belongs," she said.

Josephine's eyes followed Clea's movements, lingering on the photo before drooping in slumber.

Clea motioned to Addy and whispered, "Time to go. Grandma needs her sleep."

"I'm not late for school, am I?"

"Not if we hurry."

As they drove into the high school drop-off circle, hundreds of Belushi and Aykroyd wannabes milled about, a regular Blues Brothers convention, another Halloween caper pulled off in the best of the town's tradition.

Addy jumped out of the car. Before disappearing into the sea of lookalikes, she approached the driver's side window and said to Ren, "I know what your name stands for."

"No you don't," he returned, suspicion nibbling at the confident words. When Addy leaned in and mumbled in his ear, he went rigid. "Francesco spilled the beans, didn't he?"

"Naw. I'm better at using the computer than you think. Don't worry. It'll be *our* secret." She grinned at her mother, then ran to join the costumed crowd.

Secrets.

Usually they tore people apart, but sometimes they could draw a whole community together. In the past few weeks, Clea had experienced both, and looking first at Ren then out over the laughing students, she allowed they could also be just plain fun.

About the Author

Photo by Linda A. Mason

Carla Dietz Fortier was born in Bloomington, Illinois. She is a graduate of Eastern Illinois University where she earned a Bachelor of Arts degree with specialization in the areas of English and foreign language literature. For 15 years she successfully operated a secretarial business.

Although enjoying the writing process from early on, any serious work on fiction took second place to marriage, family and a home-based business.

In the early 1990's an adult education course at a local community college introduced her to a writers group. She joined, took up the pen, and has been at it ever since.

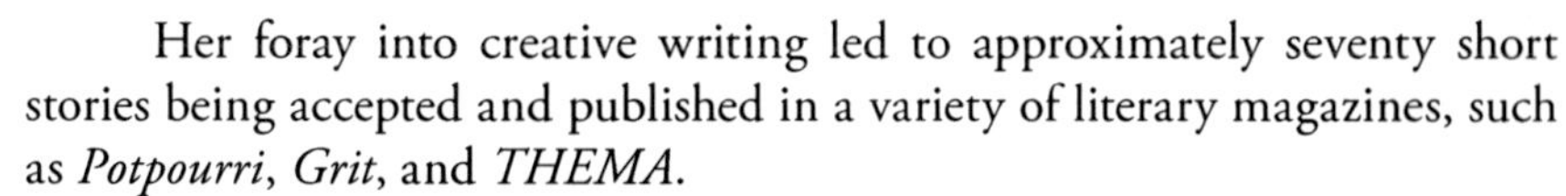

Her foray into creative writing led to approximately seventy short stories being accepted and published in a variety of literary magazines, such as *Potpourri*, *Grit*, and *THEMA*.

Secrets is her first published novel.

Currently Carla resides in Crystal Lake, Illinois where she is hard at work on another novel while she eagerly anticipates grandparenthood.

Printed in the United States
80725LV00006B/25

9 781434 300942